DON'T
HEX
AND
DRIVE

DON'T
HEX
AND
DRIVE

JULIETTE CROSS

UNION
SQUARE
& CO.

NEW YORK

UNION
SQUARE
& CO.

NEW YORK

ISBN 978-1-4549-5363-0 (paperback)

For information about custom editions, special sales, and premium purchases, please contact specialsales@unionsquareandco.com

Printed in Canada

2 4 6 8 10 9 7 5 3 1

unionsquareandco.com

Edited by Corinne DeMaagd
Cover design by Jenny Zemanek
Cover images by Shutterstock.com: Artos (car); javarman (ombre);
Kate Macate (ribbon, herbs); primiaou (scroll, quill);
StockSmartStock (leaves); Gorbash Varvara (vials)

TO MY SANITY—
For sticking with me while I wrote, revised, edited, and
proofed this book during COVID quarantine.
I appreciate you hanging in there despite the
one million times you nearly left me teetering
on that proverbial cliff.
High-fives self & drinks more wine

Chapter 1

~ISADORA~

I was thinking about purple pansies when it happened.

Just bumping along on my bicycle, down the narrow street that paralleled Magazine, while daydreaming of this particular little flower. It was right after sundown, which was my favorite part of the day to ponder things. I was a deep ponderer. Not deep thinker, mind you, because that would imply that I mused about profound, earth-shaking things. Nope. Mostly plants and flowers. And dogs. Sometimes cats. Or a more efficient way to organize our inventory at Mystic Maybelle's. But really, mostly flowers.

Did you know that pansies, especially when infused with my special brand of magic, can be brewed in teas to heal skin rashes, reduce fevers, and even help with high blood pressure? Pansies! Shocking, right?

Tia liked to tease me—and by that, I mean aggravate—by reminding me that it's also highly effective in love potions.

Ancient Greeks used pansies for love potions, giving it the nickname *heart's ease.*

"Maybe you can whip up a batch and find Mr. Right," she'd said with a cheeky grin this afternoon at her house.

To that, I'd rolled my eyes and waved goodbye, carrying my precious bundle like a newborn babe right out the door. This particular pot of pansies had been dug up in the Meteora region of Greece where they'd been growing wild and untouched for centuries. Every witch knew, especially Conduits like myself and Tia, that the most powerful of plants were cultivated by Mother Earth, not human hands.

"Almost home, my sweet angel," I whispered down to the basket attached to my handlebars.

Yes, I talked to my plants. Research proved they responded well to human speech and song. You can google it.

Okay, fine. I just *liked* talking to them. Plants and animals never judged you. Not for what you looked like, what you wore or didn't wear, what you said or didn't say, what you believed or didn't believe, or even that you preferred to travel by bicycle as opposed to car.

So that's what I was thinking about when my world turned upside down. Literally.

I didn't even hear him until it was too late. The sudden screech of tires and whip of the headlights hit me a split second before his car did. The bump against my back tire was hard enough to send me, my favorite handbag, and my sweet pot of pansies flying into the air. I was so shocked I didn't even cushion my fall with telekinesis because, unfortunately, I needed a little warning and preparation before I used that kind of magic. How fast had this idiot been driving, anyway?

Landing in a tumble of limbs, my ankle twisted painfully on the fall. "Ow!"

The simultaneous crack of pottery twisted my heart and hurt even more. The headlights of the jerk's car shone on the devasting sight of my pansies limp on their side. The terra-cotta pot was shattered, the soil spilled, her roots exposed like some horrific murder victim.

"Nooo."

A gust of wind, then, "*Hai Ram!* Are you hurt?"

It had been no more than three seconds since his car had hit my bicycle before the man's large hand gripped the curve of my shoulder. No, not a man. Not a human one anyway. Only one supernatural could move that fast. And carried that kind of potent signature. It hit me almost as hard as his car did, punching the breath right out of my lungs.

Before I could even get a good look at him, he was hovering over my feet where my knee was bent and I was holding my ankle. He lifted my injured foot gently and slipped off my flat. His long black hair fell in waves over his crisp white button-down, well past his shoulders. I tried but couldn't see his face hidden by that fall of hair. Then I became distracted by his deeply bronzed hands. Long fingers brushed lightly over my foot.

"Are you a doctor?" I winced, tugging at my foot. One, because it hurt. And two, because I didn't like strangers touching me. For that matter, I was pretty protective of my personal space even with friends. "Do you even know what you're doing?"

He ignored my questions, holding firm. "Try to point your toes."

Aggravated, I pointed them anyway before biting my lip on a whimper.

"Not broken then." He slipped my shoe back on, his fingers sliding over the injury before giving me a light squeeze.

Pulling my foot out of his hands, I accused as calmly as possible, "You're not a doctor."

When he finally looked at me, I wasn't surprised by his striking beauty. So typical. His heavy lashes framed whiskey-warm brown eyes. His perfectly square jaw and well-defined cheekbones were all ridiculously symmetrical. What did I expect from a vampire? An old one, at that. His magic hummed in the air, tinged with power and control and the trait I hated most about his kind. Seduction. They all wore it like a coat, parading it around like proud peacocks. So annoying. But this one? It sealed his aura of magic like a second skin. Like it wasn't a secondary trait at all, but a natural birthright.

Wait. Not perfect, actually. His left brow was bisected by a thin white scar that disappeared into his hairline. It was hard to see at first in the dim light. So he didn't use glamour to mask his flaws? Interesting.

His concerned expression shifted, his mouth quirking up with one of those smirky smiles that cocky guys flashed when they thought they could charm their way out of a situation. *Uh, no. I don't think so.*

"Aren't vampires supposed to have superhuman eyesight? Say, to *avoid* hitting an innocent traveler on the road?"

His nostrils flared as he inhaled a deep breath. Recognition shone in his eyes. His charming smile slipped, his expression changing to . . . amused interest? "Aren't witches supposed to have telekinetic powers? Say, to avoid being hit by cars?"

For a moment, I was completely distracted by the smooth, deep timbre of his voice and his subtle accent. Indian, definitely, but something more. The slow, intentional care of each word reminded me of a professor from Russia I had in college. His accent was strong and soft at the same time. This vampire's was similar, liquid and lilting with an undercurrent of firm control. Casual dominance. If there was such a thing.

His gaze traveled down my body, taking in my forest-green boho skirt and navy-blue top. "And why are you riding a bike at night wearing such dark colors, Mistress Witch?"

Unbelievable! He was blaming *me* for hitting *me* with his stupid car? The reason I wasn't wearing bright-colored clothes, which I did if I rode at night, was because I hadn't planned on staying at Tia's past our lunch date. But lunch turned into afternoon tea, then we'd gotten into a heated discussion about nightblooming medicinal plants, and I left too late. But this dumb *vampire* didn't deserve an explanation.

"Here, let me help you up." He leaned forward and grabbed me by the forearm, which I quickly wrenched away.

"No, thank you. I'm fine."

He eased back onto his heels and raised his palms up in a hands-off gesture, his dark eyes shimmering silver for a second. Freaking, nervy vampires. Driving around like bats out of hell. Thinking they owned the world.

5

Ignoring him, I reached for the strap of my canvas handbag and looped it over my head to cross my chest. I flattened my palms on the concrete and pushed up, hissing in a breath. I'd scraped my palms on the fall.

"Let me—"

"No," I snapped, avoiding his gaze when he made a frustrated noise in his throat.

Managing to stand all on my own, ungracefully, but still on my own, I took a step toward the front of the car and whimpered at the sharp pain. My leg crumpled, but before I hit the pavement— *again*—the vampire reached over to steady me with an arm around my waist.

"Do you mind?" I wriggled and batted at his hand to get him off.

He released me. "Look," he said, seeming to force himself to keep calm, "I'm just trying to help."

"Where's my phone?" I muttered, digging through my bag while leaning all of my weight on my uninjured leg. I could call Jules to come get me. "Dammit, where is it?"

The vampire walked away and then returned with his palm out to me. He was holding my phone, fully cracked glass and the screen frozen on the weather app for some odd reason.

"Just great!" I snatched it from him and tapped the screen, knowing I'd get nothing.

"I'm seriously sorry about this. Why don't you let me drop you off at home, at least? I'll fix your bike. I'll replace your phone. I promise."

I glared at him like he'd lost his damn mind. "I'm not getting in the car with you. Are you crazy? And, yes, you are paying for my bicycle." I shoved the useless cell phone in my handbag. "But I have phone insurance."

He propped both hands on his hips and looked up the street, his crisp white shirt standing out under the streetlight, stretching across his broad chest. "You can't live far. Let me give you a ride home."

"After witnessing your excellent driving skills? Um, no, thank you. And I don't know you. Ever heard of stranger danger?"

Plus there was the whole issue of those college girls going missing. I wasn't an idiot. Actually, I'd never seen him around this neighborhood before and suddenly eyed him with renewed suspicion. "Who are you anyway?"

His attention swiveled back to me, and then he frowned down at the ground at my foot as I wobbled.

"My name is Devraj Kumar."

"I've never seen you around here."

"I've just arrived in town. I'm a friend of Ruben Dubois. Surely, you know him if you're a local witch."

Ruben Dubois? The overlord of vampires in New Orleans? Uh, yeah, I knew him.

"You know Ruben?"

He pulled out his cell from his back pocket and dialed a number, holding the phone up to his ear. Within three seconds, he said, "Yeah, I had an incident." His dark eyes fixed on me. "An accident, actually. My fault. I hit a witch on her bike." He pivoted away so I couldn't see his face. "Shut up, man. No, she's fine. Well, except for her ankle. Will you tell her I won't kidnap or kill her so she'll let me take her home?"

He turned and passed me the phone with a seriously disgruntled look. I guess Ruben handed his ass to him. Good. A little smugly, I took the phone.

"Hey, Ruben. It's Isadora."

"Isadora," repeated the vampire king in his always-steady-and-calm voice. But then he let out a little sigh. "Are you all right?"

"Fine. Just my ankle."

"I'm glad you were cautious and didn't get in the car with him." Ruben had no idea how bad my car phobia was. There was no way I'd ever just *get in a car* with anyone. "But listen, Devraj is one of my oldest and best friends. You can trust him to give you a ride home. I'm sure Jules is already worrying since it's late."

True. She would be. Or my sisters, whoever was home right now. I eyed the vampire standing in front of me, looking somewhat innocent and remorseful, hands in his pockets.

Ruben knew our family well since he and Jules worked closely together as leaders in the supernatural world. He was a good friend to us, so if he said Devraj was trustworthy, then he was.

"If you say so, Ruben."

"I do. Let him help you. I can promise you he's already drowning in guilt. Let him get you home safely."

"Okay. I will."

"Can I speak to him again for a minute?"

"Sure."

I passed the phone back. Devraj took it and listened to whatever Ruben was saying, his gaze sharpening on me as he exhaled the heaviest sigh I'd ever heard.

"I will," he said to Ruben before ending the call and slipping it into his back pocket. "All ready to go then?"

I nodded, eyeing his intimidating-looking car. One of those superfast, fancy ones that made me cringe.

"All right." Then he swept me up into his arms, one arm under my knees, the other cradling my back.

"Wait! What are you doing? Put me down!"

"I'm getting you in the car without you injuring yourself further."

"I don't like this," I ground out, pressing my scratched palms to his white shirt, then jerked them back, realizing I'd likely stain it. Whatever he was wearing, it was expensive. "*Please* put me down."

"I will. Inside the car, Isadora. Isadora what, by the way?"

"Savoie," I muttered, gritting my teeth, my nerves fracturing on multiple levels.

"Your ankle is injured, and you can't walk. You certainly can't ride your bike." He glanced toward where it had landed, the back wheel crooked, spokes popping out. His gaze swiveled to mine as he marched forward, looking a bit more contrite. "I'll come back for your bike." He strode around his sleek car, the engine still purring as he'd never turned it off. "I imagine you don't live far."

His laugh rumbled against my side. I'd curled my hands against my chest, trying to avoid all contact. The vibration of his laugh against my rib cage reminded me how close we were. So did the scent of him. Some kind of fancy cologne. It smelled expensive and made me uncomfortable. I was ready to be rid of this vampire with his fancy car, clothes, and cologne.

"Not far," I grumbled before adding emphatically, "I'm not leaving without my pansies."

He set me down gently beside the passenger door and opened it, ignoring me. Before he could urge me in, I slammed it shut, almost taking off his fingers. The flash of silver across those dark eyes of his told me I'd made my point.

I leaned back against the closed car door. "*Not.* Without my pansies."

He braced his hands low on his hips, drawing my attention to the sheer size of him. Most vampires were built lean and trim. He fit that mold. Except he was taller. More muscular. And his body seemed built for athleticism whereas most vampires were built for indolent leisure. Looked like he scaled skyscrapers and swam lakes for fun. Who knew with vampires? They seemed to be the most over-the-top of the supernaturals. Flashy, arrogant. Except Ruben, actually. He was all right. But the rest of them, I had no use for.

He surveyed my broken pot on the street in front of his car. "And how exactly am I supposed to transport them?"

Leaning against the passenger side, I rummaged in my bag, maneuvering around my hand sanitizer, my granola bar, the duct tape, and my first-aid kit, which I'd need in a second. Aha! There at the bottom, I pulled out one of my reusable shopping bags and handed it over.

"Please move her into the bag *very* gently. If the clustered roots separate, they may wilt and die, even if I get them back into a new pot. Pansies are extremely delicate. I would just be devastated," I spit out in one breath.

He blinked at me, brows raised. Perhaps I sounded a little dramatic, but this whole freakish incident had made me, well, flustered. My ankle would be fine once I calmed down enough to heal it myself, but my precious pansies imported all the way from Greece might die because of this vampire's reckless driving.

Glancing at where my plant lay, I pushed off the door and took a limping step toward the front of the car. "Never mind. I need to do it myself."

"Wait, wait, wait." He stopped me with a firm but gentle grip around my wrist, then plucked the shopping bag from my hand. "I'll do it. You stay here."

No hint of annoyance in his voice. This vampire wasn't easily rattled, I'd give him that. Even with my less-than-kind attitude, he'd handled me gently enough. Surely, he'd do the same for my pansies.

Biting my lip, I watched him carefully remove the pieces of broken pottery and drop them in someone's garbage can at the curb. Then he scooped his large hands under the soil and roots, the entire plant fitting nicely in his palms, and placed it in the bottom of the bag.

"Don't lift it by—" I stopped mid-sentence since he hadn't hauled it up like a sack of potatoes like I thought he would have. Instead, he lifted from the bottom with both hands and walked toward his trunk. He held my gaze, arching one dark brow as he passed me by.

Okay then. Clearing my throat, I opened the door and hopped in, belting myself and staring at the spaceship-like console with more fancy gauge readings and computerized stuff than I'd ever seen in a car. Of course, this was a seriously expensive car compared to the Jeep Cherokee and the Honda sedan driven by Jules or Evie, the two I trusted most to cart me around town if I needed something beyond the neighborhood.

Deep breath in and out. I reminded myself we were only a few short blocks from the house. Surely, he wouldn't wreck again in that short space of time.

Shoving that fear away, I rummaged around in my bag and had pulled out my first-aid kit by the time he settled into the driver's seat. He'd moved my bicycle safely onto the sidewalk before getting in.

"Where to?" he asked, his gaze fixed on my lap where I'd set out my tube of homemade antiseptic, antibacterial wipes, and Band-Aids.

"The end of this block and take the first right. I was actually almost home before you decided to hit me with your car."

I dabbed at the scratches on my palms, wiping off the small amount of blood and removing any dirt.

"Believe it or not, I didn't plan to hit a witch with my car today." He shifted the gear stick into first and accelerated down the street. "It was on the agenda for tomorrow."

Pausing, I looked over at him, his gaze fixed forward but his mouth ticked up with a wicked smirk.

"Well." I folded the used wipes and put them in a Ziploc bag I had in my handbag to dispose of later. "I'm so happy I was able to get you ahead of schedule. Nothing better than ticking off your to-do list early."

"Mmm. Unfortunately, I had a brunette witch on my list, not a blonde." His gaze roved from the top of my head to down around my shoulders before he moved his attention back to the road.

"Do you have something against blondes?"

I prepared myself for a dumb blonde joke or something else equally offensive. What I wasn't prepared for was his sultry reply.

"Not at all, darling. I'm a lover of all women." His gaze caressed my face, shimmering with silver in the dark interior of his car. "I don't discriminate."

Darling? Lover? What was he talking about? *Wait.* Was he *flirting* with me? What nerve!

"Let me get this straight." A shocked laugh belted up my throat. "You speed down an unfamiliar road, hit someone with your Porsche, send her flying into the air, injure her ankle, break her expensive, imported plant, and then decide to *flirt* with her?"

He muttered what must've been a curse in another language I didn't recognize, but when he spoke, he was all silky sensuality like before.

"First of all, love. This is not a Porsche. This is a Diablo GT Lamborghini, one of the finest Italian cars money can buy." His tilted smile might as well have added *silly little girl.* "Second, why are you so sure this is an unfamiliar road to me? I could live right around the corner."

He could turn off that smooth-talking charm immediately because it wasn't working on me. "Turn right."

He downshifted and slowed on the turn.

"You said so yourself you've just arrived in town," I bit back accusingly. "And anyone who lives in this neighborhood knows not to drive their Lamborghini Devil down this road like a bat out of hell."

"It's Diablo."

"Diablo. Devil. All the same." I snapped my first-aid kit shut and shoved it in my bag, smiling sweetly at him. "It suits you well, I'd say." Then I pointed. "Stop here. This is my house."

He maneuvered onto the curb, staring at our two-story bungalow-style house, his gaze wandering to the driveway with keen interest. Kind of creepy-keen interest, actually.

"Something wrong?" I asked as I opened the passenger door.

He snapped out of whatever daze he was in. "Not at all." He flashed me a bright smile, then traced in vampire speed around the car before I was even fully standing.

"I've got it," I protested, trying to hobble.

He swept me back up into his arms, ignoring me again. I'd have objected but, to be honest, my ankle was already swollen twice its size, and it would've hurt too much to try to make it on my own. I might be stubborn, but I wasn't an idiot. Still, it was pissing me off to no end to have to depend on this guy who happened to cause my injury in the first place.

With a thorough push of magic, the familiar tingling sensation shooting through my veins, I opened the wrought iron gate at the front. He glanced down at me, all congenial and smiling, like he hit women with his car and carried them around for the fun of it every day of his life. I tried to ignore how he maneuvered me in his strong arms like I weighed nothing, his powerful strength on full display. But of course, all vampires were exceptionally strong. No need to ponder on his.

While I didn't have the fuller curves like my sisters, I was the tallest. I loved my height. I owned it, relishing the fact that I could look most men eye-to-eye. Or even down at them. But not this one. His powerful physique and easy strength made me feel strangely vulnerable. It wasn't a feeling I was used to, and I didn't like it.

Before we made the steps to the front porch, the heavy front door swung open.

"Well, this is interesting," said my sister Violet, a red Twizzler hanging out of her mouth, one hand on the door. "What did you do?"

"What do you mean what did I do?"

"I'm sorry to say," the vampire interrupted smoothly while carrying me into the house, "that I hit your sister on her bike."

Violet heaved out a breath. "I knew this would eventually happen."

"Thanks for your sympathy, Violet."

She shrugged, walking ahead of us toward the living room. "You look all right."

Kicking up my leg with my swollen ankle, now about three times its normal size, I replied, "Yeah, I'm just dandy." Then something occurred to me. I snapped my attention back to the vampire. "How do you know she's my sister?" I asked, my attention now riveted to the underside of his chin where his short beard was cut close and trim, defining the square angle of his jaw.

A fleeting glance of those mahogany eyes. "Similar shape of the eyes." He walked me to the sofa and set me down lengthwise, his gaze fixing more intently on mine. "But the shade is entirely different."

To break the uncomfortable snare of his gaze, I cleared my throat and tried to reach for the throw pillow to put under my foot. But he was there doing it before I could even ask.

"What happened?" Livvy stood in the open arch leading to the kitchen. Her long black hair piled in a messy bun, she wore a typical Livvy outfit—red-and-orange dragon-flame tights with an off-the-shoulder fitted black top and wide patent leather red belt. She held a mixing bowl against her belly and a chocolate-smeared spatula.

Before I could say anything, Violet piped in, standing above me at the head of the couch. "Isadora finally got herself hit by a car while on that bike."

"Violet. Go *away*." I wasn't in the mood for her attitude, especially with my assailant standing by my feet, listening in.

Livvy tilted her head, her full red lips smoothing into a sympathetic line. "You need to learn to drive, Izzy. You've had too many close calls, and now this." She stepped into the room, her gaze skating to my ankle.

"I don't need a lecture."

Livvy was the next oldest sister above me. And while she rarely played the big sister card, she tended to become maternal when pointing out this one particular flaw of mine. Or phobia, however you wanted to look at it.

"You need to get over this driving thing." She sighed, standing right beside me now. She gave my shoulder a squeeze. "How badly are you hurt?"

Anger rolled in my belly, spiking my adrenaline. I didn't want to have this conversation for the hundredth time, and I certainly didn't want to have it in front of the jackass who hit me with his car.

"I'm fine. And why are you baking? What's wrong?" Livvy tended to bake, especially with chocolate, when something was bothering her.

She dropped the spatula into the bowl and moved it to her hip so she could trace her fingers lightly over my swollen ankle. "Not too bad." She had ignored my attempt to shift the attention to her.

But it seemed *ignoring Isadora* was the theme for the night. "You can fix this quickly enough."

The vampire, still quiet, made a sudden movement, his brows raised. "You're a Conduit?"

I nodded, lips pressed tight. Because I knew what was coming before he said it.

"Then why not fix it back on the street?" His expression wasn't accusatory, more confused.

I'd been known to heal a number of people while they writhed and screamed in pain. That had never unsettled or stopped me from using my healing magic before. Traumatic events didn't knock me off-center. But something about this whole night had rattled me to the core. I knew I couldn't summon my magic until this vampire got the hell out of my presence. I was sure it all stemmed from the fact that I'd been hit on my bike when I'd always touted how safe the transportation was.

The opening and banging of the back door leading into the kitchen echoed a few seconds before my sister Clara walked in. "Oh no! What happened?"

Thank you, Clara, for saving me from answering the vampire.

Clara was the sweetest of my sisters. She was also the youngest, having arrived three minutes after Violet.

"This guy hit Isadora with his car," said Violet, nonchalantly, balancing her butt on the back of the sofa.

"Isadora, you poor thing." Clara knelt at my side and clasped my hand. "Are you hurt bad?"

Her worried expression zoned in on my foot. Without even knowing it, I'd bet, she pushed waves of tranquility into me with her empathic magic. She couldn't help it. Auras needed to spread joy and peace like Conduits needed to help and heal.

"I'm fine, Clara." I squeezed her hand, happy at least one sister was on my side. "Thank you."

"I know you from somewhere." It was Livvy, eyeing the vampire still standing in my living room, hands in his fancy pants' pockets.

For some reason, in the light of our living room, the force of his magic seemed to have amplified. Or maybe that was just because I wasn't so focused on the accident now that I was safe in my home.

He reeked of power. His disarming stance and charming smile did nothing to defuse it. My Conduit magic could detect potent sources of energy better than any supernatural, and this guy was pumping it out in waves. I suddenly wanted him out of our house.

"Oh my goodness," gushed Clara, wide blue eyes staring at him. "Your aura is . . ."

His head tilted, his expression softening to one of humility. As if. "I've heard from other clever Auras that it's a kaleidoscope. Am I right?"

She nodded eagerly. "Such a pretty rainbow."

His smile brightened even more. *Good Lord, Clara! Don't encourage him.*

"But I know you," continued Livvy, standing closer to him, studying his face. "I've seen you."

He offered her his hand. "I'm Devraj—"

"Holy shit!" Livvy gasped, grasping his hand in hers. "You're *Devraj Kumar.*"

With a modest smile, he nodded once and shook her hand. "I am."

"Who?" I asked. I mean, he'd told me his name, but why would Livvy know him?

She let out a laugh that sounded a little too fangirly to me. Livvy never gushed or fangirled. "Isadora. You were hit by *the* Devraj Kumar. Famous Bollywood movie star."

"Oh, a movie star. Well, I guess that makes it all right then."

"And you're a vampire," added Violet with wicked glee. "So fucking cool."

Livvy dropped his hand and held her mixing bowl with both hands again. "Do you work for Ruben?"

Was she fluttering her eyelashes? What was happening here?

He paused, charming smile still in place. "On occasion. And I'm in town to help him with a job. If I can."

His gaze skated to me on the sofa where I was sure my glare of extreme annoyance—or seething hatred rather—was more than apparent. I don't care if he'd won Sexiest Man of the Year, two Oscars, a Golden Globe, and Coolest Asshole in a Lamborghini Award. The fact that he had my sisters all swoony and girlish made me want to hurl.

"Speaking of which . . ." He glanced back toward the hallway that led to the front door. "I should be going." He rounded the sofa and leaned over, taking my hand in his. "It was a pleasure bumping into you."

"Really?" I snapped, a little too much venom in my voice.

He stifled a laugh. Just barely. "Truly." He squeezed my hand with both of his, then removed a card from his pocket and handed it over to me. "I'll deliver your bicycle to you as soon as possible. And replace your phone."

"I have phone insurance," I said again, staring at the white card with just his name in bold print and his phone number.

"Then send me the bill for the deductible. I take full responsibility for this accident."

Even though he'd mouthed off to me when it first happened, I was almost mollified as he strode for the hall.

"Wait! My pansies."

He turned. "How could I forget? Could one of your sisters . . . ?"

"I'll go," and "Let me help," and "I'll get it" came out of my sisters' mouths all at the same time.

His charming smile brightened, and I wanted to punch it off his face. His sultry gaze swept back to me.

Sighing, I said, "Clara, you go."

He dipped his head in a slight bow like some aristocratic lord from the eighteenth century, then gave me one last searing look before he left. Which made me wonder again how old he was. Vampires could live well close to a thousand years. They had the longest life span of the supernaturals. That we knew of, anyway. Werewolves could live to half a century or thereabouts. Most witches lived well into their three hundreds. Sometimes a little longer. The only one we still weren't sure of was grim reapers. But that's because we knew next to nothing about them at all. And they liked to keep it that way.

As soon as the front door opened and closed, Violet fanned her face with her hand. "Fucking hell, that vampire is hot."

"You think everybody is hot," I snapped.

Violet laughed, but Livvy shook her head, tasting the chocolate batter from her spatula before pinning me with her narrowed gaze. "Isadora. You can't pretend he isn't. Even you with your no-man-is-worthy attitude can't pretend he isn't pantie-melting."

I sniffed and straightened on the couch. "Whether he is or isn't means nothing. He's an arrogant ass who hit me with his car." I pulled down the faux white chinchilla throw on the back of the sofa and draped it over my legs. "Besides, a man with that kind of conceited personality and driving a car like that must be suffering from small man syndrome."

Violet's throaty laugh burst out hard and loud. "Are you kidding me?" She sauntered around to Livvy and tried to dip her finger into the bowl. Livvy slapped her hand. "If anyone is swinging around BDE like a fucking pro, it's that vampire, Devraj Kumar."

Livvy grinned, her red lips widening as she turned to Violet. "Even his name is sexy."

"Right?"

Traitors.

I wanted to scream with joy when Clara rushed in, carrying the shopping bag with the pansies inside. She set the bag on the coffee table and knelt down beside me, eyes glittering with excitement. "He said he carried you inside?"

I shrugged. "So? I couldn't walk."

"Oh my goodness, Isadora!" She clasped her hands at her breast, a dreamy glint in her sky-blue eyes. "It's just like Willoughby and Eleanor in *Sense and Sensibility* when he rescued her with her sprained ankle on the down."

"Willoughby didn't hit Eleanor with his car," I protested.

Violet chimed in. "Willoughby was also a total douchenozzle who dumped Eleanor for a rich sugar momma."

Clara frowned. "Oh, right." Then her expression brightened again. "Then he's like Colonel Brandon when *he* rescued Eleanor from the rain."

"This Eleanor was a bit of a klutz," Livvy added before disappearing into the kitchen. "Eighties movies are better, Clara," she called back.

Exhaling a growling breath, I said through gritted teeth, "I am *not* Eleanor. And that, that man—"

"Vampire if we're going to be technical." Violet lifted my foot and stuffed another pillow underneath.

"Whatever." I huffed out a breath, blowing a strand of hair out of my face. "I don't need rescuing."

"Says the Conduit who didn't use her magic to heal herself at the scene of the accident."

"*Violet*," Clara chastised her twin, "don't make Isadora feel bad when she's been injured." They were polar opposites in just about every way. They both had platinum-blonde hair, but Violet dyed hers constantly. Right now it was a vibrant turquoise.

"I don't feel bad," I assured Clara. And Violet's snarky comments never bothered me. Too much, anyway. "I just want to rest here on the couch a bit while I heal my ankle. I just need some quiet."

She nodded. "I'll get you some hot tea. That'll make you feel better."

I smiled as they both went off to the kitchen, leaving me alone. I heaved out a sigh of relief. I wasn't about to admit to anyone that Violet's remarks had bothered me far more than they should've. That vampire had unsettled me enough to throw off my magic. Men didn't throw me off-kilter. Honestly, they barely registered on any kind of barometer of mine at all. Whether for needs, desires, or just plain semi-interests. I didn't dislike men. I just had no need of them. I could handle *all* of my needs by myself. Which is why Devraj Kumar shouldn't have gotten under my skin at all. But he so had.

No worries. At least now he was gone for good.

Chapter 2

~DEVRAJ~

I STOOD IN MY NEW LAUNDRY ROOM, HOLDING THE WHITE SHIRT IN MY hand, staring down at it like it was a bomb. Or venomous snake. Or crack cocaine. Honestly, it might as well have been all three in one.

"Don't do it," I muttered to myself.

The mere fact that I was even standing here having this conversation with my shirt was a sign that something was terribly wrong. Hitting the witch on her bicycle hadn't just tilted my world on its axis. It had blown a city-size hole in it.

Why?

Because Devraj Kumar never lost control. Never succumbed to temptation. Hell, I never even felt temptation. As a Stygorn, I'd trained for decades to cull all basic weaknesses. I'd honed my special abilities to razor-sharp precision so the smell of blood or the scent of a woman didn't send me into a downward spiral that culminated in sweaty dreams of orgasmic proportions. But her scent had.

"Just once."

Then I would wash it.

I'd stripped off the shirt the moment I'd stepped into my new home two nights ago, right after the accident. Strangely, the compelling need—no, the desperate desire—to inhale her scent from the small stains of her blood on my shirt hadn't started until the day after. Yesterday.

I'd filled the day with unpacking. A familiar feeling I'd experienced after doing this dozens and dozens of times over the years settled with a hollow thump in my gut. And yet, it wouldn't be the last. The nature of my job kept me moving from country to country, continent to continent. Wherever the job required my skills and attention. So here I was yet again, stopping off in Ruben's hometown, wondering if I'd ever fill that longing for a home of my own. A place to dig my roots deep.

My Lamborghini was in the body shop, her bike was being repaired, and Ruben said he'd let me get settled before we met. So what had I spent the day doing? In between unpacking, I'd stalked the laundry room like a crazed serial killer. I must've marched past it a hundred times, trying to avoid the temptation in my laundry basket.

"Fuck it."

I finally, *finally*, lifted the stained part to my nose and inhaled deep.

Utterly. *Divine.*

Abort. Bad decision. Very bad decision.

I immediately threw it in with the wash, dropped in two pods of detergent, poured in three cups of fabric softener, and slammed the lid, setting it to heavy duty / hot cycle. If there was a whiff of her scent left on that shirt, I'd have to burn it.

The doorbell chimed.

I jumped like someone had caught me in a crime.

Shit!

Combing both my hands into my hair, I laughed at myself. Maybe I'd spent too many months off the grid in Romania, tapping into my natural vampiric instincts. That must've been it. I'd gone too deep, living in the Carpathian Mountains, letting the beastly side roam free too long. I'd needed the time to track an elusive vampire gone rogue for the overlord of the Bucharest coven. And yet, the time I'd spent in the wild seemed to tap into my uncivilized side.

I tilted my head and popped my neck. Time to come back to reality and focus on the new job at hand. The hiss of water filling the washing machine calmed me back to reason.

I heard the front door open and close.

"Dev?" Ruben's voice and scent carried to me.

Shaking off whatever the hell had just happened, I sauntered through the kitchen and into the living room where he stood staring at my painting of *Crann Bethadh* hanging over the mantel. I'd commissioned the Celtic Tree of Life from an old Irishman on the island of Inishmore about sixty years ago. He'd made his own paint, mixing thirty different shades of green, and flecked gold-leaf into the brown for the trunk.

That painting, along with a few other treasures, like my Grecian vase, my Icelandic wall tapestry, and my white marble statue of Shiva, always moved with me. When I'd gotten the call from Ruben, needing a favor, I'd left Romania immediately and then cleared out my apartment in Paris to make the move here.

It seemed a visit with an old friend for a few weeks was just what I needed before I moved on to the next job. There were other vampire overlords looking for Stygorn to hire in the United States. In the meantime, Ruben and I could catch up, he could show me his city, and I could lend a hand with his current case. Besides, my restlessness for something else, something more, was pushing me harder than usual these days. There was an itch I couldn't quite scratch.

"Good to see you, Dev," he said with a smile.

I met him in front of the painting, shook his hand, and pulled him in for a hard hug and clap on the back. "And you, my friend."

"How was Romania?" he asked, turning back to study my artwork with intense focus.

Ruben Dubois was one of my oldest friends and one of the few of my kind I actually trusted. I shook my head at his three-piece tailored suit in midnight blue, complete with cufflinks and personalized vest.

Ruben and his eccentric vests. This one was the same blue as the suit with silver threading in a seemingly random geometric pattern. But I knew Ruben. Nothing was random with him. Ah. It was the subtle design of the DNA triple helix. Not double like humans. The DNA code for a vampire required a third strand.

"Romania?" I sighed. "Peaceful, if you can believe that. After I'd caught a rogue vampire for the Bucharest coven. And gotten the book for you, that is."

Ruben had asked me to find a witch and acquire a rare book in heavy werewolf territory in the Carpathian Mountains. After I'd gotten the book, I stayed on in a cabin for several weeks, finding the solitude comforting but also lonely. It had twisted a bittersweet longing in my breast, though I still wasn't quite sure what that yearning was for. A desire just out of reach.

"Thank you for doing that job so last minute," he said.

"No worries. I was glad to help."

He turned to the living room, giving me a bright smile before surveying the layout. "The place looks great, though you didn't need to uproot yourself to come here."

The furniture was delivered yesterday and fit nicely in my new place. I probably didn't need to rent such a big place, but its quaintness and charm called to me.

"I wanted to," I said before admitting softly, "I needed the change."

My life in Paris was full of posh parties and wild nightlife and beautiful women. Though I'd stopped filming Bollywood movies a few years ago, I still caroused with the celebrity crowd, venturing often to Monaco, Berlin, Mykonos, and the Amalfi Coast. I enjoyed the endorphin high that the fast life provided. It kept me from thinking too long, too hard about what was missing.

Permanence. A place I could call home. Though it had been hundreds of years since my mother—my only family—had died, I'd managed to fill my life with pleasure and entertainment. Travel and parties, clubs and conquests. And though that life had lost its shiny allure years ago, I'd been going through the motions, knowing it was lacking in filling that deeper, more intimate need.

"Oh? That sounds serious," he said with a smile, though there was a pensive pinch between his brows.

"Perhaps." I laughed, noting the tone of bitterness in it.

"Tell me." Ruben was the kind of friend I trusted deeply, no matter how much time had passed between our reunions. We were brothers of a different sort.

Clearing my throat, I tucked both hands in my pockets, then faced the *Crann Bethadh*, remembering the ancient trees in the Carpathian woodlands. "After I'd gotten what you needed in Romania, I stayed on in the mountains." Pausing, I tried to find the right words to express what I experienced there. "It was so, so quiet there. I hadn't slowed down in so long. It hit me hard."

"In what way?" he asked softly. "How did you feel?"

"Very serene. And very sad," I confessed as I faced him. I wasn't surprised to find understanding there. Though Ruben wasn't as old as me, he was old enough to feel the marrow-deep hollow that came with age. And the lack of what we needed to fill that tender emptiness.

Romania was the first time I'd been alone for an extended period of time. In my everyday life, I was surrounded by people. But even amid a throng of friends, the aching loneliness found me. It always did. In Romania, the feeling was amplified, screaming through my blood like a feverish virus.

"Anyway," I added lightly, "it was time for a change. I've had other overlord vampires in the States reach out to me for work before. Seemed like now was a good time. Perhaps see what kind of trouble I can get into over on this side of the pond."

He clasped me on the shoulder with a smile. "I'm glad you're here. Even if you did hit one of my friends with your precious Italian sports car."

"Ouch." I pressed a hand to my chest.

Though I was particular about the make and model of my cars, I wasn't attached to any of them. I'd sold my Maserati Alfieri in Paris and bought the Lamborghini from a seller in Boston and drove it down here. I had been, literally, two blocks away from my final destination after two weeks of preparation, packing, and traveling when I'd run into Isadora.

Damn. I did feel bad for hitting her, no matter what she seemed to think. She hadn't broken anything, but the incident had shaken me all the same. It was the kind of mistake I never made. I'd find a way to apologize properly soon enough. For now, I had a smaller token to deliver to the Savoie sisters, which I planned to do as soon as Ruben left.

Fortunately, he'd said they were the forgiving sort. That was good to hear since Jules Savoie—a name I'd heard more than a few times over the past ten years—was the Enforcer of the New Orleans supernaturals. She kept everyone in line. Her powers as a Siphon, a witch who could suck the magic from any supernatural creature in a blink, ensured that.

Ruben bit his lip on a small chuckle, his gaze sliding over my shoulder toward the western-facing windows for a few seconds. "Come on. Let's have a drink, and I'll tell you briefly what I know about this case." He glanced at his watch, a silver TAG Heuer. "I have a dinner meeting uptown, but I wanted to check in with you."

He followed me into the kitchen. "I would've gone to the Green Light yesterday," I called over my shoulder, "but I had to wait on the furniture delivery and get it all straight."

Pulling down a bottle of Maker's Mark from the cabinet, I then grabbed two rocks glasses.

"You still like everything in order and in its place." Ruben took a seat on the stool and tapped his fingers along the granite countertop, looking around the kitchen.

I filled both glasses with ice, poured us each a drink to the brim, and then slid his across the granite. "It's the only way to keep the chaos at bay."

"As you say." He lifted his glass. "Welcome to New Orleans."

We clinked glasses and took a deep gulp of whiskey.

"While I do want to experience the pleasures of the city," I said, swirling the amber liquid over the ice, "why don't you give me a brief rundown of where you are?"

"Well said." He drained the rest of his drink in two more gulps, then set it down. That in itself was rather telling. Ruben wasn't a big drinker. But this case had him on edge. "I didn't bother to tell you because I knew you were in the middle of the move, but another girl went missing last Saturday."

After setting down my drink, I crossed my arms and leaned back against the counter opposite him. "That's, what, four girls total? In four weeks?"

"Right." His sapphire-blue eyes darkened to the color of his suit, a silvery sheen icing over them. "No bodies yet. All of them rather young." He clenched his jaw. "College age. And taken from neighborhood bars."

I flattened a palm on the countertop and began tapping with my index finger, my wide silver band tinking against the granite. "Their age may only be a by-product. Our predator may feel more comfortable hunting the local bar scene, late at night, where the easiest prey is in the twentysomething age range."

"True," Ruben conceded. "And their minds are more malleable at that age. Easily persuaded for even a young vampire."

"How are you sure it's a vampire? Could be a werewolf gone rogue."

His brow pinched into a frown. "I've got a guy who says he's got proof it's one of our kind."

"What kind of proof?"

He chuckled lightly. "He wouldn't tell me."

"This is one of your men, and he refused to tell you?"

I found that hard to believe. Ruben was a cool, calculated leader, but ruthless when he needed to be. It wouldn't be wise to hold information from him.

"Not one of my men exactly." He sipped his whiskey. "He's on my payroll, but he's a grim."

"Ah. I see."

Grims were notoriously private. Everything to them was on a need-to-know basis, including the most trivial of things like whether they took their coffee black or with cream. Yet they were founts of knowledge themselves.

"So when is he handing over this information?" I asked, suddenly curious what this grim had as proof.

"Sometime this week. I'd like you there if you don't mind."

"Whatever you need."

"How about dinner tonight?" The tightness around his mouth softened. "Then we can catch up properly. I haven't seen my oldest friend in more than three years. You've been busy."

I shrugged. "Always some asshole to put in his place. Bring to justice."

"They never seem to go away, do they?"

"Never."

He glanced behind me toward my stove. "You're baking these days? That's new."

Taking his glass and mine, I rinsed them both in the sink. "Not baking exactly. You don't bake penda."

"A recipe from home, I take it?"

Home. Varanasi, India hadn't been my home in over two hundred years. To be truthful, no place had. But Ruben was right. I tended to cook dishes that reminded me of the spices and scents of where I'd been born for the first time. And where I'd been reborn as a vampire. Cardamom, nutmeg, and saffron still scented the kitchen even though it was two hours earlier that I'd made the doughy balls of flour, condensed milk, and sugar, then topped them with cashews and crushed pistachios.

"Yes." I dried my hands on a dish towel and leaned back against the sink. "I thought my new neighbors might enjoy a welcome gift."

"Isn't the tradition for the current residents to welcome the new neighbor with some sort of baked gift? Not the other way around?"

Crossing my arms, I stared out the window that faced the side of the Savoie home next door. From here, I had a good view of the carriage house over the garage, the driveway, and the second-floor balcony with a wrought iron railing.

"I figured I'd better sweeten the deal after my incident with Isadora. Especially now that we're neighbors."

Ruben walked closer to the window, tucking his hands in his pockets. "I'm sure she's fine. Isadora is a powerful Conduit."

"It's not her ankle I'm worried about." I joined him at the window, catching sight of a small shed-like structure surrounded by chicken wire fencing. "Is that a hen house?"

His grin widened. "No hens. Just a very dominant rooster named Fred."

"Huh." Didn't know what to say to that. There was also the roof and opaque glass walls of a greenhouse tucked in the back corner behind the carriage house. I'd bet my original Pollock painting that I knew who spent most of her time in there.

"What is it you're concerned about?" Ruben asked.

Heaving out a sigh, I turned from the window and stepped into the living room. "I fear I've offended her, though I'm not sure how." I threw up my arms in exasperation. Taking a seat on the dark suede sofa, I added, "I mean, I did apologize. But she seemed even angrier by the time I'd left her safely tucked up on her sofa."

Ruben's throaty laughter snagged my attention. He didn't laugh as often as he should. "I can't believe the famous Devraj Kumar failed to win over a woman with his illustrious charms."

That had me frowning. Not because I needed to win over any woman for any reason, but because, well, I suppose I was accustomed to women being more receptive to me. At the risk of sounding vain, I never had to try too hard to charm the ladies.

"Look at you." He shook his head, standing in front of the coffee table on my red-and-gold Persian rug. "All anxious and scowling over a witch who doesn't like you."

I couldn't refrain the huff of laughter that barreled from my chest. "Are you seriously going to stand there and say that?" I arched a superior brow at him. Yes, superior. And he damn well knew why. "To me?"

His smile fell, his jaw tightened, then he glanced away, his suddenly fierce expression skating away from the windows to my three-foot statue of Shiva on his black lacquer stand in the corner.

"Ruben?" I coaxed softly.

He ignored me, his eyes trance-like, certainly chasing some memory he shouldn't be.

"*Ruben? Are you serious?*"

Stiffening his shoulders, he returned his burning blue gaze to me, not saying a word. He didn't have to. The pain was there, raw and too bright.

"Still?" I asked quietly.

He held me for three seconds longer before checking his watch again. "I'd better go." He marched for the door, his shoes clopping on the hardwood floor. "Dinner at eight? Meet me at the Green Light."

"I'll be there," I replied evenly, knowing he could hear me well enough all the way in the foyer.

The firm slam of the door told me he didn't want to talk about his old ghosts that still haunted him. Regrets that apparently cut deep and were still bleeding. Profusely. I heaved out a sigh and shoved off the sofa.

Ah, Ruben.

When would he learn that he couldn't keep running?

I pulled the Saran Wrap from the drawer beside the stove then covered my plate of penda.

I might not be able to help him with his problem witch, but I could at least make a friend of mine. No. I didn't even want that. I just wanted her to let bygones be bygones. Surely, my skills in the kitchen would win her over.

There were other skills I could employ.

No! No. Not even remotely going there.

It's never safe to live next door to your lovers. If they got too attached, it caused all sorts of problems. Though the thought had crossed my mind—say, first thing this morning after an erotic dream starring a golden-haired witch with taunting green eyes. But no. That was a terrible idea. Terrible. Wasn't it?

Heaving out a breath, I nodded to myself, ready to put that woman out of my mind.

Just make amends and move on, Devraj.

Picking up the plate, I headed for the door. Deliver the penda, smile, apologize, and be gone. That's all I needed to do, and all would be fine.

Chapter 3

~ISADORA~

After hanging the last bundle of lavender on the beam overhead, I brushed the excess pollen off my hands and counted.

"Seven lavender. Fourteen chamomile. And seven hyssop."

That should do it for this month. I'd had to double my normal bundles of chamomile, which was used for protection. Clara said she couldn't keep them in stock at the shop since the young women had started going missing a few weeks ago. My magic-infused bundles could certainly ward off a magical or psychic attack on someone's home, but it would do nothing to protect girls from being kidnapped off the street.

Still, if it gave them peace of mind, I encouraged them to use the chamomile. I also encouraged them to buy a good guard dog and stay home at night behind bolted doors.

I grimaced. That reminded me of the scolding Jules had given me when she'd gotten home two nights ago. I'll confess I really wasn't thinking when I biked home that late. Everyone knew that women were disappearing from nightclubs or bars. It wasn't exactly safe to be out that late on my own. I wasn't equipped with the kind of defensive magic my sisters were. My ability at telekinesis was negligible, making me the most vulnerable of my sisters when it came to physical threats.

"Vampires are opportunists," she'd said with more than a little bite.

I knew that snap judgment stemmed from her not-so-secret strained relationship with a certain overlord vampire. There was history between Jules and Ruben. A history none of her sisters were privy to. Not the whole story anyway. And it was a topic of discussion that was *never* on the table. So I knew her comment about vampires was more about Ruben and less about Devraj.

Still, the whole bike incident had riddled me with anxiety. Clara had told me to rest and she'd take care of Mystic Maybelle's and handle any inventory deliveries or issues on her own. When she'd told me we were already out of chamomile, I'd happily busied myself in the greenhouse all day. It was exactly what I'd needed to decompress.

Now that my ankle was fully healed, I walked around the wooden worktable littered with rope and twine clippings to see the other patient. My purple pansies.

"Now, look at you. You'll be the prettiest girls in the yard."

Smiling brightly, I lifted the pot I'd put them in, letting them soak up nutrient-rich soil before I transplanted them to the bed in the courtyard. I had the perfect place in mind near Clara's reading bench where it would get a great balance of sunlight and shade.

Taking a hand trowel with me, I carried the pansies out to the courtyard. Kneeling in my loose-fitting olive pants, I set to work, thankful the sun was out, warming my bare shoulders. Once I transplanted the pansies into their new home, I poured the excess soil from the pot around it and patted everything down. Standing, I wiped my dirty hands on the hem of my tank top, heaving a contented sigh at how perfect the pansies looked. Clara would love them right there too.

Suddenly, Evie's boisterous laughter echoed from inside the house.

I headed for the back kitchen door. Ever since Livvy and I had returned from visiting our parents in Switzerland before Christmas, Evie had been more than preoccupied with her new boyfriend. A werewolf! I'd thought she'd gone a little crazy while we were gone, but then I met Mateo and totally understood. He was, honestly, the nicest guy. Not too hard on the eyes either. And he worshipped my sister, so yes, I liked him.

Pulling open the kitchen door, the rumble of a deep, masculine voice caught my attention. Yep. Mateo must've come over with Evie. That was nothing new. They were glued at the hip most of the time.

"Then what did you tell her?" asked Evie.

But the voice who replied did not belong to Mateo. "I said, 'Madame, I don't care if you were once the lover to Vlad the Impaler or King Henry the Eighth. You're still going to put your clothes back on and come with me for interrogation.'"

"Wow." Livvy guffawed, her husky laughter carrying into the kitchen. "I can't believe that. So what did she do?"

I rounded into the archway leading to the living room to see just what I knew I would. That freaking vampire, who I'd been happy to be rid of after that nightmare two nights ago, was cozied up on our couch, his arms spread wide on the sofa back, dressed in a casual black T-shirt and jeans. Both of which probably cost a couple of hundred dollars each.

Anyone who drove exorbitant luxury cars like he did overspent on everything. I knew the type. Even stupid plain T-shirts that you could get at Target for $12. Yeah, so I might've looked up how much a Lamborghini Diablo cost. Trust me. You don't want to know. It's sinfully expensive. Do you have any idea how many homeless cats and dogs I could help with the cost of his stupid car?

Livvy perched on the edge of the lounge chair and Evie sat on his right, grinning at him with entirely too much joy. My happy mood of ten seconds ago evaporated like a whiff of smoke.

His mouth tipped at a cocky angle as his gaze slid to me standing in the doorway. "She did exactly as I told her. I didn't even have to use glamour at all."

I swallowed hard and wiped my dirty hands on my tank top hem again, aggravated that he was back. Why was he back? And *why* were my sisters so easily duped by his so-called charisma?

"Isadora!" Evie popped off the sofa and met me halfway, wrapping me in a swaying hug. "I feel like I haven't seen you in a week."

"That's because you haven't." I squeezed her back. "You've been preoccupied."

She pulled away laughing. "Maybe," she admitted, a flush of pink crawling up her neck. She wore a green T-shirt with Baby Yoda eating a frog. The caption read: *Feed me and tell me I'm pretty.* I was fairly sure Mateo did both on a regular basis.

"Where's your man?" I asked, completely ignoring the one who stood from the sofa behind her. My pulse was racing for some stupid reason. I didn't understand why he was back.

"He had a commission to deliver, and I've got a shift at the Cauldron tonight." She glanced at the grandfather clock against the wall. "Oh, crap. I need to hurry." She pecked me on the cheek and jogged toward the stairwell in the hall. "Nice meeting you, Devraj! Come by the Cauldron when you get the chance."

"Thank you, Evie. I will."

Livvy stood with a plate of something in her hand. Cookies? "Look what Devraj brought for us, Isadora." Then she turned back to him. "I'm sorry. What are they called again?"

"Penda. Also called peda. It's a milk-based confection. I hope you all like it."

"They're delicious," said Livvy. "You really didn't have to."

His dark eyes swiveled back to me. Piercing. "Actually, I thought I did."

Livvy carried the plate over to me. They were perfectly formed soft discs, like thick cookies, decoratively sprinkled with nuts, the smell of nutmeg making my mouth water. I loved anything made with nutmeg or cinnamon. I suddenly wondered if he'd somehow found out my secret love of the spice.

"He made them himself." Livvy raised her black brows, stabbing me with her sapphire eyes as if she could prod me into being nice with her dagger stare. "Wasn't that nice of him, Isadora?"

I glanced at the offending plate of sweets. And yes, they were offensive. Because why was he cooking things for us? He seemed to be trying a little too hard, wasn't he? A simple *sorry* would suffice. Or maybe he'd returned my bicycle? I knew he'd taken it to have it fixed on his own.

"Are you here to deliver my bike?" I asked in confusion as I remained half in the kitchen doorway.

"Not yet," he said with a little regret, taking a step closer. "I just wanted to bring over a little peace offering."

My throat was dry like it always got when I had to deal with strangers. I mean, yeah, I'd met him and I'd given him a piece of my mind. I'd been pissed off the other night. But we'd handled it. Now he was back in my personal space, this stranger, and it irked me.

"There really was no need for you to come all the way over here from your hotel. I wish you hadn't bothered." And I 100 percent meant it.

"Oh, that's the best part," Livvy said, lifting the edge of the plastic wrap. Nutmeg and some other sweet spice wafted up to my nose. "Devraj is renting the house next door."

I was absolutely positive that my stomach plummeted right onto the floor. I actually glanced down to be sure my organs were still contained inside my body.

"What did you say?" I whispered.

"Dev is our new neighbor. Isn't that great?"

She grinned at me like Cruella de Vil. I was sure she was about to toss her head back and laugh maniacally. Livvy and Violet were two of a kind. Evil incarnate. And there was nothing they loved more than torturing their sisters. Livvy knew this guy irritated the hell out of me, and she was gleefully rubbing in this new disaster of giant proportions.

And when had she started calling him Dev?

"Here, try one," she said, shoving the plate toward me. "They're delicious."

Ignoring the plate, I narrowed my gaze on her wicked face. "I'm not hungry."

Aaaaand, that's when my stomach decided to growl. It was a complete biological response. I'd been in the greenhouse since breakfast. It had nothing to do with the absolutely amazing delicious-smelling treats right below my nose.

"Your stomach says otherwise," said the stupid vampire, standing much closer.

I jumped. Then frowned. "Don't sneak up on me."

"I wasn't—"

"I need to go finish my planting," I said as a sad excuse to get the hell out of there.

Pivoting in my bare feet, I wandered back outside, feeling satisfied when the kitchen door slammed shut behind me. I wasn't even going to admit to myself—yet—that I was definitely going to try the penda. When he was long gone. I glanced over at the house next door where he must now be living.

It had been empty for some time since our older neighbor, Mr. Harvey, moved to Florida. He left the house in the hands of his daughter, who was having trouble finding the right renters. She was very picky, wanting only responsible professionals with fixed incomes. For which I was extremely grateful. This neighborhood attracted both quiet families and loud party people. I didn't want some obnoxious, loud person living next door, disturbing my peace. But I surely didn't want that particular vampire living there either. No matter how responsible and quiet he was. Ugh.

I knelt down and pounded the dirt around my pansies, then reached behind it and yanked out a tiny weed.

"I see they survived."

I startled again, my hand flying to my chest.

"Sorry," he apologized quickly. "I didn't mean to frighten you."

Vampires were known for moving so fast and quiet it seemed as if they appeared out of thin air. Devraj had apparently mastered that skill, and it was so annoying. He took a seat on Clara's cushioned reading bench, leaning forward to prop his elbows on his knees, clasping his hands casually between them. His hair was twisted in a man-bun today, revealing his face more clearly. His close-cropped beard highlighted the blade-like angles of his jaw and the soft curve of his mouth.

"I'm happy to see your pansies are doing well."

I was aware that my mouth was hanging open, but after the shock of seeing him there, I was now completely confused by his presence. Why? Why was he sitting there and why was he talking to me? I had no idea what to say to him.

I remember watching *Pride and Prejudice* with Clara where Matthew Macfadyen played the stoic, painfully shy, and socially awkward Mr. Darcy. Yes, Mr. Darcy truly was all these things on top of being a bit priggish at first. But behind all that, he was loving and loyal to the nth degree too. We just couldn't see it behind all of his "stay back, peasant" vibes. There was this scene where Mr. Darcy told Lizzy, "I do not have the talent of conversing easily with people I have never met before."

That was me. I was Mr. Darcy. Introverted, shy, and nervous in large crowds and around strangers. Except the difference between me and Mr. Darcy was that I had no desire to grow outside my small social circle. Content with everyone on this side of my comfort zone, I definitely had no interest in expanding it to include this vampire.

"You obviously have a gift with flowers," he said softly, warm gaze sweeping over my face, across my shoulders, and down to my hands.

I blinked heavily one more time, then returned to my unnecessary patting of the soil.

Clearing my throat, I muttered, "Thank you."

Now please leave.

"You're very welcome."

I remained silent even though the amused tone in his voice rankled. Then he fell silent too. But he wasn't leaving! Like he enjoyed just sitting there on the bench and watching me plant flowers. What did he want?

Livvy had made it abundantly clear this guy was super famous and *his* social circle included dozens and dozens of celebrities and European fashion models and all the rich, beautiful people in the ritzy parts of the world I'd never even been to or desired to ever go. Livvy had shown me his Instagram, which had included pictures of him yachting with a beautiful, smiling entourage near Monaco. The pretty, black-haired woman draped behind him in a chair, the sun setting behind them, glowing like a halo to highlight their perfection. Of course, it was one of his costars in a Bollywood movie he'd done.

And now he was sitting here in my courtyard with me while I gardened, and I couldn't figure out what he wanted. I waited him out for at least five more full minutes, yanking at weeds and patting the soil. In that time, I'd glanced up twice to catch him smiling serenely and just observing me. Quietly. Calmly. While I was screaming inside, my nerves fractured the longer he sat there.

What the hell was he doing here?

I couldn't take it anymore. I kept my eyes down on the soil and asked, "Is there a reason you're here?"

"I thought that was fairly clear," he replied evenly. "I brought you and your sisters a neighborly treat."

"Not here at my house, but here in my garden." I sat back and placed the trowel in my lap, squeezing the handle and forcing my polite face to remain in place as I looked up at him. "Do you need something?"

In the sunlight, his eyes shone more amber than the darker shade of brown they seemed the other night. The afternoon sun shot across his intense expression, highlighting the slash of his cheekbones and the beard he apparently manicured like a madman to be so perfect.

Those eyes roamed my face, the small crease pinching his brow telling me he was riddling me out. Or trying to. There was absolutely nothing to riddle. I was an open book. I was just annoyed. No secret there.

"I do need something," he finally answered, the sun glinting off something silver in his mouth.

"What's that?"

My gaze was solely focused on his mouth now, realizing with a rush of heat that his tongue was pierced.

"Your forgiveness."

I blinked. That was definitely not what I was expecting. My mind was a hazy mess from his apology and the erotic discovery of his tongue piercing.

His full mouth tipped up on one side, apparently laughing at me again. "I realized I didn't actually apologize the other night."

Gripping the handle of my trowel so I didn't fidget, I was surprised by his open sincerity. He seemed all arrogant and superior and bossy in my brief instances with him. But if he thought I'd make this easy on him because he'd finally decided to grow some manners, he was a bigger fool than I thought he was.

"No," I agreed. "You didn't."

He smiled wider. "Would you please accept my apology?"

"For what exactly?" I tilted my head as if I had no idea what that might be. My heart pounded far too fast, making my voice shaky. But I'd gotten my ass handed to me more than once the past few days from my sisters over me and my bicycle, so I actually wanted to hear this apology to the fullest.

He clasped his hands tighter, glancing down at them before spearing me with an intense expression fixed with compassion. "For hitting you with my car. You were right." His voice dropped soft and deep, a combination I didn't particularly like coming from him. "It was entirely my fault. I'd been driving too many hours without rest, which is no excuse, but I must've lost my concentration on the road. So I apologize for causing you any harm or distress."

Hmm. Well, that was a pretty damn good apology, I had to admit.

Satisfied, I wiped my right hand on my already dirty pants and held it out to him. "Apology accepted."

Without hesitation, he reached out and engulfed my hand with his own. I shook once, then pulled my hand back, not liking the fact that even his handshake was intense. Like the potency of magic that filled his frame couldn't help but reach out and zap anyone within touching distance. His aura was even pushy.

The soft clucking of Fred, Violet's rooster, drew my attention to him as he wandered behind and around me, pretending he hadn't noticed us. Like I didn't know exactly what he wanted. I tell you, a cocky rooster was worse than a cat with their snotty attitudes. He circled back to my right, posting with his head bobbing. He wore a rainbow-striped tie—that was a new one. Heaving a small sigh, I decided to put him out of his misery. "Come here, Fred."

He gave a deep-throated cluck, eyeing Devraj, like he hadn't been after my attention this whole time. Or maybe he was protecting his hen, a.k.a. me, from the dangerous vampire. What a cutie.

I rubbed a fingertip along his chest feathers. He didn't like being touched on the head. My magic responded as quick as taking a breath, flowing riverlike from my chest, down my arm, and out through my fingertip. The effortless sensation of pure magic pouring from the energy in the air around me, sending a droplet into the rooster, took all of five seconds. Fred swaggered off, fluttering his feathers with the zing of magic pumping through him.

That's when I realized I'd just used my magic in front of my annoying new neighbor / former assailant. Not that I cared that he'd watched, but it was something I tended to do in private or only around family and friends. But the look of shock and awe on his face made it worth it.

"Did you just . . . ?" He paused and pointed toward Fred retreating back to the coop in the back. "Did you just use magic to extend life to a rooster?"

I tucked a lock of hair behind my ear, refusing to roll my eyes yet again, then stood up. He stood along with me. He wouldn't understand. That rooster owned a piece of Violet's cold, snarky heart. Just like Zombie Cat did of Evie's. So yes, I used my magic to extend their lives. Not make them immortal or anything, because that was impossible, but extend I could and would do until they were ready to let go.

Ignoring his question, I gave him the first smile since our brief acquaintance. "Apology accepted. And now our business is at an end. I doubt we'll have any reason to see each other, so I wish you well."

And I honestly did. Even cocky bastards like him needed well-wishing from time to time.

"I still have to return your bike." His discerning and unsettling gaze swept over my face.

"Not a problem. Just prop it under the garage."

No need for interaction of any kind.

"I'm sure we'll see each other around the neighborhood."

"Not likely." I rocked on my heels, waiting for him to excuse himself and leave. I wasn't going to be that rude and kick him out. But I was eyeing the greenhouse and thinking of bolting to my hiding space if he lingered much longer.

He eased forward in that vampire way of his, sidling closer without being seen doing so. He tugged on a strand of my hair that dangled against my arm, then let go just as quickly. I frowned and stepped back, definitely ready to escape to my greenhouse.

But by then he was turning away, muttering under his breath, "We'll see."

Chapter 4

~ISADORA~

I STOOD SLEEPY-EYED AT THE KITCHEN SINK, FEELING OUT OF SORTS. ALL week, I'd been plagued by the presence of our new neighbor. First of all, he played his Bollywood music *way* too loud. Livvy had corrected me when I complained, telling me it's more often referred to as filmi music. I begrudgingly admitted—only to myself—that it was quite pleasant to listen to while working in the greenhouse.

But then he had to do his shirtless yoga every day! Except for Friday. I didn't catch a glimpse of him through the fence on Friday on my way to water the pansies. Instead of yoga, he decided to wash his car in the driveway. I just happened to notice when I was pulling up weeds around the front gate. There really weren't many weeds since I pulled them up a few days ago, but curb appeal is so important! My sudden interest in our front garden had *nothing* to do with the unobstructed view of a certain vampire bent over his hood, his muscular legs flexed in those shorts, his wet T-shirt clinging to his chest.

No surprise that he attracted a few admirers. I thought the girls sitting on their porch sipping iced tea across the street were going to drown in their own puddle of drool..So sad they had no idea how arrogant he really was.

I rubbed my forehead in frustration. "Jules, have you seen a package for me?" I grumbled.

I pulled a strawberry yogurt from the fridge, then opened my box of granola.

"Sorry. No." Jules sat at the dining room table, coffee in one hand, her eyes on her tablet as she scrolled through the news. Her morning ritual.

I poured a glass of orange juice and frowned when I shut the fridge door. My friendly-reminder list was half hidden by other crap. It was actually a to-do list to keep everyone organized for the month, but I always thought a friendly-reminder list sounded more positive. I moved the two papers blocking my spreadsheet. A pizza coupon for Violet's favorite take-out place. And some flyer for a poetry reading at The Boho Lounge. Definitely Clara's. I wondered when she'd ever get the nerve to read her own.

After scooping three spoonfuls of granola into a bowl, I peered out the kitchen window into our neighbor's back yard. I couldn't help myself.

Thursday morning, I'd caught him in an enticing yoga pose, shirtless, barefoot, and in a pair of loose workout pants. I'd frozen completely on the path to my greenhouse. There was only a wrought iron gate and a row of azalea bushes blocking my view, so it was hard *not* to look. I was watching the rivulet of sweat roll down the indention of his spine when I felt his gaze on me. A fleeting glimpse of his curving smile had me zipping away and hiding in my greenhouse till it was dark. I tried not to admit it to myself, but he truly was a beautiful man. And who wouldn't want to catch a glimpse of that body each morning? More a pick-me-up than caffeine, really.

Finding no sign of him in his yard, I combined my yogurt with the granola, and then picked up my orange juice to join Jules at the table.

The thought of that half-naked, sweaty, and limber vampire had unfortunately made me wonder yet again where my package was. I'd checked my tracking number that claimed it was delivered. Couldn't have been Evie since she slept over at Mateo's again last night. I needed to check with the others. Maybe it was delivered to Maybelle's. That had happened on occasion since our mailman knew us and dropped so many deliveries to the shop.

Jules's scowl, more pronounced than usual, told me she was reading bad news. What's new, right?

"So . . . what's going on in the world today?"

Jules and I were always the first up. I enjoyed our morning chats together, even if they tended to focus on the insanity going on outside our quiet bubble on Magazine Street. She read the news while I doodled my lists that somehow kept me centered.

"More details about the last girl that went missing. Did you know she was last seen at Barrel Proof?"

Taking a sip of orange juice, I shook my head. "No, I didn't." I scribbled a new list onto my Steno pad absent-mindedly. This was one was inspired by a yoga-loving neighbor.

But Jules's comment had me thinking about those girls again. Barrel Proof was only a few blocks down from our house.

"That's two girls taken from that bar. The other two also from pubs in the Garden District."

This was the first time I could remember supernaturals targeting humans in such a terrible crime. Though I didn't want to ask because I was afraid of the answer, I didn't want to be ignorant either. "Have they found any bodies yet?"

As of now, we weren't exactly sure what was happening to the kidnapped women. I mean, we could imagine the worst, but none of us had spoken about it without any evidence to go on. Not yet.

She shook her head, eyes on the article. "No."

"What does Ruben say?"

She tapped the screen to close the article and lifted her coffee, her gaze swiveling out the kitchen window. Her posture stiffened and her mouth pursed as she either considered or ignored my question. I wasn't sure which.

"Jules?" I prompted.

Turning to me, she cupped her mug with both hands. Circles were smudged under her gray-blue eyes, her focus sharp and flinty. With no makeup on, which was as typical for her as it was for me, her dark hair in a short bob framed a pale face. Whereas I spent a good deal of time outside and in the garden, she spent most of hers indoors at the Cauldron. Her lack of sun and obvious lack of sleep gave her a fragility I didn't like to see her wear.

"Ruben and his men are sure it's a vampire, but that's as far as they've gotten," she finally said. "He's brought in an expert to help. A Stygorn."

"Really?" Now that was interesting. I scribbled on my pad again. "I've never met one before."

"Yes, you have." Her brows rose in accusation. She looked so much like our mother in that moment I almost laughed. Until I realized who she meant. Which knocked the smile right off my face.

I glanced out the wall of windows that faced the side of our neighbor's house, my mouth falling open in shock. I dropped the spoon in my bowl, the metal clinking against the glass.

"*That* conceited, materialistic man is a Stygorn?"

Jules frowned, obviously not on board with my blatant character assassination.

"From those I spoke with, he's one of the best. His reputation is stellar in the field. He's never failed to find his quarry."

Picking up my spoon, I took a bite, crunching my granola angrily. "You vetted him?" I asked around a mouthful before shaking my head to myself. "Of course you did. What was I thinking?"

Jules was extremely efficient and competent as an Enforcer of the supernaturals in our district. Not that my other sisters weren't good at what they did, but Jules took her job to another level. Since Enforcers held a power greater than vampires, she was in charge of keeping the lot of us in line here in New Orleans. And she took her job very seriously.

"So you trust Ruben to lead the investigation?"

"Why shouldn't I?"

She didn't snap the question but the steadiness of her voice was a little too forced, too measured. I wasn't going to answer her with the truth, because that would open up another conversation I knew she wasn't ready to have yet. Maybe not ever.

A fleeting image from last Christmas popped into my head. Jules wasted out of her mind on JJ's special eggnog at our sisters' birthday party, her head halfway in the toilet while I held a cool rag and mouthwash at the ready.

Her slurred angry words echoed in the toilet bowl. "Does he think I'm an idiot?" When I asked who she was talking about and wiped her face with the cloth, she mumbled, "You know who. Everyone does."

When I put her to bed, she rolled over and looked up at me, stormy eyes glassy with emotion. "But it doesn't matter, Is'dora." She gave me a sad, sad smile. One that pierced straight through my heart. "Not anymore."

When I picked her phone off the bathroom floor, I couldn't help but notice who she'd been texting at the party before she'd guzzled too much of that bourbon-spiked eggnog. I also couldn't help seeing that one glimpse of texts exchanged between them before I turned her phone off and set it on her nightstand.

After finishing my last bite of yogurt and granola, I took my bowl to the sink without answering. No need to dredge up that night. She'd pretend it never happened. Or maybe she was so drunk she couldn't remember what she'd said. Anyway, best to leave it alone.

I rinsed my bowl and spoon, then loaded them in the dishwasher. "I just thought you might take the lead since this is a bigger problem than the norm. I mean, we could be talking about murdered women, Jules."

She walked over to the coffee pot and poured herself another cup. "Possibly. But Ruben is keeping me updated on the progress, and he's being vigilant. He has more access to the vampire world, of course, so it makes sense for him to continue. Plus, he's the one who hired the services of a Stygorn."

"Right," I agreed, finishing my orange juice and loading my glass into the dishwasher. "Had you met this Stygorn before?"

"Devraj Kumar?"

"Yes." I cleared my throat. I reached over to the table and ripped the list off my Steno pad, intending to throw it away. "Him."

His name sparked a nauseous reaction in my stomach. I'd sensed he was powerful, but I hadn't suspected he was one of the Stygorn. A vampire born of one of the ancients whose level of intuition, gift of glamour, strength, and speed was unparalleled by any other supernatural. The only one with more power than the Stygorn was a Siphon witch like Jules. Except the Stygorn's level of power also gave them the ability to evade and/or harm Siphons by stealth. Fortunately, most took their gift of advanced magic responsibly. To belong to the Stygorn Guild was an elite class all its own, and they kept each other in line.

She leaned back against the countertop, one hand propped on the butcher block. "No, not personally. Ruben had mentioned him on occasion. They've known each other awhile, it seems. And Devraj was the one who acquired that book we needed to help Mateo."

I frowned, remembering Evie retelling the whole story when Livvy and I had first gotten home. How some vampire had to travel into the Carpathian Mountains, full of dangerous werewolf packs, in order to get this rare book from a witch who lived there. For some reason, the idea of Devraj—perfect clothes and hair, expensive luxury car, ridiculous swagger and charm—didn't fit my vision of one of the elite, lethal Stygorn.

"Well, I'm sure Ruben has it all in hand." I grabbed my big bag off the counter, stuffed my pen and pad inside as well as that list, then looped the thick strap across my chest, double-checking I'd packed the treats. I had.

I wished her a good day, then trekked through the courtyard and out a back gate that led to the back of our shop, Mystic Maybelle's. We'd named the place after our grandmother who'd suggested we buy the empty place next door to the Cauldron and open our own shop. Clara ran Maybelle's, but I handled the inventory and bookkeeping. Livvy took care of the marketing and promotions for both the shop and the bar. Violet and Evie waitressed at the Cauldron while Jules was the chef.

When I unlocked and swung open the back door, I heard the music from the musical *Chicago* and the undeniable off-key accompaniment of Clara's voice singing "All That Jazz."

She was stacking our newest shipment of tarot cards on the square center display. But she wasn't just stacking. She was shimmying and shaking her bum to the lively twenties music and singing at the top of her lungs while she did it. Even though she couldn't carry a tune to save her life, she was the cutest thing I'd ever seen.

When she rounded the center display and saw me standing there, she shrieked and threw a deck of cards in the air. With a quick leap toward her, I caught it in the air.

She laughed and turned down the volume on her phone. "You scared me."

"Sorry. Say, did a package come in for me?"

She glanced over at the two boxes near the display. "No. I've gone through everything we have."

I needed to email the vendor and see what was up. "I'll be back soon to work on the books," I called as I headed out the front entrance.

I strode down the street under the shop awnings, only the coffee shops and breakfast cafés open this early. I'd opted for a shorter flowy skirt that hit just above my knee and a loose white tee with my lace-up gladiator sandals. The sun was just peeking between the buildings, but it promised to be a hot one. It was still May, but the temps were already hitting lower eighties midday. This morning, it felt wonderful.

I skirted around some café round-tops along the sidewalk and pulled a ponytail holder from my wrist, twisting my hair into a messy bun. I couldn't help the smile plastered on my face, thinking of seeing Archie, as I approached Ruben's Rare Books & Brew. Perhaps that's why I wasn't paying attention to the man approaching from a parked car outside the bookstore.

"Isadora."

My gaze snapped up. I gave a small wave and tried to skirt wide without stopping for conversation.

"Hold up."

No such luck. He moved directly in my path, forcing me to stop.

Inhaling deep, I straightened my posture. "Morning, Devraj." I fiddled with a loose thread on the hem of my shirt, letting my gaze skate everywhere but his face. Clearing my throat, I asked, "Can I help you with something?"

He'd worn his long black hair up in his own messy bun—just like he did when he stretched his body into inhuman contortions in his backyard—but it did nothing to make him look casual. That was probably because his steely-blue button-up had a silken sheen, and even rolling it up his forearms didn't diminish his style. His sleek black pants and shiny shoes completed the pretty persona I expected of him.

He smiled, teeth and all, though still no canines showing, thankfully. That would be off-putting to say the least. No respectable woman wanted to get too close to a hungry vampire. I'd heard the thrall of being a blood-host was completely intoxicating, but being caught in such a state with a vampire was *not* wise. They were predatory creatures, no matter how pretty the veneer. Besides, I wasn't a fan of losing control of my faculties. Or of losing anything for that matter.

"I just wanted to wish you a good morning," he said sincerely. Which was a little aggravating for some reason.

He didn't need to stop me on the street. We weren't friends. A passing "morning" with a polite wave would have sufficed.

I gave him a deep nod, grinding my teeth together. "And to you." I started to walk around him, but he moved again to block me.

Irritated, I finally looked up and held his gaze, wondering why he was messing with me. The intensity of his whiskey-colored eyes blazed bright. I arched a brow at him, wondering why he was holding me hostage.

He seemed to snap out of his daze, clearing his throat. "Your bicycle should be delivered to your house this afternoon."

Clasping my hands in front of me, I dipped my chin down, staring at the tip of my sandal, a little scuffed and worn. "Thank you. Sounds good." I moved to go around him, but he shifted to keep me from leaving. Again!

"Wait." He blew out a heavy sigh, a frown creasing his brow. "I feel like I should buy you dinner or something." He flicked a hand, seemingly frustrated with the words coming out of his mouth. "To make up for the whole incident."

"That's not necessary."

"I feel like I owe you."

"But you really don't," I explained with a shake of my head. The idea of spending an entire meal alone with him shot my pulse off like a rocket.

"Lunch?"

"No, thank you. I'm busy."

"Every day this week?"

"Yes."

"You never eat lunch?"

"I eat lunch," I injected with a touch of annoyance. "But I prefer to get something from the Cauldron. It's fast and easy."

"Ah." He bit his lower lip, drawing my eyes to the movement and the smile he held back. "I see."

"What?" I asked, wondering why I felt so disoriented and confused in this vampire's presence.

"You just don't want to have lunch with me."

Bingo. But I'd never tell him so.

I shook my head vigorously, licking my lips nervously. "It's not that. I mean, I'm busy. You're busy. I'm sure a Stygorn like yourself has plenty of work to do."

His smile widened. "You've been asking about me?"

"My sister Jules told me why you were here."

"Is that what makes you so nervous around me?"

"Look, I've got to go." Evasive maneuvers. I glanced over his shoulder, ready to be on my way.

"Is it my acting career that bothers you?"

Not that I'd seen his Bollywood movies, but the idea of him being a celebrity actually made me cringe. To have your life under a microscope where everyone watched you, wanted something from you. The thought of hanging with someone where all eyes could be on us also made me want to run and hide.

I squeezed my eyes shut, willing my heartbeat to slow her ass down. "Yes, it bothers me," I answered as politely as possible. "But even so, it would make no difference. The answer is still no."

He let out a bark of laughter, his eyes swimming with the heat rising in the morning air. He gave me another one of those charming smiles. Though they might melt other girls into puddles of goo, it didn't affect me. Much.

Then he commanded, "Have lunch with me."

I felt it. A push of magic, pulsing along my skin and breaking against my internal barrier. The sizzle raised the hairs on my arms, but it didn't have the effect he hoped for.

My mouth dropped open, and I shook my head on a scoff. "Nice try, but glamour doesn't work on me."

It never had. Only very powerful vampires could use their glamour to try to influence other supernaturals. But it had never worked on me.

His expression softened with amusement, rather than annoyance.

I reached inside my bag and pulled out my bottle of water, some of my loose notes sticking to the sides as condensation had formed on the plastic in the heat. I should've used a koozie to keep it cold for the walk. I was suddenly in need of a drink to cool off my rising temper at this nitwit holding me up.

I shoved my notes back inside, then uncapped my water bottle and took a swig. He watched, his gaze dropping to the pavement before he shifted closer, back into my space. I hefted the strap of my bag into a better position on my shoulder.

"Honestly, I'm a little disappointed you'd try to lure me with glamour," I admitted on a huffy breath, watching a woman walk past with her Golden Labradoodle leading her. So cute! I was ready to be done with this conversation and be on my way, but I couldn't help asking, "Isn't that kind of beneath your stature as a celebrity and elite vampire?"

His mouth dropped open in surprise, but laughter still shone in his eyes. "I was attempting to lure you to lunch, not to my dark lair for nefarious reasons."

"So you say," I mumbled before quickly darting around him, my skirt swishing. "Have a good day, Mr. Kumar."

Walking faster, I couldn't help but feel his eyes boring into my back. So I picked up my pace, anxious to get to Angel Paws.

I mean, what was his deal? If he really wanted to make up for hitting me with his car, he could buy me some new potting soil, perhaps some new planters. But to be honest, as long as he fixed my bike, we would be totally even. He could just let it go. Pretend it never happened, and we could move on with our separate lives. Emphasis on separate.

I swung open the glass door of Angel Paws and marched down the corridor, waving as I passed the reception window. "Hey, Trudie. It's just me."

"Morning, Isadora. They'll be happy to see you."

I rushed quickly through the gate when Trudie buzzed me in. The soft padding of feet and welcome whimpers greeted me.

"Hey, you guys," I said sweetly.

A dozen wagging tails swished and wiggled inside the kennels. I started at the end, opening my canvas bag and pulling out their treats. After crouching down, I slid my hand in between the bars of the first kennel where a new yellow Labrador mix stared back at me. The handwritten tag on her door read *Frannie*.

"Here you go, little lady," I cooed. Her tail wagged as she reached out tentatively to my open palm. As she licked the treat away, I pushed a pulse of magic into her. The energy heated a trail down my arm and tingled along my fingertips. She jumped back, shocked by the zap, then her ears perked up, her tail wagging harder.

"Good girl."

I smiled and moved on, making sure to give Oscar two treats because he was obviously older than most in here with a gray muzzle around his terrier snout. Hardly anyone adopted an older dog. If I could give them just a little longer to live, a little boost to help them with any sickness they might have, then I would keep coming back in hopes they'd all find good homes.

I'd wished so many times that Angel Paws had a bigger network or something to find homes for these guys. They took good care of them, letting them out in the yard in the back daily. But they needed love and affection, not just food and board. My heart yearned to do more, but beyond adopting them all, I didn't know what else I could do.

Finally, I reached the last cage where my favorite little man sat waiting with his sweet eyes staring up at me.

"Hello, Archie. Did you miss me?"

He wagged his short tail harder. He was so scruffy and scroungy even after Trudie bathed him. He was just one of those mutts that was so ugly he was cute. I'd thought of bringing him home a hundred times, but I couldn't imagine him getting along with Zombie Cat and Fred. Z was so old he could barely escape a good pecking from Fred when the dang rooster was in one of his territorial, ornery moods.

Archie had been caught and brought into Angel Paws as a stray "going after" a lady's cats over on Camp Street. I couldn't ask Evie to give up her beloved Z or bring in another pet who might hurt him.

"How are you doing, my best man?"

I held my palm between the bars. He licked the treat, then kept licking my palm, almost like he was lapping up the magic I poured into him.

"You like that?"

He let out a whimper-bark and spun in a circle, his little dance to get me to give him more. He blinked sweetly from under the tuft of hair covering his eyes.

"Okay," I said on a laugh. "You don't have to convince me."

I pulled out another treat and fed it to him.

"If only men were as easy to figure out as you, Archie." I scratched his scruffy goldish-red head. "But they're not. And so aggravating."

He yipped, jumping up to put his paws on the cage. I scratched him under the chin.

"I agree with you. Why bother with men at all?"

He tilted his head to the right, one floppy ear tipping up, the other down.

"If I could find a man as cute as you, then I'd be the happiest girl in the world."

He yipped again and spun in another circle. I chuckled, reaching into my bag to find him one more treat.

Unfortunately, men weren't as easy to read or as easy to please as Archie. And why was I thinking of men anyway? I'd decided I was perfectly happy without them. Nothing they could do for me I couldn't do myself.

That reminded me I needed to find my package.

Chapter 5

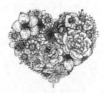

~DEVRAJ~

I LIFTED MY FOOT AND PICKED UP THE SCRAP OF PAPER ISADORA had dropped from her purse. Was it ungentlemanly to semi-steal a note that wasn't mine? Yes. But I'd glimpsed my name in a feminine scrawl which suddenly negated all rules of a gentleman.

Once I'd read what was on the paper, I huffed out a dis-believing breath, stuffed it into my pocket, then walked into the empty bookstore. I strolled past vintage bookshelves into the lounge area with plush furniture in blue, silver, and black. Dark wood tables topped with Tiffany lamps and votive can-dles gave the sophisticated but warm ambiance that suited Ruben's style.

The man himself sat in the wingback next to the blue velvet sofa in the farthest corner, dressed impeccably with a steaming cup of coffee beside him as he scrolled through his phone.

"Morning. Your grim isn't here yet?"

"Not yet." He swiped his thumb across the screen and set it aside, flashing a tight smile. "You seem to be in a pleasant mood today. Care to share?"

"Not in the least." I took a seat on the velvet sofa and stretched an arm along the back, crossed an ankle over my knee, and nodded at his phone. "Something up?"

"Not really," he grumbled, fiddling with a cuff link. "I thought Jules would want to be included in this meeting, seeing as she's the Enforcer of New Orleans. But she has work."

"You can just relay it back to her," I offered matter-of-factly. "Why so twitchy about it?"

He shot me an icy glare, but there was no true heat in it. I couldn't pass up the opportunity to tease him about his tumultuous relationship with Jules. That's what friends do.

"Anyway." He cleared his throat. "You want some coffee or tea? Barbara's back in the office and could get you something."

"I'm good."

The bookstore door opened and closed.

"There he is now."

I prepared myself for the dark push of his magic, throwing up my guards. Old vampires could counteract the effects of grim magic with their own.

Grims weren't witches, even though some called them sorcerers, but their magic was similar to Auras like Isadora's sister Clara. But whereas Auras pumped only positive emotions into others, grims did the opposite. It wasn't always negative emotions, exactly, but darker ones. Primitive, carnal urges that lived in everyone. Grims could pull those emotions to the surface and coerce a person to act on it.

Ruben's mysterious grim sauntered in, carrying a black messenger bag. His jeans looked a hundred years old. Probably were. He wore a short-sleeve black Nirvana T-shirt with the dead-man smiley face, revealing a full sleeve of tattoos on one arm and a half on the other, his hands inked too. There was even an unidentifiable tattoo spiking from under the neck of his T-shirt, like prongs wrapping up one side of his throat.

His milk-pale skin and coal-black hair and eyes gave him an otherworldly air even without his grim magic pushing and pulling on me. The intrusion of his magic forced an image in my mind. A flash of blonde hair, slim thighs, the hem of her skirt. That skirt hiking higher.

Fuck. I punched up a fortress-thick wall of magic to block it out. I sure as hell didn't need this guy's powers steering me down the carnal lane of naked Isadora. I had enough problems resisting those thoughts without his influence.

He gave Ruben a nod as he took a seat next to me, instantly setting down his bag to pull out a laptop.

I offered my hand to shake. "Devraj Kumar."

He shook my hand politely with a flick of his black eyes, then opened his laptop without a word. The laptop had no branding. Probably a creation of his own. Grims were known to be techy, since computers were the best tools to find and store information.

"No name?" I asked, knowing damn well he wouldn't give it to me.

He glanced at me sideways as he booted up the laptop. "We'll see," he answered cryptically, his voice husky and deep.

Ruben laughed.

He was enjoying this. As a Stygorn, I had access to extensive data and never had to break a sweat to get the most top secret information I needed for any reason. And here was this punk grim refusing to give me his name. I shook my head on a laugh.

Once his screen was open with a listing of video files labeled with dates, he angled the screen to face us, but he spoke to Ruben.

"You asked me how I knew the kidnappers were vampires."

"Kidnappers plural?" I asked.

"Definitely," he said with certain confidence. "My cousin developed software that tracks vampires."

Ruben leaned forward, scowling. "Say that again."

His light mood had vanished at the thought of vampires being tracked. My hackles raised too.

The grim wasn't affected in the least by Ruben's death glare. "Just listen," he commanded.

And I do mean commanded. I wanted to laugh at the balls on this guy. But Ruben must've trusted him because he eased up, lacing his fingers in his lap.

The grim tapped his laptop screen on the file labeled *Demo362*. "Watch this. It's surveillance that tracks heat signatures."

An infrared bird's-eye view of a street showed the heat signatures of people walking, some moving in and out of buildings.

"What is this?" I asked.

"This is a demo my cousin ran last year when he was developing the software. This is Bourbon Street on a Saturday night. As you see, some of these signatures are running hotter than others." He pointed to some that were outlined more red-orange than others. "Those are vampires. Possibly witches. And this guy, you can tell he's a werewolf." He pointed to one person stalking down a side street, his signature deep, full red. "But check out this group here."

He pointed to a group of five break off down an alley off Bourbon, walking for half a block before the signatures blurred, flaring yellow as they disappeared off the screen. The screen zoomed out, revealing more of the dark city and the group who'd blurred away. They streaked six blocks away, then stopped along Magazine Street before they slowed to walking again.

"Damn," whispered Ruben. "I want to buy this software."

The grim grinned, a devious glint in his eyes. "Not sure my cousin has plans to sell it just yet."

"Then why create it?" I asked.

He tapped to minimize the video. "We have our own motives for tracking." He turned to Ruben. "But in the case of these missing girls, he's definitely willing to lend a hand."

"How does he get these views of the city?" I watched the screen, realizing what a wide view he had of New Orleans and the suburbs surrounding.

"Government satellites, drones," he answered nonchalantly.

Like just anyone had access to such a thing. I glanced at Ruben with an is-this-guy-for-real? look. Ruben shook his head as the grim went on.

"So I talked to my cousin. I gave him the dates and locations of the girls' disappearances."

"He got them?" I asked, my pulse tripping faster.

"Only one." He licked his lips, tapping on the laptop. "The thing is, this software is under development and has its limitations. If we know where to watch, then we can track them entirely using our own drones. But we don't have cameras everywhere all the time."

"So if they trace out of range, then you can't follow?" asked Ruben.

"Exactly," he answered. "Our range covers the city, though."

I leaned forward, wanting a better view of the laptop screen. "I can follow a vampire's trace anywhere, as long as I'm within a few minutes of where he starts."

The grim paused and angled a questioning expression at me, but it was Ruben who replied, "He's a Stygorn."

The grim's brows raised and his mouth tilted, seemingly impressed. "Cool."

He then clicked on a new video file labeled with the name Barrel Proof and the date of the last disappearance. Emma Thomas.

"I asked my cousin to focus on Magazine Street bars last week since that's where the girls have gone missing. Since the three bars where the girls were taken were all within a few blocks of each other in the Garden District, I had a hunch our kidnappers stuck to familiar hunting grounds."

A wide view of the city popped on-screen with pinpoints of infrared movement, then slowly zoomed onto one building in particular. A few people walked casually in the parking lot toward the street.

"That's the entrance there." He pointed. "Just watch."

The time stamp at the bottom of the video showed it to be shortly after midnight when three figures left the building. Halfway into the parking lot, two of them walked on, seeming to stumble toward the street. The other remained still.

"That's Emma Thomas's friends heading for the Uber," he said.

I noticed three more infrared silhouettes surrounding the one still standing in the parking lot. "Why are they outlined in red but gray on the inside? What's up with the infrared?"

The grim grinned. "They're using glamour to shield themselves. It somehow messes with their body temperatures and creates this ghostlike image."

"Wait." Ruben frowned at the screen. "You're telling me your cousin devised a way to pick up vampires hiding themselves with glamour?"

"He's a smart guy."

"Indeed," I agreed, still absorbed with the screen.

The two girls at the curb paused for a minute, then got into the Uber and disappeared. That's when one of the hollow silhouettes grabbed the girl, Emma Thomas, and they all blurred away together.

"Bloody hell." Chills rose on my arms, watching the kidnapping take place.

"Did you track them from here?"

"As far as we could," answered the grim. "Watch. They first take her to this area near the river."

We all watched the infrared silhouettes near the river, not far from Magazine Street. They put the girl on the ground and stood around, seeming to be waiting for something.

"She looks dead," said Ruben, cold menace lacing his words.

I stared at her still image. "They could've subdued her with glamour," I reminded him. "Or with toxin if one of them bit her. Or some other human drug for that matter."

"They didn't kill her," assured the grim. "They stay here about ten minutes. Unfortunately, I wasn't watching these live. My cousin had cameras on sixteen clubs and bars that night. The day after Emma Thomas disappeared, we went through the footage and spotted this. Look, here. Now they take her away again, but we lose trace of them after they leave the Garden District."

"Goddamn it," I muttered, watching as the blurred silhouettes of vampires tracing away vanished beyond the screen of the camera.

"Like I said"—the grim shrugged—"this is new surveillance software and we haven't worked out the kinks. But basically, if we know where a crime will be committed, where the next girl will be kidnapped from, we can trace them almost anywhere." He snapped his laptop shut and shoved it in his messenger bag. "I don't need to tell you that if we're asked about this software by anyone else, we'll deny its existence."

"Then why show us?" I asked.

He stood and hooked the strap of his messenger bag over his shoulder, then fished in his pocket for a pack of cigarettes and a lighter.

"Some vampires are doing some shady shit." He lit the cigarette with a Zippo lighter, engraved with a skull wearing a crown, then shoved it in his back pocket. "If we can help catch these fuckers, we will." He dragged on his cigarette, dark eyes squinting behind the swirling smoke. He gave a wave with the fingers holding the cigarette. "Let me know when you have a location, Ruben."

He wove around the furniture in long strides and disappeared out the door.

"Interesting fellow," I commented. "And useful."

"Extremely." Ruben drained the last of his coffee and set it aside, his brow pinched in thought. "So we need a way to lure the kidnappers to one spot. Perhaps give them a prime hunting ground."

"Indeed. My concern is what they're doing with the girls. Is it just for a blood orgy?"

Blood orgy wasn't a pleasant term, but it was the common term used for a group of vampires who fed off one or more human hosts at one time.

"If so, then what are they doing with the girls after?" Ruben's voice had deepened. This mess was taking place in his territory, and there were vampires under his rule breaking the supernatural laws.

It was painful to think about what these young women were going through. But I could offer some solace. "They haven't found any bodies yet. So let's assume they're not being killed."

"That's all we can assume at this point," growled Ruben before standing. "What is it?"

He'd noticed my pensive expression. "Didn't you say that Jules had the power to null a supernatural's powers temporarily?"

"She does."

I nodded, then stood from the sofa. "I think I have an idea. But let me think about it a little while and send you the details."

"I'm open to all suggestions at this point. Anything to catch these assholes."

"I'll text you later." I left and headed to my rental sports car on the curb, my brain spinning with my still-forming plan.

I glanced up the street and couldn't help looking in the direction Isadora had gone. I wondered where she was headed this morning. All chipper and smiling. That is, until she'd seen me and I'd called her name.

Why was she so offended by my presence? I was a likable guy, dammit.

There was the fact I'd hit her with my car. True.

I found her fascinating. Was it because she seemed to want to flee my presence the second we were ever alone? I wasn't sure. Something about her made me want to know her better. Yes, I was accustomed to people liking me. Especially women. But Isadora Savoie did not, that was for sure.

And now, this fucking list of hers.

I pulled it out of my back pocket and then started the engine, wanting to take a look at her pros and cons list of "Devraj Egomaniac Kumar."

I was not an egomaniac. Just because I was better at just about everything than the average person or supernatural didn't mean I was an egomaniac. Huffing a sigh, I read to myself.

Pros:
- *Nice physique, but typical of most vampires really*
- *Somewhat considerate—after he runs people over with his expensive car*
- *Charming—but kind of over-the-top with it (note to vampire: stop trying so hard)*
- *Pretty hair*

I grinned. She thought my hair was pretty? Then I frowned. That was the only thing she didn't have a negative addendum tacked on to her pseudo-compliments. I sped the few blocks down Magazine Street but stopped for the red light next to Mystic Maybelle's. I reread the rest of the list then.

Cons:
- *Exceedingly superior and full of himself*

- *Needs to be the center of attention*
- *Too rich, clothes too fancy; obviously overcompensating for something*
- *Ridiculously expensive car and social media pics point to SPS*

Following that, there was a doodle of a man's torso and a micropenis between his legs. I couldn't help but laugh. Her illustration must have been of me suffering from Small Penis Syndrome.

I hung a right toward my rental house and then slowed as I passed the Savoie residence, grinning and shaking my head.

Isadora was intriguing. And funny, even when she didn't intend to be. The sight of her this morning, her face fresh and bare, her walk light and free, her clothes casual but pretty in that bohemian way. That's when it hit me what it was about her.

She wore no masks of any kind and a no-nonsense attitude with pride. There was no artifice to her at all. Living in a world where everyone around me had mastered the art of deception, I couldn't help but find her compelling. A strange creature I hadn't met before. One whose forthright and honest outlook made me want to stop and take note. To look. And linger.

I pulled into the driveway and stared down at the list one more time before stuffing it into my pocket. This witch loathed me on principle, but she definitely had a lot of misconceptions about me. And the gauntlet she inadvertently threw down with this damn list had my mind turning.

"Challenge accepted," I whispered to myself before marching up the walk to find a brown box sitting by the door. Frowning,

I immediately scanned with my senses to determine if this was a threat or if it was dropped off by one.

No sign of any supernatural scent on the box. And no dangerous smell emanated from within. No magical energy anywhere. Only human.

I picked up the package. Strange. I didn't order anything. Was it something the movers forgot and I'd overlooked?

I unlocked the doors, waltzed into the kitchen, and dropped my keys on the granite countertop. After lifting a knife out of the butcher block, I slit the tape and opened the box, then lifted another smaller box from within.

And stopped.

And stared.

"What in the—?"

I flipped it over to check out the package promotion that read: *Buckle up for fun with Big John! Nine vibration modes to deliver wide sensations. Waterproof for bath and shower fun. Whisper-quiet motor for wild fantasy play. Explosive pleasure-inducing orgasms guaranteed.*

Chuckling, I flipped it back over to read the vibrator's name. Some lucky lady was obviously going to miss out on nine modes of vibration to take her to ecstasy. I lifted the brown box it was packaged in and read the name and address.

My smile fell.

Isadora Savoie.

All intelligent thought stopped as blood drained from my brain and rocketed straight to my cock. The very thought of her sprawled on her back, her legs spread while she used this on herself, had my canines sharpening.

"Bloody hell," I muttered.

Slamming the vibrator back inside the box it came in, I folded the flaps, found some tape in a kitchen drawer, and sealed it as best I could. By the time I finished, my chest was heaving.

Propped under my arm, I marched for the door to go deliver it to the Savoie porch. Anonymously. As I opened my front door, I stopped and stared across their driveway to the house, imagining what Isadora would do if she knew I'd accidentally opened and discovered her new naughty toy. Then I remembered her infernal list in my pocket. A wicked smile split across my face.

"You shouldn't," I told myself.

But I already knew that I would. I stepped back inside the house, feeling "exceedingly superior" about my plan as I carried Isadora's package with me.

Chapter 6

~ISADORA~

"Oh yes," I could hear Clara saying with enthusiasm to a customer in the shop as I stood in the inventory closet. "It will not only keep enemies away but will likely turn many of them into your friends." She paused. "Hmm. One in particular, I think."

"Why would I want an enemy to be a friend?" asked the woman, obviously puzzled.

Even though Clara whispered, I could hear her clearly. "Because one will be your next lover."

The woman gasped, then stammered out, "I'll take the crystal. And two packs of the l'amour tea."

"Absolutely," said Clara cheerily. "You won't regret it."

I smiled as I stared at my inventory spreadsheet on my clipboard. Clara had obviously tapped into her minor psychic ability with the customer. Each of my sisters held power in their specific magical discipline, but they also had a touch of other gifts. Like

telekinesis and psychic ability. All of my sisters were powerful tele-
kinetics. But I wasn't. For some reason, I was a weak telekinetic
and barely possessed the psychic abilities most witches had. But I
was proud of my strength as a Conduit, even though it frustrated
me sometimes that I was deficient in other areas.

I hung my clipboard with the updated inventory list on the
nail on the inside of the closet and stepped out.

"Bye, now," said Clara, waving after her smiling customer.

I stepped over to the counter and pet Z, who was curled up
on the cashier counter in a basket with a pink polka-dot cushion.

"Why did you buy Z a pink bed?" Because Clara was in charge
of the shop, it had to be her who'd bought it. Even though Z was
technically Evie's, we all loved him to distraction.

"I didn't buy it. I made it."

"But pink?" I asked.

"Real men can wear pink," she emphasized, smiling at Z who
was now purring in that sputtering way of his.

When I pulled energy from the room, the light blinked twice.
I then poured a warm droplet of magic into my fingertips as I
scratched him under the chin before calling out louder to Clara, "I
hope you didn't tell that lady the l'amour tea would bring her true
love or anything."

Clara scoffed, moving out from behind the register to straighten
the bookshelf. "I told her the truth, of course. That it could draw
someone who is attracted to her to make his move."

"Mmm." My stomach growled. "Well, I'm going to pop over
and get Sam to make us some lunch. You want the usual?"

"Yep. Don't forget the extra pickles please."

"Never!" I called back, aghast.

She laughed behind me as I opened the shop door, the bell jingling overhead, then stepped into the alley that separated Maybelle's from our bar. I strolled to the kitchen entrance and let myself in with my key on the rubber ring I kept around my wrist during the day. I always waited till past the lunch rush because I didn't want to be a burden on Sam or Elsie, the line cooks who fixed our lunch most workdays.

"Hey, there, Iz," said Sam, stacking an open-faced po'boy with crispy fried shrimp.

My mouth immediately watered. "Do you have time for an order for me and Clara?"

Sam glanced over, giving me a smirky smile. "I always have time for you."

I grinned. Sam liked to flirt, but there had never been anything between him and the Savoie sisters. We'd come to think of him more like a brother. Same for JJ, our bartender, who'd been working for us for years. Our Cauldron family was just that—family.

"I'll have one of those today." I nodded to the order he was finishing up. "Heavy on the arugula please."

"And light on the aioli." He grinned while still dressing the sandwich in front of him. "And let me guess. For Clara, fried oyster po'boy, hold the mayo, extra pickles."

"Yep." I passed him by, grabbing a french fry from the basket on the workstation.

"Hey!" said Jules.

I spun around, stuffing the fry in my mouth and pretending I wasn't caught already.

"We're working here," she informed me with her maternal tone, turning back to her smoking skillet and pointing her spatula toward the door. "Wait out at the bar."

Jules was strict about her house rules, and I didn't blame her. She ran a tight ship and liked everything in order. I totally understood since I was the same way. In other words, we were the control freaks of the family.

As I pushed through the swinging door that opened up right beside the bar, I heard the light chatter of the midafternoon crowd and then loud, boisterous laughter off to my right. My sisters Violet and Evie were gathered alongside another waitress, Belinda, around a four-top in the corner. JJ wasn't minding the bar, but leaned against the wall, a towel hanging out the back of his jeans pocket while the four of them were riveted to the only one sitting. Devraj Kumar.

Evie huffed out a laugh. "So you were both caught with your pants down. Literally."

"With the king's mistresses," added Violet, actually looking shocked. Which never happened.

A flaming heat brushed up my neck and filled my cheeks. I gritted my teeth and listened intently while also telling myself to mind my own business. But I couldn't.

Devraj leaned back in his chair, using animated hand gestures as he held court in my family's place of business. I crossed my arms, feeling defensive and agitated. There were literally a hundred places to eat along Magazine Street. But he had to come here?

JJ pushed off the wall into a standing position. I swiveled toward the line of windows, tuning him out as he regaled them with some story about schmoozing his way out of trouble with the Spanish royalty. The foot traffic seemed light today out on the sidewalk as the heat index kicked up. More raucous laughter drew my attention back to the group in the corner.

Devraj caught sight of me at the bar and froze, his expression blank, his gaze piercing. Slowly, he swiveled back to Evie who was straddling a chair backward, her chin resting on her hands on the back of the chair. He launched into some other story, captivating them with his wit and charm.

But I wandered over to the window overlooking the side street and tried to ignore the way he rattled my nerves. A cute couple walked and laughed arm-in-arm, their perky collie tugging on the leash. I smiled, thinking of Archie back at Angel Paws.

Evie's loud, infectious laugh caught my attention. Belinda giggled along with her.

Devraj shrugged one shoulder, glancing my way as I walked back toward the kitchen door, hoping Sam would hurry the hell up.

"That's what happens when Big John joins the party."

Then they all laughed, even him before he homed in on me, heat simmering in his dark eyes, his lips parted in such a sensual look that sweat broke out on my back.

It had been a hot minute since a man had looked at me like that, that's all. I'd stopped dating a few years ago, immersing myself in happier pursuits. Like gardening. Men just didn't compare to the joy of hyacinth in bloom, sorry to say. Not in my experience anyway.

Devraj added in that teasing rumble, "Got to love Big John. Always there to give a helping hand."

Dawning realization shot through me like a thousand daggers hitting me at once. I suddenly stepped back, bumping my hip into the bar, my mouth going cotton-dry.

Big John? *Big* John. *Big John!*

No, no, no, no, no!

They all dispersed, but the he-devil just sat there grinning at me like the fiend he was. I had no idea what the hell the story was, but I knew without a single doubt his little tale was meant for me. To embarrass me. Even if he was the only one who knew what Big John was really a reference to. Heat raced under my skin, filling my cheeks.

No, Isadora. You will not allow him to get to you.

Tipping my chin higher and pretending to be far braver than I was, I cleared my throat and sashayed toward him.

"Hey, Isadora," said Evie, her ponytail swinging as she stopped in front of me. "You need me for something?"

"I just need to talk to"—I pointed over her shoulder—"him."

"You just missed the funniest stories I've ever heard." She laughed as she walked away toward a lone customer at one of the booths along the wall.

Violet was walking away, too, but she turned back to Devraj. "You're coming for dinner Sunday, right?"

Violet! I was going to skin her alive, then bury her in the back-yard in an ant bed, then resuscitate her with my magic so I could do it all over again. *Why?* Why were my sisters torturing me?

He was standing now. "Nothing would give me more pleasure." His eyes were still on me as I approached.

"Mr. Kumar," I said a little shakily, "might I have a word with you outside?"

"Absolutely." He dipped his head in a slight nod, his long hair sliding forward over one shoulder before he said formally, "After you, Miss Savoie."

I marched for the exit, not trusting my sisters who liked to eavesdrop. Pushing open the door with a little too much force, I exhaled a calming breath before I spun to face him. The amusement twinkling in his eyes and lifting the corner of his mouth made me want to punch something. Preferably his perfect face. He was lucky I wasn't a violent person.

I crossed my arms, feeling defensive and angsty. He mirrored me.

"I believe you have something of mine," I stated, low and with some bite.

"What might that be?" All innocence. Yeah, right.

"A certain *package*."

He lifted a hand and smoothed the short beard of his chin between his thumb and forefinger. "Hmm. I'm not sure. Describe what's in this package."

Really? He was going to play it this way? Unbelievable!

"I am not going to *describe* it to you, *pervert*."

He chuckled and then grinned openly.

"You are well aware of what I'm talking about." I glanced back toward the door of the Cauldron, afraid one of my sisters might suddenly appear and overhear us. Then I whispered, "Big John."

Those warm brown eyes trailed from my eyes down to my lips. "Big John, is it?" But his thoughts seemed miles away.

"You have it?" I demanded, clearing the breathiness out of my voice.

He nodded, his Adam's apple bobbing when he swallowed. "Have dinner with me."

I blew out a sigh. "No. Give me back my package."

"You seem kind of desperate for it." The wickedness was back in his eyes. Tenfold.

"You can't keep it hostage."

"Can't I?"

Hands on both my hips, I argued, "I paid for it. Are you seriously going to steal my vibrator? I'd say you're the desperate one if that's the case."

He let out a bark of laughter, his white teeth gleaming. Still no canines. That was a relief at least.

"Why won't you share a meal with me?" he asked, his voice softening. The velvety-dark timbre was unfair for any man to possess. But then, he wasn't just a man, now was he?

"Because I don't want to."

"Why not?"

Exasperating! I didn't like to hurt people's feelings, but if he was going to push me, then it was his fault. "If you must know, I don't particularly like you."

"Everybody likes me."

"Well, I don't."

He arched a brow, smiling wider. "You don't even know me."

"And I don't care to. Why is it so important that I eat dinner or lunch or whatever with you? Because I keep refusing you?"

"Maybe."

It was my turn to tilt my head back and laugh. "You are something else."

"So I'm told."

"I don't mean that in a good way."

"But maybe you really do?" He inched closer, the size and breadth of him suddenly filling up my personal space.

"You can't sweet-talk me, Devraj. I'm immune."

"You're sure?"

"*Ughhh.* I just want my package back. That's it."

He recognized the obvious frustration in my voice and posture. He measured me for several more seconds before his teasing expression morphed into sincerity. "Fine then. Swing by and pick it up this afternoon."

I frowned, not exactly keen on the idea of going to his house. Like walking into the dragon's lair.

"Or," he said slowly, "I could drop it by later, though I'm sure your sisters might get a good kick out of the fact that I accidentally opened it and found quite a surprise inside."

Flames licked up my cheeks. My sisters and I didn't hide things from each other. Or, at least, not those kinds of things. I was sure Violet and Jules were hiding a shit-ton from the rest of us. But I did not want to be the butt of the joke for them for the next month. Violet could be merciless with embarrassing things like our neighbor vamp receiving my vibrator by mistake.

"No," I said quickly. "I'll come by after work and pick it up."

"What time do you get off?"

"I'll finish about four o'clock today. Clara usually closes unless she needs me to."

"Good. Four o'clock." He smiled. "It's a date."

"Devraj." I snorted a laugh, unable to suppress it. "Me knocking on your door and standing on your porch is not a date."

He backed away, holding my gaze. "I look forward to seeing you soon."

"You're ridiculous."

"I think you mean marvelous."

"Oh. I have plenty of other names for you."

"I look forward to hearing all of them this afternoon." He winked, flashing his charming smile. "Four o'clock." Then he turned and strode down Magazine.

"What's going on there?"

I jumped and gasped at the same time. Violet held the door to the Cauldron open, watching me watch Devraj walk away. Why was I watching him?

"Nothing," I said, squeezing past her and zipping through the bar to get mine and Clara's lunch so I could get the hell out of there and away from him as fast as possible.

Chapter 7

~ISADORA~

THE REST OF THE DAY CRAWLED BY. I DIDN'T LIKE MY NEW PRECIOUS in the hands of that freaking vampire. I mean, I didn't think he was actually playing with it or anything, but his attempts to get under my skin were working. I didn't embarrass all that easily, but remembering his complete amusement at my expense had my cheeks flushing with heat yet again.

I spent the afternoon working on the books, but that didn't take long enough. I finished with too much time on my hands. So I started on payroll, even though payday wasn't until Monday. After that, I strolled back to the inventory closet and decided that the organization needed readjusting.

I mean, honestly, how can we mix the tarot cards on the same shelf as the Oracle? They're two entirely different things. Well, not entirely, but it's best not to get them confused. And the new shipment of geodes were stacked in boxes next to the crystals. If for some reason Livvy decided to fill shelf space in

Clara's absence, she'd more than likely just toss anything out there without thinking. Don't get me wrong. Livvy was brilliant—at marketing, promotion, and anything techy that we needed. But don't let her get near the products she sells so well.

By the time I finished, it was still only three o'clock. I decided to dust the shelves, much to Z's disgust. He found a table to hide under while Clara cozied up to an elderly woman in need of some pain healing. Clara brought her over to the packets of teas, the ones I'd made specifically to help with muscle and arthritic pain.

At five minutes to four, I opened the cabinet under the register, getting ready to tear out of there when the shop door swung open and in stepped three boisterous young women.

"Oh. My. God. Would you look at this place?" A statuesque blonde clapped her hands together loudly.

"Too adorbs," said the pretty brunette in a halter top. "Like it's real witchy stuff and everything."

I had a quick flashback to high school where groups of girlfriends like this found it so easy to move and talk freely in social situations. Whereas I would just break out into a sweat, trying to find the right words to say. Fortunately, I always had my sisters to lean on when I'd clam up.

The third one wearing the halter top picked up a very expensive crystal ball. "Brittany, you could totally tell my future."

"No need," replied the blonde. "You'll be slutting it up with Jared again this weekend," she said, lifting a geode of purple crystals. "There's your fortune."

"Bitch," mumbled Halter Top girl. "You're just jealous."

They congregated around the crystals, picking up and touching them. Like *all* of them.

"Maybe," said the blonde, "but I told you he was bad news."

"I don't care if he's bad news," responded her friend, picking up a deck of Oracle cards. "As long as he's good in bed." Then she knocked over several decks of cards on a standing display. "Oops."

They dissolved into giggles. I glanced over at Clara where she was still talking to the older woman near our selection of teas, then sighed heavily.

I'd backed up behind the register almost to the short hall where my office was. I hated dealing with customers like this. Okay, I didn't care much for dealing with customers at all.

My heart beat faster as I prepared to handle this, which I *didn't* want to do. It just made me nervous. This is why Clara handled the front of the house.

"Excuse me," I said, approaching the blonde. "Can I help you with something?"

I was aware my polite voice hadn't made an appearance and I came across a little aggressive. I was so shitty at this. My palms were actually sweating.

"It's okay, Isadora," said Clara, coming up beside me and putting a hand on my back, washing me with a wave of her joy spell. She fed it into me like I fed healing into Archie and the other animals.

I met her gaze and gave her my relieved thank-you-I-love-you expression. She smiled wider.

"I can help these ladies. Besides, I think someone is here for you." She nodded toward the shop door.

Standing just inside with his hands in his pockets was Devraj, taking in the whole scene. How long had he been there?

"Thanks, Clara," I whispered, then headed to the register to pull out my handbag from the cabinet beneath.

And no, I didn't miss those women ogling Devraj, maybe even drooling, as I swept toward him and the door.

"Was passing by right at four o'clock. Thought I'd walk you."

"That's fine," I said, rushing past him. Just glad to get out of there. He followed and fell into step beside me.

"You okay?" he asked.

"Fine. Why wouldn't I be?"

He arched a puzzled expression down at me. "You seemed a little nervous back there."

"Did I?"

How did I explain my social anxiety to someone who thrived off of fame and attention, who entertained strangers in bars with his wild stories?

"Hmm," was all he responded with.

I didn't know what that meant, and I wasn't about to spill all of my little insecurities or quirks, so we remained silent the short walk to his front porch. But I couldn't help but feel a warmth spread in my chest at his obvious concern. It didn't seem false, but completely sincere. Could there be more to this guy than I first thought?

"Would you like to come in?" he asked as he unlocked the door. He was wearing the sexy smile now.

Danger, Isadora. Danger.

"No. I'm good. I'll wait right here."

His smile didn't diminish. If anything, it brightened at my resistance. He gestured toward the cushioned bench on his porch.

So I settled onto the bench and waited. And waited. A long time for him to just pick up a package and bring it out to me. Right when

I was about to stand and knock to find out what was taking so long, he stepped out holding two cups of what smelled like spiced tea.

He handed one to me. "I thought you might like some tea."

The dainty cups with silver trim set on matching saucers looked too small in his long-fingered hands. I noticed he wore a thick silver band on his index finger of one hand and a gold cuff bracelet with black beading on his opposite wrist.

I was about to protest and tell him I just wanted to pick up my package and head home, but that would be pretty rude. Besides, the tea smelled divine. All that I managed to say was, "It's been a long day." It definitely sounded like a complaint.

He tilted his head slightly, raising his brow and giving me a genuinely compassionate look. "I think this chai might hit the spot after a long day."

Dammit! I couldn't dislike this guy when he was kind. And made me tea! As a matter of fact, all my reasons for disliking him in the first place seemed to vanish more rapidly the longer I was in his company.

I was the only tea drinker in the house except when someone needed my healing brews, so to have a cup I didn't make myself was a rare occasion indeed.

I was still uncomfortable in his presence. My back was stiff from sitting so straight and my neck was suddenly a little sweaty. I still wasn't sure why he was trying to spend time with me, but he was being kind. And I wasn't a rude asshole.

So I tried to relax just a little and took a deep sip of the chai. Mmm. Perfectly spiced with cinnamon and ginger and sweetened with honey. "It's very good."

He took a seat on the opposite side of the bench, not too close. "I'm pleased to hear you say so."

On a glance, I caught him watching me drink the tea, his gaze riveted. I frowned down into my cup. "You didn't try to drug me or anything, did you?"

He belted out a laugh. "No, I would never do something like that."

"Then why are you staring at me?"

"If I said it was because I find you extraordinarily beautiful, would you believe me?" His smile was teasing but his eyes were serious.

I huffed a laugh, trying not to roll my eyes at his sweet talk. The thing was, I wasn't the prettiest or the edgiest or the most glamorous of my sisters. I liked my green eyes, but I had blonde lashes, which meant, because I chose not to wear makeup most the time, I didn't dazzle the menfolk much with them. I liked my body, too, though I had smaller breasts than even Clara and not many curves to speak of at all. As the tallest, I was more legs than anything else. And that was fine by me. I had some nice assets. And some flaws, some might say. But I didn't care. I liked myself. Loved myself even. Just the way I was.

But *extraordinarily beautiful?*

I could get dolled up and make myself really pretty if I wanted to, but today with my hair that needed washing twisted in a tight bun, my baggiest mustard-yellow skirt that hit near my ankles, and a plain white V-neck shirt that had a frayed hem, I was far from the ideal beauty.

I sipped my tea and narrowed my eyes on him, which only made his smile brighten. "I would think you want something from me."

His grin widened. "Maybe I'm telling the truth *and* I want something." He crossed an ankle over one knee and balanced the tea in the crook of the bent leg, staring intently as I tried to read behind that cryptic line. I was still musing when he asked, "So tell me, how did you become a hermit?"

I coughed on the sip of chai I was swallowing and set the cup in my lap. "What on earth are you talking about?"

"I asked around about the reclusive witch, Isadora Savoie," he said with no shame at all.

"Why would you do that?"

"I was curious."

"And what? Someone told you I'm a hermit?"

He shrugged one shoulder, resting his arm closest to me along the back of the bench, his fingers brushing awfully close to my shoulder. "Some didn't even know who I was talking about. They knew all the sisters but you. Until I mentioned you were the one who rode a bicycle."

I would find this offensive if I actually cared what other people thought of me.

Angling to face him more, I said clearly and maybe a little defensively, "I'm not a damn hermit. Just an introvert."

"There's a difference?"

I licked my lips before continuing on. His gaze dropped to my mouth, which had my pulse tripping faster. And I didn't like that feeling one bit.

"Introverts simply prefer to be alone and not to be annoyed by other . . . humans."

"So do hermits." He arched an accusing brow, tapping his forefinger with the wide silver band along the back of the wrought iron bench.

"Look." I blew out an exasperated breath, not exactly thrilled about being so frank with a stranger. It was difficult for me to open up, especially to someone like him. Mr. Fancy Pants with fancy cars and a fancy life. "I just have a lower tolerance for people."

His sudden laughter shook something loose inside me. "Low tolerance for people?"

"They annoy me," I mumbled.

"Like I am?"

I pressed my lips tightly together, determined not to answer that question. But the smug expression on his face pulled it out of me.

"Exactly." I drained my cup. "Even if you do make passable tea."

It was better than passable, but Devraj didn't need too many compliments. His ego was already oversize. His grin spread, merriment written in every line of his face and in his sparkling, dark gaze.

"Passable, eh?" He reached up with his hand that had been resting on the back of the bench and twirled then tugged a loose strand of hair that had fallen from my bun. "I'll have to up my tea game next time."

His nearness and flirtiness disturbed me. I stood and smoothed the lock of hair he'd touched, then held out my empty cup and saucer. "Thank you for the tea. May I have what I came for now?"

Without hesitation, he took my cup and headed for the front door. Well, that was easy. He balanced one saucer on his forearm while opening the door, which was kind of impressive for such a large guy.

Must be all that yoga helping with good balance and limbering up. My mind strayed in a nanosecond. Sweat-slick skin, broad muscular back, tight, flexing abs, intricate chest and shoulder tattoo that I'd wanted to observe with a magnifying glass.

He'd popped back out with a brown box in hand. I banished my yoga-obsessed thoughts and sighed with relief, thankful to be done with this semi-embarrassing situation. His mischievous smile never faltered as he handed it over. I'm sure he was thinking deviant thoughts about me and my Big John or something, but I refused to be baited into another conversation about my sex toy. But then his gaze deepened to one of sincerity. "I am sorry if I embarrassed you at the Cauldron. I was only teasing you. Private joke between us."

"I know. I'm fine." Even so, my heart whimpered at his apology.

The box had obviously been opened and re-taped, maybe more than once? I offered my hand to shake his. "Thank you for the tea."

He took my hand, enveloping it almost completely, skating his thumb over the back. "You're more than welcome." He opened his mouth to say something else, but then glanced down at the box without another word.

I pulled my hand loose from his and took a step back. "Goodbye then."

He leaned against the open doorway, tucking both hands in his pockets. I glanced over my shoulder to catch him wearing that secretive smile as he watched me walk away.

Weird. I was sure he'd have some smart-ass parting words for me. But he'd done nothing more than eye my box. As I walked through the front door, I glanced down at the package in my hand, then launched upstairs to my bedroom and shut the door. Something was niggling at me. Did he do something to my new vibrator? He wouldn't.

Easily tearing open the box, I pulled out Big John still perfectly sealed in its original packaging, but then my eye caught something at the bottom of the box. A DVD movie?

Covering the DVD was a sticky note with masculine scrawl scripted in a more-than-pretty hand: *In case you need some help to accompany your new toy.—Sincerely, Devraj*

I pulled off the sticky note and read the title, *Dilwala Deewana*. And who should be starring in this sensual Bollywood movie? Yep. You guessed it.

"Seriously?"

Devraj stared out from the cover, his white linen shirt completely unbuttoned to reveal his sculpted chest and chiseled abdomen. A beautiful woman with waist-length, silky black hair kneeled at his feet, gazing up at him adoringly with one hand pressed to the bare skin of his perfectly ripped abs.

That man!

"As if I need *his* help. Please."

Like I'd ever watch his movie to get hot and bothered. The arrogance! I slammed the DVD on top of my dresser and stared at his offensively sensual smile, wicked expression, and beautiful chest, the lover at his feet staring up at him hungrily.

I started to storm from the room but then marched back to my dresser, picked up the DVD, and dropped it in my waste basket.

"That's where you belong," I muttered to my trash can.

And that's what this man had done to me. Made me into a muttering fool with pent-up aggression, and possibly repressed sexual arousal, and feeling far more agitated than was normal. And okay, I'll admit, a little hot and bothered, dammit!

The mere fact that dropping his movie in the trash made me feel satisfied and somewhat superior wasn't necessarily a good sign. He shouldn't have any effect on me at all.

I'd allowed him too much control over my own mood. So I marched off to the greenhouse to center myself. That's what I needed. And maybe a visit with Tia would help. She could always ground me when the world irritated me to death. Yep. Tia could help me relieve any anxiety or stress. Even if that stressor took the form of a yoga-fit and annoyingly beautiful vampire.

Chapter 8

~DEVRAJ~

"You want me to null a Stygorn?" asked Jules, not bothering to hide her look of shock.

"Temporarily," clarified Ruben as we stood in the back of the Cauldron's kitchen with its chef. "You've done it before."

She narrowed her gaze on Ruben. "Why?"

I glanced around the kitchen, making sure the sous chef and line cooks were too far away to overhear. They were busy shouting orders, and pop music played from somewhere, giving us plenty of privacy.

"Two of the four girls that went missing were last seen at Barrel Proof. I'm unknown to the supernaturals in the neighborhood, so if you null my powers, I can pass as human."

"And stake out Barrel Proof," added Ruben.

"Tonight?" she asked.

"The sooner the better," I told her.

Jules stared up at me. She was a petite, curvy woman. Her dark auburn hair framed her heart-shaped face. Her features were delicate, nonthreatening. Except for her sharp steel-gray eyes. Make no mistake, I knew the power of an Enforcer. If she wanted, she could do more than null my powers. She could drain my magic dry, then punch me through the wall with her telekinetic powers. Not that I thought she held any intentions of such a thing. But it made me wonder when nature put such mighty power into a small, seemingly delicate package.

Finally, she blinked heavily, apparently coming to some conclusion. "Come with me."

I followed her through the service door into a back courtyard, Ruben behind us. As soon as the door was closed, she reached out and gripped my wrists, her hands cool.

"Six hours should do it?" she asked.

My muscles bunched, my nerves already rejecting what I was about to do. "Let's make it four. I don't want to be without my powers that long."

She smiled and gave my wrists a squeeze. "Don't worry. I'm really good at this. I won't do any permanent damage."

Ruben coughed behind me. We both gave him a sidelong glance, but his smirk was fixed on Jules.

"Do you disagree, Mr. Dubois?"

"Not at all, Miss Savoie." His grin remained.

She blew out a breath that fluttered her bangs before she focused on me again. "It only takes a second."

She closed her eyes. I was about to ask her what it would feel like, then a sudden rippling jolt rattled my bones, literally shaking me in my shoes. Within a snap, I felt the change in my blood, in the beating of my heart, the strength in my limbs. There was a distinctive feeling of being less-than permeating straight through my chest.

"Fuck," I mumbled, looking down at my body, expecting to see it diminish in some way.

"It feels odd, I'm told." She dropped my arms. Her eyes glittered bright like stars in the wake of using her magic.

I pressed my hands to my chest. "It's agony."

She laughed, her head tossing back a little.

"She's laughing at my pain," I said to Ruben.

"Been there. Done that."

Her laughter faded and she glared at Ruben before giving me a pat on the biceps. "Don't worry, Stygorn. You'll be as good as new in just about four hours." She jerked open the heavy service door and called back as she walked through, "Send me a report, Ruben."

"Yes, Your Majesty," he muttered before telling me, "Let's go."

We headed down the alley beside the Cauldron toward his car parked on Magazine Street.

"I'm not lying," I said. "This feels terrible. Like something is missing."

Ruben scoffed. "It is missing, Dev. You're currently a mere human."

"Poor souls." I sighed, glancing toward Mystic Maybelle's.

Then my heart lurched. Standing in front of the building was Isadora. She glanced at me, then quickly away, trying to pretend she didn't notice me. Well, that wasn't going to work for me.

"Just a minute," I said to Ruben as he rounded the front of his car and got in.

As I walked over, she turned her head to me and smiled politely, rocking back on the heels of her open-toed sandals.

"You need a ride somewhere?" I asked.

"Oh no. Tia is picking me up." She nodded her head a little too profusely. "She's an excellent driver." Then she winced.

I couldn't help but smile. "Unlike me."

"That's not what I meant. It's just, yeah, I'm all good. You headed somewhere with Ruben?" Her voice was a little high-pitched. She was nervous again.

"Mm. Who's Tia?"

"My best friend."

I nodded agreeably. "Where you headed?"

"To get some dinner. Maybe a few drinks."

Narrowing my gaze, I accused a little too haughtily, "But you never have time for going out to dinner. Remember?"

Her green eyes rounded. She swallowed hard, her cheeks flushing pink.

She opened her mouth to say something, but I stopped her with a friendly wave of my hand. "Just kidding." I smiled. "But seriously, I'd like to—"

A horn honked behind me.

"Oh! There she is. Sorry. Gotta go." Then she swished by me, giving me one last glimpse of those emerald eyes and a deep whiff of her jasmine scent.

She was in the car and zooming away by the time I made it back to Ruben's car. I settled into the passenger seat with a heavy sigh.

"I know that feeling," said Ruben, pulling away toward Barrel Proof.

გ♪

I'd been sitting at a two-top in the back of Barrel Proof for over three hours, nursing a few beers nice and slow. Time was running out for the null on my powers, and I'd hoped I'd have had some luck by now. Barrel Proof was a rustic bar, one long and windowless room. Perfect for watching the patrons.

The polished dark wood on the floor and walls along with the cowhide rugs gave it a warm, welcoming atmosphere. They were apparently known for their whiskeys, offering over three hundred brands. It was obvious that some of the customers bustling in and out were regulars. Friendly waves to the bartenders and upbeat customers all seemed to fit here, which is why this one guy stood out among the rest.

There was a long bar that stretched almost the full length of the room. I'd watched a few loners come and go, but for the last forty-five minutes, I had my eye on one guy in particular.

Though my powers were temporarily nulled, I could still pick out a vampire when I saw him. We had a certain way of moving and observing others that was unnatural. Predatory. That's why this guy caught my attention.

Good looking with brown hair and wary eyes that glinted silver when the low light caught them at the right angle, he appeared to be in his twenties. As a vampire, he could be fifty or more with his youthful appearance. He was on his second whiskey since he sat down and kept texting on his phone. Nothing seemed out of the ordinary to anyone else's eyes. But to me, he was giving off definite vibes that had me targeting him and only him.

It was the way he watched the women in the bar. Focused. Assessing. As if he was running scenarios through his head. He was hunting.

This wasn't unusual for a vampire. However, there were rules when acquiring a blood-host. She or he had to be willing, so conversation was paramount. He'd made no attempt to speak to anyone, man or woman, since he'd entered the place.

The other trigger warning was that Barrel Proof wasn't a vampire den, like Ruben's Green Light. There were specific clubs where humans who were aware of the supernatural world and wanted to step inside our realm to engage with one of us as a blood-host. Humans experienced a pleasurable high from the toxin injected by a vampire bite. They also experienced a certain touch of youthful beauty from the toxin, especially if they engaged as a blood-host frequently.

But the humans here were oblivious to the vampire sitting at the bar, scouting for a victim. They weren't aware of our world, which made my subject awfully suspicious.

The door swung open to a trill of feminine laughter. Four lively young women swayed in and found a four-top in the middle of the bar. The vampire's gaze flashed silver as he focused intently on the newcomers. After about five minutes, he started texting furiously on his cell, his focus rarely leaving the women who bought a round of boilermakers.

I punched in a quick text to Ruben who was waiting in a dark SUV outside along with a crew of his men.

Me: We have a hunter. Could be one of our guys.

Ruben: Is he contacting anyone else?

Me: Yes. He may be rallying the troops.

Ruben: Good. Let him bring them in.

My heart pumped harder, the thrill of catching these pricks sending my adrenaline rushing fast and hard. I drained the last of the draft beer as the vampire became hyperalert.

I averted my gaze to my phone. Damn. He was definitely getting ready to take action. He had the look of a vampire taking close observation of his surroundings before he went for his target. Before he committed a crime.

I set my mug down, casually glancing at the door, then at the vampire. His gaze was riveted on me. Intense and burning. He shot off a quick text, tossed a bill on the bar, then slipped off his stool and down a corridor toward the restrooms. Probably heading for a back exit.

"Fuck."

I stood and marched after him, texting: He's on the move. Back entrance. Now.

Once in the hallway, I ran through the back door, unable to trace without my powers. Ruben's right-hand man Gabriel held the vampire from behind, his arm locked on his throat. Before I could reach them, the captive pulled out his phone and crushed it into shards of splintered glass and metal in his hand.

I shook my head. "Wish you hadn't done that."

"Fuck you!"

Ruben appeared out of the night with two of his other men, Sal and Roland. The vampire captive bared his long, sharp canines, struggling in Gabriel's grip.

"You can put those away," I growled. "Nothing will help you now."

He scanned me from the top down, scowling and heaving ferocious breaths. "Who the fuck are you?"

"You'll find out, oh"—I glanced at my watch—"in about two minutes."

His fierce expression was unflinching. That would change as soon as the null wore off and I had him all to myself.

Something caught my eye at his throat. It was a chain around his neck, but it looked strangely feminine. Reaching forward, I pulled the chain from his shirt, revealing a heart-shaped locket dangling from it.

"That's mine!" he bellowed, trying to twist away from me.

Without even thinking, I tugged it and broke it free from his throat as he tried to thrash around. Staring down at the delicate design, I said in a low, fierce tone, "This is most *definitely* not yours."

"She gave it to me."

The tiny locket weighed heavily in my palm, its psychic essence leaden in my hand.

"Who did?" As soon as the question left my lips, a jolt kicked my pulse faster with a lightning flick.

My magic poured back into me in a feverish flow. I clenched my fists on a groan of pleasure-pain as the rush of power returned, the chain dangling from one of them. Then it happened.

The memory echo still clinging to the necklace vibrated through my mind, whirling like a paper-thin photograph, coming to life. I stared down at the heart and flipped it over where her name was engraved in swirly script.

"Emma," I whispered, squeezing my eyes shut as the memory echo danced through my mind.

It's never clear when this happens. When my psychic ability merges with the Stygorn magic to bounce images through my brain, directed from a single object. Always a personal one to the owner. As if the object holds its own power from the love embedded inside of it. Memory echo was a rare gift only Stygorn possessed, but it's also uncontrollable. Like the magic deems what's worthy for me to see, for me to know.

I could see Emma Thomas, the most recent girl abducted. She lay huddled in a dirty blanket in an alley behind a garbage bin. She was unmoving. The memory blinked, flashing split-second images. The vampire standing in front of me was there leaning over her, whispering something to her as he took her necklace. He covered her in the blanket. More flashed images. A street name. Industrial buildings. Workers milling about who didn't know the girl was there, barely breathing only yards away.

I opened my eyes, hauled back my fist, and punched the fuck out of the vampire still held by Gabriel. The captive's head snapped to the side as he fell unconscious.

Before anyone could say a thing, I growled, "He's dumped Emma Thomas's body in the back alley in the warehouse district. She's still alive. Barely."

"Roland, get him back to the Green Light and into the vault," snapped Ruben. "Gabriel, you and Sal come with us."

Roland traced away with the captive vampire immediately.

Then Ruben turned to me. "Lead the way."

"Let's take the SUV." There were other images still trying to pummel my mind, rippling from the heart-shaped locket. The day her mother gave her the necklace on her sixteenth birthday. The overwhelming love the woman had for her daughter. "We need to get her to the hospital and get word to her family that she's safe as soon as possible."

Gabriel jumped in the driver's seat and I took the front passenger of the black SUV, Ruben and Sal in the back seat. We tore off toward the warehouse district, which was fairly empty at this time of night. Gabriel slowed when I started giving directions and stared intently out the window, looking for the same buildings from the vision.

"Turn here." I followed the beacon burning inside me, pounding into me from the fragile necklace in my palm. "There! Down that alley."

Gabriel jerked right. The SUV was too big to fit with the garbage bins, so he jerked it to a stop. I leaped from the vehicle and traced to the exact spot where I'd seen her in the vision, my pulse hammering with fear that we'd be too late.

But there she was, still unmoving beneath a dirty blanket that her captors had given her. Like that would be enough to keep her from dying out here all alone.

I knelt and lifted the blanket that partly covered her face, brown hair stuck to her sweaty face. Placing my palm to her neck, which was covered with bruised and healing puncture wounds from vampires, I felt the faint birdlike beat of her heart. Her skin was far too pale, her hands tucked in a ball under her chin like she was trying to get warm. It was spring and not cold at all, but her body felt otherwise. "She's alive."

"St. Catherine Memorial is closest," snapped Ruben. "Let's bring her there. Her family will be notified right away."

I lifted her and carried her to the SUV, getting into the back seat. Ruben sidled in beside me.

"We'll need to leave her anonymously," said Ruben.

"Of course," I agreed. We couldn't be connected with the girl at all, not even as her rescuers. It would be too suspicious. "She was too frail for the kind of abuse her body underwent with these assholes."

"Yes. Perhaps that's why they dumped her. That only makes me hopeful their intention isn't to kill these women at all."

"I'll find out once I get inside that fucker's head," I growled.

"We need to tend to her first," said Ruben. "Though I agree it's best we get her to the hospital and in the care and safety of the authorities and her family, she'll need a Conduit's healing."

I stared down at the still unconscious girl, knowing the paleness of her skin indicated they'd drained her too much. The fury at what had been done to her by my own kind burned through my veins.

"Isadora," I whispered.

Gabriel pulled up to the back of the hospital. Without a word, I enveloped my body with glamour and traced through the emergency entrance where an ambulance was parked. Humans might see a shimmer or a blur but I'd be gone before they could blink. I set her right by the closed back door, placing the broken necklace in her palm. Then I punched the button on the wall that requested entry into the back door and traced back to the vehicle.

When I got in, Ruben was on his cell. "Yes. Plenty of time for you to finish and close the kitchen," he was telling someone. "It'll take a few hours for the buzz of her being found to settle down anyway. We'll go after visiting hours end."

My pulse lurched at the mention of her name. Though I wasn't happy about the circumstances, I was thrilled at the thought of seeing Isadora.

"Sounds good," said Ruben into his phone before he ended the call and turned to me. "Let's grab some dinner, then we'll pick up Jules at the Cauldron and Isadora at the house."

I nodded. "After our hospital visit, we're going straight back to the Green Light."

My beast was hungry to bend that fucker's mind to find the other assholes he was in league with. Those texts he was sending were to his ringleader, preparing to abduct one of those four girls who'd come in last at Barrel Proof. Until he made me, that was.

No matter. I was a Stygorn. And I had everything I needed. One malleable mind in my hands. He would find out soon enough what one of my kind was capable of.

But first, I would have the pleasure of Isadora's company, whether she liked it or not. I couldn't help but smile at that.

Chapter 9

~ISADORA~

I WIPED THE TEARS FROM MY EYES AND HALF-SQUATTED ON OUR FRONT porch, trying not to pee on myself from laughing so hard. Tia laughed with me, though she was still standing without any difficulty. Unlike me.

"I know, right? Poor Marcus," Tia continued. "But he handled it like a champ. Even after she used that lie detector hex to make him spill the most embarrassing moments of his childhood."

She propped a hand on her hip, her face even more beautiful with the utter joy suffusing her expression. Her tight curls bounced on her bare shoulder when she laughed, her hair pulled back with a turquoise bandanna as a headband.

I shook my head. "And he wasn't angry?"

"That was the weird thing. He really wasn't. He laughed after Aunt Beryl's little test of wills was over and told her she reminded him of his own Sicilian mother. 'Tough as balls' he said right to her face."

"Wow. And what did Aunt Beryl say to that?" I asked, leaning against one of the columns by the front door.

Tia grinned coquettishly, her hazel-brown eyes glittering with dangerous glee. "She said he was fine for a white man, and since he handled himself like a class act, I was allowed to go out with him."

"Aunt Beryl–approved dating material? He must be impressive."

She winked as she reached for the doorknob, but then I wrapped my hand on top of hers, preventing her from getting away.

"So you're really dating him now?"

I was a little shocked. I couldn't remember the last time Tia had dated anyone. Like me. She and I had been united in solidarity against the opposite sex. Well, not against them really. But maybe we enjoyed a joke or two at their expense. And had been bound together in our attachment to singlehood for a long time.

She sobered, looking over her shoulder at me. "I can't believe I'm admitting this, but I am." Her little smile told me this was more than a passing fling. She hadn't said anything, but I could read Tia as well as my sisters.

She twisted the door and shoved it open. I fell in behind her, hearing familiar music coming from the living room television. The same filmi I'd been hearing coming from next door this past week.

"I guess it's convenient he's your neighbor," I continued, walking beside her down the hallway. "Easy access to your Italian stallion, right?" I nudged her playfully.

"Oh, Isadora. You have no idea." She stopped and squished my cheeks between her hands, then whispered, "You should try sleeping with *your* neighbor. You might like it."

I pulled away and marched ahead of her. "As if." I'd spent the afternoon complaining about the nuisance vampire neighbor. Rather than sympathize, she said it sounded more like sexual frustration, which I should use him to get rid of. I wasn't about to admit that the very same thought had crossed my mind earlier that day. But I'd always found men never lived up to my expectations. I'd rather avoid the hassle and just use my toys. I liked keeping things simple.

"And you hit the nail on the head with that stallion part," Tia added on a laugh. "Damn does he know how to use that body."

"Stop it! Now you're just trying to make me feel bad about my lack of a sex life." We stepped into the living room. "What in the fresh hell is this?" I murmured to Tia.

Violet and Livvy were sprawled on the giant living room sofa, popcorn bowls in hand, while Clara was facing the television with a pink scarf wrapped around her waist and shimmying her hips to the music coming from the blaring TV. None of them bothered to look up.

"I can't make my hips do that," complained Clara, swaying her pelvis in figure-eights. Sort of.

Then my gaze landed on the giant plasma screen that Evie insisted we needed for all of her sci-fi and Avenger movies she loved. I gulped, immediately breaking out into a sweat.

Devraj stared out, his lips moving, his velvet-dark voice resonating through the soundbar and filling the room. The camera panned out, revealing his white button-down billowing open. He stood at the center of a gang of seven other fine-looking men who danced and sang in unison, clapping hands and stomping feet to a heavy drumbeat, hips moving, chests heaving. And Devraj, his long hair blowing in the wind, his come-hither eyes fixed on the camera, on the viewer, on me, felt like an electric zap that pierced my chest and sizzled much farther down. I tried to swallow, but my throat was Sahara Desert–dry.

"What is this?" I was barely able to whisper.

My three sisters' heads swiveled to face me. Violet grinned with far too much glee. "It's the movie you tossed in your trash in your bedroom. *Dilwala Deewana.*"

"Are you kidding me?" I snapped. "Why would you rummage through my trash?"

Violet reached over to the coffee table and snatched my all-too-familiar weekly chores list that I'd posted on the fridge and waved it in the air like a flag.

"Just following your orders. And you tossed it out. Finders, keepers."

"Oh my," said Livvy, leaning forward toward the television.

Devraj was now circling a beautiful woman, the music having dimmed to nothing but percussion, his body an artful machine of rhythm and seduction. The woman knelt on a blanket, heaving deep breaths as he circled, trailing his fingers up her arm, over the slope of her bare shoulder, combing then fisting her hair until he firmly but gently tugged her head back, arching her beautiful neck. Then he was singing sensual words—all subtitled in English—against her lips before he ravished them. And they fell onto the blanket in a tangle of limbs and moans and complete carnal sensuality.

"Holy fuck," breathed Violet, grabbing at her chest like she might hyperventilate.

I understood because the close-up angle of Devraj devouring the woman's mouth and the lust-hazed look in her eyes told me this wasn't all acting. An unfamiliar spark of emotion shot through me like a poisoned dart. Jealousy? No way. And was that the same woman in the pictures of him on Instagram? Of course, there were quite a few other women in those pics too.

"Oh my God." Tia finally caught her breath and glared at me accusingly. "Is this the neighbor vampire? You didn't tell me he was *Devraj Kumar!*"

"What?" I was hot and sweaty and totally confused by my own emotions.

"The Bollywood superstar?" Tia's hazel eyes were wide and shocked and furious. "Are you fucking kidding me, Isadora?"

"I told you he was an actor! Why are you getting all over me?"

Tia scoffed, then growled, sounding more werewolf than witch. Then she zipped around the sofa and yanked the remote off the coffee table, stopping the movie.

"Hey!" shouted Livvy.

"What the hell?" Violet protested.

Clara had stopped dancing but her blue eyes were bright with humor and wickedness, an expression I didn't see often on her.

"Shhht!" Tia held up a palm while she flicked through Netflix, searching out a particular movie. She found it, another Bollywood movie. "You'll be thanking me in three seconds. Just you wait."

She started the movie but fast-forwarded through the opening.

"Come on, Tia!" shouted Violet.

"Just . . . wait for it." Then she stopped fast-forwarding and pressed play.

Devraj was standing in the moonlight, singing a slow, sad ballad about his lost love, while disrobing. Yes. Taking off ev-ery-THING.

"Dammit!" shouted Violet as he turned away just as the camera would catch him below his tight abs, panning to his glorious back, muscles rippling under dark bronze skin a thing of fantasies. Some women's fantasies, anyway. Not mine. Totally not mine.

"This isn't a bad view actually," admitted Livvy, crunching on popcorn.

I snapped to my sisters who were literally drooling over our next-door neighbor. Heat raced under my skin, furious with them and, I have to admit, turned on by him. Or his acting skills. That was it. Definitely just the acting skills, and the fantastic lighting and sensual music.

"He's so pretty," Clara said on a dreamy sigh.

Steam rose off the heated pool he walked into, the water sloshing around thick, muscular thighs. Moonlight bathed him, dipping into the shadows carved by his chiseled abdomen as he turned to face the camera. There was a tattoo completely covering one shoulder. A mandala in black and blue ink, an intricate design, feminine in some of the floral loops and masculine in the sharp lines along the outer edges.

Then he settled into the water, bracing his arms along the pool edge, his gaze fixed into some distant place beyond the camera lens. The water lapped at his chest, steam misting his face, his hair dangling in the water, his voice so very sad, singing about bitter longing and never having the satisfaction his body, his heart, and his soul craved.

I was completely and utterly transfixed. So much so that I didn't notice three people enter the room. It wasn't until I heard a deep, familiar voice directly behind me that I was able to snap out of my trance.

"Sorry to interrupt, ladies."

I felt the words brush against my bare neck, my hair twisted up in a bun. He was so close that when I spun around, I nearly fell forward right into Devraj. He caught me by the arms.

Oh my God!

I pulled back out of his grip, practically panting. If I could've crawled into a hole and buried myself, I would have because the smile he wore right then was the most salacious and knowing smile I'd ever seen on a man, or supernatural.

Tia paused the screen, which happened to be right as on-screen Devraj was stepping out of the pool, a close-up of water dribbling down his sculpted chest.

Jesus, Tia. Seriously?

Heat flushed up my neck and filled my cheeks. I was trying to find some sort of excuse as to why we were all so obviously ogling his body on-screen. But leave it to my sisters to make it even more awkward.

"We were just admiring your work," said Violet unabashedly, her chin on top of her folded arms on the back of the couch.

Clara sat on the arm of the sofa, her scarf-skirt billowing around her legs. "You're very talented," she said sincerely. "I've seen quite a few Bollywood movies, but not any of yours. Until now. And you have a *beautiful* voice." Clara sighed heavily like a lovesick schoolgirl, which only made me groan.

"Actually," he added, "I'm lip-syncing another singer. None of the actors are actually the singers."

"Well, you lip-sync prettily," said Clara, her cheeks pink.

"Thank you?"

"And move prettily," mumbled Livvy.

Clara slapped Livvy's arm, which made me want to hug my sweetest sister. How could they be so embarrassing?

Devraj didn't appear ashamed at all. If anything, he seemed quite pleased. Especially when he swiveled his dark gaze back to me. I hoped like mad that no perspiration glistened on my forehead because I could feel myself sweating from this entire episode. Then I noticed Jules beside him, frowning as usual, and Ruben, biting his bottom lip to hold in a laugh.

"Did you enjoy the performance?" he teased.

I opened my mouth, but nothing came out. I was speechless with humiliation.

Then Devraj eased closer. I wanted to step back because his intimate proximity wasn't what I needed right now. I schooled my features into nonchalance, the exact opposite of how I was feeling. Then I gulped hard against the dawning realization of what the scintillating emotion buzzing through my body and tingling along my skin was. *Attraction.* Intense, sweat-inducing, bone-melting attraction.

"Are you all right?" he asked, concern pinching his brow.

No. I was definitely *not.*

I nodded stiffly, clearing my throat and my frantic, runaway thoughts. "Fine."

"We need you to come with us." His expression sobered as he glanced toward Jules.

My eldest sister nodded.

"What's going on?" asked Livvy.

"We'll tell you later," said Jules. "Right now, I need Isadora."

"Oh, come on," complained Violet. "I hate it when you patronize us."

Jules rolled her eyes. "There's just no time for your one-million-and-one questions. We'll have more information later tonight."

"We need to go," said Ruben.

That's how I found myself ushered from one of life's most embarrassing moments out the door toward Ruben's car. I froze on the sidewalk when I realized Jules wasn't driving, my heart doing somersaults for a new reason now.

Too many emotions! I needed to get back to my quiet life of gardening and making herb bundles. I needed to hide in my greenhouse and burn a bonfire of calming incense.

"It's okay," said Jules at my side, giving my hand a comforting squeeze. She whispered low, "Ruben is a good driver. We're going to St. Catherine's."

I knew Ruben was a safe driver. But no one could explain that to my phobia of driving and cars. It was just one of those things.

"I could drive us," she offered.

I glanced over at Devraj holding the door open to the back seat for me and watching me with a quizzical frown.

No. I needed to be a big girl about this.

I gave Jules a little smile. "I'll be fine. The hospital is close."

Then I walked over and slid into the back seat, Devraj sliding in beside me just as Jules was about to from the other side. She was forced to round the trunk to the front passenger seat.

Trying like hell to ignore the heat radiating off Devraj sitting next to me as Ruben drove away, I finally asked, "What's going on?"

Jules twisted around to peer over the front seat. "Devraj and Ruben found Emma Thomas and brought her to St. Catherine Memorial. The doctors won't know what's causing her organ failure other than dehydration. They won't be able to treat her quickly enough if she's been bled too long. She'll need a strong Conduit."

I curled my fingers in my lap and leaned back against the seat, thankful for something else to occupy my mind and body. Something besides my spike of fear of riding in this car. And definitely something besides the traces of lust that still lingered and charged my skin. I mean, I'd have to be a zombie not to react to Devraj's acting skills.

"I see." Then I closed my eyes. "I'll prepare now. Wake me when we arrive."

Then I slid my eyes closed and began sucking energy from the air, the night, and the electrified city as we sped toward the hospital.

Chapter 10

~DEVRAJ~

I COULD'VE STARED AT THE WOMAN ALL NIGHT. ISADORA REMAINED SILENT and focused inward. Her magic whispered in the small space of the interior of Ruben's car. It felt like a sweet lullaby, a song of old, like footsteps on wooded paths taken only by her, lilting with waves of potent energy that cocooned the witch at my side. If I thought I could reach out and touch that magic that was hers, I would. I wanted to.

My God, she was so beautiful, and I honestly wasn't sure if she was truly aware. It was her frank honesty that took my breath away. In everything she did.

After her last rejection of my company at my quaint front-porch tea, I figured she truly was immune to my charms. As unbelievable as that was, I was thinking of giving up my pursuit. But not fucking now.

After seeing her reaction to watching my movie, there was no possible way I was letting this go.

Before she'd noticed we were in the room, I'd had at least thirty seconds to catalog her surprising reaction to watching me on-screen. Chest heaving with deep breaths, her heart rate galloping at a racer's pace, the sweat shimmering across the back of her neck and the edge of her hairline, but most importantly the scent of her arousal was too strong to hide.

She was turned on. By me. It took me a full minute to remember we were in a hurry to get to the girl at the hospital. And the most shocking fact was that my canines had sharpened to razor points. I'd had a hard time hiding them and my reaction to her.

Hunger. Pure, primal, feral craving. One that still ached inside me, making my gut clench with need. And unfortunately, made my dick twitch with need as well.

This scintillating witch was burrowing under my skin, and she was utterly clueless to the power she wielded over me. I stared at her, her head tilted back against the leather seat, her delicate fingers clasped in her lap. Her irresistible aura singing to my bones, beckoning me to inch closer. To smell and touch and taste.

"Devraj," said Ruben, his gaze flicking to me in the rearview mirror. "Were you able to read her memories earlier when we dropped her off?"

Ruben already knew the answer to this. He was distracting me. Somehow, he'd sensed my sanity fraying as we silently rode along into the night. Smart move on his part. Grasping for control, I focused my attention out the window to the city blurring by, refusing to look at Isadora, forcing my own pulse to slow.

"She was too fragile then." Finally gaining control of my buzzing senses, I added, "I'll try again if she's well enough tonight. But honestly, I'll have all we need once we can interrogate the man in custody."

"What man?" asked Jules, twisting to glance between Ruben and me.

"That's what I wanted to tell you," continued Ruben. "Our stake-out at Barrel Proof paid off. We captured a vampire right before your call. That's actually how Devraj was able to locate Emma."

"How's that?" she asked me, peering into the back seat.

"It's complicated," I explained. "Suffice it to say that I was able to retrieve her location through a necklace of hers that our captive had."

"What did you find out?" she demanded quickly.

"Nothing yet," I answered. "Getting Emma to safety was the priority when I discovered where she was."

"And," Ruben added, "Devraj knocked our captive out cold with one punch. So there was that." He caught my gaze in the rearview mirror.

I twisted my mouth in a wry smile, "Not a single regret. We'll deal with him later tonight."

"I wouldn't worry about how he made you at the bar," Ruben continued. "Experienced vampires pick up on signals other than magic. He might not have sensed your vampirism because you were nulled, but it's not like you look natural watching the bar from the shadowy corners of the room. He sensed you were a hunter like him."

Ruben was right. When I'd finally locked gazes with the guy, I couldn't back down as a dominant vampire. That alone told him I was something more than his senses could detect. So he'd cut his losses and taken off. Only, he didn't know I wasn't working alone.

"Well, I don't blame you for the violence." Jules turned forward as we drove into the parking lot of the hospital. "I'd have been tempted myself if I were there. And you were obviously right that Emma was the priority."

I finally looked over at Isadora and put a light hand on her arm, not wanting to scare her.

"Isadora. We're here," I murmured softly.

Her eyes opened, then she looked at me and did something rather uncharacteristic in my short acquaintance with her. She smiled at me. And my heart nearly plummeted into my stomach.

Christ. One smile, and I was devastated. Lost. Swimming in an ocean of what-the-fuck.

Ruben parked, and I took no time at all to unbuckle and get out of the vehicle, deeply inhaling the warm night air.

"Come," said Ruben. "We'll take the back entrance. My men should already be guarding every entrance to the hospital."

"And how are you managing that without causing a scene?" asked Jules.

Ruben just slid her a devious grin.

"Right." She sighed. "Glamour. It sure does let your kind get away with a lot."

"And protect the innocent," he shot back.

We entered near a stairwell where one of Ruben's men appeared out of thin air from where he'd been hiding in the shadows. "No one has tried to enter or exit here, sir."

"Good," Ruben snapped, then led us up three flights.

I kept to the rear, wanting to protect their backs. Unfortunately, that gave me a marvelous view of Isadora from behind. I tried to focus on mundane, unattractive things to keep my libido from riding me so hard. But even listing things like what was currently on my spice rack or the number of Italian cars I'd owned over the ages didn't keep me from zoning in on her long legs as we made our way to the third floor.

I strode ahead to Ruben's side as we walked down the hall to the girl's room, 310. But then Isadora stopped in the corridor, looking down the opposite hallway.

Jules stepped up to her sister and squeezed her arm to get her attention. "What is it?"

She glanced at each of us, then said, "She's this way." She walked off, leaving us to follow. Jules followed first, then Ruben and I stepped in behind them.

As we rounded the nurses' station, Ruben said, "We're here to see Emma Thomas. We were told she was in room 310." I sensed the tingle of magic in his words, using persuasion to avoid any problems if the nurse decided to deny us entrance.

"Oh yes, sir," the nurse answered automatically. "She's right down there, room 303. We had to move her earlier." Then the nurse turned back to the files on her desk like we weren't even there. She wouldn't even remember us once we left.

Ruben and I exchanged a questioning look. How would a Conduit like Isadora sense the girl had moved rooms? Could just be her psychic ability. Most witches had some level of clairvoyance, but then Jules hadn't detected it. Strange.

Isadora was already halfway down the hall, approaching a partially open door. Then a vampire appeared right in front of her, grabbing hold of her shoulder in a forceful grip. Not even realizing it, I whizzed past Jules and was suddenly there, lifting his wrist and shoving him off her.

"She's with us," I growled at Gabriel.

His ice-blue gaze challenged me for about two seconds before his focus slid over my shoulder and he stepped out of the way. "I apologize. I've been on high alert in case her captors tried to come back for her." Gabriel set his focus on Ruben and reported, "The police left an hour ago according to the nurse. We have her mother in a glamour-induced sleep inside."

With a light hand on Isadora's back, I ushered her through the doorway, fighting my urge to punch Gabriel for putting his hands on her. What was going on with me?

Ruben murmured with Gabriel behind us about the police visit, but I followed Isadora into the room where a woman was curled up in a reclining chair, sleeping with a blanket over her. She started to stir, but I whispered a sleeping incantation, and with a wave of my hand, the woman slept more heavily. Her hand on top of the covers curled around Emma's heart-shaped locket, the broken chain hanging loose. A pang of relief swept through me, that we'd gotten Emma to safety in time, that this mother now prayed for her recovery and didn't mourn her death.

Isadora glanced from me to the woman. "She won't wake?"

"No," I assured her. "I'll make sure Emma isn't frightened when she wakes."

Isadora then sat on the edge of the bed where Emma slept. The girl's face was still pale, as was expected from blood loss.

Emma stirred, her gaze landing on me first. She gasped, fear rounding her eyes and stealing her breath. I waved a gentle hand over her, willing her to calm with a whispered spell in my native tongue, "*Ham dost hain.*" I pushed a pulse of hypnotic magic into the air to settle over her, to convince her we meant no harm.

At once, she eased back onto her pillow, focusing her attention on Isadora.

Isadora glanced up at me, then back at the girl. "Hi. I'm here to help you, Emma."

"I know." My magic worked on her, persuading her that we were friends. She licked her ashen, dry lips. "They can't seem to make me feel better. I feel so sick. So tired." Tears sprang to her eyes. "And I can't remember. Not anything really. Except being in pain."

I clenched my fists till the knuckles popped.

A vampire's bite was mostly pleasurable with the euphoric toxins that released into the blood when fangs penetrated the skin. But the aftermath, once the toxins wore off, would certainly be painful. Especially if the vampire had been aggressive. Rough. Unless the vampire used glamour to ease the pain, which apparently these had not.

Glamour was a kind of persuasion that could be used to deceive the senses of others—what humans saw, smelled, tasted, felt. So it was a courtesy and a kindness to extend a glamour spell to a blood-host so that they didn't feel pain after they gave their blood. But these bastards hadn't bothered. Not only were they violating these young women by stealing their blood, but they also didn't care how much pain they caused their victims.

"I know," assured Isadora, her voice soothing and kind. "But I can still help you. Will you let me try?"

The young girl nodded, tears streaming. Isadora lifted Emma's hand in both of hers, whispering under her breath. The lights flickered and the IV shook as Isadora shifted the energy in the room and poured her healing magic into Emma. The young woman's eyes closed, her mouth falling open as she tilted her head back on the pillow, a look of almost ecstasy as Isadora fed her more and more magic.

Her pale cheeks flushed pink, then her lips, the sallow complexion vanishing, replaced with a glowing vibrancy. Isadora kept on, murmuring softly as Emma received the energy Isadora channeled into her. The vampire wounds on her neck faded, the dark purple bruising vanishing first, then the raised and reddened puncture marks. Finally, when Isadora released her, Emma sucked in a deep breath like she'd woken from a nightmare, her eyes wide in shock.

"What happened?" She was confused, which is right where I needed her to be for one more minute.

I stepped alongside Isadora and placed a hand over Isadora's where she held Emma's. "I'm going to take a look inside, Emma. But it won't hurt."

Her brow pursed in deeper confusion, but she nodded all the same, still fully under my spell.

Perfect.

Without waiting a second more, I washed her with a tidal wave of magic, letting my voice fall into a hypnotic rumble. "Close your eyes, Emma, and show me where you've been for the past week." I needed her fully entranced before I searched inside her mind.

"Of course," she obeyed, robotically closing her eyes.

I did the same, hoping like hell everything hadn't been erased. "Show me where your abductor has been keeping you."

"Yes," she agreed.

Just like that, I was in her head, stumbling into a world of darkness.

She breathed hard. She was blindfolded. I read for every scent and sound since I couldn't see anything through her eyes. I could feel ropes or bindings of some kind on her wrists. Then the sound and scent of two men drawing near.

A muffled voice of one man, then another responded as a door opened. "Thirty minutes is plenty of time."

Emma yanked on the bindings, but then the man crooned softly. Her body went limp with glamour before he punctured her neck and drank until she was listless and exhausted.

The fear riding Emma angered me the most since she remained blindfolded, but I listened intently as he walked from the door to her. It was a small room. The walls were close. She lay on a bed or mattress, but it must take up most of the room because when he moved, it wasn't very far. Then a medicinal smell. Antiseptic, which he wiped on her neck. At least he was keeping her from infection.

"Good girl," he purred again in a low whisper before latching on again and drinking deeply...

When he was done, he left the room, talking again to someone in the hall. Just before Emma fell into a toxin-fueled sleep, there was a distant sound of bells chiming. Church bells.

Her memories were hazed with glamour, like smoke cloaking her mind. There were other jumbled voices. Even another woman, not Emma, crying in the night. Then the next coherent memory was her staring at a garbage dumpster in the alley where I found her.

I pulled out of her mind and whispered soothing words to help her go back to sleep and to forget about my invasion. About our visit. Guilt hit me in the chest, having to add another layer of glamour on top of the snowdrifts our vampires had left behind. Being inside her mind was like being twisted out of shape and confused beyond reason. Her mind was so malleable it had flowed wherever the vampires took her. Wherever I took her. So easily. That's when it hit me.

"Come." I motioned for us to leave.

Ruben had remained near the door in the shadows, observing and saying nothing. Much like Jules who stood next to him.

Isadora stood and wobbled on her feet. I caught her by the arm. "Are you okay?"

"Yeah." She nodded. "It's fine. Most of the time I have no effects after transference."

I walked her toward the door, keeping a firm grip on her shoulder so she could lean on me. "But you don't usually use this much energy in normal transference, do you?"

"No," she agreed, "I don't."

She didn't fight my assistance as we headed down the corridor. With a flick of Ruben's hand, the nurses didn't see us pass, nor would they remember us coming tonight.

After making it back into the parking lot, I helped Isadora into the car. Then settled in beside her in the back seat.

Jules slammed the door, the last one in, and twisted around in her seat. "What do you know?"

"She was kept blindfolded the whole time. Most of her memories were wiped. She held on to just one. There were two voices, but I could only make out one." I clenched my jaw.

"What is it?" asked Ruben.

I met his gaze in the rearview. "This wasn't a blood orgy. It's a blood trafficking ring."

"Fucking hell," he mumbled as he pulled us out of the parking lot. "Are you sure?"

"I will be as soon as we get to the Green Light."

"What's at the Green Light?" asked Isadora.

"We have someone who may be a part of the abduction ring," I answered. "But I'll only know once I can question him."

Jules looked over at Ruben. "So he isn't killing them. Was Emma violated in any other way?"

"No," answered Ruben. "Gabriel persuaded the nurse to give him her medical chart. She was examined, and there were no signs of rape. She suffers from malnutrition and severe anemia only."

"Thank God," said Isadora, turning thoughtful. "I don't understand blood trafficking. Vampires can use glamour and their other assets. I mean, is it really that hard for you guys to find blood-hosts?"

Ruben and I exchanged a look. I raised a brow for him to answer this one. Isadora already thought I was the most arrogant ass in the world, so I wouldn't pile it on.

Ruben blew out a heavy sigh, then muttered, "Yes and no. For guys like us, it's far too easy."

Isadora huffed out a breath, smirking at me and rolling her eyes. I just shrugged. Because what was I going to do, lie and say it wasn't?

"I'll bet," said Jules, her gaze swiveling out the window.

Before Ruben could say something else to smooth over that giant foot he put in his mouth, I added, "But it can be very difficult for some vampires who are socially awkward. Or who built a reputation for being too rough. Or maybe they're just lazy. Or for that matter, just get low ratings."

"Low ratings?" asked Isadora, shifting her body to face me. "What does that mean?"

I glanced at Ruben who was shaking his head in annoyance. "Tell them," he said.

That got Jules's attention. Her head snapped back around. "Tell us what? Have you been holding out on your Enforcer?"

Ruben laughed. "My Enforcer doesn't need to know all vampire business. Except perhaps now when it might help us find these abductors."

"So tell us about these ratings. Ratings on what?" asked Isadora again.

"There's a sort of matchmaking app for vampires and blood-hosts."

"What's the vamp matchmaking app called?" interrupted Jules, pulling out her phone.

"It's not a matchmaking app as in a *love* match," growled Ruben. "It's for humans and vampires to find the right blood-host match."

"Is there a difference?" asked Jules, all ice-queen now. Ouch.

"And how do humans find out about this?" asked Isadora. "I'm assuming it's by invitation only."

"It sure as hell better be," said Jules. "The knowledge of supernaturals living among the human population must always be kept as low as possible. Who came up with this app without my approval?"

Ruben sighed. "I did. A techy guy I know developed it for me with an encrypted code so that it could only be accessed by those given invitation codes."

"Just like your club, eh?"

He slid his gaze to her, a silvery sheen glittering in his eyes. "Like you, *Juliana*, I like to keep things under my control."

"I'm well aware of that," she snapped back. If words could be laced with poison, those would've just killed the vampire overlord of New Orleans.

Isadora eased in, her voice tentative. "So what's the app's name? Ruben, can you send Jules an invitation to join? And that way maybe we can help narrow down suspects together." She was using the same voice she used on Emma in the hospital, trying to defuse the anger-bomb about to explode in the confines of Ruben's Mercedes.

He veered off Canal and onto Magazine Street. "It's called iBite."

Isadora laughed. Jules didn't.

Without looking at Jules, Ruben muttered, "I'll send you an invitation."

The rest of the car ride was steeped in heavy, burdened, angst-laden silence. And fortunately, most of that was between the two in the front seat.

When Ruben pulled up the Savoie driveway, I told him, "I'll meet you there."

He glanced at Isadora and then nodded without comment. Jules was out of the car and storming up the driveway while Ruben was peeling out into the street before I'd even had a chance to say a word. So when they both disappeared in clouds of fury, I turned to Isadora and smiled.

"It was a pleasure spending time with you tonight, Miss Savoie."

She was staring off at Ruben's taillights disappearing down the street, then turned to me and laughed. "You're such a liar."

"I'm not," I protested, smiling at her smiling. I couldn't help myself.

"I don't even know what that was, but it was not a pleasurable evening."

"For me, it was. I enjoyed your company immensely."

Her smile slipped, and that wariness reappeared in her emerald-green eyes. "You're going to interrogate that guy now?"

"I am."

She straightened her spine and tilted up her chin. "I want to go with you."

Bracing a hand on my hip, I said, "I can relate anything he says. You don't need to be there."

Suddenly, her hand shot out and planted on my chest, shocking me still.

"I *do* need to be there." Her eyes swam with anxiety and need and compassion all at once. "If you knew what I sensed when I was healing Emma . . ." Her voice broke and she shook her head, licking her lips.

My attention dropped to her mouth.

"Devraj. Please. I want to be there. I want to help these girls any way I can. I *need* to. I have to."

Desperation sang from her fingertips, pushing into me. I covered her dainty hand with my own larger one, pressing it close above my heart, warming it beneath my palm. Her mouth opened on a tiny gasp, staring at our hands on my chest as if she didn't realize she'd even put it there. I wanted to lean forward and devour her lovely mouth, but that's not what she needed from me right now. She trembled with a heady combination of despair and desire to help these women. If I could ease her pain, her need, no matter what she wanted, I would.

Gripping the back of her neck, I pulled her to me and pressed her cheek to my chest, then whispered to her temple, "Okay. Don't worry." Her hair tickled my cheek. I couldn't help but press my mouth to the crown of her head with a comforting kiss. "I'll take you."

"Thank you," she murmured, settling her weight against my chest.

We stood there in a silent hug for what might have been one minute. Maybe two. But that small moment filled me with dizzying bliss. Her slender body pressed to mine felt like holding home in my arms. I knew then that there wasn't anything I wouldn't do for Isadora Savoie.

It also dawned on me that it was getting harder and harder to fool myself. What I wanted with this beautiful witch was anything but casual.

Chapter 11

~ISADORA~

Somehow, I wasn't nervous at all as Devraj led me through the back door of the Green Light. We walked down a hallway where a few offices were, a supply closet, then he stopped at a closed door and punched in a code on a keypad.

The door swung open to reveal a short hallway where one of Ruben's men—the big, brawny one with a shaved head—sat at a chair next to another door with a keypad.

"Ruben here already?" asked Devraj, his hand on the small of my back as he punched in the other code.

"Him and Gabriel have been here for about ten minutes."

The door clicked open. Devraj took my hand and pulled me in behind him.

Ruben's icy gaze swiveled from the man who sat in a chair, his hands bound and head bowed, to us as we entered. His frown deepened. "Why is Isadora here?"

"I asked to come," I piped up. "I want to help if there's any way I can."

Ruben made a disgruntled sound deep in his throat as he turned back to the bedraggled-looking guy in the chair. "Not sure this is the place for you, Isadora."

The tall, hawk-eyed vampire named Gabriel stood behind him. His arms rested at his sides, but there was a tension to him that told me he was ready to act if their captive got out of hand. But it was Ruben fisting one hand that warned me this was about to get physical.

"No need." Devraj gripped Ruben's shoulder and squeezed then let go. "This is why you hired me. Remember?"

Normally so calm and congenial, this feral, cold-eyed Ruben sent a shiver down my spine. He cracked his neck and stepped aside to lean back against the wall, crossing his arms, which pulled his dress shirt tight over his lean torso.

The man in the chair finally looked up as Devraj lifted a chair from the wall and set it directly in front of him. Devraj settled facing the guy, his hands on his knees. There was a palpable sizzle of magic pumping into the room. All of it emanating from Devraj.

I stepped aside to the wall to stay out of the way and watch. The vampire in the chair was handsome, of course. All vampires were beautiful. But there was a savage edge to his dark eyes. As he focused on Devraj, who hadn't said a word, his eyes widened and he gulped hard, fear washing over his face.

"Oh fuck," he muttered. "You're one of them."

"I am." Devraj's arm shot out. He gripped the man by the throat, but he didn't appear to squeeze. "Tell me your name."

A pulse of pressure in the room made me suck in a breath. It was the residual magic rippling from Devraj's target.

"Darren Webber." No hesitation, but his voice shook.

"What were you doing in Barrel Proof tonight?"

"Hunting for a woman."

"What did you plan to do with her?"

Darren swallowed hard, squeezing his eyes shut, tears streaking from the corners.

"Do I need to repeat myself?" asked Devraj, his voice rough as rock.

Again, there was an electric snap in the air and a pulse of pressure swirling outward. He was using Stygorn persuasion to get the information. There was no supernatural with the kind of persuasive influence like a Stygorn. Not even an Influencer like my sister Livvy.

"No, no, no," he muttered, trying to shake his head, but Devraj's hold on his throat kept him immobile. "We were going to use her for our blood ring."

"Blood trafficking?" asked Devraj carefully.

"Yes. We get paid twenty-five percent of her sales as a finder's fee on top of the flat rate he gives us."

"Who is in charge?"

"Bellingrath."

Ruben made a subtle movement, straightening from the wall. "Blake Bellingrath?"

Darren gritted his teeth, but Devraj squeezed his throat and apparently pushed more persuasion into him.

"Yes."

"Tell us how it works from start to finish," commanded Devraj, his voice rolling hard and deep.

"Brandon, Patrick, and I find the girls."

"Full names," interrupted Devraj.

Ruben had his phone out and was typing.

"Brandon Schuller and Patrick Hobbs. We find the kind of girls he wants. Docile. Easy to pick off. When I have the target, I text Brandon and Patrick and they meet to help snatch her." Tears of frustration streaked down his face, his skin mottled red from the pressure of spilling information he didn't want to.

"Then what happens?"

"Bellingrath meets us at a different spot each time to pick up the package."

My stomach rolled with nausea. The package? These women were nothing but cattle to them.

"Where are the women being held?" I asked, desperate to find them and help heal them.

His fevered gaze snapped to me, fury riding him that he couldn't resist Devraj's power.

"Answer her," ordered Devraj.

"I don't know!" he yelled, squeezing his eyes shut. "Bellingrath doesn't tell us." He was heaving giant breaths, his face almost purple. "Please stop," he begged. "I'll answer anything. Just stop."

Devraj dropped his grip from his throat. This guy was totally defeated.

"What else do you know?" asked Ruben, his calm veneer back in place.

He tilted his head back to stare at the ceiling, despair written in every line of his face. "Only what Bellingrath tells us. We each

140

get a round with the girls. Drink off them first, then sell them to some party boys he knows before they head out on the town."

"What a piece of shit you are," muttered Devraj. "So he sells these girls to his friends for a quick high?"

He shrugged. "I don't know their names or who they are. Just that they're willing to pay the fee and keep their mouths shut. We're supposed to rotate the girls out after a while. To keep them fresh."

"You mean when they get sick?" I asked.

His petrified gaze met mine. He nodded. "That one chick seemed to get sick fast so we had to let her go first."

"Emma Thomas," clarified Ruben.

"Yeah. Her. Bellingrath said she was getting sick. Too weak to handle it."

I wanted to storm across the room and punch him in the face. Because what woman wouldn't get sick after being sold for her blood and held captive against her will?

"By let her go you mean dump in a fucking alley," Devraj clarified, revulsion in his tone.

Darren squirmed and whimpered. "Dude, we have to do what Bellingrath says. He's in charge."

"So he intends to release the others? Not kill them?"

He scoffed in disgust. "We're not murderers, bro."

Devraj struck him so fast it made me jump. My pulse pounded against my rib cage at the sudden act of violence. When Devraj spoke, his voice grated with malice.

"You may not be murderers, motherfucker, but you're kidnapping and terrifying innocent women and selling their blood for profit. You're *violating* them."

Darren shuddered, meeting Devraj's gaze with nothing but fear in his eyes. A drop of blood dripped from the corner of his mouth.

"I'll need to do a quick sweep," he told him before standing and pressing a hand to his skull.

"No, please!" he yelled.

"It won't hurt," Devraj said with disgust. "Just be still."

After one quick minute, he pulled his hand away and gestured for us to leave the room. When I pushed off the wall, Devraj turned to me, keeping his body between me and Darren. Not that this poor fool planned to do me any harm, but Devraj didn't seem to care. He put a protective hand on the nape of my neck as he guided me into the hallway.

"What did you see?" asked Ruben as soon as the door was closed.

"No more than what he said. I got a look at the ringleader, Bellingrath. And the drop-off points with the girls. Bellingrath traced away with each girl on his own. Darren doesn't know where the women are being held."

Ruben shook his head on a heavy sigh. "Blake Bellingrath. This could be a problem. We need sound evidence."

Devraj kept his hand on my nape. "His confession isn't evidence enough?"

"Bellingrath is from an old New Orleans family. Not only that, his father Harold is well-connected politically, both in the human world and the supernatural one. His wife is a witch. Marianne Baxter." Ruben gave me a meaningful look. "Her sister is Clarissa Baxter."

"Shit," Devraj muttered.

"Indeed."

Clarissa Baxter was the head of the Witch's Coven Guild over all of the districts in the southeast United States. She was well-respected and a mentor to my sister, Jules.

Devraj maneuvered his body closer to mine, his hand at my neck sliding to my shoulder. "Surely, we could bring him in quietly for a few questions."

"You know how it works, Dev." Ruben's gaze flicked to Devraj's arm around my shoulders. I blushed, not wanting to dislodge him but also wondering what Ruben might think. Ruben glanced back at the door, scowling. "Dammit! As much as I want to, I can't just bring that kid in like I normally would. Not without informing the parents of such a family. I'd have the witches on my ass if I tried. Wouldn't I?" He turned the last question to me. And though his expression was cold and fierce, I knew that look wasn't for me.

"I'm afraid so," I admitted. "Questioning him would only tip him off that you're on his trail anyway. You'll need to catch them in the act of their next abduction. Having Darren's testimony isn't enough."

"It's enough for me," added Devraj, a smirk tilting his mouth up.

I knew people like the Bellingraths. They were the kind I steered clear of. I'd rather be far from the spotlight and live my little life without all the fame and popularity. Which reminded me I was standing next to a man who lived in that kind of world. A pang squeezed inside my chest. Even knowing that, I had to admit a frightening truth to myself. I wanted him.

Glancing up at his chiseled profile, his close-cropped beard shaped nicely around that sensuous mouth. His strength and power was a potent force still resonating in a halo around him, eking from his fingertips, tingling my shoulder.

Yes. No denying it anymore. I wanted him.

"They have huge political connections," I went on. "They could say Darren's memory was tampered with by another supernatural. A witch, Influencer, who has a vendetta against the family in the political arena. No." I shook my head emphatically. "The only way is to catch Bellingrath in the act."

Smiling down, he gave me a wink. "Smart witch, aren't you?"

I couldn't stop staring, wanting to press my palm to my chest and try to force my heart to stop racing. Despite everything I knew about Devraj, and he was nothing like the man I should be with, I couldn't help but be lured into his magnetic orbit.

"What is it?" he asked, a worried line creasing between his brows.

I shook my head.

"She's right." Ruben sidled toward the door to the interrogation room. I had to wonder who else the overlord of the vampires had needed to hold and question in that room. "I need you to give him the order to pretend none of this happened and to let us know the next time they go scouting for the next target. Like Isadora said, our only hope to make this stick is to catch him in the act. Circumstantial evidence and memory reading by a Stygorn won't hold up against this family."

Devraj dipped his chin. "Fine. I'll be back shortly to take care of him. I want to get Isadora home first."

With that, he ushered me through the back halls of the Green Light, his hand on my back. We walked in silence back to my house. He'd suggested we take his car, but it was a short walk and I didn't want to confess my crazy fears of riding in cars.

The streets were busy with nightlife. Friends and couples sashaying down the sidewalk from one restaurant or pub to another. The lightness of the energy fed me somehow, lifting away the anxiety of my recent discovery. That I not only admired Devraj's glorious face and body, I admired the man as well.

His level of control during the interrogation and his obvious compassion about helping these young women showed me a side I was too blind to see when I first met him. I'd erroneously categorized him into the materialistic playboy category when there was much more depth beneath the charming veneer.

"You're awfully quiet," he commented as he opened the front gate leading to our porch.

"Just thinking."

"I gathered that." He chuckled.

Before I could step up to the porch, he grabbed my hand and pulled me to face him. Those rich mahogany eyes burned, flaming over my cheeks and down my neck, then back up to meet my gaze.

"Are you upset?" he asked softly. Sweetly.

"No." His tender tone made something ache beneath my rib cage.

"You seem so."

"And you're an expert in my moods now?"

"I'm an observant man." His hand slipped from mine to wrap around my neck. "And observing what makes you laugh or frown, what makes your heart beat faster." His thumb brushed my pulse. "It's one of my favorite pastimes." He eased closer, his voice dropping to an intimate caress. He slid his hand at my nape to cup my jaw, his thumb trailing along my bottom lip. "And you tend to fidget with the hem of your shirt when you're anxious." His other hand gripped mine where I did indeed have hold of my hem. He laced our fingers together, his broad palm against my smaller one.

Heart drumming like mad, I stared up at him, reveling in the sensuous feel of his thumb sweeping over my mouth. I wasn't a liar, so I couldn't tell him I *didn't* want that too.

Afraid to take that plunge, I simply stepped back until his hand dropped away, mourning that tactile loss. "Good night, Devraj."

I shot up the steps and into the house before he could protest, closing the door on the man who twisted my insides into a nest of mangled knots. Unfortunately, I couldn't help but lean back against the door and press my fingertips to my lips, relishing the trail of heat he left there.

If I was a risk-taker like Violet, free with my affections and wild at heart, I'd take Devraj up on his offer. To get to know each other better. But the truth kept nagging at me. He's the kind of man I could easily lose my heart to. After this job, he'd be moving on to somewhere else or jet-setting back to Europe or somewhere exotic and beautiful. And I'd be mending my heart in my greenhouse.

No. Keeping my distance from Devraj Kumar was definitely the right decision, I assured myself as I walked upstairs, touching my lips one more time.

Chapter 12

~ISADORA~

"Asshole," muttered Jules as she stared down at her phone at the breakfast table, her coffee steaming beside her.

I put the kettle on the stove, needing some caffeine this morning. I'd slept heavily last night after expending so much energy with Emma in the hospital. Still, I felt invigorated from using my magic to do such good for someone else. Don't get me wrong. I loved my quiet healing spells with plants and the strays I helped at Angel Paws, but something about healing Emma had settled a new kind of contentment in my breast. Also, the interrogation afterward at the Green Light had exhausted me further. Not to mention the fact that I laid awake in my bed for quite some time, trying *not* to think of a pair of whiskey-warm brown eyes.

I'd relayed everything to Jules that we'd learned from Darren Webber before I went to bed, so I wondered if something new had popped up.

"What is it?" I asked, shuffling in my bare feet and pajamas to the table.

Jules jerked her head up, her brow pinched into a deep frown. Then she snorted a disgusted laugh. "Oh, not much. Just perusing Ruben's ratings on iBite."

"He sent you the invitation then."

She was engrossed again, her head down. "Listen to this one. 'Mr. Dubois is so generous with his hosts, taking time to be sure the experience is as pleasurable for the host as it is for him. I highly recommend him if you're lucky enough to be selected. I'd do anything he asked.' Then there's a winky emoji. I mean, come *ON*! She's practically begging to sleep with him."

"Well, of course she is." I snorted a laugh then met her steely gaze. Oops. "Have you seen Ruben, Jules? I'll bet every single one of his blood-hosts are trying to get into his pants."

If looks could kill, her silver guillotine-eyes would've decapitated me. So I added something I knew to be true and would unruffle her feathers. Maybe. She was in quite the tizzy.

"But I know for a fact he doesn't sleep with his blood-hosts."

"How do you know that?" Her guarded expression flicked from her phone screen to me as she flipped through it furiously.

"Tia told me that one of Ruben's rules for the Green Light is that no vampires sleep with their hosts. Apparently, he says it's dangerous."

"How do you mean?" Now she'd set her phone completely down, focusing on me.

"Well, though I've never been bitten by a vampire, lore tells us that the bite itself can be addicting, right?" She nodded, then the kettle on the stove started to whistle. I hopped up to go and fix my tea. "Tia said that when you mix sex with the bloodsucking, it can be too heady a combo for humans. They become dangerously addicted to the vampire, and it's resulted in seriously unhinged stalkers and stuff. She said he has a zero-tolerance policy about it at the club and only sanctions it for long-term couples who've signed written contracts with other rules and such. You should know this," I couldn't help accusing.

I spooned some of the loose tea leaves of my own making from the greenhouse, a mixture to energize, into the silver strainer set in my cup and poured the hot water over it, the heady brew waking my senses.

When I glanced up, Jules's face was white as a sheet. "What do you mean? How would I know that?"

"I mean, you're an Enforcer. Didn't Mom ever tell you this kind of stuff? I figured you had all the intel on the supernaturals."

I set the strainer with the soaked tea leaves in the sink and settled in my usual spot at the table beside her.

She shifted nervously in her seat, sipping her coffee. Rather than answer my question, she asked me another. "How does Tia know so much about Ruben's rules?"

I couldn't help grinning. "Apparently, she's got a new boyfriend, her neighbor Marcus, and he does a lot of business with Ruben."

"The guy she put a hex on last Christmas and Evie had to intervene to fix?"

I laughed. "The very one."

Ruben was overlord of the New Orleans vampires, but he also had a hand in many businesses. I didn't even know how many, honestly, but he always had a variety of characters coming and going at his bookstore. Many of whom arrived with bodyguards and such.

As I sipped my tea, I suddenly became way too curious about something. "Can I see your phone?" I asked as I pulled it across the table.

"Sure." She hopped up. "I'm going to make omelets."

I scrolled back to the home screen of the app and realized that Ruben didn't even have his own profile. The comments Jules had found were under a forum for vamps who didn't use the app but offered a venue for blood-hosts to review them anyway.

Unable to help myself, I typed in a particular name in the search box at the top. Good grief! Six thousand and thirty-seven hits? From women all over the damn world!

The gushing and fawning over Devraj's *pleasurable bite* spiked my adrenaline. The things these women were saying! *Complete euphoria. Mind-blowing ecstasy.* And—oh, come on! *His mouth is now my go-to fantasy for getting off.* The worst was some woman named Elmira in Italy who wrote, *Ten million stars! No sex is needed with a man like Devraj. I came from his mouth on my neck and his teeth on my throat alone.*

I clicked off the phone, my heart racing. Jules was whisking her eggs furiously. And though I totally understood her angry vibes, that's not what I was feeling. It was envy twisting my stomach into knots, not anger. These other women had experienced pleasure in the arms of Devraj. Suddenly, I had the craziest thought. *Why shouldn't I do the same?*

Now that I was completely awake and feeling overly fidgety, I needed to get out. I rinsed my teacup and headed out of the kitchen. "I'm going to the market for some fresh fruit. We're all out."

"No omelet?" she called.

"Not for me. Thanks." I was too annoyed to eat.

"If they have any jackfruit, get me two or three, please."

"Sure thing."

Jules was always experimenting with new recipes, and the Asian market just a few blocks from our house had the most delicious fruit, local and imported. I was a bit of a fruit addict, so I made the trip at least once a week for fresh produce.

I pulled on a lightweight, sleeveless, chambray dress that brushed just above my knees. With small brown buttons all the way down the front, it was casual and comfortable, like all my clothes. Perfect walking dress for a lovely walking day. I pulled on my favorite gladiator sandals, grabbed my big bag, and headed downstairs and out the back door, only to stop dead in my tracks.

There, leaning against its newly polished kickstand, was my bicycle. Not only had it been affixed with a new back tire *and* front tire, but it was repainted to a bright, shiny red. And there were bright new reflectors on the spokes of the new wheels. I stepped up and ran a finger along the—yep—brand-new basket. Okay. Now I officially forgave him, and we were even. But I still refused to glance toward the house of Mr. Ten Million Stars as I zipped onto the sidewalk and headed for the Asian market.

I couldn't help but smile as I rode along. The temperature was perfect in the low seventies. People were walking their cute dogs, meeting friends for breakfast, and I was once again riding my wonderful bicycle, enjoying the breeze in my hair, which I'd left down today.

I pulled out my folded shopping bag from inside my giant handbag and wandered the produce section. I found some choice papayas. The mangoes looked a little underripe, though, so I only picked a few for later next week. My stomach rumbled as I perused the jackfruit, of all things. They were so ugly looking, but the fruity aroma reminded me that I'd skipped breakfast.

"If you're looking for a ripe one, then take this one." A large dark hand with long, well-manicured fingers reached in front of me and picked up one of the strange-looking fruit.

My breath caught in my throat as I twisted to face Devraj. I blinked a few times, not prepared for his dazzling smile this morning. It didn't irritate me like it usually did. Rather, I couldn't help notice the way his lips were so well-shaped and wondered how those lips and his canines had made a woman come without him touching any other part of her.

"It's lovely to see you," he said, his voice lower, deeper than his usual lighthearted, teasing tone.

That's when I realized I was still staring at his mouth. And he'd noticed.

"Oh." I shook my head. "Jules needed me to pick up three." I grabbed the one he held in his hand and tucked it into my shopping bag, quickly maneuvering to another topic. "Did you take care of Darren? I mean, did everything go well last night?"

"All good. He's under my compulsion not to reveal that we know anything about them. And he'll be contacting me as soon as there's a plan for their next move."

I nodded and picked up a jackfruit, but he stopped me with a hand, two of his fingers overlapping mine. I froze as he said, "This one is underripe. I can help you find two more good ones if you like."

I put that one back and pulled away. "Cool. Fine. That would be great." I tucked my hair back behind my ear. "How do you know so much about jackfruit anyway?"

"It's native to India, did you know?"

Feeling a little idiotic, I answered honestly. "No, I didn't." Glancing in his basket, I added, "Superfan of fruits and veggies, aren't you?"

"It's kind of hard to avoid when you're a vegetarian," he teased with a grin. "Well, mostly."

I couldn't help but laugh. "But you're a vampire."

"So observant, Miss Savoie." He picked up a jackfruit, looked at it, then put it back down. "You do know that vampires eat and drink human food."

"Of course I do. But a vegetarian? Really?"

"I'm Hindu," he said matter-of-factly. "Not as devout as I'd like to be, but even after three hundred years, some things never leave you."

Okay. Now I was completely fascinated with this man. I couldn't help but dig deeper, having given up my fruit perusal altogether. "What do you mean?"

He kept on the search, but his gaze skimmed to me every few seconds, leaving a trail of heat wherever it flickered. My cheeks, my mouth, my eyes, my shoulders. When I remembered the feel of his thumb brushing my mouth last night, heat filled my cheeks.

"The way I was raised, we didn't eat the flesh of any animal. My mother always taught me we should not take life when we can eat other things to nourish our bodies."

I stood there and stared at him. The way he spoke of his mother with such reverence had me speechless. But something gnawed at me. I didn't point it out to be mean-spirited, but because I was so floored by the contradiction. "You don't eat the flesh of animals, but you drink human blood."

153

His jaw tightened before he glanced at me, still sifting through the jackfruit. "I didn't choose to be a vampire. So yes, I drink blood. To stay strong. To stay alive. But I do not take lives." Then he turned to me, his amber eyes fixed heatedly. "Open up, Isadora."

I swear to you, I didn't think he was talking about my shopping bag. Stunned for a few seconds, I blinked my surprise away and opened the bag. He set two more jackfruit inside, his gaze never leaving my face. Fixed and piercing. And now it was time for me to go.

"Thank you." I cleared my throat, tucking my hair behind my ear again, even though it hadn't fallen away from the last time. "I appreciate the help."

I honestly needed to process what he'd just told me. My feelings of annoyance had morphed into sympathy and admiration in the course of a short conversation over exotic fruit.

"Well, bye then." I awkwardly waved, then beelined for the checkout register. Shaking my head, I reminded myself this was the same guy who bought million-dollar cars and hung out with movie stars. Because he was one.

"Are you hungry?" he asked from right behind me as I checked out.

"No. I'm fine."

My traitorous stomach took that moment to let out a ridiculously loud rumble.

"Your stomach says otherwise. How about I take you and your stomach out for brunch?"

"Um . . ." I was trying to find a good excuse to say no, but I was seriously struggling for so many reasons.

Namely his ten-million-star review by Elmira, the reverent mention of his mother, and the sadness in his eyes when I practically accused him of being a hypocrite for drinking blood while trying to maintain the faith his mother had taught him.

"Just brunch, Isadora," he urged as I swiped my credit card. "Then I'll have sufficiently apologized, and I'll stop bothering you."

I glanced over my shoulder where he was standing far too close, his body heat rippling off him in waves. I lifted my bag and moved out of the way while the cashier started ringing up his produce.

"Seriously. You *don't* owe me a thing. We're way past that." His face fell with disappointment because I'm sure it sounded like I was going to rebuff him again. I shocked even myself when I said, "But brunch sounds good. I could eat."

His dazzling smile reappeared with gusto, and I couldn't pretend it didn't make my pulse quicken. Hell, after falling asleep thinking only of him, I couldn't deny my attraction to him. One meal couldn't hurt, right?

"Wonderful. There's a place not far from here that I bet you'll love." He swiped his credit card. "Have you ever been to Gris Gris?"

"No. Afraid not."

He ushered me toward the door, a light hand brushing my back. I pretended it had no effect on me, but even lying to myself was starting to get seriously difficult.

"I think you'll love it."

And that's how I ended up finally capitulating to sharing a meal and my entire Saturday morning with Devraj Kumar.

Chapter 13

~DEVRAJ~

Rᴀᴛʜᴇʀ ᴛʜᴀɴ ᴛᴀᴋᴇ ᴍʏ ᴄᴀʀ ꜱɪɴᴄᴇ Iꜱᴀᴅᴏʀᴀ ɢᴀᴠᴇ ᴍᴇ ᴛʜᴇ ꜱᴛɪɴᴋ-ᴇʏᴇ when I offered her a ride, I joined her while she walked her bike the two short blocks to Gris Gris. We settled into a table on the upper balcony overlooking Magazine Street since it was such a beautiful day. The umbrella-style awning over the table blocked out the heat of the sun, and the breeze coming off the Mississippi River in the near distance made this the perfect spot for my first date with Isadora Savoie.

Make no mistake. Whether she knew it or not, this was a date.

Our waiter brought us two waters and took our drink order while we looked over the menu. Isadora stared at the brunch specials while I pretended to do the same but soaked in her lovely face across the table instead.

"So how does a vegetarian eat from a menu like this?"

Setting the menu aside since I already knew what I wanted, I told her, "I said mostly vegetarian. I allow myself shellfish on occasion."

Her lips quirked as she glanced up over the menu. "Well, that's a relief. I was feeling really sorry for you. I'm not a huge meat-eater, but I *love* seafood."

The waiter returned with two Bloody Marys. "Here you are. Are you ready to order?"

I gestured toward Isadora to go first. She blinked rapidly in that shy way she had, returning her eyes to the menu.

"Can I get the Gris Gris Shrimp and Grits? And also a house salad with extra arugula?"

"Great choice, ma'am."

"There's no iceberg in the salad, is there?"

"No, ma'am. None at all. And for you, sir?"

"I'll have the Blueberry Bourbon Pain Perdu. And can you bring us the Oyster BLT, hold the bacon on half of the order." I gazed over at her. "I thought we could share an appetizer."

"Oh, you can hold the bacon on all of it," she added.

"You don't eat bacon?" I asked.

She shrugged a slender shoulder, the sun kissing her tan skin not covered by the awning. "If we're sharing, I can do without since you don't. I might not like it, and then it would go to waste."

So considerate. It was a small kindness, but it only added to the thoughtfulness of the woman sitting across from me.

The waiter nodded. "An Oyster BLT, hold the B. Got it."

I leaned back in my chair, napkin in my lap, hands clasped on the table, unable to *not* smile in her presence. "Extra arugula, huh? And what is it you have against iceberg lettuce?"

She sneered, looking absolutely disgusted. "Iceberg lettuce has zero nutritional value. Did you know that?"

"I didn't."

"Iceberg only has forty IUs of Vitamin A." She rattled off the data she kept in that lovely head of hers. "Compare that to romaine lettuce which has six hundred and eighty, and it's a no-brainer."

"What's an IU?" I asked, amused.

"International units. Besides, it tastes like nothing. You might as well eat a piece of paper."

"I see. And how does romaine stack up to arugula in the IU category?"

She leaned forward and took a sip of her Bloody Mary. "Better in the vitamin category actually, but arugula tastes the best."

"Really?"

"You don't think so?"

She seemed perplexed by my lack of lettuce knowledge.

"I'm not that particular, though I'm not a fan of iceberg either. We have that in common."

I couldn't help but bask in the flush of pink that filled her cheeks. Why that statement would cause her to blush, I have no idea. But she blushed over the smallest of things, I'd noticed. Still, she was talking much easier than usual, so I tried to keep that going. I wanted her to feel more at ease with me. For some reason, she seemed so today.

"And you're happy to have your bicycle back? It rides okay?"

Her green eyes brightened. "Like nothing had happened to it at all." She smiled so wide my heart skipped a beat. "Thank you," she added timidly. "Especially for the wheel reflectors."

"Safety first," I said with a wink and sipped my Bloody Mary.

She had no idea but I'd ordered the biggest, brightest, safest reflectors possible to go on her bike. In addition, I'd made sure to replace her tires with wide-rimmed ones for easier balance and durability. The thought of something happening to Isadora, of her getting hurt again, had my protective instincts on high alert. It was in that moment at the bike shop where I'd interrogated the guy behind the counter over every detail of the new safety features that I realized I'd never been this insanely protective over a woman before. Without any attempt on her part, I was completely entranced.

This was no fly-by fascination. This was hardcore witchery. Oddly, she wasn't flirting or being overtly friendly or doing anything other women have done to lure me in. She was simply being her lovely self.

"Tell me, what is it you have against cars?"

Her smile morphed into that serious expression, the same one she'd worn when she conjured up lettuce nutrition facts. "Cars are dangerous."

I laughed, which caused her to frown. "And bicycles are safer?"

"Yes, they are. Did you know that over one million people die every year in car accidents?"

"No, I didn't."

"Stop laughing at me. It's over three thousand per day."

"Is that why you didn't want to ride with Ruben to the hospital the other night?"

"Yes." She sipped her drink again, avoiding my gaze. "But I know if anyone's a safe driver, it's probably Ruben. I was right. He was a very careful driver."

"I'm a safe driver."

She huffed a laugh. "Do I need to remind you that you hit me with your car?"

I leaned forward on the table, not bothered by that little fact at all. "But I had been driving for a day and a half straight. And it was quite dark. And you have to admit, you were wearing dark clothing."

"You're right," she agreed after a moment.

"Though it pains me to have hurt you in any way, I have to admit I'm quite happy that I did hit you that night," I said, letting my voice drop low. "Not that I hit you, just that I met you."

Her blush darkened her cheeks again while she stared down, stirring her Bloody Mary. She bit her lip, and I couldn't help but notice how her lower lip was quite full. Much more than her upper.

"So you don't drive at all?" I asked.

She shook her head. "I have a passport for travel and identification."

"You never even got your license?" This was unreal. I'd never heard of an adult not getting a driver's license.

"No need." She shrugged.

Our waiter delivered our appetizer, postponing my interrogation. I watched her face when she noticed the lettuce sprinkled around the fried oysters was arugula. She looked at me with an appreciative smile, and there it went again. My pulse tripled just from making her smile. There'd been a lot of things that made my pulse quicken over the ages, but a woman's smile hadn't been one of them. Till now.

"Dive in." I gestured for her to go first.

I enjoyed watching her smearing her oyster in the tomato jam and sugarcane vinegar. I tried not to stare at her mouth, but it was kind of impossible. I decided to move on to a subject that had been nagging at me since the night we went to the hospital.

"So why aren't you dating? Finding a man to fill certain needs instead of Big John?"

"That's kind of personal." She forked another oyster onto her serving plate with a small pile of arugula.

"I don't mean to pry."

"Yes, you do," she said with a tilt of the head and a casual smile.

"I can't help it. I'm naturally curious about you."

She wiped her mouth with a napkin and took a sip of water, avoiding my gaze for a few seconds. "I don't know. I don't date much."

Very closed off about that. Okay. "Who was the last guy you dated?"

I expected her to shut me down and veer to another conversation, but she surprised me.

"A witch from Metairie. We dated a little while." She shrugged that same shoulder, bringing my gaze to the curve of exposed skin. It looked so soft. I bet it was.

"He wasn't a nice guy?"

"No. He was nice. Very nice."

"Your enthusiasm is so convincing," I goaded sarcastically.

She smiled. "Honestly? I just got bored."

"So no sparks in the sack?"

"Devraj," she hissed under her breath, glancing over her shoulder at the only other couple out here who were far too engrossed in their mimosas and conversation to hear us. "That's none of your business."

"I'm just curious. But if you don't want to talk about it, that's fine." I tried for nonchalance, hoping she'd open up.

Even though a wave of pink splotched her chest and neck, she decided to anyway, much to my delight.

"It's just that I'm a private person, and I'm very particular about who I date and who I allow in my bed." She couldn't look me in the eye, but she went on. "Sometimes it's just easier to rely on myself." She sipped her Bloody Mary again before adding matter-of-factly, "I can take care of myself just fine."

She meant take care of her own pleasure just fine. My pants grew tighter while I imagined taking care of her in my own way.

"I'm sure you can." The waiter cleared the table and set down her house salad. While she busied herself mixing the greens and dressing, I leaned forward, forearms braced on the table. "But I'd like to apply for the job."

She laughed before taking a bite, then looked across the table, her smile slipping when she realized I wasn't kidding around. Damn. I really needed to adjust my crotch, but I didn't want her to know quite how arousing I found this conversation.

She examined me while she chewed, then arched a brow. "I imagine you think you could do better than Big John," she teased, trying to lighten the heaviness hovering between us. But I wasn't ready to let this go. Not even close.

"Maybe not. He could join the party if you like." I licked my lips before whispering intimately, "Actually, I think that would be a fantastic idea."

For a split second, a flash of both surprise and excitement crossed her features. The telltale blush coloring her cheeks, neck, and chest proved she was definitely thinking about my offer.

She sipped her water and wiped her mouth with her napkin. "You're being serious, aren't you?"

"Deadly." I held her gaze, green eyes swamping with heat. "Give me one night, and I'll prove it to you."

She busied herself with her salad, and I let her eat in peace. I wanted her to mull over our conversation, hoping she might come to the conclusion I truly was being serious. She had that skeptical look in her eye, glancing at me between bites, both of us watching the passersby below in between watching each other.

When the waiter cleared away the plates for the appetizers and set our main course down, she hummed in appreciation. She truly was a sensual creature. The delight in her eyes and widening of her smile expressed her pleasure before she'd even taken a bite. Yet again, I wondered what it might be like to be the cause of her pleasure.

"Would you like a bite?" she asked, watching me stare at her eat like a starving man. Little did she know, I wasn't starving for her food.

"Sure."

She pushed her plate across the table for me to reach. Lifting my untouched fork, I took a bite of her shrimp and grits.

"Very good. Would you like to try mine?"

"Even Jules's fancy french toast doesn't look that good."

I cut a bite with my fork. "It's the blueberry Bourbon syrup. Prepare to be wowed." I held the bite across the table for her to take.

She frowned at my attempt to share a bite from my fork. I wiggled my fork and raised my eyebrows. Honestly, I was 100 percent positive she was going to refuse to eat from my own hand, but I liked pushing her buttons. I prepared for a snappy protest, but then she leaned forward and opened her mouth.

Bloody hell.

I slid the bite inside and watched as she chewed and licked the syrup off her lips.

That was a really bad idea. I could barely breathe, wanting to lean across and taste the syrup from her mouth.

"You're right. I'm wowed." Then she continued eating her meal like she hadn't just punched me in the gut with an explosion of lust.

We were quiet a little while. Her enjoying her meal. Me wanting to pull her across the table into my lap and eat her for my next meal.

Oh fuck.

My tongue licked over my extended canines. I sure as hell didn't need her to notice that lapse of control. And I didn't need to be imagining what she tasted like because I was positive she wasn't up for being my next blood-host.

To be fair to myself, I hadn't taken a new blood-host since I'd arrived. As an older vampire, I could go a month or more without drinking blood to rejuvenate my magic and supernatural strength. It had been only two weeks, but that didn't seem to matter. I craved the woman sitting across the table like mad.

"That's a very unique bracelet," she said, gazing at the gold cuff embedded with gold and black beads that I rarely ever took off.

"Thank you." Wiping my mouth, I took a sip of water and pushed away my plate. It took a moment for me to force my canines to recede, but my control was something every Stygorn prided him- or herself on. Still, I was no longer hungry for food, my stomach tight with an unfamiliar knot of tension. "I made it from my mother's mangalsutra."

She finished eating and sat back in her chair, eyeing me curiously before studying the bracelet. "What is that?"

My heart clenched at the sudden flash of memory. My sweet mother and her sad eyes.

"A mangalsutra is a sacred wedding necklace in our tradition. A groom gives it to his bride." Interesting that I'd had others admire this particular piece of jewelry and ask me about it, but I'd never bothered explaining to them what it meant. Perhaps I didn't think they'd understand its importance or I didn't care to open up this particular pain. But for some reason, I found myself explaining everything to Isadora. "It was my father's promise to my mother that they would always be together. That they'd be protected from evil. In our tradition, a wife wears it until her husband's death."

She must've seen something in my expression because her own softened with sympathy. "And how long did your mother wear the necklace?"

"Until I was thirteen. The same year I was turned into a vampire."

I was well aware my voice had gone a little cold, but it was hard to discuss, even now, centuries later, without some resentment. I'd never asked to become what I was. And though I didn't resent the life I led now, it still grated my conscience that I carried guilt, being forced to drink human blood when I was once a devout Hindu. I often wondered how ashamed my mother would've been if she'd known. If she'd lived to see me now.

"Anyway, it was very difficult for my mother when he died. For any woman during that time period, being a widow was a painful struggle."

Isadora's intense expression roamed over my face, her voice a soft caress when she said, "But at least she had you, Devraj."

Yet again, my stomach clenched with some foreign emotion I wasn't familiar with. I'd wanted and sated my hungers with many women over the ages. This craving felt different. I didn't just want her body, or her blood, if I was to be completely honest with myself. Just being in her presence, soaking up her smiles and sweet company, was feeding a hunger I didn't realize I had.

"Yes," I finally agreed with a smile. "She did have me."

"I imagine she was proud of you. You were a very dutiful son, I'll bet."

"Actually, I was." Except for the blood-drinking I did behind her back.

The waiter came and dropped the check. I moved the conversation to their metaphysical shop and her role there to steer away from heavier topics while we waited for the waiter to bring my receipt. She rambled about her bookkeeping and inventory organization—yes, rambled, which was completely new for her in my presence. I realized that my shy girl only opened up like this for people she trusted. A fact that had warmth blooming in the center of my chest.

"Sounds as if you enjoy your work," I said as we grabbed our grocery bags that we'd stored at the hostess counter, then walked out of the restaurant toward her bicycle outside.

"I do. But I enjoy gardening most of all. Working in the greenhouse."

"No customers or pesky sisters to bother you."

She graced me with another of those brighter smiles she kept hidden and passed out like little gold coins. "Exactly. I like working alone."

"I gathered that."

We stopped beside her bicycle, and though I didn't want to part ways, I also didn't want her to know how desperate I was to spend the entire day in her company. One thing I'd come to understand about Isadora was that she was cautious. I needed another reason to spend time with her. Then it hit me.

"Ruben told me that Emma would likely need another treatment or two by you. I could give you a ride to the hospital whenever you need."

She pulled her bike away from the wall, after unlocking her chain on the wheel, and stowed her bag of fruit in the basket. "I'm sure I can get Jules to take me," she said, avoiding eye contact again.

I leaned my head down, trying to force her gaze up. "You mean, you don't trust my driving? Is that what you're saying?"

"No," she said quickly. "It's not that. I just." She shrugged.

"You don't enjoy my company?" I teased.

That pretty pink color flushed her cheeks again as she leveled me with those green eyes. "It's not that either."

"So you admit you *do* enjoy my company. Love it, in fact, right?"

She laughed. "You really are incorrigible."

"So I'm told. Repeatedly. By a very pretty witch."

Her eyes fell again as she straddled the bike. As if that didn't put another painfully lovely image in my one-track mind. Enough. Time for me to go. I held out my hand to her.

"Thank you for having brunch with me, Isadora."

She shook my hand, and I couldn't help but hold it a moment longer than normal, brushing my thumb over her soft skin, her quick, thrumming pulse.

"I should be thanking you. I really enjoyed it."

"My pleasure." I released her hand and tucked both of mine in my pockets, forcing myself to take a step away. Still, I couldn't help adding, "If you need anything at all. A ride to the hospital? A replacement for Big John? You can call me anytime."

Her mouth fell open in surprise. I memorized that image before giving her a wink and sauntering back up the street to my car.

Chapter 14

~ISADORA~

I'D BEEN LAYING ON MY BED, STARING AT THE CEILING FOR I DON'T KNOW how long. I couldn't get this morning's brunch at Gris Gris out of my head. No. Not the food. The company. The man. The vampire. He'd invaded my headspace and wouldn't leave, no matter how hard I tried to get rid of him.

I glanced over at my desk where Violet had set my DVD of *Dilwala Deewana.*

Sorry. Take that back. Where she'd propped it up with a hot-pink sticky note she'd grabbed off my desk and written in her swirly script: *This is NOT trash. Watch often. You're welcome. -V*

Unable to help myself, I closed my door and popped the DVD into the machine and turned on the TV on top of my dresser. Sitting back on my bed, I watched a little of the intro that was mostly about the beautiful heroine, then I fast-forwarded to Devraj. Before long, I was back at that point where I'd left off, where he took a moonlit dip. That's when I realized my hand not holding the remote was ghosting across my belly in little circles.

Glancing at the door, I hopped up and locked it, then opened my nightstand. Yep, there was Big John, sitting proudly in my nest of BOBs. I went to grab him, but then stopped. Behind me, Devraj sang with his hypnotic voice on-screen. When I looked back at the TV, the heroine had joined him in his moonlight swim, and he was sensually kissing down her throat in between singing in his silky-smooth voice.

Give me one night, and I'll prove it to you.

What would it be like to be the focus of all of that vampire's attention? Biting my lip, I watched him make love to the woman on-screen and couldn't deny the flare of jealousy burning up my skin.

Whether it was pretend or not, I was burning up with jealousy of a movie star or the relationship he might or might not have had with her off-screen. The thing was, it wasn't just his beautiful body that had my stomach twisted into knots and my libido revving to go. He was compelling on so many levels, and I just couldn't deny I honestly wanted to see what he could offer. For only one night, of course. What could be the harm?

I debated for all of two more minutes, then I shut my nightstand door, turned off the TV, threw a few extra things I thought we'd need into my purse, then headed downstairs before I lost my nerve. Someone was watching television in the living room.

When I popped my head in, it was Evie and her boyfriend, Mateo, curled up on the couch together, practically glued to each other. They were watching *Avengers: End Game* and Mateo was playing with her ponytail, his gaze on her, not the TV. They were disgustingly adorable, and so in love.

"Hey, Evie. I'm going to pop out for a while. Don't wait up."

"Headed to Tia's?" she asked.

"Mm-hmm," I lied, turning for the front door before she asked for details.

I wasn't a liar and just that teensy tiny one made my insides clench. But I sure as hell wasn't telling her where I was really going.

"Make her drive you home," she called. "It'll be too late to ride back on your bike."

"Okay!" I said as I opened the front door.

Crap. Now I had to take my bicycle to fake that I was headed to Tia's. This little escapade had already turned into something bigger than I'd planned.

It was late afternoon, the sun casting a warm glow on the houses and landscape as I rode my bicycle down the driveway, onto the sidewalk, and up the driveway next door. He'd gotten his Lamborghini back. I decided to park my bicycle well under the open garage behind the car, just in case one of my sisters passed by for some reason.

I felt like I was sneaking around, because I guess I was.

Hiking my bag over my shoulder to cross my chest, I opened the wrought iron gate that led to his back door. At the center of his pretty brick courtyard, there was a trickling fountain that butted up against the white fence that separated our backyards. Summoning courage, I inhaled a deep breath and knocked on the door.

No answer. This could be a terrible mistake. What if he already had a woman in there? A blood-host? A lover? Or both? And he was at this very minute kissing down her throat like he did that actress in the movie. What if they were going to town in his no-doubt luxurious bed, and I was standing here on his doorstep like an idiot?

Oh, hell.

I turned away right as the door swung open. Devraj stood there in his jeans, a T-shirt, and his bare feet, his long hair down around his shoulders. He had a kitchen towel in his hand and something smelled heavenly coming from his kitchen. His signature smile beamed as his warm brown eyes ate me up from top to bottom.

I didn't even think to change, dammit! What kind of panties was I wearing? Did it really matter?

"This is a pleasant surprise."

"Hi." My voice had a little squeak to it, but there was no going back now. Lifting my chin, I plowed forward. "I'd like to take you up on your offer," I said with as much confidence as I could manage. "On a one-night stand. Well, not a whole night. Just one time. Or one sitting really." A sitting? This wasn't a portrait painting. I glanced back at the darkening sky. "A one-evening stand, I suppose. I have till ten o'clock." After that, Jules would be texting Tia, frantically worrying about me because I was always in bed by ten-thirty. Always. "If the offer still stands, of course."

During my ridiculous word-vomit, I made myself hold still and not fidget while his smile slipped and his jaw slid open.

He blinked. And blinked again. Did I break him?

"Or maybe we can do it another night."

As I turned to walk away, he grabbed my hand. "Come in. Are you hungry?"

I let him guide me down the short hall and through a very clean living room. There were no signs of moving boxes. He'd settled in quickly, but I guess that was normal for someone who traveled as much as he probably did. Though decorations were sparse, he had some unique and beautiful furnishings and decor.

But I didn't have time to soak it in before he pulled me into a well-lit kitchen.

Forcing myself to relax a little since it was obvious he wasn't going to pounce on me like I imagined this happening, I said, "It smells delicious. What are you cooking?"

He dropped my hand and ambled over to the stove where he had a chopping board and some purple onions partially diced, the knife set aside. The thought of him doing something simple and domestic when I knocked on the door—rather than him ravishing some nameless woman in his bedroom—had me breathing easier.

"It's called dabeli. One of my favorites." He flashed a smile over his shoulder as he continued chopping. "Have a seat."

He gestured toward the island where two barstools stood. Setting my handbag down on his kitchen table, I took a seat at the island behind him.

"What's that there?" I asked, pointing to the mixing bowl next to a variety of ingredients.

"This is the dabeli masala and sweet chutney," he said, setting the mixture aside as his nonstick pan heated. He poured some oil in the pan. "I'm making the stuffing now."

He continued to add some mashed potatoes and diced onions to the sizzling pan, then the mixture from the bowl. His back was to me, which only drew my eyes to the broad expanse as his hands moved lithely, stirring the ingredients into the pan. I couldn't help but watch his muscles flex and move under his T-shirt that stretched a little too tight. I'd only seen him in dress shirts before.

He removed the pan from the flame and transferred the mixture to a plate where he pressed it with the flat of a wooden spoon. Finally, he sprinkled it with coriander, coconut, and pomegranate.

"Here. Taste." He turned with a small spoonful of the stuffing and held it up to my mouth, a smile ticking up on one side.

I let him feed it to me. He watched my mouth as I chewed. The flavor was delicious.

"And do you eat it just like that?" I asked, pretending I hadn't come here solely for sex and this was perfectly normal.

"No. They go into the pavs." He pointed to what looked like sweet rolls, cut down the middle. "I'll make you a few right now if you want."

This man had an unfairly sensual voice. Deep, dark, and rich. A timbre that normally rolled with sweet promises and soft seduction. But right now? It had morphed into some kind of entity all its own. A superpower he was using to lure me closer. The thing was, he didn't have to seduce me. I was here of my own accord for just one thing. And even so, his voice, his beauty, his alluring mannerisms and yes, dammit, his irresistible charm, had me completely trapped. Entranced. Wanting.

I licked my lips but couldn't seem to find any words.

"You are hungry, aren't you, Isadora?"

Those dark eyes rolled with silver.

I nodded.

"For food?" he asked. "Or something else?"

"Something else. I already told you."

And I wasn't going to repeat myself because once was all I could bear.

He set the spoon aside without removing his gaze from mine, then planted his hands on the island countertop on either side of my hips, trapping me within his embrace.

"One night?" he asked, raising his brow in question.

"Not a whole night," I clarified. "I have to be home by ten o'clock."

His mouth—wow, he had lovely lips—quirked up on one side, finding this amusing for some reason.

"Then we better get started," he whispered, leaning in.

He was going to kiss me. *Of course* he was going to kiss me. What was I thinking? Then why was my heart trying to leap out of my chest at this sudden revelation?

I don't know what I expected. Something tender? Or fierce and ravishing like he'd done to the woman in his movie? I wasn't sure. But what I didn't expect was the unbelievably slow descent of his mouth, barely open as it swept feather-soft against mine.

My eyes slid closed automatically as he continued his gentle sweep, not once landing. When he traced the seam of my lips with the tip of his tongue, I gasped. He glided one hand around my nape, holding me still, firm and possessive. He skated his thumb up my jaw in a tender caress, pausing at the tip of my chin, all the while seducing my mouth with whispery brushes of his lips. It was maddening.

Then he pulled his mouth away, making me groan in frustration. My pulse pounded a million miles a minute. I was sure he could hear it. I dared to open my eyes, knowing I'd find that smirky smile of his as he watched me come undone from a not-quite kiss.

But he wasn't smiling. No. Quite the opposite. His dark eyes shimmered with the silver of his vampire. And the lust pouring off him licked me like flame. From his open lips, I caught the glint of his tongue piercing as well as two slivers of canine teeth. Though I thought it impossible, my heart battered even harder, knocking on my rib cage with a potent mixture—mostly of excitement, but also with a touch of fear.

"Are you going to bite me?" I whispered, my voice husky.

"Do you want me to?" He trailed his thumb down my throat then back up to my chin, effectively holding me in place.

For a split second, I actually had to think about that question, which was ridiculous. No witch wants to be bitten by a vampire. It's said that a vampire bite, though pleasurable, renders a person helpless, enthralled. That sort of thing would require an inordinate amount of trust. This was only onetime sex.

"No," I finally answered. Pretty sure that was the right answer.

His expression didn't change at all, but there was a flicker of something in his eyes I couldn't decipher.

"Then no biting," he agreed.

Lightning swift, he pressed down on my chin with his thumb, opening my mouth and tilting my head before his mouth crushed against mine. He swept in with his tongue, consuming me, the combination of softness and his steel stud melting me onto the barstool.

I whimpered, only then realizing I had both hands clenched in his T-shirt, his rock-hard chest pressing closer. My feet were propped on the rung of the stool with his body slightly wedged between. He skated a hand up my calf to my knee where he squeezed, then spread my leg wider so he could press his pelvis into mine.

All the while his mouth worked me into a frenzy of need, his large hand inching upward to wrap around my lower thigh, just holding me still while he kissed me into oblivion.

I'd been kissed a lot. But whatever Devraj was doing with his tongue, his mouth, the tips of his teeth, nibbling my lower lip one second, coaxing me gently, then diving deep the next, was nothing I'd experienced before. It was like he was exploring his newly conquered territory. No hesitancy since he owned it, but definite mapping of every inch with his mouth. Then that glorious mouth trailed down my jaw to my neck.

I grabbed hold of one of his shoulders—damn, but they were tight with flexed muscle—and combed the other into that glorious mass of hair. He groaned against a tender spot at the base of my throat.

"I was going to ask you"—he scraped his sharpened canines along my shoulder, pulling aside the strap of my sleeveless dress— "if you wanted me to fuck you hard or nice and slow?" Another scrape of his sharp teeth, then a soothing sweep of his tongue. "But I've figured out what you want. What you need."

"Oh yeah?" I asked, shocked to hear myself panting in his quiet kitchen. "What do I need?"

He stilled with his mouth above my collarbone, tracing the delicate line with his tongue, the piercing a tantalizing caress.

"Everything," he whispered against my skin. "And I'm going to give it to you."

That's when I realized he'd somehow managed to unbutton the entire line of buttons of my chambray dress without me knowing. Right before he eased it open. He stood back, exposing all of me in nothing but my white cotton panties and bra. He'd inched back enough to take a long, leisurely look, his hands skating up and down my sides. His thumbs pressed low on my hips, heated desire pouring off him in waves.

I'd settled my hands on his arms below his biceps, waiting for some pretty words or a few seductive ones. But he said nothing, just stared, drinking me in.

"Devraj," I interrupted, starting to feel self-conscious.

He startled, his gaze meeting mine, a calculating intensity behind mahogany eyes.

"What?" I pushed, needing to know what he was thinking.

His grip on my waist tightened and he lifted me onto the narrow end of the island. The action shocked me so much I yipped and grabbed hold of his forearms. Now he was standing between my legs and easing my dress off my arms to drape across the countertop behind me.

"I apologize," he whispered, his hands coasting under my arms and behind my back to unhook my bra. "I was planning . . ."

"Planning?"

He pulled off my bra, then grazed his palm between my breasts, his hand spanning across my collarbone.

"All the things I plan to do to you within the next four hours." He pushed me gently, easing me back onto the island. "You might want to hold on," he suggested, placing my hands on the edges of the granite before he hooked his fingers under my panties and swiftly pulled them down my legs.

Oh boy. I was fully naked, lying on the island with the evening light shining through his window. Thankfully, it was a high window so no one could see in from the road, but the idea of being so exposed, and in broad daylight, was completely terrifying. And exciting.

I'd always had sex in a bedroom and usually in the dark. This was entirely new. Devraj had me splayed out naked in his kitchen, about to be the main course.

He gripped the flaps of my dress hanging over the island and slid my body till my bum was at the edge. He trailed his hands along the backs of my calves to my knees, bending his body and anchoring my thighs against his broad shoulders.

Oh boy, oh boy.

I caught the flash of his fanged smile as he held my gaze, lowering closer, and that was just too much for me. I dropped my head and stared at the kitchen ceiling. He glided a finger through my slickness and groaned his approval.

"Isadora," he whispered with a kind of intense adoration that had me arching my neck, the heat of his breath at my core, the scruff on his jaw scratching my inner thigh.

Gripping the edges of the countertop, I readied myself for the sensation of his pierced tongue. But when he spread me with two fingers and licked lightly over my clit, I knew there had been no way to prepare myself for this.

"Oh God." My hips came off the counter, but then he spread a hand over my pelvis and pressed me down.

"Easy. Just getting started, love."

Then he was eating me properly. No more gentle brushes. Insatiable licks up to my clit that had my hips rocking, but he held me hard, his heavy groans mixing with mine. He slid two fingers through my wetness, then pushed inside me as he closed his mouth over my tight nub, flicking wickedly with his pierced tongue.

"Oh my God." I couldn't help it. I fisted my hand in his hair and rocked my hips in rhythm to his thrusting, knowing I was about to come already. If I could've thought beyond the blinding pleasure racing through my body, I might've been embarrassed.

His responding growl of pleasure vibrated against my tender flesh, sending me over the edge. I cried out as I came so hard with his mouth buried between my thighs, his lips tugging with a sweet suction on my clit.

His finger-fucking slowed as I whimpered through my orgasm, starting to become a little embarrassed now that I realized how easy it had been for him to get me off. When my breathing was almost normal, he slipped his fingers out of me and stood. I figured he'd have a smug look and a few snarky words, but again, Devraj surprised me. His hard expression meant all business.

"My bag," I said, pointing to the kitchen table.

He walked over and then brought it back to me as I sat up. I riffled around inside until I found what I was looking for. I handed it to him and dropped my bag to the floor.

His pursed brow smoothed when he took the condom from me, looking it over before he tossed it on the kitchen counter and smiled. "That won't fit, love."

He eased to my side to lift me into his arms with one arm under my knees, the other cradling my upper body against his chest.

"It won't?" I clasped him around his neck, holding on. I was proud of being so prepared, but apparently I hadn't thought of various sizes.

He didn't answer, just chuckled as he carried me out of the kitchen into the living room. But instead of heading down the hall toward his bedroom, he walked over to his tall fireplace and settled me onto a plush white rug in front of a dark purple chaise. He stood and used a remote to flick on the gas fireplace. It was late spring and definitely not the time for a fire, but the heat of it warmed my exposed skin. That was pretty thoughtful.

Thoughtful was becoming synonymous with Devraj. And so many other words. Kind. Strong. Beautiful. I'd been too quick to judge when we first met, but the more I learned of him, the more I sank into a world of feelings. The cuff on his wrist reminded me again of his love for his mother. Why did he have to be so magnificent in every way?

I spread my palms over the soft rug. "Here?"

He reached over his shoulders with both hands and grabbed his T-shirt, lifting it over his head and tossing it aside. "For starters."

Jeesh. This man was all ripped flesh and lovely contours with a trail of sparse hair leading beneath his belt. Which he was now unbuckling.

"Not your bed?" I managed to ask, unable to keep my eyes off his progression as he unsnapped and unzipped his jeans before sliding them and his black briefs down his legs.

"We'll get there," he said, standing to his full height in front of me.

His hand went to his jutting erection where he pumped it once, nice and slow. I couldn't stop devouring him with my eyes, his muscular thighs and chiseled abdomen, the small dark circles of his nipples, tight and pebbled.

Another piercing in his left nipple glinted by the firelight. I gulped at the sight of him. I had no idea body piercings would have this sort of effect over me. I also had no clue the sight of this glorious, bare man would turn me on so fast.

His body was a love letter of perfection.

He hadn't moved since he'd removed his clothes except for the slow pumping of his hand on that perfect penis.

Finally, I moved my gaze to his face, realizing he was stalling on purpose. "What are you waiting for?"

"Just letting you get a good look since I took my time when it was my turn."

I'm not sure why, but I found that extremely thoughtful. He didn't disrobe, then pounce on me. Devraj was all about slow moves, sweet seduction, and reciprocation. He was a giver. Why that surprised me, I had no idea.

"Don't move," he commanded, disappearing down the hall and returning with what was obviously a few packets of condoms. *Five?* And a bottle of something else.

He set them on the wood floor beside the rug, then grabbed a throw pillow from his sofa and tossed it to me.

"Roll over and rest your head. Time for a massage."

I frowned up at him. He burst into laughter as he lowered to his knees. His hand spread over my hip and maneuvered me gently. "Roll over, Isadora."

Okay, then. I wasn't going to say no to a massage. I rolled over and curled my arms under the pillow, resting my head to face the warm fire.

He straddled me on his knees, which felt wildly erotic. And yet, I couldn't see him, only feel him moving above me. He poured some kind of oil from a bottle that he set on the floor near my head. I heard him rubbing his hands together right before he spread those hands on my shoulders and squeezed. The oil smelled of a clean musky scent like cedarwood but also mingled with a faint floral smell. Jasmine or lilac. Maybe both. Heavenly.

"Mmmm." I couldn't help myself as he glided his hands down my back and up my spine, the scented oil smoothing his way. The warmth seeped into my skin, and I realized the pleasant sizzle under my skin wasn't just the firelight or his hands. "It's so warm."

"It's the oil," he said. "Feels good?"

"Amazing," I admitted.

He laughed again, a throaty sound that felt so close, loosening the tension in my belly. For even though he'd just unwound me quite a bit with a mind-blowing orgasm, I knew the main event was yet to come.

His fingers worked magically on my back along my spine, then drifted lower as he pressed his thumbs over my lower back and then over my butt. I moaned again at the masterful press of his fingers. Who knew a butt massage could feel so good?

His large hands massaged me there, then stroked down the backs of my legs, pouring more oil into his hands and repeating his soothing strokes until I was humming with desire again. He pressed his thumb along the inside of my thighs, then back up along the seam of my sex and my bum.

I'd never had an erotic massage. I also had no idea my body could pulse with desire without ever touching the places I knew to be my trigger points of lust. If there was any doubt that Devraj knew what the hell he was doing in bed—or on the kitchen countertop or the living room rug—I now knew otherwise.

I had my eyes closed, but I felt him shift, leaning over my body. I opened my eyes to slivers, seeing his arm braced beside my head. His mouth nipped a trail along my shoulder, his hair trailing in erotic sweeps over my bare skin. He glided a finger along a far too gentle path between my legs. If he didn't know that he had turned me on before, he was well aware of what he did to me now. I was embarrassingly wet. But I couldn't muster any shame when he continued to make my body melt into his soft rug.

"We might ruin your rug," I murmured.

He nipped up to my neck. "I don't care." He bit my earlobe, sucking it before moving back to my throat. "I'll buy a new one."

"So wasteful." I realized my words were sluggish. I was drunk from sensation, but I still had to point out the error of his extravagant ways.

"I was right."

"Right?" I barely managed to ask.

A sharp nick of my shoulder before he licked the spot. "I wanted to see how glorious you'd look naked on this rug." His voice dropped deeper, more dangerous. "You look like a fucking queen."

That made no sense to me, but none of this really did. And then I couldn't think again while his talented fingers worked between my legs. He circled my swollen clit before skating through my folds then up to the tight hole of my behind. I tensed, having never had anyone play with me there.

"Relax for me," he whispered in that velvet-dark voice.

I did, thinking he planned to breach with his finger. But he didn't. Just rimmed softly, the heated oil tantalizing me beyond reason. Then he lifted his body away, and I felt the loss of his heat, his hands, his mere presence, like someone had knocked the breath out of me. I frowned until I heard the familiar sound of a condom package being ripped open.

I lifted onto my elbows and peered over my shoulder. He watched me watch him slide the condom on before he rolled me onto my back. With my knees bent, feet planted on either side of where he knelt, this was the moment Devraj would surge forward and take me hard and fast. But like always, I really didn't know how he worked. Always doing the unexpected.

He lifted one of my legs and nibbled a line up the inside before draping it over his shoulder. The sight of him and his slow descent over my body scattered my wits even further, if that were possible. I knew how fast vampires could move. I'd witnessed their movement so quick it was like they disappeared in one place and reappeared in another. What I didn't know was that they could also move painfully slow.

Painful because I wanted, needed, was about to beg him to get inside me. This was crazy torture that was so unnecessary.

"Now," I begged, unable to help myself.

He didn't say a word. I reached up, one hand on his biceps, the other skating down to his nipple with the piercing. I tugged gently on the tiny silver loop, seriously wanting to lick his nipple. He sucked in a hissing breath, then growled low in his throat. The reaction sparked something feral inside me.

Following instinct, which is something I'd never done during sex, always overthinking, I gripped his biceps hard and pulled myself up. I opened my mouth over the pierced nipple and then flicked the loop with my tongue before I sucked hard.

His hand was in my hair, fisting, and then he tugged me away, his gaze roaming my face, focusing intently on my mouth, his brow pinched, puzzled. Silver eyes met mine as he lowered us both, holding himself up on one elbow, scooping his hand into my hair to cradle my skull in his long-fingered hand.

"Don't rush me," he whispered against my lips, aligning the swollen head of his cock to my entrance.

"Rush you?" I huffed a frustrated breath and gripped both hands in his hair, fisting a thick handful. "Get inside me, Devraj Kumar." So aggressive, so demanding, I hardly recognized myself. All I knew is that he had what I needed, and I wanted it right now.

Something wild and ruthless sparked behind his vampire eyes, glowing with an intensity that had my pulse speeding to a maddening pace. Gripping the thigh of my leg pressing to his chest, he sank inside me, inch by slow inch.

I gasped, but he swallowed the sound with a crushing kiss, staying still a moment while my body stretched around his. Then with shallow, sinuous thrusts back out, then back in, he seated himself fully inside me. He groaned long and loud into my mouth, his tongue stroking deep. He broke the kiss and pressed his forehead to mine, narrow slits of silver devouring me instead of his mouth.

"So fucking perfect, aren't you?"

I couldn't speak at the moment, panting uncontrollably, scraping my nails down his flexed back.

"Scratch me up, Isadora. Mark me good."

Then the lithe rolls of his hips picked up speed, pounding into me with a new kind of intensity. Less controlled. More frantic. I skated both hands over his back and scratched the muscular length down his spine until I grabbed hold of the most perfect, tight ass I'd ever held.

"Fuck, Isadora." He moaned, his lips hovering over mine. "What are you doing to me?"

Then I sunk my nails in, urging him faster. He didn't disappoint, pumping hard and deep, circling his pelvis when he hit mine, which rubbed my clit teasingly. I felt a devastating orgasm building again. With my one leg planted on the floor, I rocked up, meeting him with each aggressive thrust.

"Yes," I murmured against his lips. "So good."

Because it was. He'd promised he'd make it good, prove me wrong. And I was sinking into oblivious ecstasy, thrilled that he'd been able to do so. He was so right. Sex wasn't boring. I'd been with boring partners. Or maybe I was boring with them. But with Devraj, something had ignited inside of me, pulling the wild girl out of her hiding place. As I hovered just beyond my second orgasm, I was blissed out to discover that there were men out there who made bed play exciting. Exhilarating. Necessary.

He pushed up off my body with one hand, the other sliding between my legs where he slicked a circle around my swollen nub, tightening my body further. He turned his head to place a suckling kiss to the inside of my knee where it draped over his shoulder, then focused his attention on the joining of our bodies.

His dick thickened further, growing even harder as he watched himself thrust inside me, his thumb working magic circles. I let my hands fall to the rug, gripping and holding on as he pounded me harder.

"Fuck, fuck, fuck," he said like a curse, his face contorting into one of pain, baring his teeth.

Oh my God!

The sight of his fangs out, his silver eyes glittering, his pained expression of dizzying lust fixed hard because of me had my body tipping over another cliff.

"Ah!" I let out a cry, my mouth gaping open as I came with a fierce crash, my sex clenching around him.

His gaze met mine, an indecipherable mania shining behind those vampire eyes as he fucked me even harder.

"Yes," was all he said as he thrust one last time and held, pulsing inside me with his own orgasm. "*Yes.*" His growl was gravel-deep.

He groaned, holding his pelvis hard against mine, but moving in tiny massaging circles. Then he released my leg from his shoulder and lowered down to me again. He combed his fingers into my hair before sweeping an airy kiss against my lips.

He did this for quite some time, and though it was too intimate for my comfort level, I couldn't seem to push him away. To kiss him like this felt so natural, which in itself was strange. This was hookup sex, I reminded myself. The intimacy he made me feel was a little frightening. Once again, my heart pounded erratically, reminding me that I was in a danger zone. Still, I couldn't seem to help but wallow in this lovely intimacy.

"You're quite beautiful," he finally said. He almost seemed shocked. Surprised. By his admission? I wasn't sure.

"I was thinking sort of the same thing about you," I said softly.

He grinned, staring at my mouth for a few seconds before meeting my eyes again. "I could get addicted to the expression on your face when you come."

Wow.

I slid my eyes away from his, suddenly feeling shy. The men I'd been with had never said anything like that to me before. Rather than torture me further, he gave me a brief closed-mouth kiss and lifted off me. I sucked in a breath when he withdrew from my body.

Okay, so I was definitely wrong about small man syndrome. I was wrong about a lot of things. That he was just a selfish, conceited movie star vampire. Completely, wholly mistaken.

As if to prove the point, he draped a plush throw over my body to keep me warm and comfortable. "Stay put. I'm going to feed you."

He'd put on his black briefs, which didn't lessen the phenomenal view of him walking away. Not one bit. Jeesh. Even his hamstrings were delicious looking.

I listened to him turn on the sink, obviously washing his hands, before sounds of plates clinking and drawers opening and closing poked me with another reminder.

I should go. This was like what real couples did. You know, having sex on the living room floor, then eating snacks after they'd worked up an appetite. I should really go.

But that would be rude. Right?

No. Best to stay and be polite. I wrapped the throw tighter around me, not ready to trek into the kitchen half naked to retrieve my dress laid out on the kitchen island like a picnic blanket. Heat flared into my cheeks, thinking about that picnic.

So I curled up in front of the fire, basking in the afterglow of dizzying, drugging sex with a Stygorn vampire, and waited for whatever he was cooking up for me. All the while, telling my silly, soft heart not to get attached.

Easier said than done.

Chapter 15

~DEVRAJ~

Wʜᴀᴛ ᴛʜᴇ ꜰᴜᴄᴋ ᴡᴀꜱ ᴛʜᴀᴛ?

I filled the pavs with the dabeli stuffing while trying to pick up the pieces of my flayed emotions.

I loved sex. I'd had numerous partners over the centuries. *Numerous.* So why had sex with Isadora undone me so completely? Why had this coupling with Isadora shredded all my previous sexual experiences into what amounted to a waste of time?

I felt adrift. Unmoored. Lost to any other purpose but the one that mattered. Her.

A stirring of what I could only describe as panic—though I'd little experience with the emotion—filled my body. Why? Because she'd said this was a onetime hookup, and my entire being was 100 percent against that ridiculous, asinine notion.

This needed to be repeated. Often. Every day.

I heated the dabelis on my griddle, placed them onto two plates, and then brought them into the living room.

Isadora was curled up with the blanket over her, her delicate collarbone visible through the gap. I wanted to grin like a fiend. I'd been trying so hard to get this woman to open up to me, and she finally had. But what she'd been hiding was the tigress in the sheets. In the throes of sex, Isadora was a powerful goddess. And I'd gotten to witness that. To experience it firsthand. I felt privileged in some way, having gotten a glimpse of her completely uninhibited.

"Here you go." I set hers in front of her where she sat sideways by the fire, then took a seat on the chaise lounge behind her. "I hope you like it."

She picked up one dabeli and took a bite, the blanket sliding down to her waist.

I couldn't even swallow with so much of her exposed, but I managed to somehow paste on a pleasant smile while watching her.

She closed her eyes with pleasure and smiled while chewing. "Delicious," she finally said and took another bite, some of the stuffing dribbling to the plate.

Her eyes flicked up to mine while she ate, then roamed my body before she focused on her plate. Again, I tried not to smile too triumphantly. She wasn't as unaffected as she always pretended to be. Or maybe it was knowing what our bodies could do together that made that blush crawl up her neck. Either way, it wasn't even eight o'clock, and I planned to keep her until my time was up. If she'd let me.

Before she was finished, I ate the rest of mine and returned to the kitchen to grab two bottles of water. I took a seat on the chaise again and handed her one.

"Thank you."

Back to shy Isadora, were we? Her eyes cast anywhere but on me. She took a long drink of water, then set her empty plate on the coffee table. She stood with her blanket protectively around her shoulders and stepped over to the Celtic tree painting. I didn't move. Just sat there and watched her take in the few treasures I kept close wherever I went.

She stared at my sculpture of Shiva in the corner before walking on to the Crusader's shield encased in glass on the wall.

"Your art and artifacts are lovely."

She moved on to a painting I'd bought from an Egyptian. It was the least expensive but also my most prized possession.

"Where is this?"

"That's in Varanasi, along the Ganges River. Varanasi is believed to be the home of Lord Shiva."

"Who is Lord Shiva?"

I glanced at his statue in the corner of the room before answering her. "Shiva is known as the destroyer. Or the transformer. He is one of the most benevolent gods in Hinduism. He showers his devotees with immense love. Forgiveness. And destroys those who do evil."

She must've noted the change in my voice. The tinge of regret. She peered over her shoulder, her long blonde hair hanging in wild waves. Her eyes asked the question she wouldn't voice, and for some reason I found myself wanting to tell her.

"It's the site of a pilgrimage in my homeland. It was the place where I traveled with my mother when I was turned into a vampire. A place I remained for many years."

The place where I lost my humanity for a time. A long time. And had to fight to win it back.

"The painting makes you sad," she said as a statement, not a question.

"It does."

"Then why do you keep it?"

I didn't know how to explain it, but I did my best. "It keeps me whole. It reminds me of my mother. Of a simple, sweet time in my life."

Her brow pinched together as she stared at me with some tender emotion I couldn't detect. But it swam in her beautiful eyes for some time until she cleared her throat and walked closer, eyeing the kitchen. "It's getting late. I should—"

"Don't go," I found myself spitting out quickly and moving in a flash to stand right before her. "Not yet," I begged, cupping her face with both hands, brushing my thumbs over her high cheekbones.

"I don't know if—"

I kissed her, angling her pretty face so I could do it thoroughly. I'd gotten too serious for her, I was sure, so I nipped her bottom lip, then smiled. "You said you had until ten o'clock."

I kissed up her jaw. She tilted her head back, offering me her throat. She obviously had no idea that in the vampire world, that was equivalent to full submission. For blood. For sex. I bit back a groan, knowing she had no idea what this meant. Even so, I pretended for one fleeting minute that she was mine, licking a line down her throat to the base where her pulse beat hard.

"Stay with me," I pleaded. "A little longer," I clarified.

Her breathing quickened and the blanket fell to the floor. That was all the answer I needed. Kissing her deeply, I lifted her into my arms. Her long legs wrapped around me automatically, which pulled a growl from deep in my chest.

I settled onto the chaise lounge with her straddling me, her knees on the sofa. Without hesitation, I cupped one breast and sucked the tip of the other, teasing one nipple with my thumb, flicking the other with the stud in my tongue.

Her hands were in my hair, holding my face to her breast. Yeah. Just like that, she opened up for me. The timid girl vanished as she ground along the length of my hard dick. I moved to her other breast, teasing her pink nipples into tight peaks. By the way she was rocking against me, chasing her climax, she was ready. Not to mention the heady scent of her in the air. It was enough to drive me mad.

Wrapping a hand around her waist, I dipped her back. She sucked in a surprised breath.

"Condom and oil," I managed to grit out, my canines extending again.

I'd have to feed soon, but right now there was only one thing I wanted. One woman.

She reached down and snatched a condom and the small bottle of oil off the coffee table. She dropped the condom into my hand but poured the oil into her own palm and rubbed it between her hands before spreading her palms across my chest, down my abs, back up. Before I could register the intense sensuality of her small hands mapping my body, she leaned down and sucked my pierced nipple again. I thought I'd blow right there in my briefs.

"Isadora," I warned.

She lifted her head and found my mouth, grinding her pussy down onto me. The sensation of skin sliding against hot skin urged me to get inside her. Now!

I tore open a condom package with my teeth, shoved my underwear down just enough to roll it on. Dropping some of the oil in my palm, I tossed the bottle somewhere on the floor and lubed my dick to give her more pleasure and ease on the entry.

She rose up on her knees so I could align us, then she sank down onto me on a long exhale.

Fucking hell.

This woman.

Her body.

Her soul.

I wanted it all.

I let her take the reins and fuck me like she wanted to. Her tempo was sweet like her. A little shy at first. Then confident and sure. She kissed me deep, her tongue exploring aggressively. So much so that she nicked her tongue on one of my canines.

She jerked away, her mouth agape, crimson staining her lip.

"Devraj." Her eyes dilated, the green drowned by black, as the heady toxin my body gave off during feeding slipped a drop into her bloodstream. "Oh my God," she moaned, sliding back up and down my cock, her breathing growing more erratic. Restless. Frantic. And that from a single drop.

I gripped her waist and held her still so I could pump up inside her, give her the rougher thrusts she needed. I knew the toxin made people savage, violently needy.

"Yes, yes, yes," she crooned, one hand going to her breast where she pinched her own nipple.

Fuck. Me.

On a carnal growl, I flipped her onto her back and licked the blood off her lip before I plunged back inside of her. If she was wild before, she was downright feral now, digging her nails into my back, making me insane with lust and need. I sucked on her tongue, the smallest taste of her blood like heroin, drugging me with a euphoric high as I stroked inside her.

"*Isadora.*"

I was begging her, but I didn't know what for. For more of this? To put me out of my misery? To kill me now so I'd die the happiest of men?

She whimpered as I pumped deeper and devoured her mouth. All the while, she matched my frenzied state, clawing me with those lovely nails. Down my back, my arms, my chest. All it did was make me come harder, the tingling sensation shooting from the base of my spine and tensing every muscle in my body.

Arching my neck on a desperate groan, I let go, spilling into the condom—and for the first time wondering what it would be like to be skin on skin—wishing I'd held off for her. Even so, her own orgasm swept through her right after, milking my cock with violent vibrations.

We had come almost at the same time.

That rarely happened for me. I was accustomed to ensuring the woman found her pleasure, and then I'd take my own. But Isadora and I were in sync tonight. In a way that had my mind reeling.

I stared down at her, wondering if she was feeling the same way I was. I knew she hadn't had many lovers from our previous conversations. I wondered if she'd ever experienced this before. I wanted to tell her that it wasn't always like this. This was new for me.

After that, we didn't say anything. No playful comments. No smiles. Because whatever that was, it wasn't playful. It felt like danger and providence and a shocking dose of destiny. Whereas I was perfectly ready to discuss and explore what that could mean, it was quite obvious that Isadora wasn't.

After she gathered her clothes, she went to the bathroom and came back out fully dressed, her hair tied in a messy knot on her head. I'd redressed in my jeans.

"Um . . ." she started and then cleared her throat, glancing out the window toward her own house next door, though it was now too dark to see much. "I want to thank you. For tonight."

So calm and poised. If she could pretend that didn't blow her mind, then so could I. For now.

I crossed my arms over my chest. I couldn't help but feel defensive as she pretended she hadn't experienced what I had.

"You're welcome," I said pleasantly.

Though from her searching stare, she was trying to figure out what was going on in my head. Too bad. I wasn't going to tell her. Because it would scare the living fuck out of her.

I followed her to the door and held it open.

"I'm sure we'll be seeing each other around," she said as she stepped out into the back courtyard.

Oh, she better fucking believe we would.

"I'm sure we will."

Knowing she wouldn't accept the kind of kiss goodbye that I wanted to give her, I leaned in and brushed a kiss on her cheek. The familiar flush of pink filled her face, and I wanted to laugh that a simple gesture like that could make her blush after what I'd witnessed of the vixen inside her.

"I enjoyed your company," I said, giving her my disarming smile but injecting those few paltry words with deep sincerity.

Her emerald eyes glittered under the lamplight of my porch, still searching for some sign that I might say something else.

No way. It wasn't happening.

"Good night, Isadora."

She gave a little wave, hiked her bag over her shoulder, and said, "Good night."

I watched her leave through the gate and pull her bike from behind my car. Rather than ride it, she walked it down the driveway.

She could take all the time she wanted, but there was one thing set in stone.

I wanted Isadora.

Not for a night. Not for a hookup. I wanted her glorious mind and beautiful body for as long as I was here in New Orleans. I didn't want to let her go for one minute of the time we had to be together.

When Stygorns are in training, they're always given one of many tests. One is to be dropped in the middle of nowhere, isolated dark forests or cold mountains where no humans live. Then they're given a one-inch scrap of clothing with a scent on it that belongs to someone on the other side of the continent. We're to decode the scents, categorize them into places they might come from, and track the person until we're within scent range of our prey. This test can last months until the prey is found and caught. And we always got our prey. Always.

What Isadora Savoie didn't know or understand was that one drop of her blood had set my body on fire. Perhaps my soul too. Infecting me with a drive I couldn't suppress even if I wanted to. And I didn't want to. There was something about her. She'd had me prowling and circling from the moment we met, and that fateful nick on her tongue sealed the deal.

I was now on the hunt. For her.

Chapter 16

~ISADORA~

THIS MORNING, I'D SETTLED IN AT MY DESK AND HAD WRITTEN A LETTER to Mom on parchment paper with my quill pen. If anything could settle my nerves, it was always a pen-to-paper letter to Mom, releasing some of my magic into the words. Usually, the release of emotional energy always made me feel better. Calm, cool, and in control. But it didn't work.

So I'd spent the rest of the day in my garden and was now in my greenhouse, trying like mad not to let my thoughts wander to the man next door.

I fiddled with another bunch of herbs, twining them tight for the twenty-sixth smudge stick I'd made today. I'd bundled cedar, rosemary, thyme, and lavender. Then added lemongrass, pine needles, and mugwort to a few, twining the hemp tightly. The activity had kept me busy, but my mind kept me busier, constantly drifting back to Devraj.

He was 100 percent right. My former lovers paled in comparison to him. I honestly had no idea sex could be so jarring. So earth-shaking. So intimate. And that's where the problem was.

I'd liked my other boyfriends. They were nice guys. But sex with them was none of the things I experienced last night. It was just another release. It didn't make me feel vulnerable. It didn't make me feel *feelings*. But Devraj—*sigh*—he so did. I went next door yesterday expecting to be wowed by his bedroom skills, not that we actually ever made it to his bedroom. What I wasn't expecting was the soul-deep stirring he sparked with his hands, his mouth, his body. His tenderness.

Actually, if I were totally honest with myself—because it was about damn time that I was—Devraj was so much more than a skilled lover. Hearing the touch of loneliness when he spoke of his mother, of the home they once shared. It broke down the wall I'd tried to erect between him and my emotions.

Devraj was a shiny, dazzling man used to a shiny, dazzling world. He was a Stygorn vampire who traveled the globe to hunt down dangerous supernatural criminals. Once he caught the culprit taking these girls here in New Orleans, he'd be gone. Wouldn't he?

And even if he'd wanted to continue something casual where we were lovers when he came back to town, I didn't want to be *something casual* to him.

On a giant huff, I tossed the last of the smudge sticks into the basket that was piled to the brim. I'd need to put these on huge discount to move so many at Maybelle's.

After cleaning up my mess, I looped my arm through the basket handle and left the greenhouse. I made sure to shut the door tightly since Z liked to wander in and knock my twine all over the floor.

"I thought I might find you here."

I jerked around to find Devraj standing there, smug as you please.

"Hi," I managed to say without sounding too breathy or jumpy.

"Hi there," he returned, his smile brightening further.

Maybe I wasn't so successful.

"What are you doing here?"

His smile dimmed, and I wanted to kick myself. Before I could apologize for being so abrupt and sounding kind of rude, his expression turned businesslike.

"I came to tell you that Darren Webber contacted me, and I'm meeting him over at the Green Light in an hour. I thought you might like to come along."

"Oh." I shifted the basket to my other arm. "Yes, I would. That was kind of you to include me."

"I might have a bit of an ulterior motive actually, but I'd like to discuss it with you there. Are you busy right now?" His gaze dropped to my overflowing basket, his mouth ticking up on one side.

"No. Just let me go get a quick shower and change." I glanced down at my dirt-smudged garden dress. "Um. Can you give me thirty minutes?"

"Sure. Would you rather walk or drive?"

"Walk," I snapped quickly.

"That's what I thought." He grinned. "I'll be back in thirty then."

He strode off through the gate leading to the driveway, and I took off inside like a mad hornet.

"Where's the fire?" called Violet as I threw the basket on the kitchen table and took off up the stairs.

"No time!"

Ripping off my clothes as I went up the stairs, I was completely naked by the time I entered my bathroom and turned on the shower. I tossed my ponytail holder on the counter and hopped in. I scrubbed, shampooed, conditioned, rinsed, then jumped out of the shower and towel-dried before wrapping the damp towel around my body.

When I stepped into my bedroom, Violet was rummaging through my clothes hanging in the closet.

"What are you doing?" I asked, grabbing my brush and dragging it through my wet hair.

"Finding something for you to wear on your date with Devraj."

I snorted as I scooted in next to her, yanking through some of the dresses. "I'm not going on a date with him."

"Well, after I saw him talk to you outside, then head back to his house, you tore in here like your ass was on fire, so I kind of thought you were going out tonight or something. Besides"—she faced me and tapped her temple with a mischievous grin—"Divine Seer. Something is going on between you two."

I pulled out a blue dress that had a flowy ruffle at the hem, dressier than most of mine.

"No," she said. "Wear these jeans that never see the light of day."

"Why?" I asked, taking the dark blue skinny jeans from her that I'd bought on a whim and rarely wore.

"Because they show off your cute little ass."

"Fine," I grumbled, then grabbed a white peasant blouse with a lacy V-neck.

As I hurriedly got dressed and blew my hair dry, Violet spread out on my bed, her head propped on an elbow while she watched me.

"So where you headed on this non-date?"

"It's witch business. Has to do with that case. The missing girls."

"Really?" She sat up.

I filled her in on the details, so she wouldn't think there was anything going on between me and Devraj. Even though there definitely was. Well, there was last night.

"Blake Bellingrath?" She snorted in disgust. "Met the whole family of assholes at last year's Coven Guild Summit. That cocktail party they always throw."

The Coven Guild Summit was held annually and rotated to a new district each year for hosting. Last year, it was in New Orleans while I was visiting our parents with Livvy.

"What were they like?"

"Well, Daddy Bellingrath is a pompous prick. He stood in a corner the whole night, mingling only with the superrich or famous witches at the party. I swear, he had his ass so far up Clarissa's butt, she probably got hemorrhoids."

"Poor Clarissa." I laughed while pulling on my jeans. Clarissa was the president of the Coven Guild, the governing organization for witches across the United States. She also happened to be an old friend of our mother's and a mentor to Jules on occasion. "And the rest of them?"

"Mommy Bellingrath is apparently in love with her eldest son, Adam. He's obviously the golden boy. A premed student at Tulane, honor society super-scholar, yada, yada. Whatever. She kept petting him and trying to introduce him to all the available rich witch daughters. He wore a permanent sneer on his face, like he smelled something funny."

"Charming."

"Exactly."

"And what about Blake?"

"Ha! He's the worst of them all. A total entitled douchenozzle. He got sloshing drunk within ten minutes, then ditched before Clarissa had even introduced her special guest, which happened to be her *father*, head of the London Coven. It was so fucking rude." Violet scooted to the edge of my bed and bounced up. "It was awesome to see his dad practically burst a blood vessel, though. I swear, his face turned purple with embarrassment when Blake shouted 'peace out, witch bitches' before swaggering out the door of the Roosevelt ballroom."

"Just . . . wow," I muttered, finger-combing some product through my hair so it wouldn't get frizzy in the humidity. "I'm almost sad Livvy and I missed that one."

"Tell me about it."

I tripped while trying to shove on my flats too fast, catching myself on the vanity.

"You sure are in a super hurry."

"Yeah. Well, we're meeting the guy within the hour, so I didn't want to hold Devraj up. Just trying to hurry."

"Right. Don't want to keep him waiting."

"Exactly!" I practically screeched as I powdered my face, then swept some mascara on my eyelashes.

She stood and headed for the door while I dug around in my vanity drawer.

"All business, huh? That's why you're wearing eye makeup and so desperately trying to find your favorite Passion Pink lip gloss, I'm sure."

"Go away, Violet." I found the lip gloss she was talking about then glared at her while she smiled like the demonic imp she was.

She tapped on her temple. "I can sense it."

"Out!"

She left, laughing. I swept the lip gloss on, grabbed my big bag, then dashed down the stairs and out the front door. Devraj was waiting outside my front gate, looking perfect in jeans and a white button-down and totally unruffled. Exhaling a deep breath, I pretended I wasn't either.

But then it became exponentially hard to do so when his heated gaze turned molten as he swept down my body and back up with a predatory glint. Ready or not, I was headed out on a non-date with the hottest vampire alive.

Chapter 17

~DEVRAJ~

Clearing my throat, I asked casually, "Ready?"

She nodded, then stepped along the sidewalk.

I fell in beside her. "I love it when you wear your hair like that."

She combed her fingers through the end of the still-damp strands, which streamed down to her breast. "What do you mean?"

I reached a hand up and tugged on a strand framing her face. "All wild and chaotic."

She laughed, the sound lassoing around my midsection and squeezing with delight. "That is so not like me."

"No, it's not," I agreed. "Except in bed," I couldn't help murmuring close to her ear.

"So," she said lightly, her gaze jumping around nervously, "you said you had an ulterior motive for bringing me to meet this guy. What's that all about?"

I let her switch topics, sobering a bit. "We have a plan to get the evidence we need to convict Blake Bellingrath. We'll need to catch him in the act in order to get a conviction on someone so well-connected in the supernatural community."

She glanced up at me, surely finding my expression tight as I clenched my jaw. "You don't like this plan? What is it?"

"No, I don't," I growled. "But it's the only way." I braced my arm around her lower back and sheltered her close to my side as a rowdy group of young men jostled by.

Once we rounded the group, we moved back into our companionable walk, crossing Magazine as we drew closer to the Green Light.

"Are you going to tell me the plan or keep me in suspense?" she asked.

"We'd like you to be the next kidnapping victim," I said through gritted teeth. "Ruben convinced me that you wouldn't be in danger, but . . ."

My heart hammered at the idea of her playing bait, but I understood the advantages of having someone in on the scheme rather than us finding some poor innocent.

She nudged my arm with her elbow. "But you think there is?"

I pulled her to a stop right outside the alley leading to the Green Light. I squeezed her upper arm gently, my thumb brushing a slow circle. "Ruben has a guy who can track vampires when they're tracing, so I'm positive we could follow and find you within minutes of the capture. That's if they take the bait. One reason I need to know now is so I can plant the persuasion glamour in Darren's mind. But . . ." I glanced down the alley, tightening my grip on her arm before I slid my hand down, engulfing hers in a comforting grip. "There's always a chance something could go wrong. That small percentage of unexpected error is killing me."

She swallowed hard, perusing my face. I'm sure she could see the concern written on my face, but it was nothing compared to the tumultuous storm brewing at the thought of her coming to harm in this scheme of ours.

Her eyes brightened as she gave me a reassuring smile. "Well, someone has to be the bait, right? Better me who would be prepared and in on the plan than some poor girl who could be scarred for life by the experience."

I released a shaky breath. "Somehow, I knew that would be your reaction." My gaze drifted over her hair, neck, and mouth, remembering the silken warmth of her. "We'd need someone else to come with you. It would look too strange for you to be hanging out by yourself," I added. "Maybe one of your sisters?"

"Yeah. Maybe Livvy. Blake Bellingrath saw my sisters at the last Summit cocktail party and would know them on sight."

I dipped my chin, then ushered her back down the alley where customers headed for the entrance to the Green Light.

I stepped ahead of us up to the nondescript door. The only marking to show this wasn't just an alleyway entrance to a kitchen was the gaslit lantern flickering with green flame. And the six-and-a-half foot tall, well-dressed vampire guarding it. Though his face was shadowed, his eyes glinted silver, his vampire instincts on alert as the bouncer.

"Good evening, Roland," I said.

"Devraj," he said, nodding and pushing the door open, then holding it for us.

Most vampire dens were dark and covered in red velvet and black satin, some metal band screaming in the background. But Ruben's place reflected the man himself. Sophisticated and seductive.

The decor reminded me of something you might find in a posh lounge in the 1920s, the booths and chairs luxurious and over-sized like you'd expect in a mansion, not a nightclub. The glow from warm gas lanterns and candles shimmered on the faces of the humans and vampires enjoying each other's company. Small chandeliers added an opulent touch to a dance floor centered before a small stage where a few couples danced.

The bubble of laughter and murmur of happy patrons filled the room, and the music came from the stage where a man played an acoustic guitar, his warm voice singing a masculine rendition of "I Know You" by Skylar Grey. A werewolf actually, not a man.

"Hey, there's Nico," Isadora murmured. "Evie's boyfriend Mateo's cousin. He works at the Cauldron sometimes."

I acknowledged with a nod, and then a woman stood before us.

"Mr. Kumar, I have your table right over here."

The hostess, a statuesque blonde in a white latex dress, led the way through the tables in her red stiletto heels. Though the club was posh and the employees dressed formally, people milled about in casual clusters.

The hostess stopped before a booth and lifted the Reserved placard. It was a nicely situated booth in the middle of the room where you could see the bar and the stage and anyone walking in the door with perfect ease.

I nudged Isadora into the booth, then leaned down to her ear. "I'll grab us something at the bar. What would you like?"

"Water is fine."

I wound through the tables to the bar and signaled the bartender. "What'll it be, Devraj?"

"Maker's Mark on the rocks and a water."

He nodded, then meandered back to fix the drinks, while I tuned into the conversations around the room. Nothing too intriguing at first. Just flirtations and sexual innuendo, basic club talk, then a name caught my attention from the two vampires at the end of the bar.

"Blake was fucking pissed, bro," said the dark-haired guy. "But his parents were done with them both."

"Adam too?" asked the other one.

"Yeah. Apparently, they'd embarrassed dear old mom and dad one too many times after their arrests at that vampire club at New Year's. They're using that tough love shit to try to get them back in line."

"But completely cut them off?" the other one asked. "How the fuck do they still have money? I saw Blake buying drinks for his boys last weekend at Tipitina's. Didn't look that broke to me."

Tipitina's was popular spot for small band venues uptown.

"They were for a while, but seems they've fallen into some money somehow. Who the fuck knows?"

I did. I knew exactly where he and his brother were getting the money. Or at least where Blake was. Darren had never said anything about Blake's brother nor did I see him when I read Darren's memories. But now I knew what had motivated at least Blake to start his own blood trafficking ring. I shot a quick text to Ruben, letting him know what I'd just discovered.

"Here you go," said the bartender, setting down my drinks.

I paid him, then headed back to Isadora. She looked so demure and beautiful, the sight of her increasing the pressure behind my sternum. One night wasn't enough. Desire seemed a feeble and weak word to describe what I felt for the sweet witch sitting in that booth. All I knew was that whatever this was, I wanted more. Much more.

Chapter 18

~ISADORA~

I COULDN'T HELP BUT STARE. HE LOOKED CRAZY HOT TONIGHT. DARK jeans and gray T-shirt covered mostly by a black leather jacket, his hair loose and long like it was at his house last night. He caught me staring as he headed toward me with drinks in hand, his smile deadly and knowing and his eyes burning with a silvery heat I knew far too well.

Flustered, I jerked my attention to Nico. He had a beautiful voice—smooth and deep with a touch of husky. He played his guitar with swift, elegant movements of his fingers.

I didn't look over when Devraj scooted into the booth from the other side, pressing close, his thigh a burning line alongside mine. I lifted the water and took a sip. "So this is a vampire den."

"That it is." I felt the caress of his gaze. "Not what you expected?"

"Not really. It's missing that dark Goth element."

He laughed, drawing my focus back to him. He sipped a bottled beer, his amber gaze steady on me. "Kind of cliché, don't you think?"

I shrugged. "I suppose I should've known better. This is definitely more Ruben's style." I scanned the place, almost amused that people mingled here like any other bar. "So how does it work?"

"What do you mean? How do you find and proposition a blood-host?"

Nodding, I then took another sip of water.

"Like any other pick-up bar actually. You talk, mingle, dance. When a human seems compatible and receptive, you ask if they'll be your blood-host."

I watched a hot vampire across the club in a booth like ours. He had his arm draped along the back, running his fingers along the other man's nape. The auburn-haired guy smiled and nodded, obviously enjoying his company. "Just as simple as that?" My heartbeat had skyrocketed, pumping blood through my veins like a rushing river. My emotions were a mixture of jealousy and desire, despising the women he'd drank from in the past, knowing the pleasure they'd enjoyed from him. "Then what?"

His thigh pressed against mine as he pointed his beringed finger in front of me. "Then we go behind that red velvet curtain and take care of business."

I looked where he pointed, noting the shadowy corner, covered by red velvet, one of Ruben's men discreetly placed outside the seductive entry.

Vampire dens were called such because they offered a place for blood-drinking. A safe place where vampires could drink from their host and the host could rest and recover from the high of the vampire toxin. It reminded me of an opium den. After one tiny drop of Devraj's toxin, I imagined it was a lot like that. I'd be high out of my mind. And aroused.

The hot vampire across the club stood and offered his hand to the auburn-haired guy, who took it immediately. The vampire led him, hand lacing with the other man's, to the red velvet curtain. With a subtle nod by the guard, they disappeared behind the curtain together.

I suddenly shivered, remembering the potent pleasure that sang through my veins when I'd nicked my tongue on Devraj's canine. When I turned my head to look at him, his heated gaze was fixed on me. Like he knew exactly what I'd been thinking.

"Is it all business?" I whispered.

"There is pleasure in it." Dark, intimate words.

"And sex?" I wanted to beat myself for asking, but I couldn't hold my tongue.

"No," he responded with emphasis, his silver-glinting eyes never leaving mine. "Sex and blood-drinking isn't a safe combination."

"Why not?"

"Because the host is too vulnerable, weakened but highly aroused by the toxin. It can make the host irrationally obsessed with the vampire." He swept my hair behind my shoulder, his hand covering my nape, thumb brushing gently, his gaze following the movement. "There are some vampires who may take advantage in this way, but I don't."

"Never?"

My voice had dropped so low I could barely hear myself. But he certainly did, his eyes locking on mine again.

"I would only desire and allow this kind of intimacy with someone very dear to me. I would only take that step with someone I—"

A loud huff interrupted him as someone sat on the other side of our booth. "Sorry I'm late." Darren scanned the room, his appearance ruffled, his eyes skittish. "Couldn't get away from the guys easily. We were at a party on the west bank." A devilish smile crept across his face as he perused the club. "Fancy den."

"Don't even think about stepping foot in this place after tonight," said Devraj, steel and menace in his voice as he straightened next to me. "Not that you'd get past the door."

"I did tonight," he tossed back, still grinning like the stupid kid he was.

"Because I gave the bouncer approval," he said, sounding more than a little condescending. "Tell me the plan."

I gasped at the pulse of magic that vibrated from his body, rippling over mine and across the table. Devraj eased one hand under the table and squeezed just above my knee. A comforting squeeze, but I felt it in other places I should be forgetting about.

He wasn't messing around, feeding Darren a high dose of persuasion to get to the point.

"Blake wants to wait two weeks before our next snatch. Says he doesn't want to grab another girl so close to releasing the last one."

"Does he suspect you were taken in for questioning?" Devraj shot back.

"No." He shook his head, chuckling. "Not at all. Matter of fact, he mentioned that his distributor was happy with the girls we'd gotten. He'd never mentioned he had a distributor other than himself. Said we were making good money and we could hold off to get a fresh girl for two weeks. It'll be on Saturday."

"So two Saturdays from now, you and the other two scouts will be at separate bars, looking for your target."

"Right." He drummed his fingers on the table, his dark eyes finally swiveling to me and taking me in.

A growl vibrated through Devraj, which made Darren snap his attention back to him. The alpha at the table.

"Who's she and why is she here?" he asked, apparently not even recognizing me from the night he was questioned. Devraj had erased some of his memories, so that wasn't surprising.

"This is Isadora. She will be your target two Saturdays from now."

He shook his head, sliding his focus back to me. "She's a witch. We don't snatch supernaturals. No one with powers or connection to our world."

"She'll be nulled for the night. She'll appear human."

He observed me again with a more discerning look than the lecherous one like before. "She fits our profile."

"You have a profile?" I asked.

He grinned. "Pretty. Shy." He leaned forward. I automatically leaned back, a little closer to Devraj, which made him chuckle. "Yeah. You'd be the kind of girl I'd snatch."

The very thought made me want to scratch his eyes out.

He laughed and licked his lips. "Just turn down that fire, baby. And you'll be perfect."

Devraj was out of the booth and had Darren pinned in place, his hand around his throat. A few heads turned, but the guards at each door didn't move to intervene at the sudden violence.

"Hear me, asshole." A piercing jolt of power vibrated from Devraj. I whimpered and gripped the table, his magic a terrifying force in the room, pouring into the wide-eyed vampire pinned to the booth. "You will be at Barrel Proof two Saturdays from now. At precisely 10:30 p.m., you will text your fucking friends that you have the perfect target. At 10:35, Isadora will slowly head toward the parking lot. You will make sure that you are her handler until we arrive. You'll stall the exchange to Bellingrath for as long as possible. And you will fight to the *death* to ensure no one hurts her, bites her, harms her in any way."

"No one will hurt her," he spit out quickly, fear seeping from his pores. "We don't hurt the girls."

Devraj released him and stood above him. "You've hurt every fucking one of them, you prick." He backed up a step. "Is Blake's brother Adam in on this ring?"

He shook his head. "He hasn't ever said so if he is."

Devraj stared him down for another few uncomfortable seconds before growling, "Get out of my fucking sight."

Darren immediately launched himself out of the booth and headed for the door. The few heads looking our way swiveled, the room returning to the normal murmur of voices and low laughter.

"Was it necessary to punch that much persuasion into him?"

Devraj's gaze snapped to mine, his eyes liquid silver. "Yes."

I stood, glancing toward the door, suddenly nervous at his burst of violence and fury. "I should probably get home."

I took a step, but Devraj gently clasped my hand, the anger having rolled away. I froze. He leaned over my shoulder from behind, whispering close to my ear. "Dance with me." When I didn't answer right away, he pleaded more softly, "Please."

Nico strummed his guitar, now singing a heartfelt rendition of Johnny Cash's "I Walk the Line," his eyes closed, lost in his own music.

With a stiff nod, I let him guide me onto the small dance floor. Devraj swept me into his arms, one of my hands in his, his other on the small of my back. He pulled me so close our bodies brushed together with our slow sway to the music. I had no words at the moment, sudden flashes of our night together penetrating my thoughts.

Possessive hands, roving mouth, talented tongue, him moving inside me.

Gah, stop! I squeezed my eyes shut for a second.

"Hey," he whispered against my temple. "You okay?"

"Yeah." I opened my eyes and met his concerned gaze. "Fine."

"You sure?" He swallowed hard, a soft expression pinching his brow. "I didn't mean to scare you. I just . . . I had to be sure the persuasion spell was strong enough."

A small laugh bubbled up. "I think it's strong enough."

His obvious concern for me made me want to press closer. I could easily fall for this man. And what a mistake that would be. To fall for a world-traveling Stygorn who would be leaving New Orleans as soon as the Bellingrath case was solved.

I swallowed against my desperate attraction to him. I tried to convince myself it was only because he gave me mind-blowing orgasms. A night with Devraj would scramble any woman's brains and make her dream of a heated romance. Even a long-term one. But I was too rational to let that sweep me away. Like Tia had said, he was rarely seen with the same woman twice.

"Really. I'm fine."

"You look a little . . . untethered."

I laughed. "Maybe."

"You having second thoughts about playing bait? If it scares you too much, I can get someone else." He squeezed my hand completely enveloped in his.

"No, no," I assured him. "I want to help these girls in any way I can. I *need* to."

He smiled in that tender way that made my tummy flutter. "I understand that need. That's why I asked you to do it."

Angling my head to get a good look at him, I realized he saw strength in me that not everyone did. His only hesitation for asking me to play bait was my safety, not that he didn't have confidence that I could do something dangerous to help catch these guys.

"I'm happy you asked me," I added, giving his shoulder a squeeze, suddenly remembering how it flexed beneath my fingers when he was coming inside me.

Stop it!

I was completely hopeless.

As if he knew where my mind wandered, he asked, "How do you feel about last night? Was it satisfactory?" Amusement lit his eyes, now sparkling that warm, dark whiskey hue.

Smiling, I admitted, "Well, I certainly enjoyed our, you know, interlude."

"Interlude." He rolled the word over his tongue slowly with a steady nod.

"It was amazing," I admitted, letting him see the truth in my eyes. "I'm happy I took you up on your offer. Took the chance before your business here is done, you know?"

He searched my face, skimming everywhere before landing back on my eyes. He was considering something when he eased me closer till our bodies pressed together, the contact making my breath falter.

"Yeah," he breathed softly. "I know."

This wasn't good. Because it was just *too* good. A tantalizing reminder of what our bodies could do together. But it was what he was doing under the skin that had me breaking out into a sweat. The emotions beyond lust and desire that he stoked with his magnificent body, his surprising compassion, his tender longing.

His mouth quirked up on one side teasingly. "So. Amazing, huh?"

I rolled my eyes, focusing on Nico as he sang, trying not to blush while the telltale heat crawled up my neck.

His rumble of laughter vibrated against my chest. I wanted to rub against him like a cat. I snapped my gaze back to his and frowned at his expression that showed how pleased he was with himself.

"I think you enjoyed yourself as much as I did."

"Oh, you're right about that." He leaned down on a gentle turn to the music, his mouth against my ear. "I particularly enjoyed waking up to the claw marks on my back."

"Oh my God. You didn't just say that to me."

I knew for a fact that my face was red as a radish.

He just laughed again. "I enjoyed myself immensely. And I wouldn't be averse to a repeat performance."

"That's not a good idea," I said, meeting his eyes.

"Why not? I think exploring each other is a terrific idea," he said with some amusement. My heart fluttered with a nascent hope until he added, "While I'm here, we could enjoy each other."

I glanced away, noting the sharp sting beneath my rib cage. Wow. That painful pang of disappointment was unexpected. It already hurt more than I imagined it would. He wanted to play. But I realized my heart wanted more.

I'd done plenty of playtime with men. But now, having seen what my sister Evie had with Mateo, I realized I wanted more than a fun affair. If anything, my experience with Devraj reminded me that I could feel deeply for another man. But I couldn't let myself play with a man who already had his hooks in me. Not knowing those three little words—*while I'm here*—gutted me while we swayed on the dance floor.

"Wouldn't it be better if we ended this on a high note? When there's no chance of changing expectations or hurting each other's feelings." I forced a cheerful smile up at him. "What we had was perfect, and I don't want to ruin that."

I thought he might laugh it off, but instead, he sobered, examining me again with the intensity of a vampire who'd been alive for three centuries. He was so much older than me it was terrifying. Though I looked to be in my early twenties, I was thirty-five. And that was still obviously a huge age gap between us and our experiences in the world.

He opened his mouth as if to snap off a protest to what I said. But then he only stared for another moment before his gaze slid away, sweeping the club beyond my shoulder. And, damn, did I suddenly see the Stygorn in him. I was so used to seeing Devraj the charmer that I was almost shocked to see this hard expression steeling him into sharper, forbidding angles. It was a dangerous look that made me breathless with the power and strength this man possessed, hiding behind a veneer of charisma.

The song ended, and I was ready to be out of his arms. Why? Because all I wanted to do was press myself closer, lick his throat, and then climb him like a tree. Indulging in Devraj would only hand him the scalpel to make a clean slice through my heart. No. I wasn't willing to let that happen.

I pulled away, letting my hand fall from his shoulder. For a split second, he squeezed my hand, holding me tighter, his brow pinching together. Then he let me go.

"Emma needs another treatment from you at the hospital," he said, voice soft.

I nodded. "I'll get Jules to take me tomorrow."

"I could take you."

"I'd prefer it if Jules did."

He opened his mouth to say something, then closed it. He gave me a stiff nod, beautiful dark eyes piercing mine as he followed me to the exit.

We walked home in silence, the tension a painful thrum in my breast. I hated conflict of any kind. And though this one was unspoken, I was already mourning the loss of Devraj. Not that I'd ever had him, the way I wanted him.

At my front gate, he grabbed my hand, halting me. "Thank you for helping us with this case," he whispered low, his thumb brushing across my knuckles.

"Of course." I faced him. "I wanted to help. You know I did."

"And thank you for"—he glanced at his house next door, biting his lip—"for last night. It wasn't a night I'll ever forget."

I couldn't answer, unwilling to tell him it was already seared into my memory for all time. Then I walked away from him, a painful knot in my stomach. I reminded myself that the knot would turn into a hole in my heart if I let myself be with him. While he was here.

Chapter 19

~ISADORA~

"It's seven o'clock," said Clara, popping her head into the office in the back of the shop. "I locked up the front."

"Okay." I'd been working on this month's vendor requisitions to restock our bestselling items, having managed to keep busy all day so my thoughts wouldn't wander to the vampire next door. "I'll meet you over there."

"Hurry up," she said in her light singsong voice before heading toward the back exit.

Jules closed the Cauldron up early on Sundays and cooked a big pot of something for the family and any staff who wanted to join us. They were pretty much family too.

That's just what I needed. A bowl of some good, spicy comfort food. I shut down everything quickly, locked up the store, and sauntered next door through the back entrance, finding only Jules in the kitchen, stirring something in a big Magnalite pot.

"What are we having?" I asked.

She glanced over her shoulder, her hair pulled back with bobby pins on both sides to keep it out of her face. What little makeup she wore was completely gone now at the end of the day. She looked so young like that.

"Redfish Court Bouillon. Could you grab that platter and bring it out to the table?"

"Sure thing."

I picked up the tray she was pointing to that had a steaming bowl of rice, some fresh chopped chives, and a basket of fresh-baked french bread. I heard Evie's booming laughter before I pushed open the door and smiled at the sound. She had such an infectious laugh.

I marched in, so ready to hang with my family and let my worries go for a while. But as soon as I approached the three tables put together for our large crew, my adrenaline shot through my veins like lightning. Evie perched sideways on Mateo's lap, and right next to them was Devraj.

Damn. I'd forgotten that Violet had invited him earlier this week. So much had happened, like interrogating a vampire in Ruben's secret room and having sex on Devraj's white shag rug, that it had totally slipped my mind.

Clara sat next to Jules's newest sous chef, Mitchell, chatting him up like crazy. But he didn't seem to mind one bit, probably drinking in the joy that seeped out of her skin.

"Hey, Iz," said Evie cheerily while I set the tray on the buffet table with the bowls, napkins, silverware, and a few bottles of Tabasco.

"Hey," I returned as brightly as I could manage, having had the wind just knocked out of me. When I was brave enough, I let my gaze skate to Devraj, who was, of course, staring hard at me.

"Come sit by me," Evie urged.

"You mean us," corrected Mateo, a proprietary hand spread on her thigh.

"I'm not sitting on your lap through dinner."

"Why not?"

She laughed, the husky sound making me smile again. "That wouldn't be very practical for eating."

"You might be right. Maybe I'll just eat you instead," he said low, but not low enough I didn't hear it.

Okay, didn't need to hear all that. I caught Devraj's gaze again, hotter and harder. And inviting.

Nope.

"I'm gonna get something to drink," I said, throwing a thumb over my shoulder.

Then I escaped to where JJ was still behind the bar. His best friend, Charlie, sat on his regular stool. Livvy sat beside Finnie, our busboy and dishwasher. They were facing each other, arguing animatedly about something. Violet and Belinda, our other full-time waitress, were still wiping down tabletops in the restaurant.

"Hey, guys," I said, sitting next to Charlie on the end.

"Hello, my pretty Blondie," Charlie greeted me.

I smiled, welcoming his sweetness. Charlie was the kind of guy who could always make me feel good. This was the kind of company I needed. How he was best friends with the serious and surly JJ, I had no idea. Then again, I still had a feeling there was something more than friendship lingering between the two.

"Damn!" yelled Livvy, holding out her hands in rock, paper, scissors style. "That's two for you, zero for me. But we're going to ten. You promised."

Finnie shook his head at her. "You're just gonna lose, old lady."

"Old lady, my ass. Just because you're barely drinking age. Hit me again."

"What's that about?" I asked JJ.

"If Livvy wins, then Finnie has to sing 'Single Ladies' at the karaoke contest in full Beyoncé costume."

I checked out the thin but well-muscled guy I'd known since he was hired at eighteen. This was his college job while he worked toward a degree at UNO. He was a sweet, fun-loving kid. But a little shy, like me. To stand on a stage in costume and sing would be mortifying. Then again, he had a pretty-boy face, smooth mocha skin, and long, dark eyelashes. He'd probably look amazing all decked out in drag. And Livvy was the queen of makeup and dress-up. I'd heard Finnie singing enough back in the kitchen to know he could pull it off.

"And what does Finnie get if he wins?"

"She has to make him a free website for his Dungeons and Dragons campaigns he's been writing and selling on the side."

"And she's gonna lose," said Finnie, winning a third round.

"Dammit, kid! It's like you're psychic. Are you a warlock, and I didn't know it?"

We all laughed as they went at it again. All of the workers—and Charlie, of course—knew who and what we really were. But they were our friends and protected our secrets out of love more than anything.

"Iced tea?" asked JJ.

"White wine," I corrected him. "Need something a little stronger tonight."

I refused to look over my shoulder at the dinner table, but I felt his gaze on me all the same. The exposed skin of my bare nape prickled with awareness. I'd twisted my hair on top of my head and opted for a loose cotton floral-patterned dress. I tried hard not to wonder if I looked too shabby. Nope. It didn't matter since I no longer cared what Devraj thought, right?

JJ poured me a glass of chardonnay and assessed me when he set the glass in front of me. "Anything you want to talk about?"

Deep breath in and out, I decided to share my new revelation. "I think I want to date again."

"Bravo, girl," said Charlie, angling his body toward me. "It's about time. You need to get back out there."

I nodded with a too-stiff affirmation, feeling awkward. "Yeah. That's what I was thinking. But honestly, how do I do that? I spend all my time in my greenhouse or in the shop. I'm not a club scene girl, nor do I want a club scene guy. I'm just not sure how to go about this."

"That's easy," said Charlie, tossing his blond bangs to the side. "Use a dating app. That's how I find new dates all the time. Like my new guy, Patrick."

"What?" snapped JJ, crossing his arms over his muscular chest. "Since when?"

Charlie raised his brows. "I told you I was dating."

"Yeah, but . . ." JJ didn't finish his sentence.

"But what?"

"You have such bad taste in men, Charlie."

"Oh, do I now?" He chuckled as if to a private joke. "Well, Patrick and I have gone out three times, and so far he hasn't even *tried* to chop me up and put me in his trunk, so he might possibly be a keeper."

"Don't be so dramatic," snarled JJ, leaning both hands on the bar, squaring his body and zeroing in on Charlie. "You know what I'm talking about."

"You are not going to bring him up again."

Violet butted in, tossing her rag on the bar, which JJ picked up and put away in the hamper. "Oh yes, you're totally bringing him up again. Who are we talking about, JJ? Spill."

Charlie let out a long, theatrical sigh, then regaled us with a story about a guy he met and dated from the gym who turned stalker. It was JJ who finally scared the guy off. Yeah, I wondered if these two would ever give their repressed romance a shot.

I tried to focus on the story, laughing too late at all the appropriate parts, my thoughts too fixed on the vampire sitting at the table behind me. I needed to get this guy out of my head. He didn't even have to be in the room to occupy *all* of my headspace, and it was making me crazy.

"Did you hear me?" Violet nudged me with her elbow.

I jumped. "No. Sorry. What?"

She glanced at Charlie, then over my shoulder before saying, "Come help me get the bowls."

I followed her over to the back wall of cabinets near the kitchen entrance.

She opened the cabinet and pulled out a few bowls and set them on the counter. "What's going on with you?"

"Me? Nothing."

"Something happen at the Green Light last night?"

I shook my head and glanced over my shoulder. Devraj was listening intently to something Mateo was saying, but his gaze flitted to mine like he felt me watching. I spun back to face her.

"Charlie said you want to start dating again."

Clearing my throat, I took another stack of bowls from her. "Yeah. I think I'm ready."

"And what's wrong with Devraj?"

"Violet," I growled.

"Isadora," she snapped right back. Then she froze in the middle of handing me another stack of three bowls.

I tugged, but she wouldn't let go. "Violet, what are you—"

"Well, fuck me sideways. You had sex with him."

"What?" I whisper-hissed, making sure no one heard her.

She let go of the bowls and tossed her blue-haired head back on a throaty laugh.

I stacked the bowls next to the others, facing the countertop to hide the blush blazing up my neck to my cheeks.

"Damn, Iz. Good for you, girl. Wait, was it not good or something?" She evened out the bowls into two stacks, hip to hip with me.

"God, Violet." I sighed. "It was the most incredible night of my life."

"Fucking right." She bumped her hip to mine. "I'm so proud of you. Gettin' something for yourself."

"What does that mean?"

"You're a giver, Iz. Just like Clara. I'm glad you're enjoying taking some pleasure for yourself." She glanced over her shoulder when raucous laughter built up at the bar. "I don't get it. If it was so good, why not date him?"

"Are you serious? I mean, he's a Stygorn, Violet. A fancy, famous one who likes to party in Europe and who dances like a sex god. I'm just . . . Isadora."

"You're not just anything."

"That's not what I mean. I just don't see us lasting beyond a hot affair. And he even said we should see each other while he's in town, which means he sees us as short-term too."

Violet stared hard at me, her hand sliding over mine that held the lip of one bowl. "Oh, I see. You really like him, don't you?"

Something sank inside of me at her soft, true words. Blinking quickly to keep tears from starting, I simply nodded. She stared a bit longer before a tender smile that rarely graced her face finally spread wide.

"Well, if you're sure you don't want to pursue him."

"I'm sure."

"All right. Then there is a dating app for supernaturals you should try."

"There is?"

"Yep. I've found a couple of hot vampires on Zapp. Oh, and one warlock. He was okay, but a bit tame for me."

"But I don't want to date guys like you date," I said. "No offense."

"None taken." Violet waved a hand in the air. "They'd eat you alive. You fill out a profile with your likes/dislikes. They actually matched me pretty well."

"So why aren't you still dating any of them? You never even brought one home," I accused.

"Well, I just wanted one date," she admitted with a cheeky grin.

Ah. She wanted a hookup.

"But seriously"—she turned to me—"let me help you with your profile. I'll have guys lining up at the door." Her gaze skimmed back over my shoulder, her expression thoughtful.

"Profile for what?" Devraj's deep voice rumbled behind me.

I spun, a stack of bowls in my hand, rattling at my nervous movement.

"Here," he said with a smile, "let me help you." He took the stack. "What profile?" he asked Violet again.

Violet lifted the other bowls, grinning with mischief in her bright blue eyes. I shook my head at her, but she apparently didn't see me or was completely ignoring me.

"Isadora is *finally* getting back on the dating horse. It's been like fucking eons."

"She is?" he asked, voice rumbling low.

I started walking away before he could shoot an accusing look my way.

"Yeah. I'm going to set her up on Zapp."

"What's Zapp?" he asked, voice even but not so friendly.

"Come see, Iz." She called me over as they set the bowls at the end of the serving table.

I cringed, wishing she'd drop it as I walked over. She seemed not to be aware of my discomfort as she pulled her phone from her back pocket and opened the app on her phone, facing it where he and I both could see since he'd sidled up on my left where I sat on the stool at the end of the bar.

"See? It's even got boxes where you check which kind of supernaturals you'd like to date."

I noticed she'd checked the boxes for witches/warlocks, vampires, and even grim reapers. But not werewolves. Of course, Jules didn't like us socializing with werewolves. Or at least, she hadn't. Now that Mateo and Evie were practically married and his cousin Nico was a stable part of our nightlife scene at the Cauldron, she'd changed her mind about *all* werewolves being unstable monsters. They were the only two we knew, though.

"And then there's the personality questions and so on and so forth." Violet sucked in a gasping breath and beamed her excited eyes at me. With her hair a vibrant blue, her eyes looked almost purple when she lit up like that. "Oh, Isadora. I know the perfect picture to use for your profile."

"We can deal with this later," I said gruffly.

She clicked off the app and winked at me. "Gotcha."

Devraj hovered close, seeming to want to talk to me, but I kept my gaze purposely averted. I didn't want to see a look of disappointment or hurt in his eyes. It was for our own good. Or at least mine. I knew myself enough to understand that I couldn't go further with him without wanting more than he was ready to give me. Or could give me.

"I win!" screamed Livvy, bouncing off the barstool and dancing around in a circle. Then she broke out into the chorus of "Single Ladies" while Finnie buried his head in his hands.

She propped one hand on her curvaceous hip covered in black yoga pants with tiny crystal balls on them. She wore her favorite hot-pink tank top with the phrase *I'm not bossy, I'm the queen.* A tilted crown was etched in the middle with rhinestone jewels. Evie had given it to her last Christmas, and Livvy wore it every chance she could when she wasn't in work mode. Livvy flicked the fingers of her left hand in the air as she sang.

She finally stopped on a laugh. "Don't worry, Finnie boy. I'll be your backup singer."

"Me too, me too!" said Clara, hopping over to join them. "You have to have two backup singers, Finnie. You can't have one. Right, Livvy?"

Livvy gave me the wide-eyed *oh-no* look. I stifled a laugh, easing toward the table next to Evie. Clara's enthusiasm for singing far outweighed her talent. Livvy then smoothed her face before wrapping an arm around Clara's shoulders and squeezing her tight. "Of course he does. We'll be your dynamic duo backup singers."

"It's all right," Charlie comforted Finnie. "There's a first time for everything."

Finnie lifted his head from his hands finally, his face practically purple with his deep blush. "Even wearing drag?"

"Especially wearing drag," said Charlie, patting Finnie on the head. "Just ask JJ."

JJ's scowl deepened, and even through his trim beard, I could see him clenching his jaw.

"JJ!" called Jules from the open doorway of the kitchen. JJ was the official heavy pot carrier in the house, so that meant dinner was ready.

He shoved off the bar and headed for the kitchen.

"Saved by the dinner bell," Charlie sang.

JJ flipped him off over his shoulder and kept walking. Charlie just laughed.

"Wait! Where'd you come from?" Violet had her hands propped on her hips as she glared at the werewolf across from Mateo. Nico was sitting, pretty as you please.

"From my apartment," he answered dryly.

232

"No shit," snapped Violet. "I mean, who asked you?"

"Evie."

"Stop being rude, Violet," said Evie, standing from Mateo's lap. "Nico is now my cousin-in-law."

"Y'all aren't married," she accused, scowling at her.

Mateo stood and spread a hand on Evie's hip from behind her. "Not yet," he said evenly.

"Sorry if my presence bothers you," crooned Nico. His voice was the stuff of fantasies. His smoldering grin tipped his mouth up wickedly.

"No, you're not," Violet said, scowling.

"Not one bit." He bit his bottom lip, seeming to enjoy her displeasure and staring at Violet like she was the main course.

This wasn't the first or even the second time these two had been caught bickering and snapping at each other. And even though Violet was frowning, she seemed to get some kind of strange satisfaction engaging with him this way. Something was definitely going on with these two, even if my most stubborn sister pretended otherwise.

Violet turned in a little huff toward the front of the serving line where Jules was setting a giant ladle. At least it took all the attention off me, and that's all I cared about.

What I also couldn't help caring about was the way Devraj had gone uncharacteristically quiet. He didn't try to talk to me the rest of the night, and I tried not to stare at him and worry about that pensive look of pain marking his beautiful face. And the fact that I was fairly positive I'd put it there.

Needless to say, though conversation and laughter flowed around the table, it was the worst Sunday dinner ever. But it was for the best. I was sure of it. Kind of.

Chapter 20

~DEVRAJ~

I SAT IN MY CAR IN THE HOSPITAL PARKING LOT OBSESSING OVER THE picture of Isadora on her profile on the fucking dating app, Zapp. Her sister, who'd taken her picture, had captured her so perfectly I felt a pinch in my chest when I looked at it. I was rubbing my sternum, hoping the pain would go away as I analyzed every line and curve of her face and figure.

She wore a white sleeveless dress brushing just above her knees, her long tan legs accentuating her lean beauty. There were gold bangle bracelets adorning both wrists, her sun-kissed skin smooth and beautiful. She was caught mid-laugh, her green eyes bright, the sun right behind her head, which lit her flowing blonde hair on fire, wisps picked up by the wind. One strand crossed one eye and cheek. The sunlight behind her silhouetted her long legs that could be seen through the sheer cotton. Dangling from the fingers of one hand was a yellow wildflower, one of the many surrounding her in the field at her feet.

She was breathtaking. Literally. I rubbed at my chest again, finding it hard to get enough air.

The piercing sting of this profile pic proved she wanted to date. Just not me.

Was I wrong in the attraction I sensed from her? Was it one-sided? I knew it wasn't. Even at the Green Light, her pulse raced when I pulled her into my arms on the dance floor. She couldn't fake her body's reaction, the subtle nuances I was so sensitive to as an experienced vampire. The tripping of her pulse, the labored breathing, the dilation of her pretty green eyes.

And yet, here was proof she wasn't interested in my company.

Her words at the Green Light had stung. And maybe she was right to a certain degree. We did move in different circles, lived in different worlds. But I wanted her in *mine*. Or maybe I'd give up mine to be in hers. I don't know. All I knew was that after three hundred years, I'd never felt this sort of obsessive attraction toward a woman. And what she didn't know was that I could be patient. And tenacious.

I growled, staring down at her profile. She'd checked off every box for the supernaturals she was interested in dating. No, Isadora wouldn't discriminate. That should make me proud that she was so open-minded, but all I could think of was the giant goddamn dating pool she'd just opened up. They'd be coming in droves for her.

Her profile was brief, but very telling.

- Interests: good food, gardening, cute dogs
- Turn-ons: intelligence, humor, maturity
- Turn-offs: selfishness

- Absolute musts: to be local and rooted in New Orleans

Ah. There it was. That last line explained so much. New Orleans wasn't my home. She knew that Stygorn moved often. Knew that I rarely stayed in one place too.

And cute dogs? She didn't even own a dog. Why not?

A rap on my window snapped me out of my heartsick daze. Ruben stood there, a confused expression and smirk on his face. He'd glanced at my phone in my lap. I opened the door and slipped the phone in my pants pocket.

"What are you doing?" he asked, his gaze flicking to my phone. "I figured you'd already be up there."

"Just checking something."

"Mmm," was Ruben's all-knowing response. "If you'd gone up, you'd be able to ogle the real thing rather than her picture on your phone."

"She's here?" I didn't even try to deny the fact I was stalking her online.

He dipped his chin and headed for the side entrance to the hospital yet again.

"Jules phoned me half an hour ago to make sure my guys knew she was coming with Isadora."

"So what are you doing here?"

He gave me one of those mind-your-own-business looks. Which never worked on me. "Just checking up on things."

"You could do that from the comfort of your home," I noted as we entered near the stairwell and nodded to the vampire guard, Roland, in the shadows.

"Shut up, Devraj. You're one to talk."

I laughed when he traced up to her hospital room. I did the same, cloaking myself in glamour so the nurses wouldn't even note the rush of wind as we passed. Gabriel was at the door, also cast in glamour so that no one but vampires might sense him.

I eased into the room behind Ruben, hearing soft feminine voices. The gentle timbre of Isadora's clutched me in the gut, reminding me how deep this witch had her hooks into me. The funny thing was that I was perfectly okay with being at her mercy. If she only knew, what would she do?

"I can't thank you enough," said Emma from the bed.

"You just rest up. You'll be good enough to go home by tomorrow."

A subtle glow shimmered on Isadora's skin, proof she'd been using her Conduit powers heavily. Emma's gaze shifted to us. And though I'd erased her memory of us last time, she didn't seem afraid of two strange men entering her room. Probably due to Isadora's extensive healing, calming her down to her bones.

A Conduit's power could have a similar effect as an Aura who could transform people's emotions. A powerful Conduit healing could change the energy makeup of a person so entirely that their entire demeanor changed—calmed and soothed by the witch's magical shift of earth energy into the human body.

How did I know all of this? Because I'd been doing extensive research on Conduit witches over the past week. Yeah, I had it bad.

Isadora looked over her shoulder, meeting my gaze. Those sweet eyes widened before she turned back to Emma. "We should go. Take care of yourself."

As she rose, Jules did too. But as they passed, I reached out a hand and touched Isadora's forearm, stopping her. "Will you wait a few minutes? We need to talk."

Her startled gaze shot to mine, her heartbeat spiking.

"I don't think—"

"About Emma," I clarified, realizing she thought I wanted to talk about us.

Which I did. But now that I knew why she was pushing me away, I'd have to bide my time and figure this out.

"Oh. Yeah. Of course."

Jules sidled closer. "We'll wait in the parking lot downstairs. The nurses won't understand why we're lingering."

Witches couldn't use glamour like vampires, so they were here as legitimate visitors. I nodded, then they left.

I sat next to Emma, pushing my glamour to engulf her so she wouldn't panic at my nearness. Even if she didn't remember what had happened to her, she'd have the residual effects still deep in her memory. Like PTSD, she'd likely be wary of strange men getting too close for a long while.

"Hi, Emma. Can I hold your hand? I just want to take a look."

"Sure," she said easily, even smiling, completely entranced.

I swept in quickly this time, hoping to find something new that I might've missed. Something that would finger Blake as the man we were looking for. Or one of his entourage. But nothing new. The same memories emerged from her subconscious. Mostly fuzzy. The voice of the man who fed off her. The sound of a distant church bell still ringing clear. If I could only pinpoint that bell. But there were hundreds in the New Orleans metropolitan area.

When I pulled out of her mind, she was in a deep sleep. I put my palm to her forehead, making sure she wouldn't remember meeting us this last time. Her spirit felt at ease now, and I wouldn't jeopardize her sanity or well-being by coming again. The human mind was resilient but also fragile. Especially when a supernatural started tampering with it.

I stood. Ruben asked, "Anything new?"

I shook my head. "Let's go."

We streaked through the hospital, landing outside in the parking lot beside Jules's car five seconds later.

Isadora gasped when we appeared beside them. She clutched her chest. "I hate it when y'all do that."

I couldn't help but smile. My witch was so sensitive.

My witch. When had I begun to think of her that way? How could I make it a reality? That was all that seemed to consume me these days. And yet, Ruben needed my help. There were other girls still out there in this kidnapper's captivity. I forced myself to focus. I had an idea of what to do to catch them, but I needed to see if Isadora discovered anything else.

"Sorry," I told her, restraining a smile at her skittishness. "Did you sense anything else? Something that might tie Blake to Emma?"

She held my gaze, her expression sobering. "No. She's almost fully healed, though. Physically."

"Thank God," muttered Jules.

"Not long and we'll have the other girls and bring them to safety," Ruben assured Jules. "You might want to get a few Conduits on stand-by for when we do."

Ruben's unwavering attraction to the woman was so obvious with his electric blue gaze riveted on her face.

Damn, was that what I looked like when I stared at Isadora? We two were a sad lot. But unlike Ruben, I wasn't going to wait a decade to go for my woman.

"I'll have them ready," said Jules.

Clearing my throat, I added, "I didn't sense anything new. And our plan is solid."

Jules's stance became rigid as she looked at her sister. "Are you positive this grim of yours can trace these guys? I don't want my sister put in harm's way. Especially if I have to null her so she can play bait for this trap."

"One hundred percent positive," said Ruben. "I've met with the creator of the software and I've watched it run several tests until I was satisfied. The tests were effective every single time."

"I promise I won't let anything happen to her," I said to Jules, keeping my eyes on Isadora.

My protective instincts pushed me like never before. She wanted to date supernaturals, including other vampires, and she had no idea how beastly we could all be. Take me, for example. I was concocting ideas of sabotage because I already considered her mine. Also, I worried what deviant she might fall prey to among our kind. Of the supernaturals, we were the most cunning. For a reason, of course. We hunted and seduced humans to willingly give us the blood that flowed in their veins. Our genetics demanded we be beguiling in the most irresistible of ways.

I was so wrapped up in thoughts of Isadora I startled when Jules spoke to her. "Who is going with you to pretend to be your second party girl that night?"

"Livvy said she'd do it. She's the only one who wasn't with you guys at last year's Summit cocktail party."

Jules chewed on her bottom lip a second before replying, "I know you think this plan is foolproof, but I want Violet to do a reading on you two." She eyed me and Ruben. "If she sees success in this operation, then I'll be behind you one hundred percent."

We needed the Enforcer of the district behind us, or she could call the whole operation off. And though I'd never let anything happen to Isadora, it would make me feel better if a Seer could give us a positive premonition.

Ruben gave a stiff nod. "Perhaps tomorrow?"

"I'd like to be there," added Isadora, her brow pinched into a frown. "When and what time?"

"We could meet at our house at eight. I'm letting Mitchell close the kitchen on some nights. Violet isn't closing the bar tomorrow."

Isadora cleared her throat. Her pulse picked up. She was anxious about something. "Can we do it a little later?"

Jules eyed her sister, puzzled. "Why? You got a hot date or something?"

Her fingers curled into the fabric of her skirt a second before she flexed and relaxed them. Sort of. "Actually, yes. I do have a date."

That pinching feeling was back again, twisting hard in the middle of my chest. She glanced at me, then away, tapping her hands against her sides nervously.

Jules stared at her a second longer, the awkward tension stretching. "All right then. How is ten? Eleven?"

"Oh, ten is good," she said on a quick breath. "I won't be staying out that late."

Jules turned to Ruben. "Meet us at our house at ten."

Ruben nodded.

"I'll be there too," I said, eyeing Isadora, who kept darting her gaze to me, then away. "Good night, ladies."

I gave Ruben a sharp nod, then headed for my car with only one goal in mind. To discover when and where Isadora's date would be tomorrow night.

Chapter 21

~ISADORA~

Fidgeting in my seat at the back of the Cauldron, I tried not to stare at the door, but it was impossible. I was basically on a blind date. I mean, sure, I'd seen his profile pic and we'd messaged via Zapp a handful of times before he asked me out and I accepted. But I basically knew nothing.

What *did* I know about him? Well, he liked quiet nights at home with a good meal. So did I. He also enjoyed reading biographies and books on philosophy. I wasn't a big reader, but I could totally respect that. These were quiet pursuits. But was I playing it safe again? I didn't know because that was all the information his limited profile listed.

The one thing that did set him apart from any guy in the past was that he was a grim reaper. I was going out with a grim! And his profile pic? Devastatingly gorgeous.

I'd chosen the Cauldron for our date because it felt familiar and made me more comfortable. Violet warned me to be safe because you never knew who you were meeting through dating apps. If this guy was dangerous, then I could wave to JJ to help me out. I glanced at the bar where he was talking to a customer. He tossed me a wink before pouring a draft.

I straightened my green cardigan sweater one more time just as my date walked through the door. Wow. Yeah, his profile pic didn't lie. Jet-black hair, smoldering eyes behind black-rimmed glasses, a fit but not athletic physique. More on the thinner side. But so was I. Something we had in common, right? Or was I already reaching?

He wore a gray sweater and dark pants, conservative but attractive. He looked good. He looked nice. Too nice? I don't know. My brain was racing a mile a minute and I couldn't believe I was doing this. Was this wrong?

Devraj popped into my mind. Those devastating, warm brown eyes filled with a resigned sadness when he left our family dinner on Sunday. My stomach suddenly hurt. Maybe I could still slip out the back door.

Oh hell. My date spotted me.

He gave me a lopsided smile and headed in my direction. Confident gait. Okay, that's good. Really good.

"Isadora?"

"That's me."

He held out his hand for me to shake. "Terry. It's great to meet you in person."

I shook his hand, which was warm and soft. Too soft? Well, for a bookish guy, that was totally normal. I mean, what did I expect? Large, long-fingered hands that looked and felt like they did more than hold books all day? Okay, maybe I did.

Stop it right now!

"Are you all right?" he asked nicely as he slid in the opposite side of the booth. "You said you're a Conduit, right?"

"Yeah. Oh yeah. It's all fine," I assured him. He obviously thought his grim magic was affecting me, but I'd automatically pushed out my own magic to shift it away.

Auras like Clara were completely unaffected by grims' unique powers. Conduits like myself could be, but we could also shift their energy away so that it didn't pull on our senses the way it did others.

Belinda popped over. I'd made sure not to sit in Evie's section because sisters could be too nosy. She might say or do something to make me nervous. Like now, she was staring at Terry like he was an insect under her microscope from two tables over where she was taking a drink order.

"What can I get you guys?" asked Belinda, pretending not to know me like I'd asked her. I didn't want my date to know how paranoid I was about dating a guy I'd met on an app.

"Chardonnay for me," I said.

"I'll take the same," said Terry before Belinda flitted away. "So, Isadora, tell me all about yourself."

He folded his arms on the table, and I blinked. I hated statements like that. I mean, *all about myself?* That was a lot. If I summed it up, I'd sound so boring. So I went for a semi-shortened version. "Well, I live with my sisters and work at our metaphysical shop right next door actually. I spend a lot of time in my garden and greenhouse when not working."

"Really?" His dark eyes were nice, but they didn't make my pulse trip faster the way Devraj's did.

Why was I thinking of him? I was on a date with another man. I had to stop comparing.

"Interesting. What kinds of plants do you grow? Is it all for potions? What kinds of potions do you make? Do you write your own spells for customers?"

Hello, Mr. Interrogation. I wanted to ask if he was collecting data because that seemed an innate need for grims. Then again, I guess it was his nature to gather all the info he could. So I told him about the plants I grew, the different bundles I made for the shop. This was no big state secret or anything. I explained the different items we sold as well and kept answering all of his questions until I had to hold up a finger to pause him so I could take my first sip of the glass of wine Belinda had dropped and I hadn't touched.

Before he could dive back in, I reversed the tables. "So, Terry. What about you? What do you do?"

He stared at me a minute, taking a sip of his wine, then answered, "I teach philosophy."

"Oh wow. That sounds cool. Where at? UNO? Loyola?"

"Wherever I can."

Um, what?

"So are you a university instructor?"

"Of sorts." He let his smile widen. Okayyyy.

"That's like being sort of pregnant."

"Is it, though?"

Oh my God. This guy.

"So you don't want to talk about your job. Tell me about being a grim. I've never actually met one. What's that like?"

"It's quite . . . nebulous."

I let out a little laugh. "That makes no sense."

"Doesn't it?"

Now his cutesy smile was irritating. Was he playing games with me? Or was this really what he was like?

"Well, tell me anything about yourself. Like *anything*. That wasn't already in your profile." Which was only two things.

He must've heard the frustration in my voice, and yet his answer frustrated me even more.

"I can tell you that I find you very beautiful."

Is this guy for real? How could I date someone who refused to tell me about himself? I enjoyed a good intellectual debate as much as the next woman, but I didn't want to play mind games just to find out where the hell this dude earned his paycheck.

It's funny how some gorgeous guys lose their attractiveness the more you saw their flaws. It's also funny how some guys grow more attractive the more they showed you their humor, their intelligence, their sensitivity, and compassion. Like someone else I knew.

"Well, tell me about what kinds of philosophy you teach."

His eyes widened with a spark of interest, and then *finally* he started talking. Unfortunately, the topic had my eyes glazing over. By the time he'd covered existentialism and Jean-Paul Sartre's brilliant definition of this cultural movement, then moved on to relativism and realism, I'd finished my second glass of wine and was internally screaming to be released from captivity.

"Excuse me," he said, taking a sip of wine and setting it down. "I'm going to run to the restroom."

I was inwardly sighing with relief to get a break from the philosophy lesson. Then suddenly Terry's seat was filled by the man I couldn't stop thinking about.

"So how's the date going?" asked Devraj with the most perfectly amused smile stretching across his handsome face.

I whipped my head around to be sure Terry hadn't seen, then faced the grinning vampire.

"What are you doing here?" I whisper-hissed.

"I was just at the bar having a drink, talking to JJ, when I saw you over here. He told me you were on your first Zapp date," he said casually, which eased my guilt a little from how he looked last Sunday. "So have you decided?" He propped his perfectly trimmed, bearded chin on his hand thoughtfully. "Are you an existentialist or a realist? I really need to know."

I clamped my jaw tight and narrowed my gaze. He chuckled to himself and grinned wider, continuing on. "As for myself, I'd like to hear more about Freud's sexual theories." He arched a salacious brow at me. "Is your superego hiding any dormant sexual fetishes that I should know about?"

"Shut. Up." I glanced at the restrooms again while he laughed at my expense, then snapped my attention back to him. "For your information, he's a very interesting guy."

"Very. If you like listening to dissertations."

"How could you hear from over at the bar?" I stared accusingly.

"I'm good at lip-reading," he answered with a shrug.

"He's telling me about his work," I defended, trying not to smile at his obscene intrusiveness. "This is what people do when they date."

"Is it?" His expression morphed into confusion. "But I thought the point was to actually *attract* the person you're dating."

"Stop being mean. And leave. Before he gets back."

"Don't worry." He sat back in the chair and gave me a wistful smile and a wink. "I won't ruin your date."

He already had. Just by being here, he'd shown in glaring con-trast the difference between my date and who I really wanted.

I couldn't do anything but glare at him as he stood and brushed his fingers along the curve of my neck exposed above my cardigan sweater. He gave me a friendly squeeze that I felt zing all the way to my toes.

"Enjoy the rest of your date, Isadora," he said sincerely and then marched for the door.

A few seconds later, Terry took up his place. "So where were we?"

Then he launched into his thoughts on Friedrich Nietzsche, expounding on his views on traditional morality, and he truly lost me.

It's not that his thoughts weren't interesting. To many women, he'd be reeling them in with his immense brain, but I was a simple girl. And I honestly didn't want to debate whether a fallen tree really made a sound in the woods if no one was there to hear it. I'd rather discuss what kind of tree it was and if it held any medicinal properties that could be brewed into a healthful tea.

The real problem wasn't so much that Terry's long-winded philo-sophical history was boring—but sorry, to me it was. The real issue was that my mind kept wandering to someone else. As I sat there, I compared Terry's rather unremarkable voice to the sexy timbre of Devraj's. Terry's eyes, though intelligent and nice to look at, didn't carry the same weight and heat of Devraj's. Even his smile didn't com-pare. Not to mention the fact that I'd checked out of this conversation at the third reference to Sigmund Freud's Oedipus complex.

I was bored. And annoyed. Perhaps even a little sad.

Since Devraj had strolled up, I couldn't think of anything else but him. It was all his fault!

Okay, that was a lie. Terry and I just weren't meshing, which is why when he asked if I wanted another round, I politely declined and told him I needed to get going. After Terry paid the bill, we walked out together.

"That was lovely, Isadora," he said politely, and I cringed inside when I realized he had enjoyed this far more than I had. "Should I call you again?" he asked with that hopeful look in his eyes.

This was one main reason I hated dating. When I didn't return the guy's feelings, I hated rejecting them. But I wasn't the kind of girl to lead a guy on either.

Swallowing against the discomfort, I said, "I'm sorry, Terry. But I don't think so."

"Ah." He looked down with a tight smile, then offered his hand to shake. "It was a pleasure nonetheless."

"Thank you," I said, giving his hand an apologetic squeeze, then withdrawing. "I'm sorry."

"Not necessary. Take care." Then he sauntered off toward his car.

Devraj leaned back against the wall of the Cauldron, one knee propped up with his foot against the brick behind him, arms crossed. That's when I noted he was wearing dark jeans and a black Henley, his hair in a man-bun, looking far too fine for words. Somehow, that irritated me more.

His expression was one of concern as he watched Terry walk away. "Ouch," he said, finally looking at me.

"Why are you here?" I sauntered over.

"Moral support?" He raised his brows innocently, his charming smile beaming.

"No, you're not. You were waiting for me."

Looking a little sheepish, he admitted, "I wanted to be sure you were safe. These guys aren't always who they say they are on those dating apps."

"Same thing Violet told me." I couldn't actually be mad about that, but still.

Blowing out a breath, which lifted a wisp of my long bangs, I said, "But you interfered. And you—" I bit my lip.

"I what?" he asked, all innocence.

Please.

"You distracted me," I admitted. But his aggravatingly knowing smile made me go on. "And I don't like you butting in and acting like the protective big brother or whatever."

He opened his mouth to say something, then stopped. He tilted his head, dropped his foot from the wall, and tucked his hands into his jeans' pockets. "Were you enjoying his company?" he asked, expression serious. "Was this going to lead to a second date?"

There's no way in hell I'd be going out with Terry again. I had already been contemplating excuses to leave early when Devraj had shown up.

I glanced up the street, heaving out a sigh, propping my hands on my hips. "That's not the point."

"I'm sorry."

His sincerity cooled me off. Some of the steam had blown out of me. "I don't like you interfering."

His smile disappeared. He took a step toward me into my personal bubble, forcing me to tip up my chin. I didn't back down, though. I wouldn't let any vampire intimidate me. If that's what he was doing. But the flash of heat in his eyes told me that might not be what was on his mind.

"Maybe not," he said in a low whisper, his voice silky smooth and sweet like a chocolate river. "But I care about you enough to make sure you're safe. I'm sorry if I crossed a boundary." He reached up and tucked a lock of hair behind my ear, his fingers trailing along the shell. I barely repressed a tingly shiver. "Some of these guys make up their profiles to hide who they truly are. What they're really like."

Swallowing hard against the emotion I saw in his deep brown eyes and heard in his unfairly hypnotic voice, I asked, "And you know this from experience? On your own dating profile?"

His fingers had trapped a long strand of my hair, which he rubbed slowly between his thumb and middle finger. My gaze was drawn to that cuff bracelet, the one made of his mother's mangalsutra.

A little throb beat in my chest for this charismatic man who still loved his mother so much. I would say he was a contradiction, but that wasn't really true. He was exactly who he showed to the world. A brilliant, charming, and stealthy vampire who lived life fiercely. Too fiercely perhaps. His light shone too brightly. It burned.

He scoffed, his gaze on the lock of hair he toyed with between his fingers. "I don't use dating apps."

"Only the blood-host app, iBite."

His smile became that wide, all-knowing force that made me all melty inside. He'd caught me.

"Now look who's stalking. Have you been checking me out on iBite?"

"Please." I rolled my eyes. "Not stalking. Jules was on there, so I happened to check and see, you know, if you had a profile."

"Why was Jules on there?"

"To check Ruben's profile, of course."

Somehow, he took that in stride with a nod. Huh. I wondered what he knew about those two.

He twirled a lock tighter around his index finger and tugged, drawing me an inch closer. "You read the forum reviews."

I shrugged a shoulder, giving him my I-don't-care look.

"I see." His dark gaze roved down to my lips, coasted lower to my throat, then back up. "Have you ever thought of donating a little to team vampire?"

"No," I snapped.

"Liar."

"Don't call me a liar."

"Even if you are one?"

"Okay, maybe I thought about it after that one time. You know."

He arched a black brow. "No, tell me. I don't know."

His fiendish grin was unbearable. He was having so much fun taunting me, and for some dumbass reason, I was enjoying it too. A stark contrast with the rest of my evening with Terry.

"I think you can guess," I added flippantly.

"Okay. I'll play," he said, his hand drifting under my hair to wrap loosely around the base of my throat. "You enjoyed it when you nicked your tongue on my fang. You enjoyed it so much you've wondered what it would feel like if you went all the way."

I clenched my thighs tight at the phrase *all the way* because that conjured up our one-night stand. The most fantastic sexual experience of my life.

He brushed his thumb along my pulse, heat pouring off him. "You've thought about it more than once. You want to know if what those women said about vampire toxin is true."

"Maybe," I said, aggravated with his arrogance. And the fact that he was totally right. I pulled away till his arm dropped from me, refraining from groaning at the loss of his sensual touch. "Maybe I need to try a vampire next on Zapp and see for myself." Then I turned and walked up Magazine Street toward home.

That was a bitchy thing to say, I know. It was really unlike me. But Devraj needed to understand he didn't have rights over me. We weren't in a relationship. We were friends. Who'd happened to have had mind-melting sex once. Twice, really. And that was that. I needed a man I could fall in love with. One who'd stay.

Chapter 22

~DEVRAJ~

DAMN. THAT WOMAN WAS GOING TO KILL ME. AFTER COOLING MY head and biting back a string of curses in ten languages, I caught up to walk with her back to her house. I changed the subject to something lighter so I didn't lose my shit over the thought of her entertaining some other vampire. Her letting another vampire touch her, bite her. The burning jealousy that thought stirred in my gut was crippling.

So I steered us onto something else. "You like dogs?"

She glanced at me as we passed by Maybelle's and through a laughing group of friends going somewhere. I placed a light hand on her back, and she let me, thankfully. So maybe she wasn't that angry with me. Perhaps she was just giving me a little payback for ruining her evening with Terry the Witless Wonder. Maybe it was a dick move to butt in, but I had zero regrets. That idiot had no business with a woman like Isadora, who was so far out of his league.

"How'd you know I like dogs?"

"Your profile on Zapp."

"You read my profile?"

"Of course I did," I answered shamelessly.

My bold admission sent a flush of pink crawling up into her cheeks. I wanted her to know I was interested. I just couldn't let her know *how* interested. How fascinated. That would terrify her.

She hiked her bag on her shoulder again nervously as we turned the corner onto our street. "Yeah, I love dogs."

"Then why don't you have one?"

"Well, I do sort of—" She glanced at me, biting back what she was going to tell me for some reason. "It's just that we have Z and Fred, and they're enough right now. I'm not sure how a new pet would fit into the mix, you know? I mean, being a pet owner is a big responsibility. I wouldn't want to bring him into the house if he wasn't going to fit in well with the others."

"Him? You have a dog in mind already?"

Her focus remained straight ahead, but I caught the widening of her eyes as though she hadn't wanted me to pick up on that. This woman had no idea how hard I listened to her. How much I obsessed over every word that came out of her mouth. Over every lithe movement of her body, every soft expression, every blink of her haunting green eyes.

We were turning up her walk through the wrought iron gate. "You're coming in?" she asked, surprised.

"It's almost time for Violet's reading."

She squeezed her eyes shut with a little shake of her head as we stepped up to the porch. "Right, right."

She was a little more scrambled than normal. I wasn't sure if it was me interrupting her date. Or if it was just me. What I did know was that her pulse always picked up the pace when I got close to her. And that was definitely a good sign.

I followed Isadora into the house and down the foyer to the living room.

"Hello? Anybody home?" she called out.

"In my study!" yelled Jules.

Rather than head into the living room, Isadora glanced over her shoulder and pointed down the longer hallway. "This way."

I gave her a reassuring smile and followed, happy to sense her anger had subsided. When we arrived in what must be Jules's library, Violet was already there, the wooden coffee table set up for the reading. White pillar candles sat staggered on the table, a smudge stick burning upright in a bowl of black sand. Incense filled the room with spice and sage.

Violet sat cross-legged on one end, shuffling her tarot cards. They were all facedown on the table as she roamed her fingers over them, moving them under and over each other. Already I sensed a pulse of magic sizzling in the air.

Jules sat on the other side of the coffee table on the floor, her demeanor calm and watchful as always. "Isn't Ruben with you?"

"We came separately."

Isadora scoffed. Jules eyed her with a raised eyebrow, but Isadora just shook her head. She would most likely wait till we left before she spilled about my interference.

"How was your date?" asked Violet, grinning down at the cards as she scooped them up.

"We'll talk later," Isadora promised with a hint of warning.

Violet smirked, then glanced at me and winked. Somehow I felt like Violet was on my side. She was now my favorite sister.

"Would you like a reading while we wait for Ruben?" she asked me.

My pulse tripped. I wasn't sure why. Then I glanced at Isadora who took a seat in a chair behind them near the bookshelf. "Why not?"

I settled into a wingback chair on the opposite end of the coffee table, suddenly very nervous. "What do I do?"

Violet grinned, her catlike eyes shining by the candlelight. "We're doing three cards. One for personal. One for professional. One for your heart's goal."

"Heart's goal?" I asked with skepticism. My gaze darted to Isadora again, the magnetic pull she had on me in a room so overpowering I could hardly focus on anything else.

"To catch the kidnapper, of course," Violet answered, her gaze on the cards, her voice amused. "That would be the goal that weighs most heavily on you. Right?"

"Right. Of course."

She bit her bottom lip, holding the cards in one hand. She tucked some of her blue hair behind her ear, revealing a row of piercings up the cartilage.

"Whoa. That's new. When did you get that?" Isadora asked, leaning forward and pointing at Violet's arm.

Violet stretched out her left inner forearm. I recognized the image because I'd just seen something similar on one of the tarot cards.

"The High Priestess?" asked Jules, leaning forward and holding her wrist so she could inspect the ink.

The priestess wore a horned crown and held a crystal ball in one hand, her gown embedded with stars, a crescent moon over one shoulder.

"Isn't she beautiful?" asked Violet with a huge smile.

"Who's the High Priestess?" I had to ask.

Violet went back to flipping her cards from hand to hand. "She's the queen of intuition, sacred knowledge, and the divine feminine. I need her on my side."

"It's beautiful work," said Isadora. "Did you use your regular guy?"

"Nah. Someone new," she said evasively.

As she shuffled, I noticed some Celtic runes inked on her index and middle fingers. Though I'd spent some time in Ireland, I didn't know much about runes. But I did recognize the upward arrow for the spiritual warrior.

"Okay, Devraj. So first you'll pull a card for your personal self."

She fanned out the cards in front of her on the table, her silver nail polish sparkling. The charge of magic in the room amplified, pulling my own to the surface. Moving my hand on instinct, I tapped a card and slid it out from the deck. Violet flipped it over to reveal a man hanging from a gold cord by a tree. The card was upside down.

"The Hanged Man. But reversed." She angled her head at me. "This means resistance and indecision. There's something in your personal life that you're stalling about. If you really want it, you're going to need to get over that hump. Make the decision and go for it."

I made no response. I was totally confused. The only personal thing in my life was my hunt of Isadora. And I wasn't stalling about it. Was I?

"That's kind of vague," I said. "What if I have no idea what you're talking about?"

She nodded her head definitively. "You will." She pointed to the deck. "Now for your professional self."

On a heavy sigh, I leaned forward, tapped the card my fingers were drawn to, then slid it forward. Violet flipped it.

"Ahh. I like this one. Strength. Not a great mystery in meaning. You have strength, courage, and compassion in your work." Violet tapped her index finger on the card three times. "You have an enormous amount of influence too."

"On who?" I asked.

"On everyone," she answered flippantly.

My gaze moved to Isadora who had her eyes on the deck, her expression calm. But the wringing of her hands in her lap told me another story.

"Last one, Stygorn," said Violet. "This is for your heart's goal. So hold it in your mind as you seek your card."

I thought of Blake Bellingrath and of Darren Webber and our plan, which immediately led to the thought of Isadora acting as bait. Which then led to the anxiety I felt putting her life in danger. The fear, even, that I wouldn't be able to get to her before something happened to her. Then my thoughts flickered to Isadora in my care, under my protection, in my home, in my bed. In my arms. In my heart. I reached over and tapped a card, pulling it forward out of the deck.

When Violet went to flip it over, it flew up into the air, spun, and slapped back down directly in front of me. There was a collective gasp among the women, but I just stared down at my fate.

"Wow," said Violet. "That one had some emotional power behind it. The Chariot. That's interesting. Control. Willpower. There will be success in your action." She reached for the card, which slid away from me on its own until it stopped in front of her. Magic sparked the air with sizzling energy. She placed one finger on top of it and closed her eyes. "Yes. Definite success. But only *if* your determination and will matches genuine intentions. Otherwise, you'll lose." Her eyes sparked an electric blue as she seemed to stare straight into my soul. "Hear me, Stygorn. You'll lose."

I swallowed hard, mouth gone bone-dry at the thought of losing Isadora. I was more than determined to keep her safe, to make her mine. So what the hell did that mean?

"Well," said Isadora, "we know he's determined to catch this kidnapper, so that should be easy enough."

"You're right, sis," Violet said evenly, ethereal gaze boring into mine, telling me she knew what goal I was after. "Should be easy enough for a Stygorn who knows what he could lose if he fails. You best be all in, vampire."

I swallowed hard, my heart hammering like mad. I'd thought of possessing Isadora's body. I hadn't thought of her owning me instead. But that's what this felt like. Over three centuries, no one had beguiled me like she did. And without even trying. Some part of her spoke to some part of me. And I hadn't realized it until Violet asked me to think of my heart's goal. Not on this level.

Fortunately, Ruben stepped in, breaking the awkward moment between Violet and me. And Isadora, who had no idea what was really going on. The Seer witch knew, though. And she was warning me to be careful. To understand that I could fail if my intentions weren't true. I wanted Isadora. There was no doubt. Was that not true enough? Not according to the blue-haired witch who still had her cat eyes fixed on me.

"Apparently, I missed something interesting," said Ruben.

Isadora piped up. "According to Violet, Devraj's goal to catch the kidnapper will be successful."

Violet shuffled the cards and arched a brow at me.

"Is that so?" asked Ruben. "Then we don't need my reading, do we?"

"Sit down, Ruben." Violet fanned the cards in front of her.

I moved to lean against the bookcase next to Isadora, letting Ruben have my place. The candles flared when Ruben sat. Magic reacted strangely to the elements. Or maybe the elements reacted strangely to magic. A vampire's was an aggressive, intrusive sort of magic, so it didn't surprise me when the wind shifted angrily. Especially in the presence of three witches so attuned with the elements. There was a palpable undercurrent of energy humming in the room.

Violet flattened her palms on either side of the fanned deck and looked at Ruben. "As I told Devraj, you'll pull three cards. One for personal self. One for professional. And one for your heart's goal to catch the kidnapper."

"Easy enough," he rumbled pleasantly, pulling at the cuff of his starched shirt. He wore only a deep red vest, no jacket. His silver skull cuff links winked in the candlelight.

"So you say," mumbled Violet. "Pick a card."

Ruben appeared poised and smooth as always, but the narrowing of his gaze on the cards like they might be the enemy revealed he wasn't quite as calm as he appeared. He tapped a card with his index finger.

Violet flicked her hand, flipping it telekinetically.

"Oh dear." She bit back the smile overtaking her face. "The Emperor, reversed. That means domination, excessive control, inflexibility."

Jules coughed, nearly blowing out one of the candles before righting herself with a serious smile on her face. Ruben's gaze grew darker, his blue eyes more the color of midnight.

"That doesn't bode well, now does it?" he commented easily, even as he clenched his jaw.

"Well, yes and no, actually," said Violet, reaching out and flattening her palm over the card, fixing her attention on it, concentrating, listening to her magic. "It's true, you can be inflexible. Domineering." Her voice vibrated with a haunting sort of echo. "But it's only because you are unfulfilled. Frustrated." She removed her hand to her lap, her voice going back to normal. "Once you're fulfilled, you'll be balanced again. Though you'll never lose the dominant factor."

Ruben said nothing. Nor did he look at Jules when I knew he wanted to. He gestured toward the deck. "Shuffle."

Violet grinned. "See? Domineering."

Ruben blew out a heavy sigh. Violet and Isadora laughed. Jules didn't.

When Violet stopped moving the cards in a circle on the table, he reached over and flipped a card himself. Yes. Definitely domineering.

Then I couldn't hold back a chuckle at the card.

"Emperor again," said Violet. "This time upright. You're quite the leader, Ruben. The Emperor is so dominant in your house.

This shows you to be authoritative in your professional self. A sort of father figure to many. Role model and well-respected."

He made no comment, but the aura of anger eased around him.

"That's no surprise, though," she murmured. "But now the last one. Your heart's goal. To catch the kidnapper, mind you."

Ruben's gaze sharpened on her. "No need to remind me, darling."

"Just checking." She shuffled without touching the deck, spinning the cards on the flat surface with a swirl of her finger. When they settled flat, she gestured with a dip of her chin. "Pick one."

He leaned forward and tapped one on the outer edge. She flipped it to reveal the Tower.

It was a tower on fire, flames pouring from the windows, lightning flashing in the sky, and a woman falling.

"This means there will be an upheaval and great chaos. But also, revelation and awakening." She frowned before saying, "Yes, I believe you will get him."

"We will get the evidence we need for a conviction? We'll find the girls?" Ruben snapped.

"I'm sure." She gestured down at the cards. "But it may not play out exactly how you plan."

That had my gut tightening. I didn't want any surprises, especially when Isadora was involved. I'd be more than diligent and prepared that night.

"Has he killed any of the women?" asked Ruben. "Can you at least tell me that?"

"I can ask," she said, arching her brow as a warning of sorts. Ruben's aggression was spilling into the room.

Violet closed her eyes and raised her palms facing out. The pull of magic sharpened, a firm pressure building in the room, pressing on my chest. She inhaled deeply. The candle flames all leaned toward her, as if the fire were drawn to her. She whispered in French, an old incantation, calling to the elemental spirits.

The tattoo of the Empress on her forearm shivered and rippled, looking as if it moved. Did the inked Empress blink her eyes? Isadora gasped, also staring at the strange phenomenon. Then Violet popped open her eyes, burning bright blue, then set her hands in her lap. The candle flames righted themselves.

"No," she said. "The girls are all alive."

Ruben and I both exhaled with relief at the same time.

He gave me a nod and stood. "Thank you, Violet." He tugged on the cuffs of his shirt. "That's more than I could ask for." He glanced down at Jules. "Does that meet your satisfaction?"

She held his gaze, then nodded.

"Good evening then."

Jules said nothing, having been extremely quiet this whole time.

"Devraj, if you'll join me," said Ruben as he walked out.

I stood and couldn't help but brush a hand on Isadora's shoulder as I passed. "Good night."

She gave me a small smile, but that was it. I wondered if I'd made her seriously angry by interfering with her awful date. That's what was spinning through my mind when Ruben and I made it outside and he stopped on the porch.

"I don't like the card's reading that there will be chaos. We'll need to plan for every possibility."

"Agreed. As long as I'm on the team following the trace when they take Isadora."

"I understand," he said, glancing back at the house.

"And have your men had any luck tracking him?"

"No. I knew that would come to nothing. I have two men watching the Bellingrath estate, but Blake seems very wary. We haven't caught sight of him at all, going in or out."

He glanced once more toward the house, unable to hide the intensity of his expression.

"Why don't you just tell her?"

He huffed a sad laugh. "She knows."

"Does she? I mean, truly?"

He locked on me for a second before heaving out a sigh. "It doesn't matter anymore."

"Like hell it doesn't."

"Good night, Dev." Then he traced away, leaving me on the porch alone.

Ruben might be content to leave well enough alone, but I wasn't. Especially after that peculiar reading from Violet, her words making me sicker by the second as I walked to my home next door.

He knows what he could lose if he fails.

Pretty, lovely, wonderful Isadora.

"Then I won't lose," I vowed, more determined than ever.

Chapter 23

~ISADORA~

WHEN I PICKED OUT MY DRESS FOR DATE NUMBER TWO, I WONDERED if Devraj would've liked it. I wondered if he'd happen to be at the Cauldron tonight like last time. Then I had to admit to myself that I liked him watching out for me. Or maybe I just liked him watching me. And that was bad. Dangerous. I kept telling myself I couldn't hook up with him again. He was too . . . too Devraj.

I stood at the end of the bar next to Charlie while JJ tended to customers. Meeting at the Cauldron gave me a sense of security that calmed my nerves.

"Okay, that's him." I bumped Charlie with my elbow. "Remember, the signal is, if I tap my fingers on my knee three times, you come save me with some family emergency."

"Got it, Blondie. Don't you worry." He turned sideways on his stool. "Ooh. He's a pretty one. Go get him."

He patted me on the behind, a little encouragement. My date, Christopher, was searching the bar, but stopped when he saw me. Whoa. Now that was a beautiful smile.

"Christopher?" I asked, knowing it was him. He looked exactly like his profile.

"That's me." He smiled wider, his dimples popping. Mercy. "It's a pleasure to meet you, Isadora."

He held out his hand so I shook it. A good shake. Pleasantly firm grip.

"Um, I saved us a booth over here." I gestured to the corner near the stage. Nico was set up but wasn't playing just yet.

We settled in, and I felt surprisingly at ease. Strange that it should be with a vampire that I felt most comfortable.

"Nice place," he said, looking around. "Never been here before."

"It's my family's place," I admitted.

His blue eyes widened. "Really? That's so cool."

"Yeah. Me and my sisters own it together. I do the bookkeeping for both the Cauldron and Mystic Maybelle's next door."

"That's a great setup. A family business. Or businesses, actually." When he chuckled, it was a pleasant, rumbly sound. "I'm an architect for a larger firm, which isn't always that great. I imagine the family business is rewarding, even if it's hard working with your sisters sometimes."

"True, it is. What firm is that?"

"Bentley and Marks. We're based in Kenner actually. Do mostly commercial work for Metairie and Kenner."

Wow. A well-put-together guy who answered my questions and everything. This date was going amazingly well. And still,

I didn't feel that spark of attraction, that undeniable chemistry that I'd hoped for.

"Hey, Iz." Belinda sidled up to us. "What can I get you two?"

Christopher turned to me. "What do you have good on draft?"

"The Witch's Brew is really good."

He turned to Belinda. "I'll take that then."

"A glass of chardonnay for me," I said.

"Any particular brand?"

"JJ knows what I like."

While she marched off, I caught Devraj sitting at the bar next to Charlie. He was turned sideways on the stool, one hand wrapped around a tumbler of what looked like JJ's Blood Orange Old-Fashioned. He was listening to Charlie, but as if he knew my eyes were on him, he looked directly at me. I held his gaze for just a second, then turned away, a little shocked to catch such a somber expression on his face. Last time, he'd found my whole dating thing amusing.

"You all right?" asked Christopher, reaching across the table and touching my hand.

I drew back on instinct.

"I'm sorry," he apologized. "You just looked upset."

"No, it's okay. It's nothing."

Nothing but the realization that seeing Devraj sad made me suddenly *very* sad. Was Mr. I-Could-Charm-the-Panties-Off-Anyone more interested in me than I'd thought? Maybe something with the case had him looking that way. Maybe it had nothing to do with me.

"You sure?" asked Christopher.

"Absolutely. So tell me about blood-drinking," I charged ahead. "What's that like?"

"Wow. So we're just going there right away."

"Yep." I wanted more answers about this side of the vampire, and Christopher could give them to me. "We are."

He laughed, dimples popping, which was endearing as he fiddled nervously with the napkin in his lap. Note to self: a blushing vampire was adorable.

"Can I be totally honest?" he asked, chin down as he peered up beneath long eyelashes.

"I prefer that."

He shifted anxiously and set his clasped hands on the table. "It's a lot like sex actually."

"For the vampire or for the blood-host?"

"For both."

"You've been both?" I asked curiously.

I'd never thought of a vampire being bitten as well, but of course anyone could serve as a blood-host. Humans were just more open to the idea.

"It's very intimate," he said. "And pleasurable. For both parties."

Belinda strode up and set down our drinks. "Here we are. Enjoy!" She smiled and sauntered off just as Nico settled behind the mic, hooked his guitar strap over his shoulder, and started to play. I recognized the soft tune of a familiar song. Then he began to sing KALEO's "I Can't Go On Without You."

Christopher drank a little of his beer. "I have to say I'm a little surprised you're interested. I mean, are you interested?"

His demeanor remained friendly, but his blue eyes rolled with silver, his vampire very much liking the idea.

The fact is, I was interested. But not with him, I didn't think. I needed to be sure.

"Let's dance." I took an unladylike gulp of my wine for courage, then set it down and stood from the booth.

"Okay."

He seemed caught off guard but stood and took my hand quickly enough. He led me the few paces to our small dance floor.

We slid into each other's arms easily, his hands on my waist, mine laced around his neck. He wasn't quite as tall as Devraj, bringing our faces closer together. He was a seriously good-looking guy. Hot, even. And nice. Friendly. Normal, not a nut job. And yet, still, I swayed in his arms, wondering why he couldn't make me feel the way Devraj did.

My gaze skated over his shoulder to the man forefront in my thoughts. He stood beside Charlie now, back to the bar, both elbows resting behind him. He was *not* happy. But all I could do was eat up his perfect physique in dark jeans and black fitted T-shirt. Good heavens, that man was fine. And sweet and gentle. My pulse tripped faster, and not because of the man I was dancing with. This was so unfair to Christopher.

Nico's voice, normally so deep, crooned the lilting melody of KALEO's desperation in his high-pitched key when he sang the chorus. Nico's eyes were closed as he sang with heavy emotion, drawing the attention of everyone in the restaurant. The incessant chatting had lowered, and I couldn't do anything but stare at Devraj, wishing I was dancing with him.

"Isadora." My gaze snapped to Christopher. Damn, now *his* eyes were all sad. "You're a lovely woman, but I'm pretty sure your heart isn't into this." He lifted a hand and gestured between the two of us. "Am I right?"

"No, Christopher. I mean, maybe. I don't know."

"I think I do." He looked over at the bar at Devraj, who unashamedly watched us, his expression stoic, steady. Not threatening, but still, a touch too intense before he turned to something Charlie said beside him. "I think that vampire at the bar staring daggers through the back of my skull might be the reason."

"I'm so sorry," I stammered. "I didn't mean to waste your time."

"You didn't." He smiled, and I wished I could be attracted to this uncomplicated, great guy. But I knew I couldn't. "Let's finish our drinks, then I'll be on my way."

I nodded, and we ambled back to the booth and did just that. Christopher talked about trivial things, the last St. Patrick's Day parade in the French Quarter where he watched a friend drink from a woman while she downed a green beer, both of them getting wildly drunk on booze and boozy blood. I smiled and laughed where appropriate, but all I could do was hope he'd leave soon. Devraj was still there, and I couldn't focus on much while he was.

Before long, though, Christopher pulled out a twenty and set it on the table and stood. "It was such a pleasure meeting you, Isadora. I hope he deserves you."

"Not sure he wants me the way you're thinking." In the permanent way, my poor heart whimpered. But I was starting to realize I wanted him for as long as I could have him. And no amount of dating other people was going to make me want someone else.

Christopher came to my side, cupped my cheek, leaned over, and pressed a slow kiss to my lips. It was nice. Really nice. But it wasn't Devraj.

He pulled back, still holding my cheek. "Maybe that'll get him moving." He caressed my cheekbone with his thumb. "If it doesn't work out, please give me a call." Then he flashed one of those dimpled smiles and left.

Three seconds later, Devraj was standing beside me, examining my features with somber intensity. "Can we talk?"

I gestured toward the spot where Christopher sat a minute before. He stared at it, clenching his jaw.

"Somewhere else?"

"Sure."

When I stood, he laced his fingers with mine and led me out the door and up Magazine where people meandered to and from bars.

"How'd your date go?" he asked, a roughness in his voice I wasn't used to.

"Fine."

"Just fine?"

Sighing, I pulled my hand from his and faced him. "I liked him. He's a nice guy. Has a steady job here in New Orleans. He's attractive." When he winced, I continued, "So yeah, it was fine."

A laughing couple brushed past us. He took my hand and tugged me around the corner of the Cauldron into the alley. "Then why did it last barely an hour?"

"What are you getting at?"

He shoved his hands in his jeans' pockets. "I just want to know if you're really interested in him before I offer a proposition to you."

I leaned back against the brick wall behind me. "What kind of proposition?"

He eased closer. "So you're not going out with him again?"

No reason to pretend I was, I shook my head. His dark eyes flared with silver before he pressed closer, placing his hands on either side of my head, caging me in.

"I think you're looking for excitement," he said. "But you're not going to find it with those men on Zapp."

I didn't contradict his statement. No one lit me on fire like Devraj. "Excitement, yes. But I was hoping to find more than that."

He stared, silver eyes blazing, his thoughts seeming to whirl as he cataloged my features.

"I could give you more." Whether Devraj was capable of anything *more*, I couldn't pretend I was already willing to take whatever he had to offer.

"While you're here, you mean?" His brown eyes glinted with silver, but I went on before he could respond, placing a hand on his chest. "Look, I want to be totally honest. After our first night, I didn't want to do it again or let it go any further with you, because I was afraid."

"Of me?" His hand spread over mine, pressing hard. His heart drummed erratically beneath my palm.

"No, not of you. More of myself really." I gave a little laugh. "Of letting my feelings grow too strong before you had to leave."

He licked his lips, drawing my gaze to his luscious mouth. "Isadora, I feel . . ." He cleared his throat and started again. "I enjoy being with you. *Shit*, that sounds so small compared to what I'm trying to say." The raw vulnerability in his expression had me gulping hard. He was being serious. So intensely serious. "I don't want to waste any more time. I would never disrespect you or hurt you—"

"I know that," I assured him. "And I've thought about it. I can handle this, the intimacy. I'm a big girl." My smile was shaky, much like my nerves. But I couldn't deny what I wanted anymore.

His heated brown eyes intensified as he caressed my face, zoning in on my mouth.

"So what I think you're saying is, let's not waste any more time." He hovered closer, his hard chest pressing into mine. "Is that the wonderful news you're telling me right now?"

"If I said yes, what would we do first?" I asked, my voice a breathy whisper.

His mouth brushed mine as he murmured against them, "I'll lick you and fuck you till you come so hard you pass out wherever I take you."

My knees buckled. He gripped my waist.

His lips brushed, coaxed, eased my mouth wider. "Tell me yes, Isadora." He nipped again, sucking on my bottom lip before he scraped a fang along it. "Tell me you want that."

I moaned when he pressed his mouth heavier to mine, sweeping in with his tongue. The tease of his piercing as it trailed along my tongue made me see stars.

Pulling back, he pressed his forehead to mine. "Tell me you want me." There was earnest desperation in his plea.

"For how long?" I needed some sort of parameters. I couldn't just go headlong into this without having some sort of boundaries. Or end date. If I could control that, then maybe I could keep my emotions in check. Maybe.

"For as long as we've got." He skimmed his lips up my jaw to my neck, sipping at my skin, making me dizzy. "Say yes."

I clutched at his T-shirt, wondering if I could really do this and keep my heart intact. I mean, sex was sex. I'd been able to compartmentalize it in the past. But none of my past lovers had managed to invade my heart. They also weren't the kind of lover that Devraj was. Could I become his temporary lover and be fine with it when he left?

Knowing this was the biggest mistake ever, but completely unable to resist him, I murmured "yes" against his shoulder where I'd let my head fall.

He gripped my head with both hands, lifted and cradled gently, then he slanted his mouth over mine for a deep, penetrating kiss. I groaned at the intensity, especially when he pressed his hard body fully to mine. Chest to breasts, hard cock to my pelvis, thick muscular thighs to mine, his mouth devouring me with deep strokes of his pierced tongue.

Jesus, I was a pool of burning need.

By the time he pulled away, I was clinging to him to keep upright. He'd pressed one thigh between my legs to steady me, inching up the hem of my dress.

"Let's start tonight," he said, fiery eyes boring into mine.

"Okay," I agreed, suddenly shy.

Then I was tossed over his shoulder caveman style, and we disappeared from Magazine Street, reappearing on his doorstep seconds later. Only I knew vampires couldn't disappear. He'd just traced with me so fast I barely blinked before we'd moved several blocks. The sudden dizziness when he righted me had me falling back against the wall next to his back door.

"Sorry," he said, fitting his key into the lock.

"In a hurry?" I asked on a laugh.

"You have no idea."

He wasn't laughing.

Chapter 24

~DEVRAJ~

Slow down, slow down, slow down.

I had to repeat the mantra, but it wasn't working. I wanted inside her right fucking *now*. It felt like an eternity since I'd touched her. Tasted her.

As soon as we were through the door, I slammed it shut and pressed her into the wall in the foyer, swallowing her little moan when I delved in for a deep kiss, skimming my hands over her body. Her breasts, waist, hips. I slid my mouth down the slender column of her throat, loving the taste of her, the rapid fluttering of her pulse against my tongue. I slid one hand up her thigh and under her skirt, then dipped between her legs and into her panties.

"Fuck, Isadora," I growled. "So wet already."

She fisted a hand in my hair. Fucking right. My tigress was back. I fingered her slick cleft and sucked on her pulse till she was breathing good and hard. Dropping to my knees, I lifted the hem of her dress. "Hold this."

She gripped it with one hand, the other still in my hair, her breath ragged in the quiet space. Holding her gaze, I slid her panties down her legs, slipping off her sandals at the same time.

Skating my hands up till I gripped the tops of her thighs, I urged her to widen her stance. "Open up for me, love."

The growl in my throat was practically menacing, but my witch didn't flinch. No. She tightened her grip in my hair and urged me closer.

I couldn't keep the grin off my face before I leaned in and licked the sweetest pussy in the whole world.

"God, Devraj," she panted.

Her knees buckled, but I held her hard and licked her harder, flicking my piercing over her swollen nub.

"I can't . . ." Her head fell back to the wall, her pelvis rocking forward to meet my eager mouth.

She was climbing fast, thrusting faster.

"I need, I need it, Devraj."

She was panting, fisting my hair tight, her body thrumming and wanting to get there. But today I was being selfish. The beastly side of me wanted her to come on my cock alone. I needed to feel her come undone while I was buried deep inside her, and nothing else would satisfy.

When I let her thighs go, she wobbled, but I grabbed her hands and put them on my shoulders to steady her as I stood and reached for my wallet in my back pocket. Her face was flushed, splotched with pink, her mouth agape as she panted, her eyes half-lidded.

"Please don't stop," she begged, a little sluggish and slow to respond.

"Not planning on it." I had the condom in hand, then unzipped my jeans and freed my cock.

"You were prepared," she commented with a hint of sarcasm. "Someone was sure he'd get lucky."

"Hoping, Isadora."

The condom rolled on, I gripped her by the waist and lifted her, pressing my chest to hers, trapping her body between me and the wall. She wrapped her legs around my waist right before I notched my cock at her entrance. Her eyes widened as I gripped her thighs and thrust in with one deep slide.

My lips pressed to hers, still holding her gaze, I whispered, "Always hoping."

Then I moved in her slick heat, the sound and smell of sex pushing my limits of control. I almost laughed at myself. Control? I'd lost it the minute she'd said yes.

I needed to pump deeper. Harder. So I did and buried my mouth against her neck, inhaling her sweet skin as I licked and nipped every inch I could. The desire to bite her, mark her, spun my head like a top. Growling deep, I scraped my canines down the slope of her shoulder. "I want to bite you."

She cradled my head closer, but said, "Don't bite me."

"I want all of you, Isadora." I pulled back on my thrusts, moving with intense slowness. I licked the sweet beat of her pulse. "Let me take all of you."

She shook her head, rolling her pelvis, urging me to speed up. "Not yet."

Yet? I groaned at the very idea she was considering it.

"Move, damn you," she demanded, clawing her nails against my nape and scalp.

"With pleasure, love."

I fucked her fast and deep, sliding one hand between us to rub circles around her slick clit. She squeezed her thighs tighter, panting harder until she came while crying out my name. That was it for me. I drove deep while her sex pulsed around me, dragging my orgasm out of me a few pumps afterward.

I speared her one last time, crushing my mouth to hers as I came hard, kissing the fuck out of her, not near ready for this to end. Unable to hold back my thoughts, I whispered in her ear with a nip on her lobe, "Not ready to let you go yet."

She laughed, the sound making my heart clench tight in my chest. "Then don't."

Two hours later, we'd made it to the living room and no farther. Once more, we were on the white rug, which I'd had cleaned since last time, curled up with a blanket and a plate of grapes, cheese, and olives that I'd put together quickly for us. I knew she hadn't eaten with her date. I would've paused to cook something more, but last time when she was left alone with her thoughts too long she'd made a quick escape. I didn't want her to leave. Ever.

I couldn't ignore the nauseous sinking sensation I'd gotten when I saw her on a date with that guy tonight. He wasn't a buffoon or fool like the other one. He was actually potential dating material, and the very thought had made me want to scream, punch something, and weep all at the same time. If that wasn't an eye-opener, then my uncontrollable need to pound into her the second we crossed the threshold of my doorway did the trick.

Violet's strange reading made no sense. I knew what my intentions were. To make Isadora mine. So her warning that I could lose her seemed like nonsense. But Violet was a powerful Seer. Still, I had her in my arms now, didn't I? So maybe Violet was wrong.

Her fingers traced over the hand I had spread over her bare belly. I'd gotten her dress off, but her bra was still on. Though I was pleased there was nothing beneath the blanket spread over her lower body. I wanted one more time before she left me. Who was I kidding? I was conjuring ways I could convince her to move in with me while I was still in New Orleans. Or perhaps, I could stay here longer. *Should* stay longer.

The idea of settling here permanently suddenly had great appeal. Ruben was my dearest friend. The Savoie family had all but welcomed me with open arms. And Isadora.

Fuck. *Isadora.* The thought of her name, of her smile, of her tender heart and sweet soul had found permanent residence in my own thoughts on a daily basis. The idea of leaving this behind, of leaving her, widened that gaping hollow that lived deep inside me. Funny how the opposite, of imagining a life here with her at my side filled that aching loneliness I'd been carrying around with me for centuries, from place to place, country to country. Ever since I'd lost and left my first home, I'd been subconsciously seeking another. My heart squeezed at the possibility I may have just found it.

"This must be for Stygorn, right?" She fingered the silver ring on my index finger with the onyx center and strangely scripted S.

"Yes and no." My voice was rough with heady emotion as I soaked in her beauty, her lovely presence.

She smiled, tilting those gorgeous green eyes in my direction. "It's an S, Devraj."

I laughed. "Yes. But it stands for Styx, actually."

A frown pinched her pretty brow. "Why Styx?"

"That was the name of the first known Stygorn."

"Really?" She flipped sideways, propping her head on her elbow, her wild wavy hair falling across her chest. "Tell me about him."

I shifted to do the same, relishing that her gaze flicked down my naked body, certainly noticing I was half-hard already.

"You want some covers?" she asked, lifting the edge up.

I wasn't cold or embarrassed in the open, but I wanted an excuse to be closer to her, so I shuffled under the blanket with her. She blushed, her gaze dropping to my biceps, which made me want to lean forward and kiss her sweetly. But I wasn't sure how she'd react. Sure, we'd just had sex three times, but the last time she was here she'd distanced herself when the physical intimacy felt too intense. I didn't want to scare her off again.

"Not a him. A her."

"Really?" Her face brightened.

"Oh yes. Styx was a born vampire, not made, a millennium ago. Her parents, a vampire and a witch with gifts as a Seer and an Influencer, brought her to their respective Guilds, saying she demonstrated heightened gifts. At two, she could make a seasoned vampire do her will. And she could track deer in a blizzard at age five. But like most gifted vampires, supernaturals began to fear her."

"She was too powerful," said Isadora, nibbling on a grape.

I focused on her lips as she held the grape between her teeth.

"Indeed, she was. A faction of vampires sent out their best trackers when the family fled. Eventually, they tracked them down. When her mother and father were nearly killed trying to defend their child, Styx, now eight years old, beheaded every vampire with a single swing of her knife."

"Wow."

"Indeed. After that, the Guild instilled a protection law." I lifted a lock of her blonde hair, rubbing the silky strands between my fingers. "Later, after her gene was passed down, by blood or bite, the Stygorn were formally named. Our name is a loose variation of stygian, the origin of the mythical river of the underworld Styx." Pressing her lock of hair to my lips, I met her quizzical gaze. "Then they began to be trained by ancients."

"And the rest, as they say, is history." Isadora got that dreamy look, watching me sweep her lock of hair against my closed mouth. "It's hard to imagine such a brutal world that would allow that to happen to Styx and her family before our laws were put into place. Before the Stygorn became revered instead of feared."

"We're still feared," I admitted. "I'm not always as welcome as I am here with Ruben's coven. To be honest, I'm not so sure how welcome I am even here."

"Seriously?" She sat up, seemingly affronted by this fact. "Vamps give you shit for being Stygorn."

I laughed. "Some do. The ones who fear us still."

Her frown deepened. I pressed my thumb to the spot, smoothing it out by rubbing softly. "Don't worry. I'm fine."

"But I don't like the idea of people mistreating you. You can't help that you're a stronger vampire. That's ignorant prejudice. It's stupid."

"Lots of people are stupid for less reasons than that, love."

"Well, I don't like it."

Something buoyed up inside my chest, lifting me with the thought of her care for my well-being. "You learn to ignore the fools and cherish your friends."

I laced my hand with hers, palm to palm. And she let me.

"You're wise, Devraj. And more forgiving than me."

I smiled. "I've lived a long time."

She nodded. "So the S is for Styx."

"But also, the ring is a symbol of my status as a Stygorn. We're given the ring after our training is complete."

She stared at our laced fingers. "And how did you become a vampire?"

"That's kind of a sad story. I'm not sure you want to hear it."

"I do." She stared at me, sincerity written in her eyes.

I'd told this story to only a handful of people, all of whom were dear friends and confidants. Like Ruben. And never a woman I had bedded. Strange that I felt as if I were walking across a line in the proverbial sand. A place of no return by sharing this intimate part of my past that I clung to and hid from the world.

"I was young, only thirteen, and I took my mother on our annual pilgrimage to Varanasi. This was the first time since my father had died of illness the previous year. We were nearing the temple and set up camp on the outskirts of the city. I told my mother I'd find fresh water for us to wash with and drink. So I went inside the city, wandering the streets filled with people. Somehow, I found myself being lured down an empty alley and then a stone stairwell. I don't know why, but I knew I had to follow the whispering in my mind."

I paused, remembering the bone-deep fear and allure of that voice, guiding me toward my fate whether I wanted it or not.

"A Stygorn vampire."

"An ancient one," I added before going on. "He sat upon a throne deep in the earth, his hall lit only by braziers. There were other vampires, beautiful ones draped in the shadowy spaces on luxurious silks. Golden platters of food and drink sparkled, filling my senses with the opulence of this place, the majesty of this man. Gorgeous women, stunning men, all seemed to be worshipping the one on the throne. I thought I'd fallen into a dream because I couldn't resist when he held out a hand to me, covered in jewels. His eyes were pure liquid silver."

I huffed out a laugh, the memory smarting.

"I went to him so easily. So, so easily, Isadora. A poor man being summoned by a king. So I'd thought." She squeezed my hand before I went on, "I took his hand, and he said, 'One day, you will thank me.' Right before he hauled me to him and bit me hard, drinking so long I passed out. When I woke, I was still in that room, the braziers of torches lighting the room. But there was no beautiful entourage at his feet. No golden platters. Only cobwebs and the musty dank smell of decay. Just the beast himself in ragged clothes. When he saw me wake, he stood, his eyes glowing bright silver, his face flushed and healthy after feeding. The rest had been a mirage created by his glamour. There was such pain and such thirst, but all I could do was look up at the vampire. He smiled down at me and repeated, 'One day, you will thank me.' Then he walked away and left me there.

"I remember wrapping my scarf around my neck to hide the mark and stumbling my way back to my mother. I'd found a well along the way and drank furiously, trying to quench my thirst. But nothing would do it. Not until I stole a goat and drank from it when the thirst had nearly made me mad. That was when the guilt set in."

"What was wrong with him? Vampires don't behave like that anymore."

"He was an ancient who'd been in a trancelike sleep for centuries, waking to smell me near. I don't know why he pinpointed me out of a city full of people, using his power to lure me, but he had. The bite had nearly killed me, but he'd also transferred the magic and power of the Stygorn."

We paused for a few minutes, neither speaking, till she asked quietly, "Did your mother ask what happened to you?"

"Oh yes. She did. She knew something was wrong, but I'd returned. I was alive, and that was enough to pacify her. As a widow, she had a very hard life in that time. I'd already sworn to never marry while she was alive. I was her only child. I had to stay close and keep her safe. Now that I knew what monsters lived in the world, I was determined to keep them away from my mother. The only problem"—I gulped hard, staring down at Isadora—"was that I'd become one of the monsters."

"No." She squeezed my hand, hauling it closer against her breast. "Of course you weren't."

"Can you imagine the kind of guilt I felt as a Hindu to live as a vegetarian, who vowed to hurt no living creature for my body's sustenance? Then I'd sneak off into the night to steal and kill a neighbor's sheep or drink from his goats. I avoided killing when I could, but in the beginning, I couldn't stop myself. I had no one to teach me. The only option was to stop altogether and die. But I couldn't do it."

"I'm so sorry, Devraj." She loosened our hands and pushed a long lock of my hair over my shoulder, her palm settling over my tattoo there. "You can't help who and what you are. I'm so glad you did what you needed to do to survive."

I didn't know quite what to say to that other than, "Thank you."

The tension stretched into something heavy. But I couldn't spin away from the thoughts of my origins while she traced the intricate mandala covering my shoulder, biceps, and part of my back.

"Why did you get this?"

"Because it's pretty," I teased.

Her gaze shifted from the tattoo to me. She laughed. "Really?"

"That . . ." I tapped her nose, then traced my finger up one cheekbone and down her jaw, drawing the sharper edges that shaped her lovely face. "And the circle represents the universe. A deeper connection to self and the world at large." I finished tracing her lips and dropped my hand, fixating on her mouth.

"Devraj, the deep thinker? I don't know if I believe that."

I tossed my head back on a deep laugh before responding to her bright smile. "It doesn't fit your perception of me?"

"Not at all."

Then she leaned forward and pressed the sweetest, softest kiss to my lips. "I better go," she murmured, not pulling away.

"Not just yet," I begged, a nip of her bottom lip. "Stay."

"Maybe just a little longer."

I rolled her underneath me. "Just a little longer."

As I kissed her, savoring the feel of her plush lips moving against mine, the softness of her lithe body opening beneath me, I realized I would have never met her if I'd lived out my life as a human and never suffered those early days as a vampire. I couldn't help but hear the ancient one's words ringing over and over again in my head.

One day, you will thank me.

Chapter 25

~DEVRAJ~

"Saturday feels too far away." Ruben stood beneath the awning of his bookstore entrance, hands casually in his pockets. "But we're all set."

"And your grims are tuned in to the full plan?" I asked.

"They're ready. A little excited about the prospect of catching the culprits actually."

"As long as there are no glitches in their tracking software, they can be the ones to put the cuffs on for all I care."

"They might take you up on that." He grinned.

My next thought vanished when I saw a swish of sun-gold hair and long, tanned legs traipsing across Magazine, heading in the opposite direction. She was wearing another one of those light, airy dresses that barely touched her body, hiding the slight curves beneath that made my mouth water.

Ruben snapped his fingers in front of my eyes. "Hello? Anyone in there?"

"What's that?"

"I've been speaking to you, but apparently you didn't hear a word I said." He followed my gaze over his shoulder. "So you've got it pretty bad."

He honestly had no idea.

"Have a good day, Ruben." I patted him on the shoulder and walked briskly past him.

"I thought you were going to have lunch with me," he called out, laughter in his voice.

"Rain check."

Then I picked up the pace, following her down Magazine and right onto Pleasant Street.

Bloody hell, I really was a stalker, wasn't I? This was a terrible revelation. I was reduced to being the creepy guy. Unless I caught up to her like a normal friend to find out where she was going.

I might've been just a little paranoid that she was off on another date, the very thought stabbing me with a claymore-size sword of envy. No. She wouldn't do that. Not after last night, I was sure of it. Still, we hadn't discussed whether or not we were exclusive. I needed exclusivity. Quite a bit more than that if I were honest.

I jogged ahead to catch up. "Isadora!"

She paused in front of a thrift shop, the windows painted with sunflowers. When she turned, her beaming smile nearly made me trip. I was finding it more and more difficult to play it cool where she was concerned. Since when had a woman's smile made me breathless and giddy?

"Hi," I said when I'd caught up to her.

"Hi," she returned brightly. "What are you doing out here?"

"Following you."

Her brows shot up. "What?"

Grinning, I tugged on a wild lock of her hair. "I was talking with Ruben at his bookstore and saw you heading this way." Forcing indifference into my voice, I asked, "So where are you headed?"

She smiled and marched on. "I have an appointment with someone."

"An appointment? So not a date then?"

Her laughter filled my chest with an infectious joy. I couldn't help but smile even though I still wasn't quite sure if she were off to meet some guy.

"Not really," she finally said. "Though he is awfully cute. The sweetest brown eyes I've ever seen." Then she glanced at me and said in a low voice, "Well, maybe not the sweetest."

By heaven, I wanted to grab her hand and lace our fingers, feel the warmth of her delicate hand tucked in mine, brush an intimate kiss along the back of her knuckles. But that was what a boyfriend would do. Not fuck buddies. Even if I understood we were well beyond a simple sexual relationship. But did she?

"Mind if I tag along?"

"You already are, Devraj."

She hiked onto her shoulder that crazy, giant bag she carried everywhere with her. I heard something crinkle inside.

"And we're here anyway," she said, opening the door below a sign reading *Angel Paws*.

Hmm. An animal shelter.

I followed her as she waved to the lady at reception. "Hey, Trudie! I have a friend with me."

"No problem, Isadora. Tell him to take a few home with him."

Isadora laughed and kept going through a closed door where I heard the pitter-pat and yipping of lots of dogs.

"Hello there, guys," she cooed, stopping at the first empty pen. She pulled out a bag of treats, which was what was making that crinkly sound. "Oh wow. Looks like Frannie found a new home." A beagle yipped in the next pen over. She crouched and gave him a treat.

"Who's Frannie?" I asked, still standing and watching her.

"A pretty yellow lab mix that was here last week. Didn't think she'd be here long, though."

The beagle licked her fingers tenderly. That was when I sensed the soft wave of magic wafting around Isadora. I watched as she went from one pen to the next, crooning soft words, her skin luminous from expending energy to the cute little beasties. She was giving them health with her magic. Her pretty face lit up as she gave two treats to one she called Oscar.

"And there's my handsome boy," she said, obviously loving the scruffy-looking terrier mix in the last pen. "How are you this week, Archie?"

The dog did a cute spin, wagging his stub of a tail, soaking in her affection. He was obviously completely in love with her. I didn't blame him.

"So this is where you get your doggy fix, eh?" I asked, crouching down and sliding my fingers into the pen.

Archie sniffed my fingers, then wagged his tail harder, letting me scratch him behind the ears. Friendly little guy.

"I can't take them all home obviously, but I figure I can keep them in good health and spirits while they wait for their forever homes. I wish I could do more."

"Like how? Seems you're doing quite a great deal already."

She shrugged a shoulder. "I don't know. These guys spend too long in pens, waiting to be loved. It makes me sad." Her voice took on a wistful lilt, which tugged at me to make it better.

"My," I said in wonder, "what a great big heart you have, Isadora Savoie."

Her shy gaze slid to mine, our faces close. Intimately so. She blushed and looked away. The fact that she was possibly the most selfless woman I'd ever met amplified my obsession. She hid from the world, doing her good deeds without the need for notice or praise. I wanted her more with each passing minute.

Archie licked my hand, pulling my attention to him. "This guy is awfully friendly."

She smiled brighter, her face still flushed a pretty pink, then swept a hand over the scraggly reddish hair on his head. He looked like he had bushy eyebrows and a bad comb-over.

"Yeah. Archie is the sweetest. I told you so."

I gave an exaggerated sigh. "Well, if you're to two-time me with an overly attentive redhead like this guy, I suppose I'm okay with it."

She made that soft throaty chuckle I loved, glancing at me while we both showered Archie with affection, our fingers brushing together. Then she was studying me a little too closely.

"You thought I really was going on another date, didn't you?"

I tried to shrug nonchalantly, but my body tensed anyway. "Maybe."

"Devraj, as long as we're doing this thing we're doing, I won't see anyone else."

"Good." I wanted to pass out with relief.

"And I expect the same from you."

My gaze sharpened, first on her electric eyes pooled with magic and then on her pink lips. I leaned forward, unable to control myself, needing to taste her sweet mouth like I needed my next breath. I brushed my lips against hers, then slowly coaxed them apart. After a slow, melting kiss, I pulled back and cupped the sides of her neck, my thumbs brushing along the line of her jaw.

"There is no other woman I want. No other will share my bed as long as we're doing this *thing*," I teased.

"I still haven't shared your bed," she teased back with a quirk of her lips, then a bite of my bottom lip.

Growling, I gripped the back of her head and crushed my mouth to hers, angling for a deep, devouring kiss. She whimpered as I stroked over her tongue, then sucked on it before breaking apart. What I felt for her was fierce and unrelenting, demanding all of her.

"You're lucky we have so many innocent eyes on us in here. Otherwise, I'd take you against that wall."

She laughed again, but it dissolved quickly when she caught the fire in my eyes. I was sure my heady desire was written all over my face. I simply couldn't control myself when it came to this woman.

Archie barked and stood against the pen, both paws up, trying to give us puppy licks between the bars.

"Down, Archie," she said, reaching into her bag for one more treat to give him.

She stood afterward. So did I.

"Hold out your hand," she said, producing a bottle of hand sanitizer.

"Always so prepared." I rubbed in the sanitizer while she did the same.

"Thank you for coming with me," she said with a smile. We were back outside, sauntering toward our homes. "Do you want to grab some lunch?"

I glanced at my watch. "I actually have an appointment as well."

"Oh, what for?"

I spun her to face me and combed my fingers into her hair, pulled her body into mine. Before she could fully gasp, I had my mouth on her again, tasting all of her sweetness.

Well, not all. But soon enough. Right now, I just wanted to feel the rightness of her body against mine, in my arms where she belonged.

It hadn't escaped me that my thoughts were becoming exponentially proprietary where Isadora was concerned. The thought of this ending and me leaving New Orleans sent a panicky, sharp feeling into the pit of my stomach. So I kissed her hard, delving into the softness of her mouth, wanting to dive into the softness of her body.

But there was something I needed to do first. Pulling my lips away, I kept her pressed against my body, needing it for a moment longer.

"I'll see you soon," I assured her.

"Okay," she replied softly, her eyes glazed with lust.

I loved that look, but I wanted even more than that.

"Are you on the pill?" I asked.

Her eyes widened in surprise. "Um. Yes."

"Good." With another soft kiss, I stepped away. "I'll see you soon," I repeated with a smile. Then I went to take care of my next order of business.

Chapter 26

~ISADORA~

I SAT AT MY VINTAGE WRITING DESK AGAINST THE WALL, WHICH DOUBLED as a vanity with a narrow ornately-framed, oval mirror just above it. I wore my knee-length nightie, my favorite camphor-scented candle was burning, and I was writing to Mom with my blue quill pen. The night was pleasantly cool, so I'd opened the french doors that led out onto our second-floor balcony.

I kept starting and stopping because my thoughts continually strayed to the paper unfolded and sitting at the upper corner of my desk.

I hadn't seen or spoken to Devraj since yesterday when he'd left me in a hurry outside of Angel Paws. I didn't understand why he needed to know if I was on the pill since we'd been protecting with condoms. Not until that piece of paper had arrived with a personal note inside.

I set the quill pen back in the inkwell and picked up the note, rereading for the hundredth time.

Dearest Isadora,

Since I'm aware of your affinity for charts and graphs and every-thing spelled out in black and white, I'm sending you the results of my testing as of today. Though I knew already, I wanted you to have all the chartly and grapherly evidence that I'm 100 percent clean. (Yes, I made up those two words especially for you.) That being said, with you on the pill and with your assurance that you're also in the clear, I formally ask if we can dispense with the condoms from here on out while we explore this "thing."

If that's not clear enough, Isadora, know this. I want you, to be inside you, skin to skin. I want you all the time. You invade my thoughts every minute of the day. I crave you like I've never craved another woman. So yes, this is my plea, a vampire on his knees, begging you to let him come inside you with nothing between us. No boundaries.

Think on it.

Yours, Devraj

The chart that came with the note was dated yesterday after-noon, two pages long, and completely thorough with the doctor's stamp of approval on each page. As if I'd think him a liar without it. He'd also added a handwritten smiley-face on the bottom of the chart on the second page, which had made me smile like a Cheshire cat.

He'd gone to extraordinary lengths to get the testing completed so quickly. He'd hand-delivered the note to Clara to pass to me last night. Then he'd made himself scarce all day today. I'd expected a text, a call, a visit. Anything after that note that had set my thighs on fire. I was eager to give him my answer, even if the thought of condomless sex seemed so intimate. Too personal. Especially if this thing was just a temporary fling.

I mean, in theory, the sex could be better without a condom, the sensations more intense. Yet again, I squeezed my thighs together, heat pooling between my legs at the thought. I'd been like this all day, a complete mess of hormones and flaming, unrequited desire. How could he send me that note and then just leave me totally alone all day? And afternoon. And night.

It was the longest, most torturous day I could remember. Not only had I been considering his proposition, I'd been thinking of other things I wanted to do with him. I was rather shocked at how wild my sexual appetite had gotten. I'd never been shy in the bedroom, even though I'd had less than enthusiastic partners in the past. But Devraj had set something free, finding the sensual woman I'd buried beneath hours of gardening and bookkeeping and healing.

As someone who always cared for others, expending magic to heal and nurture other people, it was shocking to discover I'd been ignoring my own needs. And that Devraj was the one who could satisfy them, tend to me with unwavering care and passion. He'd delved inside and called to that carnal creature I kept tucked away. And I wanted more of him. So much more. I ached. I burned.

Prickly awareness tingled along the bare nape of my neck since my hair was tied in a messy bun. I spun halfway around on my stool to find Devraj standing in my open doorway to the balcony, leaning against the jamb, hands in his pockets and the devil in his eyes.

Wow. Did he look delicious. Faded jeans low on his hips, white T-shirt form-fitted to his muscular chest, wavy black hair around his shoulders, and lust cloaking him from head to toe. I wasn't sure if he was putting it off or if it was coming from me or both, but I was suddenly aware I was in a sheer spaghetti-strap nightie with nothing but lace panties underneath.

"You got my note?" he asked casually. Like he wasn't ready to eat me alive.

"I got it."

His gaze strayed from the note on my desk to the letter I'd been writing to Mom. Trying to write, anyway.

"What's that?"

Glancing at my desk, I lifted the thick fibrous paper I used for writing and opened my desk drawer. "Just writing a letter to my mom."

He chuckled. "You know you can text or email her, and it would be much more efficient, right?"

Ignoring his sarcasm, I said, "I prefer handwritten letters. They're more personal."

He walked slowly to the edge of my bed behind me and sat. It was strange. Usually, there was a lightness between Devraj and I. His charismatic nature causing a buoyancy that inflated the air around him. But tonight, there was a distinct heaviness between us. A density that weighted the air with serious thoughts. Serious desires.

"I should've known," he said with a hint of wonder, voice a low rumble. "You can infuse your magic into writing, can't you?"

As a witch who was weak in telekinesis and psychic abilities, the basic magic every witch wielded without even blinking, I cherished this second gift as a side effect of being a powerful Conduit.

I was still sitting sideways to him, feeling quite shy all of a sudden. I'd thought I'd gotten past this feeling with him, but the note, coupled with my near-nakedness and him being in my bedroom, my personal haven, had me speaking soft and low.

"I can," I answered.

I picked at a frayed thread on the green cushion of my stool, but I could feel his stare burning with intensity.

"I've heard of Conduits who could do this, but it's a rare gift, Isadora."

It was true. Magic infused onto paper could make spells more powerful, could render the bearer of such a spell formidable just from possessing it. I'd given all of my sisters, my parents, and my grandmother incantations of protection the Christmas after I figured out I held this power. If they recited the incantation on a regular basis, they inhaled my magic from the pages, my energy. It was a unique way of transference of magic. One I didn't advertise because I didn't want any extra attention from the witch community. I preferred to remain in the background.

"I'll bet you keep this all to yourself, don't you?" he asked, as if reading my thoughts. "Except for family."

"I don't want the attention," I defended.

"I know you don't," he said softly. "You don't want the world to see too much of you." His voice was a whispering caress, searing along my skin. "But I see you."

I glanced at him sharply. "What do you see?"

"A lovely woman who knows the meaning of humility and kindness and true beauty."

I swallowed hard, unable to look away.

He leaned forward, elbows on his knees, holding my gaze as he asked softly, "Can I hold the letter you're sending to your mother?"

With a stiff nod, I picked it up and set in his hand.

He made a soft sound in his throat, something like surprise. "Incredible."

"What?" I asked, glancing at him in the mirror. "What do you feel?"

"Magic. Your love for her." His gaze softened, holding me with reverence. With awe. "You're so amazing."

"Me?" I huffed, trying not to let his beauty steal my breath. But it was so, so hard. My God, he was gorgeous.

"Yes, you." He licked his lips. "So quiet. So unassuming. Lingering behind the bold front of your sisters when you hold such power in that pretty body of yours. That pretty mind. That pretty heart."

My pulse throbbed in my veins, adrenaline spiking at his description of me. I couldn't speak.

"Write my name," he commanded softly.

My gaze sharpened on his in the mirror. I shook my head. The thing about this type of magic was that it didn't always obey your will. It wasn't just energy that poured onto the page, but emotions. A Conduit was most closely related to Auras, the magic wanting to escape and heal with power and heart and soul. Sometimes my magic cut loose from me, spilling more than I intended.

"Please, Isadora," he begged, his brow furrowing in a pained expression. "Write my name."

I couldn't deny him, no matter how afraid I was of what he might discover. I pulled a blank piece of the thick parchment from the drawer and tore off a strip at the top. Sitting up straight and leaning closer to the desk, I lifted my quill pen from the inkwell and tapped it on the edge to release any loose drops from the nib.

After a concentrated inhale and exhale, I put the nib to paper and looped a flourishing D with an extravagant tail, my heart pounding hard, my magic pulsing harder. I didn't think of any one thing at all as I scrawled the rest of his first name with purposeful loops and curves, not daring to write the second, my hand already shaking. I set the quill pen in the inkwell and picked up the paper, blowing to dry the ink, noticing the pale glow of my skin, my magic pumping hard enough to shine.

Sweat broke out on the nape of my neck. I was afraid of what he'd pull from the parchment. He was a Stygorn after all. What could his senses read? But it was just his name. Not much to go on. I hoped.

"Here you go," I tried to say lightly, passing him the paper, then turned back to the mirror.

Pressing my hands between my bare knees to keep them still, I watched his reflection as he held the torn piece of paper. I couldn't see his eyes, his head bent as he stared down, his long hair hiding his face, but his shoulders started to rise and fall. His chest heaved deep breaths, and he was so quiet as he swept his index finger over his inked name. Almost with reverence.

With his head still down, he stood, folded the piece of paper, and slipped it into the back pocket of his jeans. Then he moved behind me, one hand sweeping lightly to my throat, his fingers curling gently, the other hand cupping the round edge of my shoulder. When he finally looked at me in the reflection, I gasped. His eyes were pure silver, vibrant and flickering eerily by the candlelight. When he spoke, I saw the distinct flash of fangs.

"Isadora. Have you thought of my request?" His voice was husky silk.

I glanced down at the note and his charts, my body singing with every touch and brush of his fingers along my collarbone. "Yes."

He slid his hands to my spaghetti straps and pulled them down off my shoulders, baring my breasts.

"What's your answer?"

I held his gaze, not looking at my naked torso. This was almost unbearably bold for me. Vulnerable. Still, I sat with my back straight, my chin high. "My answer is yes."

A scintillating wave of heat crossed his expression. Pure male and feral and predatory.

"Stand up, Isadora," he commanded softly.

When I did, he knocked the stool out of the way onto its side, his hands gliding over my hips, pushing my nightie down. It dropped to the floor. He stood inches behind me, his body heat soaking into my back and thighs. He hooked his thumbs into the sides of my black lace panties and shoved them down, letting them fall to the floor as well.

By now, I was breathing fast, but remained perfectly still, wound so tight my body thrummed with need. He dipped his mouth to the curve of my shoulder and throat, keeping his gaze on me in the mirror.

"Look at you," he whispered against my skin, licking, then placing a sucking bite hard enough to leave a mark.

I moaned, then reached back and curled my fingers into the sides of his jeans, needing something to hold on to, to sink my nails into.

"So goddamn beautiful."

Then his focus was on the line of my neck. He cupped my breast, rolling his thumb over the tight tip. His other hand slid across my stomach, the sight of his brown skin against my pale torso so stark and lovely I bit back another moan. He dipped lower, gliding his middle finger along my cleft. I tried not to be too embarrassed by how wet I was. His strangled groan told me he was pleased with the discovery as he dipped inside me. He pulled out again to slide between my folds, driving me utterly insane.

He was so masculine but gentle, fierce but careful, intense but attentive, sure and purposeful with every brush of his hands, mouth, and tongue. I was melting into a pool of lust and need and willing female.

"Devraj," I begged, body trembling.

Still, he moved with such concentrated focus, brushing his nose up my throat to my ear where he growled, "I'm going to fuck you right here, love."

I nodded, totally done with words.

"Put your hands on the wall."

I must not have moved quickly enough. He reached down and circled my wrists with his long-fingered hands, then placed my palms on either side of the oval mirror.

"Keep them there," he breathed heavily into my hair above my ear.

The distinct sound of him unbuckling his belt and unzipping his pants tore through the silence, only muffled by my labored breathing. I felt so exposed, so open, so raw, and he wasn't even inside me yet.

Anchoring me with one hand wrapped on my hip, he slid his cock through my wet folds, teasing twice before thrusting in deep.

"Ah." I pushed against the wall, bowing my spine to take more of him in.

His responsive groan had my sex quickening already, seeking that pleasurable high only he could give me. I watched him in the mirror as he stared down where our bodies joined before his eyes slid closed with pained intensity. The sensation of him filling me up with nothing between us was almost too much, setting my entire body on fire.

"Oh God," I whimpered, loving the way he felt as he pumped so hard, so deep.

He caught my gaze again, then hauled me up against him, one arm wrapped across my chest, mounding my breast on the opposite side. His other hand dipped between my legs, circling my swollen clit, his dark hair mingling with my blonde as he nipped my neck. I covered his hand over my breast, a need to have him deeper, closer, an undeniable desire gripping me with a wild force.

"Bite me," I demanded.

He froze, stopped pumping, his vampire eyes catching mine in the reflection. "What did you say?"

"You heard me, Devraj."

He started to shake his head, wanting to deny me. Deny us. I wasn't having it. My body wanted all of him. I reached back with the hand not covering his possessive hold on my breast and fisted it in his hair, pulling him closer.

Tilting my head to the side, offering my throat, I ordered more gruffly, "Bite me. I want you to." I caught his preternatural gaze in the mirror. "I want you."

There was a split second of hesitation where I watched his control snap like a taut leash. His eyes flashed bright, pure silver. On an agonized groan, he opened his mouth, fangs flashing as he sank into me with sharp teeth, pumping deeper inside me with his cock. I gave a little whimpered cry as the pain in my neck immediately morphed into unparalleled pleasure.

I slurred his name as he bent me forward more, his mouth sucking my throat, his hands clenching my hips as he drove inside me deeper and deeper. I wasn't paralyzed, but I sort of was. I could no longer move. His toxin filled me with such ecstasy, his body even more. His feral grunts and groans marked me with the pleasure he felt, but all I could do was lean into his embrace, my hand in his hair holding him to my neck. Then I arched my spine so he could go deeper inside me. He took what I offered, gripping my hips as he pumped with sensual thrusts, moaning against my throat.

When my orgasm came, it threw me so high my body locked as I choked out a cry and held him hard, feeling him pulse inside me on an aching moan. I didn't know I could faint from coming so hard, but I did.

ꙮ

I woke under my covers, naked. Devraj lay atop my bedspread, propped up on one elbow, combing my hair across my pillow, his brow furrowed with concern. His eyes were no longer silver, but they were still fully dilated, his adrenaline running high.

"Wow," I whispered, smiling.

He clenched his jaw. "Are you okay?"

I laughed. "I passed out from pleasure, Devraj. I'm pretty okay."

"I was afraid." He stopped and licked his lips. "I was afraid I hurt you."

"How?"

He shrugged a shoulder. "I don't know. It's just never been like that for me."

I remembered that he'd told me he'd never bitten a woman while having sex. Actually, it was fully on my mind when I'd begged him to bite me. He'd said he'd only do that with someone dear to him.

"Do you regret it?" I asked softly.

"Not for one second." He stared intently, fingers still working my hair. "It's just never tasted that good. Been that good. Ever."

Exhaling deeply with the heavy emotion swelling in my chest, I whispered, "Same for me." I slid a hand along his jaw, his scruff tickling my palm.

His mouth tilted into a half-smile. "Maybe we're blood-mates."

"What?"

"The legends about vampires finding a pleasure mate in sex and blood-letting."

I shook my head. "I don't keep up with vampire legends."

He grinned wider, leaning down to sweep an airy kiss over my lips. He whispered, "Allegedly, there is only one for every vampire. One who sets his blood and soul on fire when he drinks from her. When he comes inside her. As some have told it, the experience chains her to him as well."

I closed my eyes and received his kisses indolently, still spent from before. He teased me with his mouth. And his words?

"So basically, they're soul mates."

"Mmm." Another lazy kiss, nibble of my bottom lip. "For a vampire, the blood is tied to the soul." A slow trace with his tongue, his piercing flicking my bottom lip lightly. "So I suppose so." Then he lifted up, mahogany eyes capturing mine. "Would it be so bad?"

If we were tied to each other by blood and pleasure? Yes. It would be terrible. Because Devraj would be leaving soon, rejoining his glittering world where he was a movie star and much-sought-after Stygorn. His expertise was in high demand as Jules had told me, so there was no doubt he'd leave New Orleans. Leave me behind. Because life outside of my gardens, my shop, and my life with my sisters didn't work for me. I'd never leave. Never. Not even for a legendary blood-mate.

The sharp tang of fear merged with a swelling of hope. I swallowed against the sudden lump that had formed in my throat, then I looked away, focusing on the sharp angle of his jaw, the masculine lines of his neck.

What the hell was I going to do with myself now? I was already hurting from the loss of him, and he was still here.

"I'm really tired, Devraj."

I could feel his gaze pouring over my face, but I couldn't look at him. I didn't want him to see what I truly felt. He was too astute at reading people. After an awkward, tension-filled moment, he brushed a hand from my crown and down to cup my cheek. Leaning forward, he pressed a tender kiss to my lips.

"Good night, Isadora."

"Good night."

He swept off the bed in vampire speed, standing in the open doorway of my balcony. "Lock these doors when I leave."

I nodded. Scooting to stand, I realized I was naked. I wrapped a throw at the end of the bed around me and met him at the open doorway, reaching to close the doors. I jumped when I felt his knuckles sweep down my jaw again.

"Look at me, Isadora."

Bracing myself, I did, trying not to let my depth of emotion show there. He gave me one of those sweet smiles, the one that felt like it was just for me. One that told me maybe, just maybe, he was feeling the same way.

How could a man like Devraj fit into my world? We were just too vastly different. I'd never want to be with a man who lived in the spotlight. And there's no way he'd ever want to be with a woman whose highlight of the week was visiting an animal shelter. Would he?

"I'll see you tomorrow?" he asked sweetly.

"Tomorrow," I said, forcing a smile.

With one more lingering glance, he disappeared over my balcony. I shut and locked the doors, then crawled into bed. I traced my fingers over the puncture wound in my neck, unable to deny the sigh of pleasure and sad smile it brought me.

Devraj had marked me well, and it would be hard to hide our relationship now. I wanted to laugh and cry at the same time. I'd known I'd fall hard if I took that step back into his arms, so I had only myself to blame. Still, it didn't make this any easier. I knew without any doubt that when he left, it would crush me. Break me. I closed my eyes, feeling a tear slide down my cheek, knowing no other man would ever compare to my beautiful vampire.

Chapter 27

~DEVRAJ~

I WAITED FOR ISADORA. VERY IMPATIENTLY. PACING IN THE LIVING room, I checked the clock on the wall again. I'd texted her first thing this morning, and she said she'd try to come by. When I'd texted back in all caps I NEED YOU TO COME OVER, she'd simply sent back a smiley face.

She probably thought I wanted to fuck her into the stratosphere again, which I did, but that wasn't why I wanted her to come over.

I glanced down at my new roommate who'd been keeping pace with me in the living room, his brown eyes partially obscured by the scruffy tuft of red hair on his head.

"Not sure she's coming, buddy."

He yipped. Then I heard a knock at the back door.

Tracing in a split second, I swung the door open, my heart tripping at the sight of her as it always did. Today, she wore well-worn jeans and a loose T-shirt with a thin yellow cardigan. I rarely saw her in jeans, and I had a split-second thought that she was denying me the easy access of her little dresses and nightgowns, but that would be ridiculous, right? We had the most intense sexual experience of our lives together last night. I knew she'd felt it as much as I did. She'd come so hard she fucking fainted.

And I'd fallen so hard, I knew she had to be mine. For as long as my heart was beating.

Her magic in my name. When I got home, I pulled the paper out and traced her handwriting with my fingers before pressing it to my lips. Isadora cared so deeply for me, and I knew it from the powerful punch of magic that pulsed from my six-letter name. It screamed from the scrap of parchment—deep, possessive feelings of longing and want. And more. But I couldn't think about it too much because it made my chest ache.

She was conflicted; there was no doubt. She wanted me, but she didn't. So I was going to do everything in my power to pull her over to my way of thinking. Because I had forever on my mind.

She gave me a tight smile, then her gaze fell to the little guy at my feet who greeted her with a tilted head and wagging stubby tail like he'd lived here all his life, not less than twenty-four hours.

"Archie!" she squealed and fell to her knees right inside my doorstep.

He barked and twirled enthusiastically in a circle before planting both paws on her lap as she showered him with love. Yet again, my heart ached as I crouched beside her, soaking in the pure joy on her sweet face.

"How—?" she started, then laughed when Archie licked her hands, then darted to her handbag, nudging to get inside. "How is he here?" She looked at me with disbelief, still petting him.

"Believe it or not, Miss Savoie, I'm an upstanding citizen, and some people deem me responsible enough to adopt a dog."

"I just . . . I can't believe he's here." She scooped him into her arms and hugged him tight, then looked at me curiously. "I didn't know you even liked dogs."

I shrugged. "There's a lot you don't know about me."

While petting Archie, her focus on him, she added, "But who will take care of him when you're off doing Stygorn business? Or Bollywood business?"

Hmm. Lots of tells there, sweet Isadora.

I crouched down next to her and scratched him behind the ear. "I'm sure I can find someone to puppysit for me."

"So everywhere you move, you'll have to find someone new to watch him? That seems difficult to manage for someone like you."

"What do you mean, someone like me?" I watched her face while she avoided mine.

"You're just very, you know, busy. Moving a lot can also cause animals stress. Did you know that twenty to forty percent of dogs suffer from separation anxiety? I mean, Archie will get attached to you, then you'll go off on business or pleasure or whatever, and I just wouldn't want him to be lonely. At least at Angel Paws, he had his canine friends and my weekly visits."

Bloody hell. She was working her way up into her own fit of anxiety.

"Well, there's an easy fix for that. You'll just have to come over for frequent visits, won't you?"

She finally glanced up at me. I was on my knees, sitting on my heels, hands fixed on my thighs so I wouldn't grab hold and kiss the hell out of her to stop her insane cycle of what-ifs.

She let out a sad little laugh, sounding similar to how she did last night before I left her. "Sure. I could do that. Until you move off to Bolivia or Nepal or something."

"Why would I move to Nepal?"

"I'm sure there are bad vampires to chase in places like Nepal."

Her predictions of specific faraway destinations almost made me smile. Except she actually believed I was about to ship off thousands of miles away to remote, exotic locales.

"I suppose I'll just have to stay here in New Orleans then."

Her eyes rounded. "Why would you do that?"

"Can't you guess?"

Her pulse quickened, thumping faster as she held my gaze, a frown forming as her mouth hung open in confusion. How could she possibly be confused by that? Didn't she know I was crazy about her? I wasn't ready for this to end anytime soon. I just needed her to take a chance on us.

"Devraj, we don't fit . . . long term."

Acid burned in my stomach. But that had nothing on what her words had done to my heart, slicing it with soft little syllables.

"Why not?"

"Seriously?" She raised her brow, looking at me like I was a child. She petted Archie, who was now curled quietly in her lap, absent-mindedly, her gaze sweeping the living room beyond the foyer. "You drive million-dollar cars and collect ancient relics and marble statues and hang around with movie stars. Hell, you *are* a movie star. While I like to plant pansies and make herb bundles and visit dogs in shelters. I mean"—she scoffed in disbelief— "come on."

"So you're saying I'm too shallow and materialistic?" Though my words might've been biting, I kept my voice soft and calm while a storm raged inside.

"No!" Her frown deepened. "That's not what I'm saying. We just don't match, don't you see?"

"I think we've been matching rather well."

"That's just sex, Devraj."

"Really? Is it?"

Again, her face flushed with confusion and a deep blush. "It's good."

"It's better than good," I said with conviction.

She nodded. "I'll admit that. But you'll get bored eventually. This is exciting because it's new, but over time, you'll see we don't mesh beyond the bedroom."

She was literally tearing me apart. I could feel something crushing and crumbling inside of me. That's when I realized she honestly didn't know me as well as I knew her. Yes, I'd told her about my past, but I didn't tell her about my present. That the reason I dragged these ancient relics around the world with me was because I longed for a home, longed for a place that always made me feel welcome and not so very alone. Like I'd been feeling since the night I'd met her.

My career as a Bollywood actor had been over for several years now, but she didn't know that either. I hadn't bothered to tell her because I was too busy spinning my web of charm as I liked to do with a woman I pursued. I needed her to know that this *thing*, as she'd called it, was far more than a brief sexual arrangement.

Get bored with her? She was out of her fucking mind. Didn't mesh beyond the bedroom? Then she hadn't been paying attention last night. Or every other moment we'd gotten lost in each other. But she wasn't ready to hear my protests. She didn't believe I could stay. That I would stay. That was the real obstacle here. Not the truth. But her perception of the truth. And sometimes, that's all that mattered.

Time to lighten things up and move away from this. I was a patient man. I would prove her wrong. Actions speak louder than words, after all. "But we actually haven't even made it to the bedroom." I arched a brow at her and grinned.

She smiled back. "True. But whose fault is that?"

"Entirely yours. You're just too irresistible for me. Beguiling me with your witchy ways."

She laughed. "Right. That's me. The seductress."

"You have no idea." I reached over and took her hand, standing and tugging her with me.

Archie hopped down and promptly trotted toward the kitchen with a clickety-clack of his toenails on the wood floor. Probably going to eat from his bowl that I'd had to refill at least twelve times since he'd moved in.

"Come on, love. Let's get out of the house. I want to take you somewhere."

She looked toward the kitchen. "Do you need to kennel Archie? Is he house-trained?"

"Come here." I pulled her into the kitchen and pointed to the back door that now had a newly installed doggy door leading to the gated courtyard that also had a moderately large square of grass. "He can take care of business on his own."

"Well, you've been busy." She aimed a bright smile my way, steamrolling over my will to keep her at arm's length.

I pulled her in for a kiss, which started sweet and turned serious in three seconds. I slipped my hand beneath her fall of hair and squeezed her nape, then skated my mouth down her neck to lick and kiss the mark on her neck she'd tried to cover with her hair. She moaned, clenching a hand in my T-shirt, arching her spine and bending her body toward me.

"Like I said," I told her lightly, pulling her through the door toward the garage, "I'm much more responsible than you think I am."

"I never said you weren't responsible."

"Just shallow and materialistic," I teased.

"I didn't say that either! Jeesh, I had no idea how sensitive you were. Wait, where are we going?"

I now had the door open to my Lamborghini. "We're going somewhere in my million-dollar car."

"I don't like cars."

"I'm well aware. Did you know that the Diablo has a forty-three–fifty-seven percent front/rear weight distribution, making it aerodynamically safe on the road? It also has Brembo servo-assisted four-wheel disc brakes, adding to its safety as well. I can stop on a dime."

"What's Brembo brakes?"

I chewed the inside of my cheek to keep from laughing. "Brembo is an Italian manufacturer of automotive brakes, specifically for high-performance cars. Best of the best, love."

"Are you throwing stats at me to try to impress me?"

Fucking right, I was. "Am I impressing you?" I held the door open for her.

"Kinda."

"Please get in so I can take us very safely and responsibly to our destination."

She eyed me and then my car, as if it truly was a demon, sighed heavily, then flounced inside, putting her bag on the floor.

I closed the door and whispered, "Gotcha."

Time to show her that even she could break out of the safe and somewhat stifling box she'd built for herself.

Chapter 28

~ISADORA~

"So what were you and Ruben talking about the other day outside the bookstore?" I asked, just needing some random topic of conversation.

He turned into a mostly empty parking lot near Loyola. "Just making sure we've got everything set for Saturday night. Is your sister Livvy willing to be your partner in crime?" He downshifted, the car purring as we slowed.

"More than willing. Livvy is always up for adventure."

He wheeled to the back of the lot where there were only two or three cars parked.

"What's wrong? You seem tense."

Devraj shook his head, unbuckling his seat belt. "Just the reading Violet did. I want to be ready for anything."

"I'm sure your Vampire Justice League can handle anything unexpected."

"Oh, we can. Vampire Justice League? Is that an Avengers thing or something?"

I laughed, thinking of Evie. She'd like the label. "I don't think so, but it should be. I don't know what you call your little party of vampire cops."

He eyed me like I was crazy, then said, "Get out of the car, Isadora."

I unbuckled and met him around front. I glanced around, wondering where he was taking me. This was just an empty parking lot for students near the university. He took my hand and led me around to the driver's side.

"What are you doing?"

He opened the car door. "Teaching you how to drive." He gave a little shove to the small of my back.

"What?" I backed up into a hard wall of Devraj. "No, no, no, no."

He laughed, spinning me by my waist and pressing my back to the side of the car. He cupped my face, pinning me with his pelvis and his gorgeous eyes.

"Do you trust me, Isadora?"

I gripped his wrists. "Not if you're trying to teach me to drive, I don't."

He kicked the inside of one ankle, spreading my legs, and settled against me, possessing my mouth with dizzying speed. I pressed my blunt nails into his wrists in defiance of this crazy-ass idea. Still, I kissed him back, my appetite for him as voracious as ever. When our kiss mounted to that frenzied state, his tongue piercing making me want his tongue in other places, he pulled away and pressed his forehead to mine, still holding my face, his gaze so warm, so steady, so sure.

"You trust me with your body." He pressed his closer to mine, rubbing against me, as if I needed a reminder. "And with your blood." His gaze flicked down to my neck. "Now trust me with your fear. I can help you with this."

"You think me wrecking your million-dollar car is going to help me get over a lifelong phobia? You're nuts, vampire."

He nipped my bottom lip with a fang, not breaking the skin, but stinging all the same. "Isadora." He licked the sting, rocking his hard body into mine, dragging a whimper from my throat. "Trust me."

I was breathing heavily, panic running amok. "I can't do this."

"You can."

"I might wreck your car."

"It's insured."

"I'm scared."

"I'm here for you."

I half-laughed, half-whined at that. "You're *insane*."

"I want you to trust me. I'd never let any harm come to you. You'll be safe."

His crooning words vibrated straight through my rib cage and encircled my heart. I *did* trust him. I *did* feel safe with him. I knew he'd never let harm come to me. All of these things sung in my soul like magic, pulsing with his sweet promises. As sweet as the ones he'd made with his body, his hands, his mouth, his tongue.

Why did this feel so monumental? Trusting him enough to teach me to drive? It was a trivial, minor thing. To most people. To me, it was an irrational fear that had morphed into my way of life, settling me into a world where I avoided cars and preferred to shop as far as my bicycle would take me. And he was asking me to just, what, jump off the cliff with him and drive his freaking Lamborghini?

"Trust me," he cooed against my lips, sipping softly now, tracing my jawline with his thumbs in soothing sweeps. "You can do this, Isadora."

My heart tried to pound through its cage of flesh and bones. I squeezed my eyes shut and said, "I can do this," just trying the words on for size. My pulse immediately slowed.

"You can do this," he repeated with supreme confidence. And affection.

I opened my eyes and inhaled a deep breath. "Okay. I'll try."

The smile he gave me was galactic in its brilliance. "Good girl."

One more soft kiss, then he ushered me into the driver's seat. I sat there stiffly, trapping my hands between my thighs, staring at the insanely complex console. When he lowered into the passenger's seat, he reached over and buckled my seat belt. Probably because I hadn't moved yet, stiff as a robot.

"All right, first step," he said, obvious amusement in his voice, "put your hands on the steering wheel."

I whipped my head toward him and warned, "No. Laughing."

His expression sobered with wide eyes. "Never."

But there was still a twinkle in his eye. I arched a brow at him before returning my focus on the car, gently placing my hands on the wheel. "I'm not driving outside this parking lot."

"Absolutely not. Baby steps. Today, we're practicing right here, nowhere else."

Blowing out a heavy breath, I nodded. "Okay. Now what?"

"Press your left foot down on the clutch, your right on the brake."

I did. "Okay."

"Now, start the engine. And put your hand on the stick."

I arched a brow at him. "Is that code for something?"

"My, oh my, Miss Savoie. What a dirty mind you have. Get your head out of the gutter and focus. And wrap your hand around my stick."

He taunted me with a hot look and a waggle of his eyebrows. I couldn't keep myself from laughing. And just like that, some of the tension eased from my shoulders.

"We should be starting with an automatic," I said, grabbing hold of the gearshift.

"Where's the fun in that?" He leaned an arm along my headrest but kept some distance so I didn't feel crowded. Just close enough to feel comforted. "So, because this is a rather luxurious, high-performance car and expensive, as you've reminded me on a number of occasions, it has a very smooth transition from gear to gear. All you need to do is ease up slowly on the clutch as you press the gas pedal at the same time. Go as slow as you need and take your time."

I faced forward and did as he said, eased up with the clutch and pressed down on the gas pedal. When I felt the car moving, I pressed too hard and the car jerked, then stalled out.

"Oh, hell!" I had the clutch and the brake down to the floor. "I can't do this."

"Yes, you can."

"Stop laughing at me, Devraj!"

"I'm not laughing."

He was so laughing. *Hard.*

"Okay, okay. Let's do this first. Take your feet off the pedals."

"Are you crazy?" I shrieked.

"The car is off, so we're in no danger. Take your feet off."

"All right."

"And close your eyes."

I snapped my head to him. "What are you planning?"

"Nothing nefarious," he crooned, edging closer, one hand on my thigh. "I want you to relax."

"Your glamour doesn't work on me. I've told you that."

"Just a little guided imagery to help you relax."

I pressed the back of my head to the headrest with a huff of frustration. "It won't work."

"Let me be the judge of that." He tugged a lock of my hair. "Close your eyes, love."

"This isn't going to work." I closed my eyes anyway.

"So little faith." His hand on my thigh tightened, but didn't move up, thank goodness, because then my mind would've been somewhere else for sure. Already, his proximity and body heat and electric energy filled up the space with a heady concoction of sexy vampire.

"Imagine you're walking through the courtyard to your green-house." His voice was close to my ear, rumbling low and deep with a hypnotic tempo. "But instead of the door you normally see leading into the greenhouse, there is a door made entirely of golden light. When you open the door, you step through into a wilderness made of vibrant color. A field of purple wildflowers wave in a summer wind to your right, a brook with crystal-blue water rushes into the woods to your left. The trees on the leaves rustle as you walk barefoot on the plush grass."

He went on, detailing the beauty of a fairy forest where magic lived and thrived. My body eased at the cadence of his sensual voice.

Finally, he pressed a soft kiss to my cheek. "Now open your eyes, beautiful."

I did, heart skipping at his endearment.

"How do you feel now?" he asked.

"Good." What an understatement.

Damn, this man. If someone had told me I'd let a guy teach me to drive after he'd once hit me with his car, I'd have told them they'd lost their damn mind. My sisters had begged to teach me in the past to my constant, resounding *no*. But here I was with little more than a nudge from him, slipping into a relaxed state with only a few words. I could barely believe it.

But Devraj. He was the unbelievable. The man I never expected but wanted more than anything. More than anyone.

"Good." He squeezed my thigh, then eased away from me back into his seat, giving me space. "Now, let's try it again."

I did, only to stall the car again. But this time, I laughed rather than got nervous. I'd actually made it more than two feet.

"Again," he said calmly, his gentle demeanor seeping into me.

By my fourth try, I actually managed to shift into second gear.

"I'm doing it. I'm driving!"

He laughed. "You are. Now, as you come to the corner of this row, just ease down on the brake, no need to downshift here, then speed up a little, that's it. Now in this straightaway, let's go for third."

"You sure? That's so fast." I cut him a sharp look. "No laughing, Devraj!"

But he couldn't help himself. "You're right. It's *so* fast. Let's see what you can do."

I cut the corner a little sharp, but not on purpose, pulling Devraj over to my side. He just laughed again, but I managed to right us and gently speed up, shifting into third gear as he'd instructed.

"I can't believe I'm doing it!" I couldn't take my eyes off the road. Well, the parking lot. But the crazy feelings of elation pumping through my veins had me giddy and grinning like a loon. "I can't believe this."

Someone pulled into the parking lot a hundred yards away, so I screeched to a halt, jerking us both forward, the seat belts locking and pulling us back.

"I got it," I told him, pressing the clutch and brake to the floor and restarting the car before easing in the opposite direction of the other car.

"Yeah, you got it. I knew you would."

That's when I finally chanced a glance at him, and my insides melted at the blazing look of pride and adoration on his handsome face.

After my third lap around the parking lot, I was so high, feeling beyond confident at this. Chuckling at myself, my fear. I mean, yeah, we hadn't left the parking lot and the thought of cruising on an actual road made me want to vomit, but I was *really* driving a car. I did a fourth lap, then pulled into a parking spot at the end of the lot. I put it into park and turned it off before leaping over the console to straddle Devraj's lap.

My skyrocketing excitement didn't seem to faze him. He grabbed my hip with one hand and cupped my nape with the other, diving into my mouth with a soft groan. I rocked my hips on his quickly hardening erection, the denim between us giving the perfect friction between my legs.

"Devraj," I nearly cried, dipping my mouth to his neck and giving him a suckling kiss below his ear.

He hissed in a breath, thrusting his hips up and grabbing hold of my hair, but not pulling me away.

"I can't believe I did that," I said, still licking and sucking his neck, the salty taste of him driving me mad.

"I can." He nuzzled into my hair and nipped my earlobe. "You're incredible." His hand on my hip slipped under my T-shirt and mounded my breast over my bra, pinching my nipple lightly. "Amazing."

"It was just the parking lot." I scooped both my hands under his shirt, lifting so I could see his gorgeous chest while my hands roved frantically.

"You overcame a lifelong fear in minutes, Isadora. You're stronger than you give yourself credit for." His eyes glowed silver, his voice deep and growly. Then his gaze dropped where he unsnapped my jeans and unzipped me. "Why did you wear jeans today?" He slid his hand beneath my panties, skating his middle finger through my wetness.

My eyes slipped closed when he glided to my entrance and pumped a finger inside me. I'd worn jeans because I'd planned on not having sex with him today. I needed a break after last night's earthshaking experience where I'd felt him capture my heart at the same time he'd conquered my body.

He gripped my chin and whispered, "Open your eyes."

I did, but I wanted to look away again.

"You never wear jeans." He slid out of me, circling my clit with my own slickness.

I didn't say anything, mouth falling open on a sigh. It was true.

"You wanted some space from me after last night?"

I bit my lip as he pumped two fingers inside me, nice and slow. I should've known this Stygorn would've seen through my sad attempt at creating boundaries. All it did was make it more difficult to get him inside me, and I was regretting my ridiculous outfit choices with every pump of his long fingers.

"No space between us, love." His voice was soft, melodic, but his expression was fierce. Determined. Dominant. "Do you understand?"

I nodded, riding his hand with little pumps, gripping his shoulders tight.

"Now, get your fucking jeans off so I can come inside you."

I shifted off him onto the other seat. I'd barely wiggled them over my bum before he'd grabbed hold of my panties and jeans together and ripped them off my legs. He had his jeans unzipped and pulled down below his hips, his cock out, before I'd made a move to straddle him.

He gripped my waist to pull me across but I shoved away his hands. From the moment we met, he'd been a giver. From baking, to his kindness, to teaching me to drive, to his lovemaking, he was constantly giving. Always giving. I wanted to give something to him.

Maneuvering till I leaned over the console, I wrapped my hand around his cock.

"Isadora," he growled, thrusting up into my hand.

I ignored his warning, stroking once before I slid my mouth over the head and down his shaft till it bumped the back of my throat. He hissed in a breath.

"Fuck, fuck, fuck." His hand cradled my skull, pressing gently as I bobbed and sucked him deep.

I moaned at the pleasure of giving to this man, slowing my tempo so I could take him deeper each time.

"Christ, you're going to kill me."

When I came back up and sucked the tip hard before letting it pop free, he made a feral sound deep in his chest.

"I can't take it."

He moved me up, grabbed me around the waist, and hauled me onto his lap. I went easily, straddling his lap. He gripped my hip with one hand, his cock with the other, then pushed me down as he thrust up.

We both groaned in unison at the drugging sensation of his hardness plunging inside me. He reclined the seat to give us room.

"Ride me," he ordered, his hands on my bare hips, moving me up and down.

I skated my hands back underneath his shirt, hiking it up so I could watch his abdomen tighten with each thrust inside me. The man's body was a marvel, but the man himself—his warm eyes, his deep compassion, his lethal power—was breathtaking. Bone-melting. Soul-stirring. Heart-stealing.

He captured my gaze and held me with him as he rocked up, our bodies riding a frantic rhythm, both of us climbing faster and faster. I came with such lightning speed it shocked me. I cried out. Devraj wrapped my nape and pulled me down, devouring my moans as he ground into me with punishing thrusts. After he came on a deep groan, he sucked on my tongue before he let my mouth go, but kept me close.

"Don't tell me we don't match," he ground out against my lips, squeezing my nape. "Don't tell me this is just sex."

I almost laughed because his cock was still throbbing inside me. But he was right. Whatever this was—this connection, this craving, this obsession—it went beyond the physical. I knew that, which was why I was trying to build a little distance. But Devraj would have none of it. He wanted all of me for the time we were together. And I honestly couldn't deny him. Not anymore.

My heart pounded hard against his chest where I could feel his own. I pressed a palm there, willing to surrender all to him. He was more than sex. But I still couldn't say it aloud. Somehow, I knew that would make it that much harder when this assignment was over and he was off to the next.

His gaze softened. "Come here." He tucked my head in the crook of his shoulder and brushed a hand over my hair, his other arm anchored around my waist, our bodies still joined.

Anyone could've walked up and seen us, especially my bare ass on full display. It was only late afternoon. But I didn't care. His strong arms and gentle hands, his mouth pressing into my temple was the comfort I needed. I decided I'd enjoy today and worry about the pain of tomorrow when tomorrow came.

After he soothed me for what felt like a half an hour but probably wasn't quite so long, he whispered, "You really know how to use my stick."

I laughed against his chest. "So do you."

His dick jerked inside me, and I gasped, sitting up with my elbows on his chest. I could feel him growing harder by the second.

"Again?" I arched a brow at him.

His hands slid to my bare cheeks, grabbing hold and slowly rolling me forward. "Definitely again." He kissed me hard. "And again." He nipped down my jaw to my ear. "I'm never letting you go."

And for one blissful moment, I believed him.

Chapter 29

~DEVRAJ~

By the time we got our clothes back on, Isadora had slipped back into her distant, quiet mode. And I didn't like it.

Too frustrated to talk about it now, I opened the door so I could walk around to the driver's side. A sound hit me like a punch to the chest.

"What is it?" she asked.

I'd frozen in place with her door open, listening to the familiar bong of the church bells from Emma's memories.

"Devraj?"

Pulling out my phone, I called Ruben, my blood racing like mad, pushing me to hunt. He answered on the first ring as I rushed around to the driver's seat.

"Track my phone and get here now. Bring three men."

"On my way." Then he clicked off.

I revved the engine and took off, rolling the windows down.

"What the hell is going on?" Isadora asked, belting herself in.

"Those church bells. They're close to where the other women are being held."

"How do you know that?"

She stared a moment but then went silent, realizing I needed to listen. I charged out of the lot and wound my way toward the chiming bells down St. Charles Avenue. I veered to a sudden stop in front of a small Catholic church just as the bells died.

"Are you sure those are the same bells?"

"Positive." My sense of hearing was so acute I recognized the twangy ring of the third bell in each chime, exactly as it was in Emma's memory. "He's holding them within hearing of this church. Northwest of here, I believe."

We both hopped out and stood on the sidewalk in front of the church, peering one way and then the other. I closed my eyes and inhaled deeply, catching a very faint, familiar scent. Jennifer. The young woman who'd been captive the longest.

My instinct was to bolt, but I couldn't leave Isadora alone. Not this close to the kidnapper's lair. When I looked at her, she seemed to read my mind.

"Give me your keys. I'll lock myself inside. This isn't exactly a dangerous part of town."

"I'm not worried about you being accosted by college kids, and you know it."

She held out her hand. "Give me your keys. I'll be fine."

Just as I did, Ruben appeared, a wake of wind nearly knocking me over, whooshing Isadora's hair. Then Gabriel and two of his other men, Roland and Sal, appeared.

"Perfect timing. I need one of you to stay with her."

"I'm fine," snapped Isadora, opening the car to slip inside.

I glared at Ruben. "Leave one of them with her. We're too close to this asshole's nest to leave her alone."

I was probably being unreasonable because this crew's MO wasn't to nab a girl off the street. But I wasn't taking any chances.

"Roland. Stay with Isadora."

Roland was big and badass with a shaved head, the most intimidating on first glance of Ruben's men. I breathed a sigh of relief, then traced at minimum speed down a side street, the scent coming from that direction. I stopped, Ruben, Sal, and Gabriel with me.

All vampires had extraordinary senses, but they didn't hold memory scent like Stygorn did. I'd memorized all of the women's scents the day after I arrived in New Orleans, so they'd need to rely on me to take the lead until we were very close.

They watched and waited in silence while I sought their scent. Once I found it, I traced again, slow enough they could follow, trailing Jennifer's faint smell on the wind. Her scent grew stronger again until we all stopped in front of a tall, non-descript building.

"Looks like a dorm," said Gabriel, peering in a window. "An abandoned one."

An orange Renovation in Progress sign was pasted on the double doors. Looked like renovation got put on the back burner due to lack of funding or some other bureaucratic issue.

Ruben and I shared a glance before I nodded. "This is it."

Gabriel wrenched the locked door open with a metallic crack, then we stood in a lobby/lounge area, musty and moldy from disuse. There were doors on the right and the left marked as the stairs leading to the upper floors.

"Ruben and I will take the right, you both take the left."

Sal and Gabriel nodded and took off, then so did Ruben and I, tracing down the hall of the first floor, then up to the second and repeating the process. Still, I could smell her presence close. So close. By the time we reached the landing to the fourth floor, I halted in my tracks.

Ruben stopped and marched back to me. "What do you—?" Then he glanced up the stairs, his nostrils flaring. The scent of humans in the building was detectable to him as well now. "Fifth floor."

We moved as one, tearing up to the fifth floor and tracing directly to an open room. An empty room. No lights or signs of life anywhere. We didn't need light to see anyway.

"Here." Ruben crouched on the floor and lifted a blanket, bringing it to his nose.

I met him and did the same. "That's her. Jennifer."

A drop of dark blood stained the edge of the blanket. Ruben reached over to the bed and lifted a leather cuff chained to the bed. "For fuck's sake."

He'd kept them chained. Fury lashed through my chest at the fear this asshole had instilled in these girls, at him taking what wasn't rightfully his. Ruben traced out and to the next room. His fuming growl dragged me there too.

An empty carton of Cup-a-Soup littered the floor next to an empty water bottle, but what had Ruben's silver gaze cutting the room with rage was the paint chipped away by someone's fingernail to write her name: Kara.

"I'm going to beat him bloody once we get him," promised Ruben. And I didn't doubt him for one second.

This was Ruben's territory, his responsibility to protect humans from our kind getting out of hand. Not only was this a sin against these girls, it was a challenge to his authority. I had no doubt he'd use Blake Bellingrath as an example once we found the fucker.

I swept the room but found nothing, then went to the next where I smelled the remaining scent of Emma. When I scanned the room, there was nothing but old mattresses on the single beds, but I did find a half-empty cup of soda sitting underneath one bed.

I was sniffing its contents when Ruben asked behind me, "What is it?"

"Coke. But something else too." I inhaled deeply, trying to dissect the scent. Then it hit me, and I cursed under my breath. I'd come across this smell before in my dealings with lowlife motherfuckers around the world. Most vampires didn't need it. They could use glamour or the paralysis of their bite to subdue their victims, but some still dabbled in man-made drugs.

Ruben took the cup from me and smelled. A glint of silver rolled over his eyes, his jaw clenching as he said, "Rohypnol."

"That would definitely make his victims go quietly from the places he abducted them."

Because they'd likely be unconscious. Yet, he was still using it on them during captivity. The women were likely still fighting back. Good.

Gabriel and Sal suddenly appeared in the doorway, slightly winded since they must've completed the search of their entire wing, then come to meet us.

"He's moved them," said Gabriel.

"He's cautious, I'll give him that," I said to Ruben.

"Yeah, enough not to stay in one place too long with the girls. He may not want his customers to know where the girls are after their feeding."

I couldn't help the sneer at the thought of these terrified women being hauled around like cattle.

"Let's head back." Just the look of this place, thinking of these women in captivity, had my beast clawing to get back to Isadora. I didn't like her so near here.

We traced back within two minutes. Roland was leaning his back against my car, his gaze vigilant on the streets while he chatted with Isadora, who had her window down.

"No luck?" he asked.

"Some," said Ruben.

Isadora popped out of the car. "You found where he was keeping them?" Her green eyes rounded with shock.

"Was," I emphasized. "He's moved them." I turned to Ruben, all of us gathered beside my car now. "He likely has several places scouted so he can rotate their locations."

"I wish it was Saturday. Time to catch this asshole," Ruben ground out, his eyes stormy blue. "Are you ready, Isadora? Still want to do this?"

My sweet girl looked at each and every one of us hard-ass vampires, resolve set in the upward tilt of her chin. "Damn right, I'm ready."

If I wasn't aware yet, I knew then and there that I was deeply and wholly in love with this woman. Once this operation was over with, I'd make damn sure she understood I wasn't going anywhere.

Chapter 30

~ISADORA~

"READY, GIRL?" LIVVY STOOD NEXT TO ME IN THE PARKING LOT OF BARREL Proof looking like a 1940s bombshell. She'd come straight from a photo shoot at Belle Chasse Navy Base. She modeled for a friend of hers who did pin-up girl photo shoots for his ultra-popular website who cross-promoted the Cauldron and Maybelle's.

While she was decked out in a tailored red dress, tight in the bust and waist, then flared at the knees, I was wearing tight black jeans and a white halter top that revealed a lot of skin but also could be tucked in. If I was going to be carried and traced away by a vampire, I wanted to be dressed for the occasion.

"Ready," I said, leading the way into the bar.

We found a two-top in the middle of the bar. The point was to be seen tonight. The place was already starting to fill up.

"I'll grab us a few drinks. What do you want?"

"Old-fashioned."

"Something that strong?" I whispered.

"We're supposed to look like we're partying it up, right?"

"True."

I made my way to the bar that stretched the length of the place. Most of the stools were already filled, but Darren wasn't here yet. "Take What You Want" by Post Malone and Ozzy played from the speakers. I glanced at my watch. 10:10.

"What can I get you?" asked the good-looking bartender.

"Two old-fashioneds please."

There were several different gatherings in the bar. Couples and mixed boy-girl groups. So far, there were no other girl-only parties. That made Livvy and I good targets, which again had my heart pounding. I was actually doing this, and I couldn't pretend it didn't have me on edge. As it was, it was strange to not feel the sweet hum of magic under my skin. Jules had nulled us both right before we left, informing us she'd be in constant contact with Ruben to monitor the operation.

I was carrying the drinks back to the table right as Darren entered the bar. And another vampire right behind him. A cold sweat flashed across my neck and back. I tried not to stare, catching in a single glimpse the arrogant tilt of the second vampire's head. Blond hair, pretty face, predatory eyes. Blake Bellingrath.

When I sat across from Livvy, I whispered, "That's him that just walked in. And the other guy is Bellingrath."

She leaned forward and took a sip of her drink, her red lipstick leaving a mark on the rim. "I thought they scouted alone."

"I did too. This is weird."

A second later, my phone buzzed on the table. I'd carried in my phone rather than have my big handbag, knowing I wanted to go light. The phone was actually a burner phone that Devraj had given me. I unlocked the phone with my fingerprint.

Devraj: Bellingrath is with him I'm sure you see.
Darren said it's nothing to worry about.

Me: If you say so.

Devraj: We're still a go. Unless you don't
want to. ???

I paused, glancing at the bar. Darren was ordering drinks. Blake was skimming the bar, looking for his next victim. Burning fury blazed through my belly, thinking of those poor women he had in captivity. And I could help set them free tonight.

Me: I'm a go.

There was a pause, then the ellipses looped on-screen until his last message popped up.

Devraj: I'm so proud of you. I'll show you
how much later tonight.

I smiled, then locked the phone and slid it into my back pocket. Leave it to Devraj to try to distract me from imminent danger with thoughts of naughty sex.

"That's a saucy smile." Livvy had drained her old-fashioned by the time I slipped my phone in my back pocket.

"Might want to slow down there."

She switched our glasses. "Now you go up there, stand right next to Bellingrath, and order another."

My stomach sank. "You come with me."

She shook her head. "I want his attention only on you. I'll be unable to stop my word vomit."

True. With or without her Influencer magic, Livvy beamed. She was the kind of person you wanted to look at, wanted to listen to. And though Darren had a serious compulsion glamour spell put on him by Devraj, we didn't need any complications.

"You've got this," she said, pulling out her phone and pretending to be distracted, even though I felt her attention and awareness of the room in her posture and fleeting glances to the bar.

I walked steadily toward the bar where Darren and Blake had settled. Not looking at either of them, I maneuvered on the left side of Blake, lifting a hand to get the bartender's attention.

I felt his gaze sweeping over my face. Rather than look his way, I flipped my hair over my shoulder, knowing he'd have full view of my fading bruise from Devraj's bite. This was a big gamble, but Devraj argued it would be good for them to see. According to him, a "human" who already engaged as a blood-host would be the perfect target. She wouldn't be as traumatized by feeding their clients. Not like Emma, whose fragile mind and body couldn't handle being a host for the kidnapper's clients.

I wasn't sure I agreed with his logic, but he knew how vampires thought better than I did. And criminals, since he spent his life hunting them down and bringing them to justice.

"So, beautiful, you like to play?" came the sultry voice next to me.

Apparently, Devraj was right. The term play was used when a vampire courted a potential host.

Glancing at him shyly, which wasn't entirely an act, I said, "Sometimes."

"Another old-fashioned?" asked the bartender.

"Yes, please."

I pulled the cash from my pocket, but Blake put his hand over mine on the bar, trapping it beneath his. I was using cash only so I wouldn't get caught with my real name on anything.

"Let me get it for you, sweetheart."

"Thanks," I muttered and put the cash back in my pocket.

"So what's your name?"

"Isabelle." I finally met his gaze dead-on, wishing I hadn't.

There are some people who hold their sins in their eyes. Piercing with all the wickedness he'd committed and desired to commit, his gaze held me hard. "Why don't you stay and party with us, Isabelle?"

I shook my head and grabbed my drink from the bartender. "I'm with my friend. Sorry."

Darren remained still and focused on the other side of him, nodding to me. He'd relayed to Devraj that I should play it submissive tonight. Blake didn't want fighters.

I felt his eyes on me all the way back to the table. I settled and took a deep sip, needing the whiskey to take the edge off.

"That seemed to work," she said. "His eyes are burning a hole through you."

"Awesome. Now I want to throw up."

"Hang on, Iz. We've got him."

She then tossed her head back and laughed like I'd said something hilarious. I joined in the laughter, though not quite as enthusiastically. Checking my watch, I had eight minutes to be outside.

Livvy smiled playfully and leaned forward. "It's all going to be fine. Don't you worry."

I knocked back most of the drink in the next few minutes, listening to Livvy carry on about the karaoke contest she had planned to promote the Cauldron. I already knew about it, but it was something to ramble about while time ticked down. Finally, she set her glass down with a loud clink and stood, lifting her vintage clutch off the table.

"It was so good to see you again!" she yelled, opening her arms for me.

I gave her a big hug. She whispered in my ear, "Now go get those motherfuckers." Then she pulled away, laughing wildly like I'd said something hysterically funny. "We'll catch up next month."

She sauntered off toward the bathrooms. I refused to look at the bar, but I felt them watching as I headed out to the parking lot by myself.

I'd prepared for this moment, but it didn't take away from the solid knot of dread twisting my insides. I walked slowly through the dim lot toward my car, knowing Devraj and Ruben were monitoring not far away.

My arms were clasped from behind and the growling whisper of a vampire brushed my ear. "Time to go to sleep, beautiful."

A jolt of persuasion punched out of him. Strangely, I figured I'd be susceptible to it since Jules had nulled my magic. But somehow, it still didn't work on me. Perhaps because this was a passive form of my magic, not like the potent healing power I used on others.

I let my body go limp and pretended to fall under his glamour spell. He lifted me in his arms, behind my knees and my back.

"Let's go."

For some reason, Darren wasn't in charge of this hit. We were told they typically worked as a group, the three scouts coalescing on the one target. But tonight, it was just Darren and Blake.

I remained unmoving in Blake's hard grip. Not that I could do anything against him anyway. Not only was I nulled from using any telekinetic magic, which I wasn't powerful at to begin with, but he was remarkably strong. I sensed that well enough in the ripple of his muscles as he traced away.

When the dizzying sensation of tracing stopped, I kept my body still, my head against Blake's shoulder. He smelled of some too-strong cologne. Other men's voices overlapped.

"Got a good one, Bellingrath?"

"Let's see her."

"Yeah. Wasn't trusting Webber this time," came his rumbling reply as he walked toward the voices with me in his arms. "Not after that last chick was a dud."

"Dude," said Darren. "I can't help it if some of them can't take it."

"This one can, though," assured Blake. "She's already a player." He laughed, the menacing sound raising chills on my arms.

"Sweet," said the voice of a guy I didn't recognize.

"She smells sweet too," said Blake.

I refused to flinch when I felt him lean in and whiff the skin of my neck.

"I'll take her," said someone I hadn't heard in the mix.

This voice was deep and commanding, more so than Blake.

"What the hell?" swore Darren.

"Boys, meet our secret partner."

One of the others laughed. "No fucking way."

342

Another guy clapped his hands. "Finally, we meet the king-pin. How am I not surprised, fucking Ivy League."

"I guess we should've known it was you," said Darren. "Damn Bellingraths."

The new vampire didn't respond to them, but I felt the heat of his body right in front of Blake when he said, "Give her to me. No time to fuck around."

Then I felt the cold, long-fingered hand of this new vampire, who could only be Blake's brother, brush the bite on my neck. That time, I couldn't suppress the shiver that trembled through me. His magic was powerful. He had more than just vampire magic. He gripped me under the jaw and forced my face toward him.

"Fuck, Blake. I know her. She's a witch."

"No, she's not. She's reading like a human. She's out cold."

His long fingers slid to my throat and squeezed till I couldn't breathe. I coughed and opened my eyes, staring up into Adam Bellingrath's sinister eyes.

I'd checked out the entire family on their Facebook pages before tonight. I knew his father was a powerful vampire and his mother a witch, a Divine Seer like Violet. Which meant he very well could possess some of her psychic abilities.

"This little bitch is definitely a witch," he said, steel-blue eyes slit like a snake's. "What are you up to?" A wave of persuasion glamour pulsed against my skin.

I glared, refusing to say a word, his glamour bouncing off me.

He pulled something from his pocket. "Open wide, sweet-heart." He gripped my jaw in a bone-breaking clasp.

"No!" I tried to pull away, but he was far too strong.

He shoved a pill in my mouth and forced it closed with his cold hand clamped tight. He peered closer, his face right in front of mine. "Swallow it," he commanded. "Or choke on it."

I shook my head, but the pill was already dissolving, my head feeling foggy. When I couldn't help it any longer, I swallowed, but the pill had already started to work, my eyes slipping closed with unnatural drowsiness. The last thing I remembered was Adam tossing me over his shoulder with brutal force and tracing away right before I fell into darkness.

Chapter 31

~DEVRAJ~

WE FOLLOWED THE SPECIAL TRACKERS STRAPPED TO OUR WRISTS LIKE watches, which took us to an empty pier near the river. But when we came out of the trace, there were four vampires there and no Isadora. Rage pumped hard through my veins. This operation was different from the beginning with Blake scouting alongside Darren.

"What the hell is this, man?" croaked one of the scouts, Brent, fear skittering across his eyes as Gabriel zip-tied his ankles, shoving him to the pavement.

Roland and Sal had the others bound and on the ground by the time I swept the area for signs of her. This didn't make sense.

"I have rights. My dad—" said Blake, the only one still standing.

Ruben gripped Blake's throat, silencing him at once. "Listen to me, son." His voice was quiet and deadly. I'd heard Ruben sound like this before, and it was when he was teetering on the edge of control. "Where is the girl? Where is she being taken?"

Ruben tilted his head, staring the boy down, and whatever Blake saw in his eyes, it had him gulping hard, his eyes widening. "Tell me now."

Ruben removed his hand as I strode over and stood in front of the ringleader.

"You have two fucking seconds to speak, or I'll take what I need by force."

"Wh-what?" asked Blake.

I didn't have time for this shit. I stunned him with glamour, knocking him unconscious, and crashed into his brain, flying through the last month of memories at lightning speed. If he was conscious, the effect would make him spill his stomach, so this was me being nice as I punched through like a runaway train.

I watched with harrowing fear and fury pumping through my veins everything that had happened in the bar tonight up until one minute ago when we arrived on scene following the trace.

When I pulled out of his mind and let him go, he mumbled, "I'm going to puke."

"I don't give a fuck. Where's your brother taking her?"

"Where the other ones are, man," whined Blake, rubbing his head, hands bound.

"And where is that!" I screamed.

"I don't know. He moved them again. I don't!"

I glanced at Darren, who glanced at the others before he said, "We never even knew Adam was the kingpin till tonight."

Scorching flames seared through my body. I wanted to follow her scent, still fresh on the wind. My fists balled, needing to wrap around the throat of that motherfucker. He was a dead man if he hurt her.

Ruben appeared beside me.

"I'm going to sever his spinal cord from his body," I ground out, fangs long and sharp.

"We need to find him first," he replied calmly, glancing at his phone. "Incoming from my grim."

My body was vibrating with rage and the need to move, to act. To find her. Fuck's sake, I was going to lose my mind. But I didn't know where to go. He could be taking her anywhere.

"Speak," Ruben answered, then listened. "You're fucking kidding me." A pause as he looked down at the tracker on his wrist. "That's not good enough. Get me a signal." He hung up, gritting his teeth.

"What?" I demanded.

"They lost track of them. Bellingrath took her beyond the camera's lens, past Metairie. Fucking technology."

Just at that moment, two black SUVs pulled up to the end of the pier on the street. Ruben's other men who'd followed the coordinates by vehicle were just arriving.

Ruben barked orders while I honed in on the scent of Isadora, filling my lungs with the traces of her floral aroma in the air.

"Sal, you make sure these men get back to the Green Light while we go after the last one."

Sal nodded, taking Blake by the arm and heading for one of the SUVs where two black-clad vampires were striding our way.

My magic burned a white-hot line through my blood, urging me to hunt down Bellingrath, to find my woman. I strode across the lot in the direction he'd taken her.

"Hey!" called Ruben. "Where are you going?"

I snapped my head around. "To fucking find them. I don't need a tracker." He nodded, then I traced away without waiting. He'd taken her beyond the city limits. Unfortunately for him, he didn't know a Stygorn was on his trail. There was nowhere he could go that I wouldn't find him. Find her.

The wind pushed against me, resisting my insane speed. I powered forward with the strength that ancient vampire had bestowed on me, racing into the night and following my prey.

While minutes stretched, feeling like hours, my mind slipped to Isadora. My Isadora. Her sweet smile, her curious looks, her pensive expressions that made me want to kiss her until she smiled again. The very thought of something happening to her set my gut on fire. Put poisonous, deadly thoughts in my head.

I couldn't live without her. There was no doubt of it now. No matter that she was afraid or didn't trust our relationship, I'd make her see reason. When I found her. When I got her to safety. When I'd pummeled Adam within an inch of his life.

The scent of her veered off the interstate into the city of Slidell. I zipped off the interstate's shoulder and blurred onto a frontage road off the next exit, easily following her scent. I traced right onto a dark road, which led me to a large fenced-in, solitary lot. A storage unit. He'd moved the women to fucking storage.

Jumping the fence, I crept forward stealthily and followed her scent, weaving down the rows of garage-style units. This close, I could smell her so powerfully, like she was standing right next to me, calling to me. But her scent was actually coming from the back side of the lot from a storage container facing some woods. I also instantly scented the other girls. This prick.

Without hesitation, I ripped open the corrugated steel door, tearing a gap from the floor halfway to the ceiling. Within two seconds, I bent it back so that I could step through. And there was Adam, staring at me with wide eyes and a sudden jolt of fear.

"You better be scared, motherfucker."

Isadora was unconscious on one mattress on the floor, her hair hiding her face. Another girl was curled into a ball, watching with a similar expression as Adam. But she had nothing to fear. Not anymore.

Then I was on him, pummeling him to the floor with one punch to the face. But I couldn't stop. Falling to straddle him, I kept on whaling. I had enough sense to pull my punches so I wouldn't crush his skull. He would stand trial. He would face the Guild Court because I wanted the Bellingrath name to be dragged through the mud. Killing this asshole was so tempting. So very, very tempting. But public humiliation and the removal of his powers by Jules would make a deeper mark than a Stygorn losing his fucking mind and killing a blood thief. I didn't want to waste a minute of my time facing the Stygorn Guild to defend my excessive actions. But I still wanted him to pay.

I'd moved my punches to his ribs, cracking a few with great satisfaction when arms grabbed mine and hauled me back bodily.

"Stop, Devraj," growled Ruben.

I did, standing over the bloody mess of Adam Bellingrath, fallen son of a high family, blood thief whose time was up.

"He's unconscious," said Ruben.

"He's lucky he's not dead," I growled, heaving in deep breaths and trying to come back from the maddening rage. "How'd you get here so fast?"

"My grim got another signal right after you left." Ruben let me go and nodded toward Adam. "I've got him. Go to Isadora."

Isadora.

I wrenched away and marched to her. I knelt in front of the mattress, trembling with uncontrollable fear at the thought of her in harm's way. Ruben had arrived on scene first, his speed much faster than his other men. He was older and stronger than them.

I brushed her hair away from her face, which had fallen from the ponytail. Moving my hands to her neck, I checked for new wounds with trembling hands, but I found none and breathed a shaky sigh of relief.

By the time I'd gotten my shit together and pulled her into my arms, Ruben had zip-tied Adam's wrists, though he was still comatose and would be for a while if the sting on my knuckles had anything to say about it.

Ruben crooned to the girl paralyzed with fear, "It's all over, Kara. You're safe now." She didn't believe him, but then a wash of glamour draped the room as he pulled her into his web. It was necessary. These girls had been through an ordeal and would need glamour to wipe the fear away so Ruben could get them out of here and to a supernatural healer. Then they'd need their memories erased before they were delivered back to their families.

"I'm taking her home," I told Ruben as he removed the restraints around Kara's wrists.

"I'll text Jules and tell her you're on your way." He stopped and looked up at me. "Is she unharmed?"

Meaning, did that fucker have time to bite her?

"She is. Though she'll have a headache from the heavy dose of Rohypnol he obviously used on her."

He gritted his teeth and pulled his phone out to send a text, Kara now sleeping from his glamour. "Jules is going to kill me."

"What's new?" I asked, trying for levity now that Isadora was cradled safely in my arms.

Ruben had a fucking mess to clean up and set straight with the vampires under his district. And no doubt, Jules would give him hell for letting it get this out of hand.

Roland, Gabriel, and two others suddenly appeared, a gust of wind coming with them. They quickly scanned the open garage.

Ruben nodded to the container next door. "Get the other girls. Use glamour to put them to sleep. They'll fear your intentions. Let's get them out of here. Gabriel, text Barbara and tell her we need the cleaning crew down here ASAP."

"Done."

Then an unexpected but familiar face appeared in the torn doorway. In stepped the black-haired, black-eyed grim who'd helped us track and catch these assholes. He walked into the enclosure, surveying the situation, especially Adam, bloody and unconscious on the floor.

"Nice work." He seemed pleased and impressed by my carnage. Not sure what to think other than I liked this grim.

He stepped over to me where I crouched with Isadora half across my lap, her head in the crook of my arm. I held out my other hand for him to shake. "I can't thank you enough for your help." And I sure as hell meant it.

"Looks like you didn't need it in the end." He leaned over and shook my hand. "Henry Blackwater." Then he exited, pulling out a cigarette to light as he watched the rest of the rescue unfold.

I glanced at Ruben as I lifted Isadora in my arms, snickering at that strange exchange. "Did you see that?" I'd finally gotten the grim's name.

"You have a grim's admiration. Not an easy feat," said Ruben, grinning while wrapping a sleeping Kara in a blanket.

With that, I nodded to Ruben, then took off, tracing as quickly as possible back along the interstate shoulder. Once I'd gotten off the interstate, I took back roads through neighborhoods to finally make it to Magazine Street and then the doorstep of the Savoie house. As if she sensed me, the door was wrenched open, Jules standing there with a furious glare. Thankfully, she didn't bite my head off. Just said, "Come with me."

I followed her upstairs to Isadora's bedroom, the other four sisters right on my heels.

"What the fuck happened?" demanded Violet, hot on my tail.

"Is she okay?" demanded Livvy, still wearing the dress she had to the bar.

"He dosed her with Rohypnol, but she'll be okay," I said as I entered Isadora's bedroom and set her gently on the bed.

Clara had already peeled back the covers. Evie stood on the other side, worry creasing her brow.

"Clara, go call Tia and get her here at once. I know she's on standby for the other girls, but I want her here."

Clara zipped out of the room.

I leaned forward and put my palm to Isadora's forehead. "It should wear off soon." I wouldn't admit that I was worried too. Knowing Adam, he was aware she was a witch and probably dosed her too much to ensure she'd go out quickly. The thought of him snatching her right underneath me, the fear she must've felt before she went under, had my blood boiling again. I fisted one hand, relishing the sting on my knuckles from pounding his face.

352

"You seem to care quite a bit about our sister, Devraj," said Livvy, her big blue eyes focused on the way I had one hand on Isadora's cheek, the other spread across the blanket over her torso.

"Because he does," said Violet on a heavy exhale.

Evie, Livvy, and Jules all swiveled their heads to her. Violet just shrugged. "What? I'm a Seer. They belong to each other."

At that moment, I loved that foul-mouthed sister almost as much as I loved Isadora Then I looked at my girl, remembering the tarot reading Violet had done for me. She'd said my determination had to match my intentions. Otherwise, I'd lose.

She was right. And there were a few things I had to do to make that happen. She'd given me a gift with spilling her feelings onto a piece of parchment, weaving my name with the magic in her heart. Now it was my turn.

I leaned closer, pressed a long kiss to her forehead, and then stood and marched for the door.

Violet grabbed my arm as I passed her. "Where are you going, Stygorn?"

I glanced back, recognizing that sting in my sternum for what it was. The clenching of my heart. The longing to be with this woman for all time. I huffed out a breath and turned back to Violet. "Need to take care of some things." Then I gave Violet a wink. "So she knows I'm all in."

Her eyes gleamed, sparkling with her Seer magic, as she smirked. "It's about fucking time."

With that resounding vote of confidence, I set off to find Ruben.

Chapter 32

~ISADORA~

I woke to the sound of low voices and light laughter. When I peeked open my eyes, the sunlight pouring through my open balcony doors had me squeezing them shut again against a piercing pain.

"There she is," said Tia, hopping over and sitting on the edge of my bed. "How do you feel, sweetie?"

"Like crap," I muffled, my head pounding like mad. "Nauseous."

The headache was so bad I wanted to vomit. Tia put both her hands on either side of my head, cradling me in her palms.

"You need a little Tia love, my friend," she said sweetly and then washed me with her Conduit power.

"Oh my God," I moaned, the relief so fast and so wonderful my adrenaline spiked. "That feels so good."

"That's what Marcus says all the time."

I giggled, the painful throbbing having vanished with her magical hands. "You still got that Italian stallion?" I asked, opening my eyes to find Jules and Clara sitting at the foot of the bed, both smiling.

"Yes indeed. Once you've got a good man, girl, you don't let him go."

I scooted up to sit against the headboard, my heart lurching at the realization that one person was definitely absent from the room.

"How'd I get back here? What happened with Adam?"

Jules sat forward on the chair she'd brought in from Evie's bedroom next door. "Devraj, Ruben, and his men were able to track the trace to where Adam had taken you."

"Track the trace? I didn't know that was possible."

"Neither did I until very recently," Jules said calmly. "Apparently, Ruben knows a grim who has this technology I wasn't aware of before all of this."

"Oh," piped up Clara. "The cute one who's always on the corner of Ruben's bookstore?"

Cute? The grim we met the night we went to the Green Light was seriously dark and mysterious, striking in his sharp features, but I'd never describe him as cute.

"Yeah, that one," said Jules. "Anyway, he followed the trace where Adam had brought you to a storage unit where the other girls were."

I sat up straighter, afraid for them. "How were they? Have they been healed? How much damage was done to them?" My heart ached for those young women, having to live through the nightmare of captivity and forced blood-drinking.

Tia put a calming hand on top of mine. "Aunt Beryl and I took care of them. And the guys used glamour to wipe the painful memories away before delivering them to their parents' doorsteps."

"Yeah, you should see all the wonderful articles being posted to the internet," said Clara, beaming with joy. "The happy tears and reunions. It's been so amazing."

"How long have I been out?" I asked.

"Two days," said Tia. "You had a lot of Rohypnol in your system. I've been slowly purging it and had to keep you under longer than normal."

"Two days?"

And Devraj wasn't here. No, he'd be packing. Hell, maybe he was already gone. No. He wouldn't leave without telling me goodbye, would he? Tears welled in my eyes. Tia leaned forward and pulled me into a hug.

"Don't worry, my sweet friend. All is well."

But it wasn't all well. It was miserable. My heart was cracking in two, realizing that Devraj was leaving. Or already gone. He hadn't even waited till I was awake. But he was busy. Maybe he was at the trial. Supernaturals handled these things swiftly, unlike the lengthy trials in the human world.

"Did they have the trial for Adam yet?" I asked Jules, leaning back out of Tia's arms but still holding her hand for comfort.

"Not yet. Adam is still recovering."

"Recovering?"

Jules smiled wickedly. "Devraj beat him pretty badly. They needed to wire his jaw shut, and Ruben wouldn't let him have a healer. And since he's getting no blood to strengthen his own magic for healing, we're waiting for the swelling to go down. And his ribs to mend, so he can at least sit up in trial before the Guild Court."

Yeah, Devraj would've been upset. I knew he cared about me. So maybe he wasn't gone.

"Is Devraj staying for the trial?" I asked, heart in my throat.

"He has to as the Stygorn on the case," said Jules.

Then he'd be gone.

"I need to take a shower," I announced, emotions welling up too fast.

I didn't want to cry in front of everyone.

Tia popped up and helped me stand, but I was actually feeling remarkably well. Normal.

"I've got it," I said.

Her brown eyes reflected sympathy, catching the sorrow in my own. Tia knew me so well. Before Clara could juice me with one of her happy spells, I started to walk toward my bathroom.

"I'll go make you something to eat," said Jules. "What do you feel like? I have some of that Redfish Court Bouillon frozen that you love. Or how about a shrimp po'boy with extra arugula?"

I laughed, the sadness leaking through. Arugula made me think of Devraj. The Redfish Court Bouillon too. How long would it take to get over him?

"Whatever is easiest," I answered, seeing my phone set on the charger on my nightstand.

Hoping, I lifted it and checked for messages. No such luck. He hadn't messaged. Nothing at all. My heart sank again, the pain of losing him already too sharp. Too raw.

When I closed the door to the bathroom, I shed my clothes and stood under the steaming-hot shower, wondering how I was going to pretend I was fine when he said goodbye. I couldn't handle it. I just couldn't.

I let the tears come, scrubbing my body clean. I tried to wipe away the sorrow of losing him, but it was too painful. How had I not seen that Devraj meant far more to me than I'd ever realized? The thought of him really and truly leaving made me want to curl into a ball and forget the world. Somehow, the fact that he lived this flashy, glamorous life didn't matter anymore. Maybe he'd be okay with visiting? We could do long distance maybe. At this point, I was okay taking whatever he'd give me.

All of this was spinning through my head as I ventured out of my bathroom with a towel wrapped around me, finding my bedroom empty except for Clara. I pulled on some panties and one of my loose, comfy dresses I wore in the garden, not even bothering with a bra. I moved like a zombie. A sad, broken-hearted zombie.

"Here, let me do your hair."

I sat in front of the oval mirror, remembering how Devraj had taken me right here and had stolen my heart at the same time. I wiped the back of my hand across one cheek as a tear slipped.

Clara combed through my hair, pushing some of her euphoria into me. I smiled, my vision blurry, knowing she was worried about me. I looked so pale, circles under my eyes even though I'd slept for two days.

"It's okay, Clara," I said, voice cracking. "I'll be all right."

She beamed at my reflection. "Oh, Isadora. You're going to be fantastic. Just wait and see." She winked at me, which was a little odd. First, because she didn't know how to wink, so it came across as an awkward double-wink. And also because Clara wasn't the winking kind.

I exhaled on a heavy sigh and stared back at my sorry reflection, wondering what I was going to do with myself. Then music blared from the front yard. I jumped and turned on the stool. Clara let go of my damp hair.

"What the hell?" I asked, staring out the open balcony doors. "Is that—? Is that Peter Gabriel?"

"Sounds like 'In Your Eyes.' Might want to check that out," she said sweetly.

When I faced her, I realized she wasn't at all surprised by the eighties hit blaring from the yard. I walked through my french doors and out to the balcony, my heart falling right out of my chest, tumbling over the balcony, and falling at the feet of the man below.

There, standing in my yard, wearing jeans, a white T-shirt, and a gray trench coat was Devraj. Over his head, he held high Archie, who saw me and yipped happily, his stubby tail wagging right over where Devraj supported his bum with one hand.

My mouth dropped open as the eighties anthem from the most romantic boom box serenade pumped out into the neighborhood. Walkers had even begun to gather, watching the spectacle.

"What are you doing!" I yelled down at the beautiful man holding his dog over his head.

"Come down here, love," he said just loud enough for me to hear, his smile blinding and beautiful.

I just stood there, shaking my head, then Clara popped me on the behind. "Well, go, Isadora. Don't keep him waiting!"

I disappeared back into the house, my heartbeat racing as fast as my feet as I hurried down the stairs, through the foyer, and swung open the front door, only to find Livvy operating her karaoke system and Violet grinning beside her. Glancing to the right, Evie and Mateo sat on the swing, Mateo's arm wrapped around her shoulders, both of them grinning and enjoying the show.

"Better get out there," said Jules behind me, pushing me forward a step.

Her, Tia, and Clara stood in the doorway, smiling like fiends. All the while, Devraj hadn't moved, watching me with love in his eyes. Yes, definitely love. I couldn't catch my breath. Then Archie started to wiggle furiously when he saw me coming closer. As I stepped off the porch, Devraj lowered the unwieldy Archie, setting him down at his feet.

When I finally made it right in front of him, I asked, my smile achingly wide, "What are you doing?"

"I heard this is what American girls like." His hands cupped my cheeks, fingers threading into my damp hair, thumbs brushing over the semidry traces of my tears.

"I don't need that."

"What do you need, Isadora?" His mouth was an inch from mine, his chocolate eyes pleading, imploring. "Tell me what you need, and I'll give it to you. Anything."

Lacing my hands around his neck, I whispered, "You. That's all I need."

He swept me close, banding an arm around my waist and kissed me deep. Like he craved me. Like he cared. Like he couldn't do without me. Like he loved me.

I barely heard the hoots and applause from my sisters and the crowd that had gathered over the pounding of my heart and the rush of emotion. New Orleans was the kind of place where people wanted to share in each others' joy. And today, it seemed, they were all sharing in mine. In ours. In this moment where I let go of all my fears and let my heart have what it wanted.

"Devraj," I whispered against his lips. "I was wrong about us not being a match."

He chuckled, holding me tighter, smiling against my lips. "I know, love." Another soft kiss. "I was just waiting for you to figure it out. But I couldn't wait anymore."

"I'm sorry it took me so long."

Then his face sobered as he pulled the cuff bracelet from his wrist, the one that had been the wedding necklace his father had given his mother. My mouth fell open because I knew what he was doing. Again, I could hardly draw a breath.

"Will you take this and wear it as a promise? Until I can get you a proper ring? Until I can wrap you in your own mangalsutra?"

There was zero hesitation this time. I knew what I wanted, and I wasn't letting him go.

"Yes." I nodded furiously. "Yes, yes, yes!"

He slipped the cuff around my thinner wrist, tightening it at my forearm. Then I attacked him, kissing him like mad. He lifted me off the ground, and my legs wrapped his waist, never breaking the kiss as my sisters yelled out catcalls and Peter Gabriel sang about love.

"Get you some," yelled Tia.

"Show him what you've got." That was Violet.

I heard Evie and Clara laughing hard, my sisters' laughter one of the best sounds in the world. Right next to any sound or word uttered by the man in my arms.

"And now for another eighties favorite, people, from one of the best movies ever made, *Pretty in Pink*," Livvy said into the mic, launching "If You Leave," a song she'd played a million times around the house. "And don't forget about the upcoming karaoke contest at the Cauldron."

I was half laughing, half kissing Devraj. Leave it to Livvy to use this moment for a little PR for the business. I glanced back, seeing she was filming on her phone, grinning like crazy and giving me a thumbs-up. Meanwhile, Archie was hopping around us in circles, barking and prancing in a frenzy.

I leaned my forehead on Devraj's. "I'm sorry for my family. It's a circus."

He pulled me flush against his body, seeming not to care about our very large crowd. People actually started dancing on the street, others singing to the song. Evie and Mateo danced in each other's arms on the porch. Clara now had Archie in her arms, upright like a baby, holding one paw and singing terribly to him as she twirled around to his puppy delight.

"I'm not. They're wonderful." He pressed a kiss to my temple. "They're a part of you. And fortunately, now a part of me." He sighed sweetly. "I've longed for a place of belonging for many years. For a home. Now, I've got that, and my blood-mate." He pressed another soft kiss to my lips.

"Blood-mates? Like the legend?"

"Exactly like the legend. It was all true," he whispered against my mouth, sweeping his tongue in for a lingering kiss before pulling back and pressing his forehead to mine. "Plus, you're moving in with me soon, and we can get away from this circus."

"Oh, am I," I said breathlessly. "You're letting me into your mysterious, hallowed bedroom?"

His smile softened, his expression serious. "I love you, Isadora. You're already into my everything."

I gushed out a shaky sigh, my eyes brimming with happy tears. "I love you too."

Then he took one of my hands in his, keeping a grip around my lower back, and we started to sway, dancing and making a spectacle of ourselves. But so was everyone else. And for some reason, with Devraj holding on to me, there was no fear at all. I didn't care that others were watching or what they thought of me. I didn't care about anything but him. But us.

I had Devraj. I had his love. He had mine. And that's all that mattered.

Epilogue

~ISADORA~

"And now! What you've all been waiting for. Drumroll, please!" Livvy glanced at Clara, who stood next to her onstage in front of another mic. She proceeded to make the drumroll sound with her mouth while the rest of us pounded the tabletops. "The man of the hour is none other than our very own Finnie, tonight performing as the queen Beyoncé."

The crowd lit up with a roar while Livvy grinned like a demon. A very beautiful demon. The outfits she and Clara were wearing were definitely something she'd put together. They were bodysuits made entirely of black sequins with red sequins stitched across their boobs in the logo for the Cauldron.

Then Finnie stepped onto the stage to a series of loud catcalls, the loudest from JJ and Violet by the bar. And I had to admit, he made a very beautiful woman, his tawny, smooth skin glittering under the spotlights. I do mean glittering because, apparently, Livvy had smoothed glitter lotion all over his arms, chest, and bare legs.

"You've got this, Finnie baby!" shouted Evie, sitting on top of the table at my back, Mateo standing behind her with his arms wrapped around her upper chest.

When Finnie stepped up to the mic, the jeers died down, but hoots of laughter still rippled in our packed bar. Livvy was a PR genius. Her online promotion had pulled every singer and non-singer out of the woodwork to join our competition tonight. The winner would win $1,000, a Cauldron T-shirt, and bragging rights till next year's competition since Livvy had decided this would be an annual thing. And it would all be prominently promoted via social media. Tonight, they were streaming live.

Finnie stepped up to the mic and said with his deep voice, "Uhhh, I lost a bet."

More laughter, and a group of guys whooped down front. Livvy told me those were his best friends from UNO, here to support him. And embarrass him. And laugh at him. One of the guys was bent over so far and laughing so hard I thought he was going to hurt himself.

"So," said Finnie, very awkwardly. "Here it goes." Then his mouth tipped up into that signature cute Finnie smile and he said, "This is for all the single ladies."

"Yeah, baby!" a girl from the back yelled with a whoop, her friends joining in.

Then the music started and Livvy, Clara, and Finnie all started to move, hands on hips Beyoncé-style, and the crowd lost it. So did I. And Devraj next to me.

"Oh my God!" I yelled into Devraj's ear. "Finnie can sing!"

The bar went insane, clapping and whooping while Finnie killed it. Sure, it was a few octaves deeper than it should be, but it was awesome. And hilarious. And his dominant voice even drowned out our very off-key sister Clara. Still, she had some moves, shaking it like she just didn't care. She and Livvy had more attitude and flair than was fair to the rest of the world.

I leaned close to Devraj and whisper-yelled in his ear. "I could never do that."

He gripped the nape of my neck and put his mouth right next to my ear. "You'll do it for me tonight." Then he nipped my earlobe, rocketing my libido into the stratosphere.

"People are watching," I hissed.

"Let them watch," he said, completely amused, while he drew me into his lap.

Rather than fight him, because that was pointless, I wiggled till I was sideways and wrapped my arms around his neck while we enjoyed the show.

When the song ended with the three onstage thrusting their hips out and a wink at the audience, there was really no contest. Still, we had judges at a front table, who now had a decision to make. The judges were Nico, who had a background in music; Tia, who didn't but had volunteered for the job; and Charlie, who knew showmanship better than anyone.

Livvy stepped up to the mic, breathless. "Okay, guys. Go get another round at the bar while our judges deliberate. Let's give it up for all our contestants!"

A loud cheer went up, then the house music came back on, and I was itching to leave. But I still wanted to see who won.

Then Violet marched up onto the stage, motioning to bring the house music back down.

"Hey, you guys. Since we've got a captive audience tonight, I wanted to let everyone here know first since my announcement means I'll be cutting my hours back here at the Cauldron."

Some guy groaned, "Nooooo!"

"Yeah, I know," she said, grinning. "You all love me. But uh . . ." She licked her lips, nervous.

I glanced at Devraj, who mirrored the quizzical look on my face. I said to Evie over my shoulder, "You know what this is about?"

"No. But I think we're about to find out about her secret she's been keeping from us."

Leave it to Violet to do it this way. With a public audience so there was no going back from whatever it was.

"Anyway, the really cool news is I'm opening my own tattoo shop!"

Her favorite customers clapped and encouraged her. But her glance went sideways to Nico at the judging table. He'd stopped looking down at the ballots, his eyes on her.

"And I guess I should mention that I'll be partnering with none other than your favorite local musician, Nico Cruz."

He shot her a look but then shook his head in exasperation. He laughed and stood, giving a casual wave to the crowd.

"So if you guys want the perfect tattoo from the best tarot reader in town, I'll hook you up. Check out my website for Empress Ink, coming soon. Right, Livvy?"

I jerked my neck around to see Jules with her jaw hanging open. Of course Livvy had known about this all along. Then Jules was beelining toward Violet, who hopped off the stage right where Nico had motioned her to come down.

"You know what?" I whispered to Devraj. "I think this would be a good time to make our exit."

"You sure you don't want to tell them about your little enterprise too?"

I laughed. "Um, no. Jules can only take one shock at a time."

I'd saved a good bit of money, and Devraj said he wanted to invest in my small business. Something I'd always dreamed of, but never had the guts to do. Devraj didn't make me braver, but he showed me that I was. I should go for my dreams, let my worries and doubts and fears take a back seat.

So I did. I contacted the owners of Angel Paws and offered to buy the place. I planned to renovate the kennels and set up a website, with Livvy's help, to start a foster program so they wouldn't spend so long waiting for their forever home. I had big plans. And Devraj was with me 100 percent. I couldn't imagine what the hell I was thinking when I thought we didn't match.

Devraj was my perfect other half, encouraging me when I needed it. And I loved him, offering him the home, the place of belonging, that he'd always wanted. He was buying the house and staying put here in New Orleans. He'd work for Ruben and also serve other contracts abroad when needed. But he was in semi-retirement as a Stygorn, keeping close to home. After three hundred years, I told him he deserved a little relaxation and leisure. He'd kissed the hell out of me and told me he agreed.

Devraj hummed in agreement, whispering close to my ear. "They might try to drag you into some Savoie sister family meeting. And you're mine tonight." He lifted me in his arms and headed for the door.

"I can walk, you know."

"Where's the fun in that?"

Then he traced to his back door and opened it with one hand, balancing me with one arm and leg. Once inside, Archie yipped and danced for our attention.

"Oh no you don't," said Devraj, dropping what was obviously half of a po'boy from the restaurant into his bowl. "I'm getting all of her attention tonight, little man."

"Where'd you get that?"

"JJ. He loves me."

I laughed. "So do I." I nuzzled his neck as he headed toward the hallway. "What's the big plans tonight?"

"They entail my bed and no clothes. And Big John." He quirked a naughty smile when I laughed. "And no work or gardening or shelter plans tomorrow. We're sleeping in, and I'm feeding you every meal in bed."

I smiled, sweeping a lingering kiss on his neck, relishing the shiver I gave him. "I feel so privileged. Taken to your bedroom and everything."

He pinched my ass. I yelped.

"Keep it up, and you won't leave my bedroom. Ever."

"Promise?"

Then he was all Devraj smiles and Devraj eyes, heated and intense. "Promise, love."

Then he did just that, and I couldn't imagine anyone ever being more perfect for me than my charismatic, passionate, and devotedly loving vampire.

Acknowledgments

A special thank-you goes to Farah Heron and Mona Shroff, who kindly and patiently answered my bazillion and one questions about Indian culture at the beginning of this project. And to Mona for doing that essential beta read of my first draft. So sorry for that hot mess!

Also to Korrie Noelle for her wonderfully encouraging spirit and for introducing me to my sensitivity beta readers—Nikita Parikh, Paramita Patra, and Sonal Dutt. You ladies were beyond amazing in cheering me on and correcting important details to make the story and Devraj more authentic. I can't thank you enough!

A special shout-out to my Instagram friend Nilika (@LiberLady) who gave me the perfect name for Devraj's fictitious Bollywood movie! He totally fits the title translation, "Crazy Good-hearted."

And finally to my phenomenal beta readers—Jessen Judice, Christina Gwin, Naima Simone, and Malia Lilinoe. Your attention to detail and genuine feedback helped me make this story the best it could possibly be. Sending you all tackle hugs and big kisses!

Author's Note

So, researching for this book was "so hard." I was *forced* to watch a ton of Bollywood movies and to stalk Ranveer Singh constantly on Instagram. Not to mention my weekly search for "hot Indian men" on Pinterest to keep my inspo board up to date. SUCH a hardship, you guys, but I endured all of it for you, my readers, determined to get my research right.

All sarcasm aside, I LOVED writing this book. I loved delving deep and discovering what made Devraj and Isadora tick. Not to mention how fun it was exploring the sisters and secondary characters more. Writing in the Stay a Spell world gives me pure joy. Yes, writing is still hard work and editing is a living hell, but the bohemian, eclectic characters on magical Magazine Street speak to me in a special way. Book 3 is already calling me, and I can't wait to get inside Violet's head and Nico's heart. Thank you so much for hanging with me, guys. More to come.

About the Author

JULIETTE CROSS is a multi-published author of paranormal and fantasy romance and the co-host of the podcast *Smart Women Read Romance*. She is a native of Louisiana, living in the heart of Cajun land with her husband, four kids, her dogs, Kona and Jeaux, and kitty, Betty. When she isn't working on her next project, she enjoys binge-watching her favorite shows with her husband and a glass (or two) of red wine.